VEIN OF JUSTICE

BY SHARON LANGDALE

To Katie,
Hope you enjoy
my story
Sharon Langdale
2017

ISBN 978-0-578-14595-2

Edited by: Lorna Collins

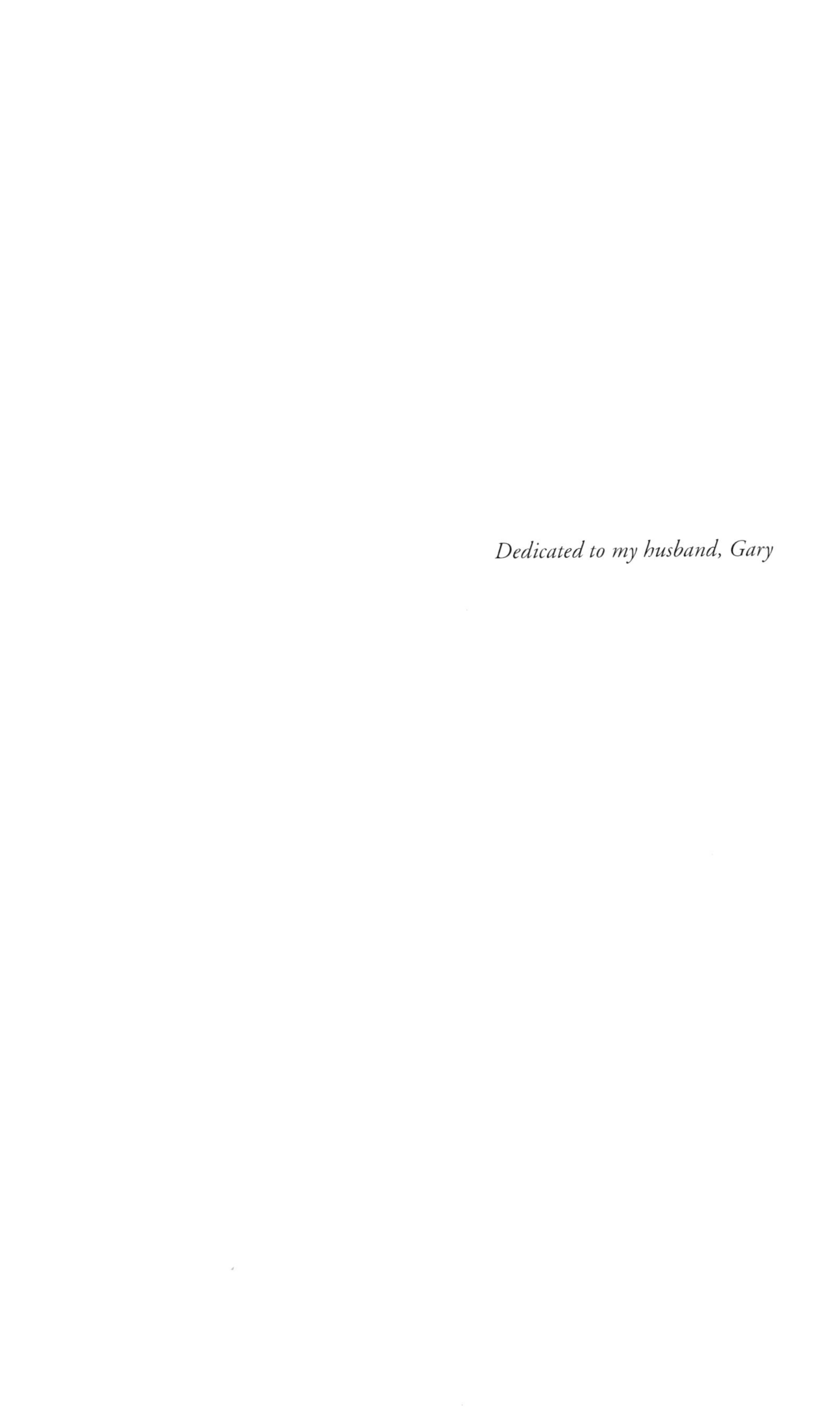

Dedicated to my husband, Gary

ACKNOWLEDGMENTS

Thanks to the following without whose efforts this book would not have been possible:

• Deseret Book Company for the quotes used in this book with permission on pages 70, 235. ("So Well Expressed" compiled by H. George Bickerstaff, Bookcraft, Salt Lake City, Utah copyright 1964, 9th Printing, 1975. Pages 9, 64.).

• My critique group members of Orange Coast Writers, Word Wizards, my creative writing classmates and teachers for their suggestions and encouragement.

• Lorna Collins, editor, for her patience and expertise.

• Note: Page 192, http://en.wikipedia.org/wiki/Circumstancial_evidence

•Note: http://en.wikipedia.org/wiki/Gunnison_County,_Colorado

"High Country Spring"

Spring begs release as lacy ice recedes,
rivulets seek rivers open to breathe.

Freed from beneath white blankets,
denizens of lakes, streams awake,
break surface, nature's hatch to partake.

Oft unseen, through time repeated,
minus man's intervention, captured
perfectly into sparkling facets.

Sharon Langdale 2014

CHAPTER 1

Deputy Maggie Hernandez slowed her Jeep to an idle and scanned the scene fifty yards above the dirt road. The old mine building appeared abysmal. Her attention focused on the vacant windows and missing boards forming a lopsided face reminiscent of a gap-toothed jack-o'-lantern left to rot. The scene evoked a wry thought. Who's to say whether the past is gone, or lingers still?

The pre-dawn cold sent a shiver through tired shoulder muscles as she drained the last drop of tepid coffee from her thermos. Duty pushed her to continue to search for any sign of Betty Clay's vehicle along Bright River. Her patrol vehicle was less than a hundred yards past the abandoned Fist-Full-of-Nuggets Mine when the ground rocked. Involuntarily, air fled her lungs as pressure pushed then pulled at her chest. Instinct took over, and both feet hit the brake. She cupped hands over her ears to muffle the loud booming that bounced from crag to cliff. The ground heaved and convulsed, causing the Jeep to sway as though in a porch glider-swing. Craning her neck, she caught sight of the concrete dam spanning Bright River rupture along its reinforced spine. Behind the relic, the riverbed bulged as it belched years of refuse and fine black silt.

Maggie's heart pounded in her chest. Beside her, loose butterscotch-hued soil trickled down the cliff, and a small avalanche of loose rocks tumbled across the road. She stomped on the gas pedal. Risking a glance into her rearview mirror, she gasped as water rose across the width of the river, striking like a rattlesnake at the trunk of a thirty-foot pine, and sucking it into the boiling fury. She drove dangerously fast alongside the twisting river, hoping to outrun the torrent. The roar of rushing water became louder as she raced the three miles to town. As she reached the edge of Elk Hills, she swerved sharply to the left onto Nugget Top Road and reached safety on higher ground. The black wave passed by her, spreading from bank to bank. Trees and brush buckled from the turbulent flow and disappeared into the maelstrom as it transformed the town's peaceful creek into a menace.

Above the roar, she rasped into her cell phone. "The dam on Bright River just collapsed, and the river is surging through town. Violet, get word to the sheriff we've got a major emergency here. I'll be at the road-maintenance building in five minutes. Ask him to call me."

Next she called Lynn Mason. "Can only talk a second. Want to let you know that Deputy Hayes, Sheriff Carlson and I have been out all night looking for any sign of your mother. So far we haven't found her or the car. We'll continue to search, but can you and Don come into town? Something extraordinary has happened on Bright River."

"Of course, we'll be there in twenty minutes. Want us to meet you at the station?"

"No, at the fork of the river. If I'm not there, wait for me."

"Maggie, I'm so worried. I tried to reach Arnold but got no answer. We want to help search. Tell us where we can look."

"Can't right now. There's an emergency. I'll explain when I see you. Need to coordinate with the sheriff. See you soon."

The deputy followed the narrow road that bordered the creek as it cut through town. She witnessed fish caught by the fury, tossed upon the gouged banks, mutilated, and dead. Silvery, sequin scales glinted in thin morning sun. She turned into the maintenance yard and parked.

Standing on the gravel levee alongside the river, she concentrated on dialing Deputy Jones. Debris passed by her. She squinted into the light, following the passage of a curious tangle, but failed to identify the item entwined in tree branches and brush being borne by the rough current into the historic mining town. The journey from the dam, which took less than an hour, became a silent eternity, as the bruised corpse came to rest among willows lining the convergence of the town's two rivers. Half-submerged, shattered trees, uprooted by the ebony water, failed to dislodge nature's makeshift grave, as severed pine limbs cradled the lifeless form ripped from the present, now entombed between still boulders.

By six thirty a.m., Don and Lynn Mason, newcomers to the mountain community, raced to join the startled residents milling along the embankment at the river fork. Their Colorado morning had arrived bright and sunny as a crush of tourists filled the town's cabins and motels, eager to celebrate the Memorial Day weekend. Rudely roused from their beds, befuddled visitors mixed with the local residents. All around them, shocked faces mirrored the scene of carnage and destruction.

"Oh, God." Lynn grabbed Don's arm. "What happened?"

"Hell if I know. The water's black."

Edging through the crowd, they reached the large rock levee alongside the swift current. Speechless, they tried to comprehend the ghastly scene of hundreds of fish floating past belly-up. Angry cuss words and moans issued from the crowd. Previously a home to native rainbow and brook trout, the unnatural charcoal ribbon of water from Bright River had suffocated its inhabitants with silt. In a death spiral, it twisted into the crystal waters of Mineral Creek. Now, the braided rivers carried disaster farther downstream.

Hal Adams hurried up to Don and Lynn.

"All the fish are dead. Our river's been killed." His face was ashen. "Nothing can live in that muck." He removed his eyeglasses and used a large hanky to wipe them clean. "Did you hear the dam break at your restaurant?"

"No." Lynn said, "Sound must have been blocked by the canyon ridge between the lake and town. We came in to meet Deputy Maggie. It's important. Have you seen her or the sheriff?"

"No. Someone said she went back up Bright River. Maybe the sheriff's with the Fish and Game warden. This is unimaginable."

Don stood with his fists clenched. "What in the world could cause this mess? You'd think crude oil's been poured in the water." He paced back and forth, his handsome face granite hard.

Hal said, "No one knows. I was jolted out of bed when I heard a loud rumble around five thirty this morning. I thought someone was mining right under the bed. Lived here eighteen years and never seen anything like this." He shook his head. "I walked from our living quarters into the gift store. Couple of glass figurines had fallen off shelves and broke. I thought an earthquake had hit or maybe a landslide. Drove to the bridge, and when I looked down, the water was black as tar. What will we do if all the fish are dead?"

A muddy vehicle pulled up near the creek.

Lynn pointed. "That's Maggie's Jeep. Come on we need to talk to her."

Lynn and Don joined the crowd that surged around the vehicle, and questions zinged through the crisp air.

"What happened?"

"How bad is it?"

"How far up did you get?"

The deputy's uniform was black from the knees down. Waving her arms in the air, she asked the crowd for quiet.

"The dam below the old Fist-Full-of-Nuggets Mine burst."

"But how?" someone asked. "That dam's concrete, at least three feet thick."

Another man's voice rose over the chatter. "And it's been there fifty years or more. How could it burst?"

The crowd hung on Maggie's words. "All the black water you see is from silt that built up behind the old dam over many years."

A voice asked, "Did you see the dam?"

"I was close by when it happened. I managed to get out of the way, but I could see the road was being washed out in several places. I tried to get back up there, but the road is too unsafe. The Forest Service sent their helicopter to check it out.

They radioed the station to say trees are uprooted and flattened below the mine, and the banks are covered with all kinds of debris and busted chunks of concrete."

A man called out, "Do they think someone blew it up? Sounded like dynamite going off to me." Many nodded in agreement.

Maggie raised her hand. "They don't know what happened yet. They'll check out all possibilities. It's not safe to go up there now. The road crew will need to grade the road and make sure it's drivable."

The owner of The Sport Stop asked, "How much water do they think came down the canyon?"

Maggie answered, "Right where the dam was, the pilot says black silt extends ten feet up both sides of the stream. Below the mine, the flow is pinched by steep cliffs. He could only guess at the height the wall of water reached as it was forced through the rock sides. May have been fifteen feet."

Hal's gravelly voice rang out. "That dam's been on the map since 1874. It was reinforced back in the thirties. Miners didn't worry much about what they threw in the river. All they wanted was gold. Could be some toxins in the water."

Lynn whispered to Don, "Poison in the water. What's going to happen to everyone?"

"We could all be ruined, that's what."

People talked back and forth. The deputy pulled herself up ramrod straight, and her voice carried over the conversations. "Along with mining machinery and trash, the old sediment holds chemicals used years ago in the mining industry." She scanned the crowd. Her sharp eyes located a big man in back. "Burton, you know mining. What might they find?"

Burton rested his hands in the bib of his overalls. "Hard to say." He spat tobacco on the ground. "Small amounts of arsenic, lead, cyanide, zinc, and chlorine was used for sure. That stuff would have dissipated years ago—unless they dumped leftovers still in drums—then, who knows?"

The crowd stirred. A man's voice boomed out. "What about our well water?"

"Officials will test the water in the stream and all the wells in town today. The Fish and Game wardens have only checked a portion of Bright River. They have a lot more tests to do, but so far, it looks like all the trout are dead."

Her words seemed to affect everyone. No one spoke.

Don asked, "How far down river does the black water and damage to the fish extend?"

A man shouted, "My place is eight miles downstream from town, and the water is black as ink. I was lucky I got my fish ponds closed before much of it flowed in."

A young woman holding a baby said, "Is the town water safe?"

Maggie said, "Our town's reservoir water supply should be safe. There's plenty to last us until this...uh, emergency is over. Mayor Steele has called a town meeting at noon. We may not have all the facts by then, but we should have more information. The city council contacted me, and our Monday parade will go on as planned." She put her shoulders back and cleared her throat. "We're a small town of just over five thousand people, but we can overcome this tragedy if we pull together."

Someone called out, "Yes, we can." A few people clapped.

Maggie spoke up, "My office will contact all motels, cabin rentals, and the campground, to see if anyone is unaccounted for. Sheriff Carlson already sent word to the sheriffs in Tin Cup and Crested Butte in case some of their visitors were on Jeep trails on their way down the east side of Bright River. I didn't pass any vehicles on the west side. We hope there were no casualties. We need workers for cleanup along the stream. The road crew will also need extra men. Anyone who can help, contact the road department."

Don whispered to Lynn, "Burton didn't mention all of the possible contaminants in the debris. Damn, I wanted our first full summer season to be a good one. Poison in the water..."

"Like what?"

"Mercury. They used it to pick up their gold, and some used the stuff to catch it on the riffles, to meld the small pieces together."

Lynn blanched. "Good Lord, mercury's toxic."

"The miners panning along the streams used it. It's outlawed these days."

Lynn wrinkled her nose. "There must be thousands of dead fish. It smells already."

"They'll decay soon." Don picked up a small rock and tossed it into the dead stream. "Our best fly-fishing river ruined. I bet there won't be any fishing all the way into Gunnison."

Lynn scanned the disaster area. "This is terrible, but I'm really worried about Mom. We need to find the sheriff right away."

"Let's see if Maggie knows how we can contact him. I'm sure he's knee-deep in this mess. You could call Arnold again. Maybe he's heard from Betty."

"Mom wouldn't just take off. She'd call me and let me know if she was leaving town. They must have had an argument. Maybe she took a room in town to get away and think."

Don put his arm around her. "Try not to worry. She may be home by now."

"I sure hope so..."

A scream cut the air. Fifty feet away, two teenagers close to the water's edge scrambled up the embankment. A boy shouted, "A body, a dead body."

In one motion, the crowd coiled like a school of fish and rushed toward the embankment.

Maggie yelled, "Get back! Stay away. I need to see it first." She waded through the rubbernecks and knelt by the body.

Don moved with the crowd closer to the site, but Lynn stood apart. She couldn't see through the crowd or down the embankment. Then Maggie stood and looked right at her. Their eyes met. Maggie clambered up the rocky slope and grabbed Don's arm. They both rushed to Lynn.

Moaning, Lynn's hands covered her face. "No, no. Please, God. Not Mom." She took a step then swayed and crumpled to her knees as though her spine had been severed. Shaking with sobs, her voice rasped. "It's a mistake. It has to be. This can't happen. Not Mom." Her head shook in refusal.

Don knelt and cradled her in his arms. He whispered soothing words, stroked her hair, and held her tight against his chest. "Honey, I'm here. I'll take care of you."

Maggie patted and rubbed Lynn's arm and back. Her voice quaked with emotion. "What a lousy damn thing. I'll find out how this happened. I promise. Be strong, Lady Bear. Don will get you home. I'll call as soon as possible."

After a few moments, Don asked, "Can you stand? Let's go home."

Lynn tried to struggle out of Don's arms. "Let me go. I want to see her. She's my mother. I want..." She pushed against Don.

"No, no, you mustn't. Not now..." Don resisted her shove. "We're leaving."

He helped Lynn stand, and slowly they walked to their truck.

As Don backed up, Lynn tried to see past the crowd hovering near the discovery. She caught only a glimpse of Maggie walking back to the site carrying a roll of yellow tape and motioning the curious back. Some men in the crowd turned away and wandered in the direction of the road department service yard, a short distance down Quartz Street. Others stood in small knots, talking, hands in pockets, still gawking at the river. Lynn's temple throbbed as they pulled onto the highway and headed home.

Don spoke more to himself than to Lynn. "Couldn't let you see such an awful thing. Unbelievable. I'm damn angry. I'd like to squeeze the neck of whoever did this. I'm taking you home. Maggie's calling the sheriff right now. They'll find out who's responsible."

Lynn sat in a stupor as they left the two river convergence and drove through town. They traveled four miles north to their home and restaurant on Mineral Lake. Her tears blurred the familiar sight of pines hugging the edge of the cascading Mineral Creek, the second creek in the small town which flowed from Mineral Lake into town and which fate had spared from the disaster that had befallen Bright River.

"Why Mom? I can't stand to think of her suffering." Lynn struggled to speak through her sobs. "Who could do this? She was gone all night. Someone took her."

"Try to calm down. The sheriff and Maggie will sort everything out. I think you should lie down for a while, get your breath back."

"I don't understand. Mom dead. It can't be true."

They reached their home, and Don parked under a fifty-foot pine tree. "We'll be inside in a minute, and you can rest." He walked around to the passenger's side.

Lynn slumped against the door. She didn't move. Pine boughs waved as a gentle breeze strummed green needles. She closed her eyes. *Mom gone. Why, why? Someone here hurt her. This peaceful place is all a lie. I'll never feel safe here again.*

Chapter 2

The moment Lynn and Don left, Maggie got busy. She cordoned off the crime scene and located Deputy Jones. Surrounded by yellow tape, she squatted on the river edge and surveyed the blue-gray corpse. Black water swirled past, and all she could see were small areas of skin, a bit of ankle, a slice of wrist. Her senses recoiled in revulsion and she looked away from the vacant eyes and open mouth, sucking on a plastic bag. *This is my best friend's mother, murdered, her life force taken, dumped like garbage into the river among broken tree limbs and soggy dead leaves. Betty, this is not how it should be. I promise to avenge this wrong.*

Softly, Maggie sang prayer words in her native Ute language, spiritual words spoken to wrap around Betty's soul and help her find her way to the Great Spirit.

Shortly, she heard the deputy's patrol car park nearby. He stepped down the embankment, loose gravel flowing around his boots, and she reached out to stop the chubby man's slide into the passing current.

"Came as quick as I could."

"Glad you're here. Coroner will arrive soon."

The young deputy swept his hat off in respect. "Pitiful." He moved close enough to notice the large splotches of eggplant-colored skin and the bulging, eyes of the elderly woman. He spoke softly. "I'll take pictures of the body and the area, but it may be contaminated by all the debris in the water. Maybe forensics can find something."

Hands on her hips, Maggie's gaze went upstream. "I doubt this is where the body was placed. Too close to town. Killer might have hid the body way upstream sometime last night. Unexpectedly, the dam breaks, flushing it downriver, where it snagged here. It would help if we could find even a small bit of evidence, a piece of clothing, something that might indicate a struggle. We'll have to check both sides of Bright River from this spot to the dam—when the road is cleared. A small vehicle can make it partway up the east side, after that it becomes a narrow hunting trail."

Jones followed Maggie's glance upriver. "On the east side, trees go right down to the river. Water must have gushed past everywhere. Might be almost impossible to find any clues."

"We'll need some luck, all right." Her thoughts darkened.

The two of them kept a solitary vigil over the victim until the coroner arrived. For an hour, he worked silently to finish assessing the body and scribbled facts in his notebook.

Deputy Jones looked over his shoulder. "Doc, I've seen some corpses, but I've never seen such a horrified expression."

Dr. Handle snapped his notebook closed and put his equipment into his satchel. A hushed silence wrapped around the trio as they studied the victim's face.

"Until I do a more thorough examination, I can't tell if she died from the blow to her head or by suffocation from the plastic bag." He rubbed his chin. "If she gained consciousness after the killer placed the bag over her head, the terror of trying to breathe could account for her expression. Then again, she might have been startled to see the killer's face, or perhaps, on a subconscious level, terror set in as she realized she was dying."

Jones said, "Yeah, whatever the reason, it's creepy."

Doc said, "I've got what I need for now." He made his way up the embankment. Alongside him, the young deputy wheezed from the exertion.

Doc frowned. "Lose some of that belly now, before it becomes cement."

"You're right Doc, I'll try harder."

Maggie said, "Jones, Forensics just called. Be here in five minutes. It's close to noon. I'm going back to the station. Doc, we'll look for your report as soon as it's ready. We've got Deputy Hayes out looking for her vehicle. It may provide more to go on."

"Sure thing. Hayes better watch his step, this killer knew what he was doing."

****

At home, Lynn struggled with her grief. She tossed on the bed in fits of crying and angrily pounding her pillow. Her thoughts went back to early March when her mother had announced she planned to marry Arnold Clay.

She'd anxiously told Don. "Mom and Arnold are getting married in Las Vegas."

Don had scooped up his thermos and zipped his jacket. "Got to go. Need to open early. A customer will be there at eight for his material." His long stride had carried him quickly to the front door.

"Don, what do you think?"

The front door had closed before she finished her sentence. *Damn, he's taking off in such a rush.*

She'd followed him down the stairs then stopped on the bottom step as he hurried across the parking area "Wait a second," she called out. "I want to talk to you."

"About what?"

"About Mom and Arnold." Irritated, she added, "You never listen to me." She pulled her jacket tighter for warmth and walked to his truck. "They're getting married soon, probably next week."

"You don't sound very happy. You met him. What's he like?"

"He's a retired policeman from Denver. Remember? I mentioned how interested he is in gold mining."

"Sounds to me like a good step for Betty." Don had checked his watch and gotten into his truck.

"Mom said they just want a simple ceremony, by themselves. I know I couldn't leave now but I feel left out not to be invited. Don, I wonder if he's the best choice for her. She really likes him, but…"

"So, what's your problem?"

"He's a lot younger, and her divorce from Dad was such an ugly mess. I don't want her to get hurt again." She added, "Mainly, I got a funny vibe from him."

Don started the engine and listened for the idle to slow. "Come on, Lynn, stay out of her business, okay? She's old enough to know what she wants."

"Why would you say that? I'd never interfere with her decisions." She backed away from the vehicle.

"Just saying, let things go along and don't screw up her plans."

She'd started to argue that it was not her intention to interfere in her mother's life, but Don had driven off. The silhouette of his truck had become faint as the lingering morning mist formed a thin barrier between them.

She pushed the memory from her mind. It was another reminder that her own marriage wasn't all she'd hoped for. Don's habit of only half-listening to what she said gnawed at her regularly. *Today, knowing I've lost my mother, what does it matter how or when she'd married?*

Lynn tried to rest for several hours more. Failing, she went upstairs. Don fixed her a sandwich and placed a glass of milk in front of her.

"Try to eat a little. The sheriff called. They're still looking for her car. Maggie's going to come by tomorrow. I told them you were too upset to talk to anyone today."

"Did he know anything?"

"Not really. They've talked with Arnold. The sheriff may call us later today, but he wasn't sure."

"Did Arnold call?"

"No. You'd think he would, but he hasn't."

"He must be devastated. Someone hurt Mom so bad..." Her sobs began again. Don held her in his arms. She whispered, "I can't think of being without Mom.

Everything is destroyed by this horrible…" She looked at Don. "I feel like a mountain has fallen on me."

"Try not to think about it. If I could change what happened, you know I would."

"I know. I just feel so useless, and my nerves prick me like needles."

"You need to calm down. The sheriff and Maggie will find out what happened. Neither of us can do anything."

"My heart breaks for Mom. It's unfair. I'm angry, so angry. She should have had many more years ahead..." She let the thought hang. "I'm selfish. Feeling sorry for myself. I won't be able to see her…"

She let out a big sigh. "And the people in town, I'm sorry for them, too. What a mess with the river…"

"Today has been a double whammy for you and me. Along with our own loss, we have to face what the rest of our town has experienced today. This disaster can ruin everyone."

"You think some folks won't make it?"

"I'm sure of it. Cross your fingers we'll be able to hang on. Listen, you don't have to talk about this stuff. You've had a really rough day. Try to eat something and see if you can rest again."

"Can't sleep. I…" She took a small bite of her sandwich then set it back down. "Talking about something else might help. When I close my eyes, ghastly pictures appear."

She took a sip of milk. "I heard people say they thought they heard dynamite. I recognized one guy, William Short. He was in here last year eating with Scott Lee. He's a hard-rock miner and should know. What if someone blew up the dam on purpose?"

"For what reason?" His lips tightened.

"I don't know, maybe to keep people from coming here, to keep this town small and quaint—maybe some kind of environmental freak."

"That's pretty far-out. Do you really think someone would kill fish to make an ecology statement? It sounds pretty stupid."

"Maybe. A fringe group might figure sacrificing one small river is worth it to make their point. There could be some other reason we'd never think of or expect."

"It's odd, that's for sure, but after Fish and Game do their investigation, I'll bet they verify the old dam just finally gave way."

"You're probably right, but the timing is cruddy. Summer's just begun, and the whole town may dry up if fishing is gone. We've worked like crazy to get ready."

Don gave her a smile. "Try not to worry too much. The cleanup crew will remove the downed trees and any debris they can. The water will clear up eventually. They could declare a state disaster and provide money to replenish the fish. Sure won't arrive in time to help us this year, but if the replant next year succeeds, we'll all be fine."

"And if not, we're finished, along with the rest of the town. I wonder how long it will take to repair the Bright River road so tourists can travel to the ghost towns and over the pass." Absentmindedly, she traced her finger over the tabletop. "I'm worried. If Bright River is ruined for good, will fishing on the lake be enough for people to come here? Will you still have customers at the lumberyard buying material for remodel jobs or new homes?"

Don began to scrub hard on the stovetop. "Who knows?"

"We might lose everything, the restaurant and the lumberyard if tourism stalls."

Don stopped cleaning and leaned against the work counter. "We both have to think positively."

"I can't be positive about anything right now. I've never been so low."

"Give it time." His reply was cut off as the phone rang. He listened to the caller and smiled at Lynn as he hung up. "Greg's calling a businessmen's meeting at his store for tomorrow night. We're going to work up a plan with newspaper advertising in the major Texas papers. He thinks our loyal customers will continue to come this summer. All we need to do is promote all the other trout-fishing locations that circle our town." Don rubbed his hands together. "That's what I like, a good offense."

"Once a football player, always a football player. Your confident attitude helps."

Don was across the room, halfway out the front door, and missed her remark.

That night, customers were sparse. Lynn stayed downstairs while Don, Wendy, and Mike handled the restaurant. She was surprised to see Don close early.

"I sent the help home. We counted the number of dinners on one hand."

As Don lay next to her in bed, her thoughts clashed. *I'm not optimistic like Don. I'm afraid we might lose everything. I've already lost my mother. What could possibly be worse?*

CHAPTER 3

Just past midnight on Sunday morning, a mile from downtown Elk Hills, Deputy Hayes heard a coyote's howl. The round notes hung in the night air, and evergreen trees, lit by moonlight, moved in the night breeze. An indigo sky arched over the slumbering mountain town as he cruised silently up and down dark streets, looking for the missing vehicle. On his second pass through this part of town, his headlights pierced the gas station's broken windows and gaping repair bays. He slowly circled around to the back under a canopy of stars and a full moon, which illuminated a streak of silvery chrome on a parked vehicle in the silent yard.

The deputy cautiously shone his light around the back of the abandoned building, checking for anyone who might be hiding among the discarded boxes and rusty barrels. The area appeared deserted.

His patrol vehicle rolled closer to the Buick SUV, and his searchlight skipped across the metal body. The column of light pierced the interior, which was devoid of occupants. The beam passed over a woman's purse on the front passenger seat of the empty car.

Exiting his vehicle, he opened the passenger side door, found the registration, and called in his discovery. He found no wallet in the purse, but the car was registered to Arnold and Betty Clay, the woman found dead in the river the day before.

Hayes finished his notes and sat in his vehicle, waiting for a forensics tech to arrive. He knew the small town wouldn't stir for several hours. The morning mist accentuated the charcoal outlines of shuttered homes where residents slept. He caught sight of the imposing crest of Divide Mountain, one of several peaks that loomed over the valley bordered by Bright River, which flowed nearby. His mind turned on the thought that the mountain, a lone sentry with a cloud-veiled peak, was quite possibly the only witness to the grisly murder of Betty Clay.

CHAPTER 4

On Mineral Lake, Sunday morning struggled to burst through chilly air. The muffled flap of outstretched wings sliced the air as the golden eagle circled above the peaceful water. Sharp eyes scanned the hillside and narrowed. Once chosen, the marmot never knew what hit it. Wingtips nearly touched the flowing surface as the large bird carried its paralyzed prey in steely talons upward to an unreachable crag. The predator's scream careened off the boulders and cliff face as the unchallenged eagle declared its victory.

The bird's cry woke Don, and his eyes flicked open just in time to see the morning light cover Lynn's face in a golden glow. He tried to rise, but the twisted sheet pinned him to the bed. Kicking his bare feet, he unraveled the snare woven by a fitful night. Lynn slept curled in a fetal position. She let out a soft whimper.

Don gently rolled his wife onto her back. "Lynn, you're having a nightmare. Wake up. You're dreaming. Come on, honey, you're okay."

Lynn focused on Don's face, only inches away. Her voice cracked. "I tried to scream." She shook her head. "I can't believe...I was choking." Her hand came up then covered her eyes. "I wish it was a bad dream, not something so real." Tears welled up in her puffy eyes.

Don put his arm around his wife. "The sheriff's call really upset you. You cried yourself to sleep."

"Someone killed my mother. It's so wrong."

"I know honey. It's crappy. Do you want to sleep longer? Or, I'll make some coffee."

"Coffee. Awake, maybe I can keep the pictures out of my mind."

Don set his cold feet on the wooden floor and wasted no time pulling on warm clothes. He stood at the kitchenette, and in a few minutes the aroma of coffee being brewed filled their small bedroom.

Don placed the coffee mug in Lynn's hand. "Are you all right?"

Lynn didn't meet his eyes. She stared into the hot drink.

Don sat beside her. "I don't know what to say that will help. You're probably still in shock..."

"Must be." Lynn swirled her spoon round and round. "I feel like I've been in a car crash, or a building fell on me. I don't know what to do or say. How can Mom be murdered? I want it to be a mistake, someone else, not her."

Her fingers trembled as she wiped at tears. "I'm angry. It never should have happened. Not here. It's supposed to be safe here. Why her?"

"It's normal to wonder. Not always possible to understand. Things just happen." Don touched Lynn's forehead. "You're pale, but no fever. I'll stay home with you."

"I feel a little better. Yesterday was gruesome, thoughts so mixed-up. There's nothing I can do but deal with it. You need to be at the yard today. No need for you to sit and hold my hand."

Are you sure you'll be okay by yourself? I can stay home if you need me. "

Lynn produced a thin smile. "I feel rough right now, lack of sleep and all. But, Sheriff Carlson said Maggie would come by later today. It'll help to talk to her. She's such a rock."

Don's eyebrows went up. "And I'm not?"

"Of course you are. I just mean, she's had experience with these types of cases. I'm all upside down, and we're so close. Sometimes I'm shocked at how she understands me when I can't explain something."

"I'll stay with you." Don pulled the quilt up under Lynn's chin. "At least, I can stay until Maggie gets here. I don't want you to be alone."

"I want to pull myself together. She'll be here in a bit. It's past nine and you need to open the lumberyard. The parade is tomorrow. Someone may want stuff for their float, and people need supplies for their weekend cabins. How I feel isn't going to change anything. I have to face this—as bad as it is—and somehow go forward."

"I'm proud of you. This is a hard time and a horrible loss."

"I'll be okay. We depend on the lumberyard. Lack of fishing's going to impact us and every business."

"Point taken." He stood and opened the bedroom door. He pulled his jacket from the coat hook. "I wouldn't leave if Maggie wasn't going to be here with you soon. I can be back by six tonight. I think you should let Mike and Wendy handle the restaurant. It may be a holiday, but with the river damaged, some tourists will check out early. Business could be slow."

Lynn closed her eyes. "'Right now, I just want to keep my mind occupied. I need to get up and start doing something."

Don sat next to his wife and pulled her close. He squeezed her tight. "Honey, I'm sorry. Betty didn't deserve this."

Lynn nestled into his embrace. "The sheriff didn't tell me much other than they found the car. I need Maggie to answer so many questions, and I can't wimp out."

Don kissed her forehead. "Maybe you're right to keep yourself busy."

Lynn's answer was muffled by his heavy wool shirt. "I'm going to miss her so much. I keep seeing her face and thinking how much I love her. She was always there to help me. She was the best mother ever. Dad left everything up to Mom. It should have been a lot different. Last night I kept thinking if she and Dad were still married, maybe she'd never have been a target. It's so tragic. She'd just found love and started a new life with Arnold."

Don wiped away salty droplets from her cheek. "Having you for a daughter made her very happy. I don't understand why Kurt left her. But then, after his heart attack, he changed."

Lynn's voice was bitter. "He bailed on all of us. I think he wanted to outrun old age, and his personality flip-flopped. He wasn't the same anymore. Amy called me a couple of weeks ago and said Dad's spending his time flitting around like a thirty-year-old, seeing one woman after another."

Don stood up. "He's an old goat. Forget about him. He made his choice, and he's out of our lives."

"I know you're still mad at him. I am, too. I haven't spoken to him in over a year. But do you think I should call him and tell him about Mom?"

He faced Lynn with his jaw set. "No. He'll hear about it soon enough, and a call to him right now will just open old wounds. You don't need the aggravation."

Don opened the sturdy wooden door of their ground-level bedroom, and a rush of cool air filled their living quarters along with the pungent scent of pine laced with the smell of burning wood. "Our neighbor has a fire going this morning."

Lynn drew her legs up and circled her arms around them. She rested her chin and inhaled deeply. "I'm sure Mary's been up for hours feeding everyone breakfast. Their cabins are probably full, and the boys are working hard with Dave to get a start on summer."

She sipped her coffee. Her mind rebelled. *The world is going on as usual, without Mom. Will anything ever feel normal again? Everything has changed.*

"I've got to take off. Call me if you need me. Promise?" Don hesitated in the doorway, his muscular frame blocking the filtered light. "Your face is awfully pale."

"I'm fine, just kind of numb. Go ahead."

"All right. See you tonight."

****

The door closed with a thud. Lynn got up, covered the bed, and went to the bathroom to shower. An image of her mom lying in the river flashed through her mind. *God, spare me those visions. It isn't right. She died so horribly.*

She covered her face with a washcloth and fought back a sob. *I can't help her. She's gone. She died alone. Someone should have been with her.*

After the warm water eased her tense muscles, she pulled on jeans, a Pendleton shirt, and lightweight boots. She opened their living quarters' door and surveyed the silent lake scene. She breathed the clean air. Moist vapor drifted upward from the surface and collided with sunbeams as the world prepared for another day.

Even the glorious morning couldn't improve her mood. She closed the door and slowly walked up the stairs into the restaurant.

She moved past empty tables to face the scene filling the large picture windows—each a giant postcard. The azure water tugged at her. This morning, she welcomed the sensation, hoping it might give her strength. A wave of helplessness went through her, and her knees wobbled. *Mom will never see such beauty again.*

In a haze, she stabbed at cleaning and completed routine duties, but she was unable to concentrate. *I've got to see Maggie. Questions are driving me mad. I want answers.*

She grabbed her car keys and walked down to her vehicle. The lake was bluer than the mountain lupine that sprang from the granite soil in spring. As she closed the car door, she looked critically at their restaurant. The two-story structure mimicked the vintage mine buildings with their sloping roofs cascading down hillsides in cubistic sections that housed the chutes used to move rocks laced with gold. She contemplated their frugal five-hundred-square-foot living quarters on the ground level of the restaurant. *This is our home now. It's tiny and lacks amenities, but living this close to nature, I've become fused with the lake and mountains in mind and spirit. I'm at once a captor and a captive of the delicate rhythmic heartbeat of the living lake and a witness to the changing mountains constantly on stage before me. A place of peace and tranquility. Has it all been an illusion?*

She started the car and drove along Mineral Creek until she reached town, then crossed the bridge at the convergence of Mineral Creek and Bright River. Eyes forward, she avoided the spot where her mother's body was found only the day before.

She passed by frontier-style storefronts, some made of logs and many using river rock. The historical mining town was a mix of sturdy brick buildings and newer wood-sided structures, often painted white with cheerful trim of red or green. Most sported high front facades, trying to look more impressive than they were. Half of the town enjoyed paved roads, but sidewalks didn't exist, and a gap-tooth assortment of Swiss chalet shops connected to gray stone buildings built a hundred years before during the Colorado gold rush.

Main Street ran alongside the town square, a football field-size area dotted with pine trees. In honor of Memorial Day, the park was decorated in red, white and blue banners. Tomorrow's parade would go past the park and in front of Hunter's Bar, a two-story red brick hotel and restaurant, situated on Treasure Street at the southwest corner of the central hub. The largest building in town featured eight tall, thin windows on the second floor and provided excellent views of the picturesque community nestled between large mountains. Log-cabin rentals and small historic homes filled the streets throughout town. Two church spires pointed to the heavens, their worship buildings hidden by thick leaves of cottonwood trees. To the west, Bright River sliced through town then flowed south for thirty miles into Gunnison. Steep hillsides circled the small valley and blue spruce marched next to Douglas fir as the town's eight-thousand-foot elevation meandered up to Nugget Top Mountain. Its peak, a lofty fourteen thousand feet, would remain covered in frothy snow until July.

Lynn parked in front of the sheriff's office and hurried inside. Maggie wasn't in. Frustrated, she left a message and returned to the restaurant to await her friend.

****

While waiting for Maggie, Lynn tried to keep busy. She plodded through her chores, checking the supply of steaks and crab legs for the entrées. She stacked twenty russet potatoes on the sink and cleaned and dried each one. Robotic reflexes kept her moving with little thinking. She refilled the dressing containers for the salad bar and prepared sliced carrot sticks, mushrooms, and chickpeas. Several times she passed by the kitchen phone and touched the handset, but retracted her hand. *I can't call anyone and explain Mom is gone. Not yet.*

Evening preparation completed, Lynn gazed out the side window facing the bridge. Her emotions teetered, her grief a stark contrast to the bright sun and images of aspens quaking in the gentle breeze.

A white Jeep crossed the bridge, entered their lot, and parked close to the restaurant. Soon, boots trod the wide stairs leading up to the entrance. Lynn opened the door before a knock sounded. Without a word, her good friend enveloped her in a warm hug.

"Maggie, I'm so glad you're here. Sheriff Carlson called early this morning. Since his call, I keep picturing my mom in pain, and I start to cry again. I need you today. I went by the station…"

The women, so different in appearance, Lynn willowy and blond, Maggie, short with a sultry beauty, entered the restaurant. They chose a front window table and sat down across from one another on cane-seat chairs with curved mahogany backs. A tissue box sat on the table. Lynn slumped with her head bent and arms crossed, hugging herself.

"I wanted to be here earlier, but for a Sunday morning it was hectic." Maggie leaned forward. "Give me your hands." Her strong ones rubbed back and forth, bringing warmth to Lynn's ice-cold fingers. "I'm your friend and want to be here with you. I'm so sorry for your pain. I didn't get to know Betty well, but I could see how much you loved her."

Lynn brushed at tears. "I thought her move here would be a new start with new friends. Dad's behavior and the divorce hurt her deeply. She was embarrassed around her old friends in Piñon. We planned to spend time together once she lived nearby." Her brow creased. "But after Arnold stepped into the picture, we hardly visited. I didn't expect her to marry again so soon. And now, we won't have..."

"Lynn, I'm sure you have good memories. Hang on to those."

"Yes."

"Unfortunately, today I also have a job to do." She cleared her throat. "Officially, Betty's death has been declared a murder."

Lynn scanned Maggie's face. Any trace of the attractive smile the deputy was known for was missing. Instead, her lips formed a tight line. Whether because of her Native American heritage or her police manner, she projected complete control and her straight posture reinforced her direct speech and no-nonsense manner. Her long hair was pulled back and tied. When not on duty, her loosened raven black hair shimmered past strong shoulders.

Maggie asked, "Is Don here?"

"No. He said he'd stay, but he needed to open the lumberyard. Even though it's Sunday, people will want items for the parade tomorrow and his helper is out of town. He has to be there."

"I expected him to be here with you. Will he be back later to help you with the evening dinner service?"

"Oh, yes, by six. I was relieved when he left. He made me nervous hanging around listening to me cry. I'm embarrassed. I'm not being very strong."

Maggie laid a hand on hers. "Give yourself some time. Your employees will be here, won't they?"

"Yes. Mike and Wendy can handle things. We may not have much business with the river ruined."

For a moment, they both observed the lake. The late-May scene outside did nothing to calm Lynn. She wiped at each eye as tears began to flow again. "I thought I was safe here in Elk Hills, and I'm sure Mom did, too. I'm angry. Instead of peace, it brought death."

Lynn yanked out a tissue and blew her nose.

Maggie carefully placed a notebook and small recorder on the table. "Murder in Elk Hills is unusual. Highway 50 runs not far from town, and we get our share of drifters and vagrants, especially in the summer. But still, even on the weekends, by nine o'clock, the town is asleep. Our crime rate is very low."

"Obviously not low enough. I have huge questions."

"I know you do. I'm sorry. Sheriff Carlson gave you a little information regarding your mother's death. He wanted me to tell you in person what we've learned."

"I need to understand."

"I'll record our conversation so I don't miss anything that may help our investigation. As you know, Betty's body was discovered in the river Saturday morning during all of the commotion over the river damage. Arnold had called the Elk Hills Sheriff's Office about eleven o'clock Friday night. He reported he was concerned his wife hadn't come home from shopping and requested a search for their vehicle. As the deputy made his rounds Friday night, he kept his eye out, but it wasn't until early this morning, Sunday close to 1:00 a.m. when the car was found."

"The sheriff called me early this morning around five o'clock and said it was found but not where."

"It was behind an abandoned gas station southwest of town, on Wagoneer Street. It was well-hidden in the back."

Lynn leaned forward. "I know Mom. She'd have struggled. She had spirit..."

"Possibly. It's hard to tell you this, but she was suffocated with a plastic bag."

Lynn gasped. Maggie's words stung as if a Band-Aid had been yanked off her heart. She pressed her eyes closed and rocked. A choked sob escaped the hand covering her mouth. "It makes me sick. Don didn't let me near her body at the river, I never dreamed. The sheriff only said she'd been killed prior to being placed in the river. He didn't tell me how she was killed."

Maggie moved to sit next to Lynn. Her arms held her friend.

"I'm really sorry. If it helps at all, she passed away in only a couple of minutes." Barely audible, she added, "Also, she wasn't raped."

Lynn's eyes closed. Her body trembled. "Thank God. I prayed..."

Maggie got up and went to the kitchen. She returned with a glass of water.

"Here, take a drink. I hate having to tell you all of this."

Lynn sipped the water and blew her nose several times, then rubbed her swollen eyes.

Maggie studied her friend. "Are you all right? I can come back later if this is too much right now."

Lynn took a deep breath. She held the table edge tightly. "Please stay. It's such a shock. I feel helpless and...guilty I wasn't there to help her. I guess I'm afraid, too."

"Your feelings are understandable. We want to find out who did this, just like you do. No one ever fully recovers from this kind of loss, but you'll get through. Don will help, and I'll be here if you need me."

Lynn formed a fist. She spoke rapidly. "I keep thinking, if Mom and Dad were still married, she'd be alive. She would have been safe in Piñon, not living in Elk Hills. After thirty years of marriage, the breakup was a shock. I wanted to help her, but there was nothing I could do. Dad galloped off with another woman. Gossip spread through town, and it hurt her deeply. Now, just when she's starting over with someone who loves her, she's killed."

"Being in law enforcement, I've seen things people have done that don't add up, no matter how you view them. Do you want me to tell you more about what we've discovered?"

"Yes. Go on."

Maggie sat back and took a breath. "The coroner estimates the time of death at between ten p.m. Friday night or early Saturday morning. Once the final autopsy report is complete, a more definitive time may be evident, but being in the water may blur the time. Betty's wallet and jewelry appear to have been stolen. We don't have complete information yet."

"Do you think it was a mugger?"

"It's a possibility. The investigators are checking her car for fingerprints."

Lynn frowned. "I read in the paper last week about the two inmates who escaped from prison in Salida. What about them?"

"Sheriff Carlson is checking with the corrections facility regarding the escape. We're also checking all reports of any suspicious persons seen in the Elk Hills area."

"Did anyone hear screams? See anything?"

Maggie shook her head. "Nothing of any help. The station did receive a call around ten Friday night reporting a loud argument, and a deputy was dispatched, but..."

"He didn't see her car?"

"No. Not until this morning."

Lynn's voice was barely audible. "If only someone had been there to help her." She rocked back and forth.

Silence stretched between them as the regulator clock on the wall nearby ticked away time at a funereal pace. Maggie placed her hand on Lynn's. "It's a deserted area of town. A few homes here and there." She cleared her throat. "I need to ask you a couple of questions."

"Okay."

"Lynn, you're not a suspect, but I need to ask just for the record, where were you between seven o'clock Friday night and early Saturday morning?"

"Here with Don all evening and night. Why did Arnold wait so long to call the sheriff?"

Maggie shut off the recorder. "Lynn, I have to do this interview in steps. Help me, okay? I'll answer everything I can once I'm finished."

"I'm sorry. Go on."

Maggie restarted the recorder. "How long have you known Arnold Clay?"

"I met him in September of last year, so about eight months before he and Mom married in April."

"Describe your relationship with him."

"Not much of one, really. I didn't have any problem with him, but there was something funny about him." Lynn lifted a shoulder. "I didn't want to challenge Mom's decision to marry, but he just didn't seem the right man for her."

Maggie stopped writing. "Lynn, can you be specific? Did he do or say anything that alerted you to some kind of agenda or major personality flaw?"

Lynn took her time to reply. "Nothing huge. It was more like they didn't seem to go together. Mom was delicate. He's big, barrel-chested, and bald, with heavy eyebrows. He seemed overpowering, her opposite and so different from my dad. I didn't see why she was attracted to him."

"You've given me a general physical description of Arnold. What was your impression of him as a person? Did anything in particular bother you?"

Lynn hesitated. "It's hard to say. I don't want to sound like Arnold seemed dangerous, just rough around the edges. Before they married, I met him twice, so my opinion is based on little contact. I don't want to point fingers."

Maggie's eyes sharpened with interest. "Even a small item may be important. Tell me about anything you sensed and let me decide, okay?"

"There was one time. They'd dated for about a month when she brought Arnold by the restaurant to meet me. After a quick handshake, he walked out onto the deck and stared at the mountain across the lake. Mom and I joined him. He asked me, 'How much is your side of the lake worth?'"

"What did you say?"

"I was shocked by his nosy question and mumbled something like, 'It's hard to know today's land prices.'"

"How did he respond?"

"He didn't skip a beat. He said to Mom, 'Your land, with all the old mines on it, is worth a lot more than this side.'"

Maggie said, "It sounds like Betty had told him how you and Don split the property with your parents. What did Betty say?"

"She acted flustered...no, embarrassed. She told him as far as she knew; the old shafts above her land were abandoned failures. Arnold smiled, put his arm around her, and gave her a squeeze. They stayed about fifteen minutes. Then they left."

"Lynn, did you have any other contact with him?"

"Carol and Wendell Trim invited Don and me to dinner at their cabin here in Elk Hills in January. Arnold and Mom were also invited. Don couldn't come, but I showed up, anxious to see if my feeling about Arnold was right, or if I'd exaggerated."

"How did Carol and Wendell know Arnold?"

"He rented a small cabin behind their home, and Carol introduced him to Mom. Once Mom and Arnold met, they discovered they both had ties to the Aurora and Piñon areas."

Maggie frowned. "Did you think it odd that two people from Piñon would bump into each other in this small mountain town?"

"I never thought about it. It's true we don't get too many tourists from the Denver area, and Piñon isn't exactly a metropolis. Mom explained to me they knew of each other but hadn't been acquainted. Mom was in real estate in Piñon for a few years, and she was also in a number of clubs, like the art association. Dad was in the Elks. She knew a lot of people. She told me from their first meeting, she and Arnold spent a lot of time with Wendell and Carol Trim. They all went for some fun four-wheel rides through old ghost towns and mining camps last fall. She said they got along well."

"How did Arnold act the evening you joined them for dinner?"

"Pleasant. Wendell's stories thrilled him. You know, the ones about the high-grade ore found on the old mining claims across from here on Golden Cross Mountain. As you know, Mom and Dad owned the property on the other side of the lake from us. When she and Dad divorced, he let her keep the land. He didn't want anything to do with Mineral Lake."

"What kinds of stories did Wendell tell Arnold?"

Lynn smiled. "I'm sure you've heard them all. He started off with Tin Cup's discoveries. Next, he brought up St. Elmo and then the Golden Cross Mine right above us here on Mineral Lake. Arnold's eyes bugged out as Wendell came to the part about the millions in gold ore that came from those areas."

Maggie smiled. "It is exciting history."

"We all know the abandoned mines are played out, just hollow shells of past riches, but I'm sure Arnold caught gold fever that night. He said he'd been to Tin Cup, and Wendell had to tell him the stories about the Twin Pines Mine there."

Maggie said, "Try to remember exactly what Wendell told Arnold. It could be important."

"Well, you know how Wendell loves an audience, and he's a good storyteller. He started with tales of miners gone mad with greed. He bragged how just up the pass, between 1895 and 1910, Tin Cup held the spotlight as the largest gold district in Colorado, and the Twin Pines Mine's big strike made history when miners blasted into the Chapel Vug, a living room-size underground void with two tons of crystallized gold along with crystals of the gold telluride minerals."

Lynn rose and stood in front of the large window as she tried to picture the scene. "Arnold sat on the edge of his chair and urged Wendell to go on with what he knew about gold there and in Elk Hills."

Maggie said, "Keep going."

Lynn cleared her throat. "Wendell brought up the story of 'Loopy' Joe Stock, the old prospector who discovered gold around Tin Cup. The statistics he reeled off were mind-boggling. Finally, Arnold wanted to know if any of the rich mines were still operating. Wendell said by 1960, the last one had closed down."

Lynn leaned back. "Don and I have read several books about this area, and we've heard all of this history many times—from Wendell as well as others—but the story still gives me goose bumps."

"How did Arnold act?"

"He seemed entranced. I'd swear he almost swayed. He begged Wendell to continue, so Wendell explained how the future is still bright for the Tin Cup area, due to the rise in gold prices. Gold has sold for over fifteen hundred dollars per ounce and silver is nearly twenty-five dollars per ounce. Wendell said the computer industry is using rare earth elements, called REEs, like tellurium in circuit boards, and there could be other applications for the unique elements found in these mountains. He said foreign representatives are buying up lots of mines to corner the market on REEs. But as to physical mining, the time it takes to get mining permits keeps activity down."

Maggie's pen stopped. "What did Betty say to all the gold lore?"

"She seemed just as excited as Arnold, wanting to know if any rich ore had come from the Elk Hills area and if any old mines still had a possibility of producing again."

"I'll bet Wendell recounted the story of the mother lode in this area."

"Of course he did. Every newcomer hears how 'Loopy' Joe Stock spent time here in Elk Hills after he cashed out of the Tin Cup area."

Lynn sat down. "They both became excited, especially when Wendell embellished his yarn with history of the Golden Cross Mine. When Arnold heard Wendell mention Mom's property, his jaw dropped."

"How did Betty react?"

"She squeezed Arnold's arm. Next, Wendell pulled out a book with pictures of the Golden Cross Mine and said it had a pure vein of gold six feet high. It went into the center of the mountain for a good three hundred yards. Wendell put the cherry on top when he mentioned the area above Mom's property had been the richest ore-bearing site in southern Colorado."

Lynn jumped up. "I've got a book with the same pictures. It's in the bar. I'll get it."

She produced the book and thumbed through until she found the section on the Golden Cross Mine.

"Here it says, 'High-grading at the mine became a big problem. When miners left their shift, they were searched. With ore so rich, stealing became common.' Arnold's eyes bugged out at the pictures."

"Yeah. I think the way the mine played out at the end left hope someday the big 'ribbon of gold' would appear again."

Lynn said, "Imagine an internal slide, which cut the ribbon of gold like a pair of scissors. It left miners digging all over the mountain, hoping to find the spot where the vein would start again. I've heard dynamite now and then. Unfortunately, none of the new miners have found anything like the thick vein of gold in the Golden Cross."

The deputy tapped her pen several times. "Did Betty mention she knew this history?"

"No, she didn't. When Don and I, along with my dad and Betty came here, we purchased four mining claims. After the divorce Betty retained one claim, the Cross Basin. Its located at the base of the mountain up several hundred feet from the county road, you can see the many abandoned mines farther up. Arnold asked who she bought the property from, and she indicated through local Realtor Sandra Steele."

Lynn waited while Maggie wrote. "At the time, I thought it was funny how excited Arnold seemed about the gold history, but now I wonder if he went a little mad over the stories."

"He may have. It's happened a lot in the past. Gold fever can twist a person's mind." Maggie stopped writing. "Was Betty a wealthy woman?"

"Not really. She owned the lake property here and a small home in Piñon. She got both from my father in the divorce settlement. She found success with a small art gallery in Piñon, and I'm sure she had some savings put aside. With her Social Security and savings, I'd describe her as comfortable but frugal. She never spent much of anything, no trips or expensive things. She always saved for a rainy day. She told me she opened the art gallery on a shoestring."

"Do you know of any life insurance?"

"I have no idea about that."

"Are you in her will?"

Lynn gulped in surprise. "Gosh, Maggie, I'm her only child, but I have no idea. She never discussed her will. She and Dad didn't like prying. They kept their finances private. You might ask Amy, her closest longtime friend. She lives in Piñon, and she may know about Mom's will or who she's used as her attorney since the divorce."

"Thanks, Lynn. That's all I need to know for now."

"Can I ask some questions?"

"Sure."

"Did Arnold say why he called the sheriff's office so late?"

"I can only tell you Arnold's statement indicated he was at home that night working in his garage on a woodworking project. Close to nine o'clock, he realized how late it was. They only have one vehicle, so he was unable to drive around to look for her."

"Did he say where she went to shop?"

"Yes, to the art supply store in Alpine Shopping Center on Third Street. Arnold said he thought she might have stopped to visit someone and just lost track of time. Then he became concerned she'd had a flat tire or car trouble of some kind."

Lynn interrupted, "Why didn't he call her cell phone?"

"She didn't have it with her. So, by eleven o'clock, he called the sheriff's office asking for their help."

Lynn pondered the explanation. "Then Arnold has no alibi? Or was someone with him?"

"Nope, all alone."

Lynn slowly rocked. "Is Arnold a suspect?"

"In a murder case, the spouse is always considered a 'person of interest.' They're usually first in line to inherit the estate. I can't tell you anything more."

Both women were silent. Maggie studied Lynn's face.

"I didn't like the guy much. I was uneasy about him," Lynn said. "But I never dreamed he'd harm her. For God's sake, he's a retired policeman. I expected Mom to choose an honest man. Someone she could trust."

Maggie said, "Yes, it's a fair assumption. I'm not saying he's guilty. But he also has a lot of knowledge about murder. We have to examine all possibilities."

Lynn stood and paced again. "I can find out some stuff about him. There must be people in Piñon who know him. They said they had mutual friends there. I'll try to figure out who they are and call them."

Maggie motioned for Lynn to sit down. "Lynn, it's very important for you to stay out of this investigation. Our office is handling it. If you think of someone we should contact, let me know. You're not to get involved. Promise me, please."

Lynn tore at the tissue she held. “But I feel so guilty. I didn’t speak my mind to her about Arnold when I had the chance. I was uneasy about him, but I said nothing. Now it’s too late.” Tears shone in her eyes. “If I think of something, I’ll make sure you hear about it. Is that okay?”

“Promise me you’ll keep your distance, and I’ll keep you informed as much as I can. Trust me.”

“I will. I know you want to see justice for her like I do. She deserves it.”

“Don’t be reckless. This is a murder. There may be real danger here.” Maggie took Lynn’s hand. “If a person has killed once, he—or she—usually won’t hesitate to kill again. Think not only about yourself but also about Don.”

“I hadn’t considered our personal vulnerability. You’re right.”

Maggie gathered her things, and they walked downstairs together.

The detective opened her car door. “Don’t hesitate to call if you’re upset or need to talk to someone.”

“Thanks. Later today, I thought I’d give Mom’s friend Amy a call and let her know what happened. I’m dreading the call, but I have to do it.”

Maggie gave Lynn a hug then slid behind the wheel. “I think you’re doing pretty well. You’re stronger than you realize. We’re anxious to solve this crime. It has all of our attention.”

Lynn said, “It’s just so sad. She died with no dignity. It makes me boiling mad to even think her husband might have killed her. He might have gotten away with it before, but I hope not this time.”

“What did you say?”

“I figured you’d already discovered his second wife died mysteriously.”

“No, we hadn’t. How do you know that?”

“When Mom told me about their involvement, I asked if Arnold was divorced. She said no, his wife had died. I asked, ‘Did she die from an illness?’ She said, ‘No, she died in a house fire.’”

Maggie’s eyes narrowed. “What did you say?”

"Before I said anything, Mom quickly told me Arnold had mourned her death and was hurt by the ugly rumors that circulated afterward."

"Did she tell you what the rumors were?"

"She didn't say much, other than he and his second wife had no children together. Arnold inherited her home and business in town. I think she sensed my concern, but she brushed it all off as unwarranted gossip and jealousy, typical in a small town."

"Lynn, did this worry you?"

"It definitely concerned me, but she chirped like a happy bird. I didn't know Arnold and she did, so I trusted her opinion. I gave her my best wishes. I was elated she'd found love and someone who cared about her."

"So, this situation didn't worry her."

"Not at all. I did tell her it seemed a little soon to jump into marriage after knowing him for such a short time, but Mom just laughed and said, 'At sixty-nine, what's the point in waiting?'"

"Did she mention Arnold's age?"

"No, but I think he's at least fifteen years younger, maybe more. But with her facelift, Mom appeared younger and very attractive. I'm her only child. She had me at forty-one. I was a real surprise. The only other family she had left was a cousin. Mom did mention that Arnold had a son from his first marriage. They don't see much of each other."

Maggie added to her notes.

Lynn said, "I'm really upset now. If Arnold did it, you'll have to tie me up to keep me from hanging him from the highest tree."

"Please, keep our conversation private. I'll keep in touch on any progress. Remember what I said. Leave this investigation to us. We're experienced, and you're not."

Lynn held the car door. "You're going to investigate Arnold, aren't you?"

Maggie said, "He's more than a person of interest, He's our prime suspect. He has an attorney."

"Can you tell me who his attorney is? Someone local?"

"His son, Trent, is handling all inquiries. He's from Denver. Have you ever met him?"

"No. I'm real surprised, though. Mom said he refused to meet her when she and Arnold stopped in Denver on their way back from their marriage in Las Vegas. She said Arnold and Trent argued a lot and weren't even on speaking terms for years at a time."

"Well, he's put up road blocks to keep us away from Arnold. I've got to go. I'll call you soon, I promise."

As Maggie's vehicle faded from view, Lynn concentrated on a patch of cloudless sky. She pictured her mother and rode with the tears that carried her back to her childhood. *Oh, how I wish yesterday had never happened.*

CHAPTER 5

After Maggie left, Lynn dialed Arnold's home number.

"This is Betty's daughter, may I speak to Arnold?"

The voice replied, "I'm Arnold's son. Sorry, he's not taking any calls today. Please call back later."

"Sure, of course. I will." Hanging up, she stared at the phone. *So much for any mutual consolation of shared grief.*

Wandering around the restaurant, inertia set in and images of a bleak future filled Lynn's mind. Her grim thoughts were cut short when her mother's friend Amy called.

"Oh, Lynn, I'm in complete shock." She began to sob. "I had a call this morning about Betty. It's horrible. Sheriff Carlson said they found Betty's phone book in her purse, with my phone number written in red, so they assumed I was family." Choked sobs came over the line.

"I'm sick, too. I'd planned to call you. I didn't know Sheriff Carlson had reached you already. Deputy Maggie Hernandez just left."

"Poor Betty. I never dreamed in a million years…something like this would happen to someone so good. No sweeter angel than Betty ever lived. She's been my best friend for fifty years. I'm going to miss her so much."

"There's no way to understand it. I'm at a complete loss."

"I wish I was there now to comfort you. Your mom loved you so much."

Only their sobs broke the silence. Finally, Lynn said, "I tried to reach Arnold to express my condolences, but his son was screening his calls and said he wasn't taking any today. I can understand. I'll try again tomorrow."

Amy's voice rose. "The sheriff told me the most awful things. He said they think a mugger attacked her." Lynn heard her blow her nose. "I'm not surprised. I let him know how Arnold made Betty park his precious new car off by itself so no one would put a ding in the door."

"When did she tell you that?" Lynn tried to calm the quiver in her voice.

"Last month I was on my way back from visiting a friend in Jeanville and I stopped to see Betty for just one night. I don't get to see her much since she moved to Elk Hills. We went shopping in town at the new shopping center, and she parked on the edge of the parking lot. I explained how unsafe it seemed, but she said Arnold insisted. Some husband, he cared more about a car door than he did about Betty."

"I hardly know Arnold, but that sounds pretty controlling. I'm surprised."

"I never trusted Arnold. I wish Betty had never met him. I always thought he was hinky."

Lynn pressed fingers to her temple. "What are you saying? Have you known Arnold for a long time?"

"He lived in town ten or twelve years, but he wasn't around much. He was married to Blue Bird."

"Blue Bird? The Native American lady who owned the gift shop in town?"

"Yes. She was a lot older than Arnold, and after she died, he leased out her store and left town. She didn't have any children or family, so he inherited all of her property, even her cabin in Gold Creek, up near Idaho Springs. Neither of them socialized much, and they didn't have any close friends."

"Mom mentioned Arnold had a wife who died. Do you know any details?"

"Her house behind the store burned almost to the ground. The authorities said a cigarette started it. We all thought it seemed strange since no one remembered her smoking. In fact, in her store, she sold herbal remedies to maintain good health. Some even considered her a healer."

"Amy, the sheriff thinks in Mom's case it was probably a random mugging. But what you've just told me might point to Arnold's involvement."

"Oh, my God. Poor, poor Betty." Her voice became a wail.

"Don't say a word to anyone about this. Promise?"

"Oh, I promise. How sad if Betty put her trust in this man, and he plotted to end her life. Oh, I wish I was there. I'd like to smack him in the face."

"The sheriff may call you again. They're gathering information."

"Well, I'm the executor of Betty's will. I didn't mention it when he called. Should I let him know? Of course, you were in Betty's will. She wanted to leave you the home your father built in Piñon. She only had one distant cousin, Nanette in Indiana. I don't know how much money Betty had left. She gave Arnold bundles since they got married."

Lynn almost dropped the phone. "What? Why? They were married less than two months."

"Well, at first she said they needed to fix up the cabin in Gold Creek to store their stuff."

"What stuff?"

"Mostly Betty's furniture from her place in Piñon and a little furniture from his condo in Denver. Arnold said it would cost less than renting a storage unit."

"What did she have to fix?"

"Oh, the roof leaked, and Betty said field mice came in. She was afraid they'd eat all of her nice furniture. Also, the shower came out in a trickle, so she helped get the well improved. She told me they might use the place as a summer home in the future. Arnold also needed help for his nutty invention."

"Invention?"

"Some kind of sluice-box contraption for gold mining. After they got married in Las Vegas, they stopped by to visit with me, and he showed me a drawing of it. I didn't see anything special about it. My father used to do gold panning and dredging. He put together a nifty sluice box of his own."

"What did Arnold say about his?"

"Oh, he bragged it worked in a special way, and Betty just beamed and said she thought it showed such genius and innovation. Privately, she told me she preferred to go along with it and help finance the patent expenses rather than fight with Arnold. She added if he didn't get his way, he pouted and wouldn't speak to her for days. She was frightened he might leave her. After she gave him the money, he'd be nice again."

"I don't understand why Mom put up with him. Why was she so desperate to be married again?"

"I probably shouldn't say anything. She made me swear I wouldn't tell a soul, but now that she's gone, it might explain why she let him control everything. She had a medical problem."

"Mom didn't say anything to me about being sick."

"She didn't like talking about it, but even before her marriage to your dad ended, she'd developed depression. She called it 'the big D.' She was devastated and told me no one would want her if they knew about it. I think Arnold held her condition over her head. She told me she was so embarrassed at her age to have a mental disorder. She thought her life was over."

"God, this is a nightmare. It sounds like Mom was so depressed she got involved with a man who meant to take her money, as long as it lasted, or as long as she went along with it. If only she'd confided in me."

"Lynn, I tried to talk to her. I explained that lots of people have depression, but she seemed blind. She thought with Arnold she could be happy again. I didn't know what to say to her. They hadn't been married very long. I hoped things would iron themselves out as time went on, but her time ended."

Amy took a breath then spoke rapidly. "Arnold's a rat. I'm sure of it. I'm going to call the sheriff and tell him everything I know about the man. It's been years since she gave me a copy of her will, but I'll find it. I'll get right back to you. I love you. Take care."

Lynn closed her eyes and hung up the phone. Her fist hit the counter.

With so much to think about, Lynn had forgotten the time. She glanced at the clock and quickly prepared for the dinner hour.

Mike, their cook, showed up and found Lynn behind the bar. Without a word, he walked around and enveloped her in a hug.

He shuffled his feet. "Lynn, you know how this town talks. I'm sorry to hear about your mother."

"Thanks, Mike."

"I just want you to know I've lived here all my life, and this kind of thing has never happened in our town. We're good to people. Had to be a stranger. They'll catch him."

"I hope you're right. I'm praying they find whoever did it."

Lynn put down her dishrag. "Mike, I need you to manage the restaurant tonight. I don't expect Don until after six o'clock, and if we have any customers, you and Wendy will have to handle them. I'm wiped out."

"Don't worry. We'll see to everything. You should take it easy."

"I've got to. Thanks."

She walked downstairs to their bedroom and opened the curtains to search the night. The setting sun stroked the mountain to the west, and the sky held only a smudge of lingering light, which outlined the jagged ridgeline in pink. Higher up, a deep vault of purple hung in a hammock of white stars. Lynn closed her eyes. *Mom, I pray that you find peace and God has His arms around you.*

Later that night, when Don entered their living quarters, he found Lynn sound asleep. He pulled the quilt around her shoulders and settled beside her, careful to not disturb her.

Chapter 6

Memorial Day in Elk Hills spread rays of morning sunlight across Arnold's kitchen table. Hands cupped around a mug of black coffee, Trent sat across from his father. Silence stretched between them. Arnold hunched forward in his chair.

Trent finally spoke. "They'll have your car for several days. Do you want me to take you somewhere to get a rental?"

"Yeah, best to do it today. Need to get around somehow. Only rental place is at the airport."

"I plan to stay here as long as you need me. Plenty to be done as soon as they release the body."

Arnold snapped, "Don't call her a body. She was my wife. At least you can say her name. Betty. Hear me? Betty."

"Sorry, I didn't...only meant that after the autopsy, you need to decide on burial or cremation."

"Just because you didn't know her...still need to respect her memory. You couldn't spare a couple of hours for dinner to meet her. Now it's too late."

"Sure, Dad, sure. Now it's my fault she's gone. As usual, I screwed up. Never could please you."

His father harrumphed. "You try to please me? That's a laugh."

Trent walked outside to smoke. His eye twitched from holding back his anger, which hovered dangerously near the surface. *Dinky town and tiptoeing around*

Dad is wearing thin. If I don't get out of here soon, I'll explode. He thought of the two-hundred-mile drive he'd made Saturday from his home in Wildflower to be with his father during his time of need. *Morning sun's coming up now. It'll set the glass-mirrored office buildings of Denver ablaze brighter than idols to the Sun God. I miss the city already. I'll take traffic over the boredom offered by this hick town anytime.*

Trent's mind went back to March when he'd returned the urgent message left by his father on his office phone. The conversation was etched in his mind. He'd asked what was so important.

His dad had fairly bubbled over with his news. "Just got married in Vegas to a wonderful woman. Met her in Elk Hills. Next week, we'll be in Denver, and I thought—hoped—you'd meet us while we're in town...have some dinner and—"

Trent had cut him off. "Oh, want to bury the hatchet and behave as father and son again, all family-like? Sorry, can't make it. I seem to remember you didn't find the time or wherewithal when I begged for help to keep my life from falling apart. It's all one way with you—Arnold Clay's way or nothing."

"Son, don't say that. You know why I stopped giving you money, and anyway, I don't have any to spare. Twenty-five years on the force, busted-up back, and my lousy pension barely pays the rent. I'm just scraping by. It was Betty that bought us a decent car. Mine was ten years old, and I don't even have the money to fix the leaky roof on the Gold Creek cabin. All I know is police work, and at my age, that means some dopey security job."

Trent fired back, "And, clearly, no money for your deadbeat gambler son, who's about to lose his house, wife, and child. Admit it. You're ashamed of me." He switched gears. "If you're so broke, how'd you find a woman to marry you?"

"I caught Betty on the rebound from a nasty divorce. She's well-off, and she believes in my sluice-box invention. After some convincing, she's even willing to back it. She's quite a bit older than me, but keeps herself up good. I'm lucky anyone's interested in a bald-headed, potbellied ex-cop walking around with empty pockets. Any sexy beauty queens I pass look right through me."

"So, two lonely souls found one another. Well, lucky you. Next time you call, make sure it's urgent. I'm busy digging out of deep shit in my own life."

He'd started to hang up, but his father continued. "I'm here for you, Trent. I'm still your father. I know I wasn't there much—"

"Sure, talk to you whenever." Reflex had taken over, and he'd slammed the phone down. Even now he remembered the pressure in both temples and how they'd pulsed with pain, the normal reaction to any conversation with his father.

Different day, same response, sitting on the porch with his distant parent inside, his headache grew, and he tried to massage away the residue of years of disappointment as a boy raised without a mother and, on top of that, a cop's son. Memories of a father always on duty or working overtime, empty seats at baseball games or birthday parties flooded his mind. *I tried to get close to him, even joined in training the K-9 dogs he brought home. But, as usual, I wasn't good enough. Dad loved those dogs more than me.*

Trent rubbed out his cigarette and held the stub in his fingers. *Little did I know when I talked to Dad that day how bad things really were. I was a hooked fish, ready to be gutted.*

He paced back and forth on the porch and remembered how he'd expected to get popped by one of Salvatori's men. He'd decided then and there what he had to do.

With no way to pay the rent on his office, he'd terminated his lease and moved his computer and files to his home. *I know I stopped and bought some tequila, then drove home. It was quiet inside. Everyone slept, and I spent the night drinking. It was late morning when something woke me. I remember the bleached light spilling through blinds left open to the morning as my optic nerve screamed surrender and planted a white flag in the base of my skull. Damn tequila had turned my mouth into cotton and killed enough brain cells so all I could pull together were jangled thoughts about the night before.*

The sound of the garage door opening had pulled him from the abyss. Stiff from sleeping on the couch, he'd gone from den to kitchen and managed to hit his toe on boxes stacked against the wall. He'd opened the connecting door to the garage just as the car trunk banged shut.

His fogged brain took in the sight of Christina as she bent to buckle Kendra into the child car seat. His fist exploded against the garage wall, and he wiped the blood on his pants. All he saw was Kendra's lower lip as it trembled and her SpongeBob T-shirt damp from tears.

His worst fear was right in front of him. He'd begged Christina to wait. Talk it over. But she'd ignored him. She screeched, "No. I've had it with your problems, and I'm through paying for everything. You've sucked me dry."

"I'm begging you for more time, some kind of intervention."

She snapped, "You're ridiculous. Five years isn't long enough? You ran from every kind of help I suggested." She slammed the Volvo's door. "You're a sick gambler and diligently working towards alcoholism. I'm not wasting the rest of my life on you and suffocating in a crappy marriage. I deserve a hell of a lot more than what you're giving." She started the car and shouted, "You want an intervention? Have one with the movers. They'll be here tomorrow."

Desperate, he'd peered at her through the tinted window, told her he'd change, and that Salvatori would need him, and money would come in. She wouldn't listen.

She started to back out of the garage and then stopped and rolled down the window. "Some lawyer you are, big shot. Salvatori uses you, and you don't even get paid, so now we've lost our house. I hired a real attorney. He's sending bankruptcy and divorce papers. Look for them." The car jerked backward out of the driveway.

Standing on the curb he watched as his daughter's faint silhouette disappeared, her face buried in the curls of her Barbie doll. All he could do was blow a kiss to the only perfect being in his life.

Powerless fists clenched as the car speed down the street, ripping his baby from him. The memory tore at his manliness, and bile rose in his throat. A grisly scene flashed across his mind of Christina on the garage floor, thrashing like a gaffed fish, his shoe on her throat. There was no reason to say anything more. Kendra was gone, house, money, all gone.

Trent wanted to shake off the fading image of his child. He lit another cigarette and meandered around his dad's front yard, still lost in thought. Before that hideous morning was over, his client Tony Salvatori had called to rail at him. The casino owner reminded him how much money he owed and the job he'd been given. Even now, months later, Trent remembered how he kowtowed throughout the conversation.

Tony shouted, "I'm not sitting around on bail forever. I got places I need to be. If you don't get me off on the murder charge, I'll have you cut up in so many pieces your mother will rename you *Cuisinart*." The big Italian had paused, then added, "You got my meaning, college boy?"

Trent had to yank a reply from the pit of his gut. "I assure you, I'll have it worked out soon." The last comment he heard from the casino owner was the hiss of his ever-present Havana being extinguished in a glass of booze. A dial tone ended the call.

Sweat had rolled down between his shoulder blades. He'd thrown papers and files into his briefcase. A name had caught his attention: Jake Dixon. *No time to piss off Tony. Better tidy up that deadbeat's case*, he'd cautioned himself. *Got to figure some way to get Tony out of the murder noose or I'm road kill with my toes sticking up from a grave somewhere in the forest.*

Trent had barreled south down Highway 25 from his home to Denver. The carnival-colored carpet of wildflowers spread along the foothills never pierced his concentration as he grappled with the likelihood his client had killed his casino partner, George Wilson. Fear had gripped him as he realized his dilemma. *Damn, I've only handled small issues for Tony: labor disputes or property acquisitions. Old Ned took a convenient time to become too sick to manage this ball of wax for Tony. Cagey bastard knew when to fade into the background and let me step up as head attorney. And risk getting disposed of if I fail.*

He'd spent less than an hour at his office then he'd driven eight blocks to West Colfax Avenue. He parked and entered the Denver Downtown Detention Center. Immediately, the familiar stench hit him. Slumped into an uncomfortable chair in the visitation room, he tried to get a grip. The morning disaster marched through his mind as he stared at the ceiling. A fly circled over the metal table. The grating buzz irked him. After the fly made several midair loops, its erratic movements slowed and the insect spiraled to the floor. Trent casually pressed his shoe over the flopping creature. The half-severed body stuck to the sole as frantic wings tried to rotate. He placed his middle finger next to the maimed fly, aimed, and flicked it across the room. It stuck to the wall. His thoughts went to Christina. *Did you have a good flight, Christina*? His reverie was cut short as Jake Dixon entered the room.

Trent only took one look to size up Jake Dixon. *He's less than zero to me. The homely guy standing in front of me just begs to be used.*

"How 'bout deese?" Jake said as he held his hands up.

"Guard, take the cuffs off."

"Dat asshole judge gave me four months for beatin' dat slime-bag Paco. How I gonna do four months? Two punks already jumped me."

"Yes, he did, and yes, you can. You pled guilty. Did you expect to get a medal?"

Trent pushed the paper and pen to the lumpy-faced bouncer. "Sign the form. It's a formality for your final Gold Bar Casino paycheck and termination of your employment." Trent coughed. "Between the disinfectant, BO, and piss smell in here, you might not even make it four months."

Jake signed the form. "My girlfriend needs help and money while I'm in this shit-hole. Our baby..."

Trent stuffed the papers into his briefcase. "You're too ugly to have a girlfriend, and what baby?"

"Maria Garcia, she's a dancer at the Gold Bar Casino in Oreland. Dat's how we met." He took a scrap of paper from his shirt and pressed it into Trent's hand. "Dis here's her phone number. Ya gotta call her. Tell her I'm here."

"Call her yourself. You get one call a week. Anyway, with you in here, she'll hook up with some other guy. Best to forget her."

"No, ya don't understand. She's my woman. We got a baby."

Trent motioned to the guard. "Forget her, it will—"

"Wait. Salvatori said you'd take care of everything."

"Tony Salvatori doesn't want to see your face again. What use are you to him? You blew it. Don't you get it? The man you punched into mush, Paco, is important to his organization. You're not."

Jake interrupted, "No, let me—"

"Listen, there's an avalanche of shit called a murder charge coming down on Salvatori. Neither of us have time to deal with your stinking jail stay."

"I worked for Salvatori six years. I done my job. Dah punk got outta line." Leg shackles clanked as Jake tried to reach Trent.

"Back up, you punch-drunk slob. You got rough with the wrong man." He walked out the door as two guards cuffed the inmate again.

Jake yelled, "Ya gotta help Maria."

Trent continued down the hall and rounded the corner.

****

All that week, Trent had boxed up the last of his files and made arrangements for them to be shipped to a small office he'd rented in Piñon. He mentally reviewed his plan to stall the foreclosure on his home in Wildflower as long as he could, then find an apartment in Piñon. His old home town was close to Denver and rent was cheap.

In his den, he poured over Tony's arrest papers and statement. By Friday, he received a call from the Denver Downtown Detention Center infirmary medical administrator.

Trent had barked into the phone, "Who? Jake Dixon? Why the hell are you calling me?" He listened as Dr. Andrew described the attack.

"Four men jumped Jake. He received multiple kicks to his groin along with a deep stab wound to his genitals. He'll live, but there's infection. Probably be able to raise his flagpole, but children are out of the picture. He's asking for you."

"Crap. I'm up to my neck in problems. Don't have time to deal with the jerk."

"Says right here you're the guy's attorney. It's your job to listen to him. Judge won't like hearing you refused to see an injured—"

"Okay, no need to send in a complaint. I'll stop by later today."

Trent pawed through his file on Dixon and found the note Jake had given him. There was no home number, only the number for the Gold Bar, where Maria worked. The backstage manager at the Gold Bar picked up his call. Trent introduced himself as Tony Salvatori's attorney.

The manager became cooperative. "Okay, seen you around here a lot. Yeah, Maria Garcia. Jake's girl. She's a pretty one. She left a week ago to start work down at Tony's place in Towaoc."

Trent affirmed, "Flaming Arrow Casino?"

"Yeah, just south of Cortez, before you get to Four Corners. Need their number?"

Trent said, "No. I've got it somewhere. That's a tiny place. Why'd she want to go there?"

"Wasn't her idea. Jake was a bulldog around her. When she came off stage he'd hustle her out the door to her car. When he got arrested, Maria flew into Salvatori with claws out. She was real mad. Don't know what she said to Salvatori but it was the only time I've seen Mr. Big's face turn purple. He told her to either work at "Flaming Arrow Casino" or pick up her severance."

"Thanks, Rod." Trent found the casino's number in Tony's file, punched in the number for the manager.

"Trent Clay, attorney at law. I work for Tony Salvatori. I need to find one of your dancers, Maria Garcia."

"Yeah, so do I. Scheduled her to start work a week ago and no call or nothing. We replaced her."

"Do you have a home number for her or know where she lives?"

"No, they're all flakes. Probably got picked up by ICE. We lose dancers right and left. Our choreographer loves the Mexican ladies, and they sure can dance, but no papers, they disappear."

Trent called the Denver Sheriff's Office. He waited for a connection to his insider. Mick answered, and Trent heard him shuffle through the past week's list of deported undocumented workers.

"Yep, she was picked up first week in March at the Gold Bar Casino in Oreland. We shipped her to Juarez. Sure didn't want to go. Kept screaming her man's here and her family would hurt her if she showed up there. But once we found her birthplace, back she went."

"Any parents or relatives here in Colorado?"

"She didn't mention any. Last place of residence came up as Ciudad Juarez. That's all."

"Thanks, Mick. I owe you one."

Trent tossed his office items into his trunk. Next, he drove to the Denver Downtown Detention Center. Fluorescent lights reflected across the infirmary's tiled floor. An orderly pointed out Jake's bed in the corner. Pillows propped up the ex-boxer. His face matched the gray walls. He appeared catatonic as he stared at his groin. His only movement was his right hand, flopping back and forth on the sheet. His ugly face was now grotesque. Trent moved a chair close to the bed.

Jake whispered, "Gotta get me out. Shit-bag Paco's got family here. Help me, I'll do anything..."

Trent studied the man. Finally, his lips formed a smile. "Jake, I can try to get you sent to a different facility where it's safe and you can recover. I assure you, I may also be able to help Maria. It took a great deal of work, but I've found out she's been deported."

"Argh." An animal moan erupted from Jake.

Trent rose and backed away from the man's bed. "Now, Jake, I may be able to get her back across the border—back to you—where she belongs."

"Dey will...kill...her."

"You mean her family? So, home is not a safe haven. That's unfortunate." Trent let the image of Maria being killed float between them. "In appreciation for my help, along with the considerable cost to bring Maria home, I will need a small favor from you. Try to remember where you were on the night of January tenth, just three months ago."

Jake faced Trent. "Yeah, I was somewhere..." His bloodshot eyes watered.

"With Mr. Salvatori at his home in Denver, all night, working."

"Yeah, we got lots of work to do and..."

Trent snarled, "Don't get fancy. I'll tell you exactly what to say." He leaned over the big man. "We'll talk again. Keep your mouth shut, and I'll work to get you out in three months instead of four."

The next day, Trent had presented Jake with a typed statement. Jake glared at Trent but signed it. The Gold Bar Casino was located in Gilpin County. Tony Salvatori and George Wilson had been partners. Trent had to get to Central City. He drove the thirty-eight miles in less than an hour. He walked into the Gilpin County Justice Center and entered the new evidence with the district attorney.

He slapped the paper on the desk. "This shows Tony had a witness who swears he was at home the night of the murder. You have to drop your charge."

The DA's face turned purple. "You're a disgrace. We have to interview Mr. Dixon and if his alibi proves to be factual and credible. We will let you know if charges can be dropped."

"Make it snappy. Mr. Salvatori has business to conduct."

****

The following morning Trent received the call he needed. He hurried to the Gilpin County Justice Center. His hands were sweaty as he grabbed the dismissal papers that would remove the target from his back.

Faking bravado he said, "Face it, your case was Swiss cheese anyway. Guess you guys will have to find someone else to pin the Wilson killing on."

Elated he was out of some hidden assassin's crosshairs, Trent took the courthouse steps two at a time. He jumped into his car and hit the steering wheel hard. He snorted. *Hah! I got Salvatori off. He'll wipe clean my gambling debt and I won't have to worry about being shot in the back. It's a start. If I can save my home, I can get visitation with Kendra. Christina won't be able to keep me from seeing her.* Rummaging for his favorite head-banging CD, he slid it in, cranked it up full blast, and peeled out of the parking lot. A few miles out of town, a billboard advertising Blue Spruce Lake caught his eye. Thick trees caressed the cobalt lake, and at the back of a large pontoon boat, a man and woman sat, holding fishing poles poised over crystal water. Nearby, a secluded cove beckoned. *Maybe I should take a day off and go fishing. Do some trolling and catch myself a rich woman. Oh, yeah, Dad's already hooked one.*

Trent was proud of the work he'd done during the next ten days. He'd produced proof that Jake was in extreme physical danger at the Denver Downtown Detention Center, having suffered a severe attack by inmates there. His demand for placement in the Pueblo County Detention Center with special circumstances was approved. Finally, Trent visited the DDDC again and waited in the visitation room. Jake entered.

He faced the prisoner. "You look better. I have news for you. I pulled some strings with the Commission on Correctional Health Care, and they agree your stay here is life-threatening. Your physician, Dr. Andrew, verified how severe your injury was. It took pulling in a lot of favors, but you'll soon be moved to Pueblo, out of reach of Paco's family. Your cooperation in the Salvatori case lent weight to consideration of a shortened stay. Salvatori, out of kindness, presented a letter with a strong recommendation for you and even offered to put you back on his payroll when you're released. So, if you stay out of trouble, keep your head down, and mouth shut, by around May twenty-third, you'll be out and have a job waiting."

Jake slumped. His shoulders were stooped, but his eyes glowed. "Did ya see Maria and my baby?"

"That's another matter. You forgot to mention Maria's real name is Arellano. Oh, and one other fine point: her father is in the Mexican Gulf Cartel. She's also not alone at home. She has seven brothers and four sisters, all nasty people."

Jake squinted. "You promised you'd get her back."

"I'll try, but it's more difficult. I'll need to spend much more time and money." Trent picked invisible lint off his suit. "It's possible I may need another favor from you, which will, shall we say, be more involved."

The former bouncer squirmed in the metal chair. "What?"

"When the time comes, I'll let you know."

Jake's face twisted. "Why me?"

"I might need someone with your special skills. Listen, I got everything you asked for, you're set to move to Pueblo County Detention Center in just a few days. Of course, if you don't want my help, I can reverse all of that, and you can find Maria on your own—when you get out on July first. That is, if she's still alive."

Jake's neck cords pulsed. Between the two men, body heat radiated across the space. The prisoner's hairless skull glistened with sweat, and his thick wrists twisted against the manacles.

Silently, Trent gave a nod to himself at his forethought to keep Jake's hands bound during this visit. He glanced sideways as Jake opened, and then closed his mouth.

Jake sank deeper into the chair. His words slid over half-healed scabs and a missing front tooth. "Okay. I got no choice."

Trent focused on Jake's slack mouth. *He reminds me of a toad, all bumps and oozing bruises.* He held back a smile. "Correct." Trent stopped as though finished, then added, "Considering your…unfortunate altered condition, I imagine you are extremely anxious to have your baby in your arms as soon as possible and will work with me in the most cooperative way."

Jake's pupils were pinpoints. "Yeah. Screw me over, and I swear, I'll kill ya—like a pig—in a way ya can't imagine."

"I'd be surprised if you didn't make that threat." Trent stood. "I'll speak with you the day you get out of jail."

Trent had left the jailhouse and sailed into bright light. Before entering his car, he removed his jacket and shook it violently, trying to rid himself of jail stink. He cranked the key and slid in a CD. On the steering wheel, his fingers tapped out the beat. He smiled, remembering his final thought. *Good to have an ace in the hole. You never know when you'll need it. What a mush-head, and he's all mine.*

CHAPTER 7

On Tuesday, Sheriff Carlson asked Lynn to come by the office to discuss the murder case. The two-lane road from Mineral Lake to Elk Hills formed a double helix and wound for four miles through pines, which gave way to cottonwood trees and aspens. A strong breeze danced through new spring leaves clinging to branches arched over the fast-moving Mineral Creek, swollen by the spring snowmelt.

She drove south down Main Street and then turned west to 300 West Pioneer Street. At the Gunnison County Elk Hills Justice Center, she parked under a stately tree. Scattered leaves, disturbed by strong spring winds, lay on the ground. Lynn strode quickly across the lot, which served both the superior court and the jail annex.

She had enjoyed her previous visits to the historic building, which, prior to 1881, was used by the territorial Indian Agent to hand down justice. Now the western town had a full-time judge.

Located in the basement, the old jail had housed gunfighters, rustlers, and bank robbers. In comparison, the new jail, usually sat empty. This fact made the quiet town, perched on the western slope of the Continental Divide, attractive to new residents wanting a safe community. Inmates of the jail were now likely to be drunks, poachers, or petty thieves.

The old courthouse had been demolished in March and construction on the new courthouse had begun. She looked over to a pile of debris, remnants of the broken granite steps. She squinted as mica flakes, embedded in the matrix of the native stone captured sunlight for a nanosecond. She paused before entering the jail annex, thinking of her attraction to the town. *Everything tries to out-sparkle the next thing: snow, rivers, and minerals.* Only the north side shelters shadows. The reason for her visit quickly returned to the forefront of her mind, and she shivered despite the sunshine. .

Lynn stepped through the annex's automatic glass doors. Within a few minutes, the secretary escorted her to the sheriff's office. Metal keys jangled as Sheriff Carlson stood and took her hand with a firm shake. He motioned for her to sit as he lowered his bulky frame into his desk chair.

"Thanks for coming by, Mrs. Mason. I have some news I wanted to share with you. First, please accept my condolences for your loss."

"Thank you." Lynn studied his broad face, brown and crinkled by sun exposure. She noted a faint Texas drawl in his deep voice.

"I didn't know Betty Clay, but I've heard nice things about her. I'm sure my call shocked you. I realize it was painful to hear about her death. I want to assure you my office intends to keep our full attention on this case."

"I appreciate your help, Sheriff."

"Please, call me Larry. I understand Maggie filled you in on some of the initial details we gathered from the crime scene."

"Yes, she did, but I still have so many questions."

"I'm sure you do. What I have to tell you is from our interviews with her husband, Arnold Clay, and Betty's cousin, Nanette Hanks. You know Ms. Hanks, of course."

"Actually, I've never met her, but Mom told me about her. She visited my mother every couple of years."

"Arnold said a few days before the murder, Ms. Hanks arrived, and the three of them took a drive to Oreland. They wanted to visit the old mining town and gamble at the new casinos there."

"Mom didn't mention her cousin's visit to me."

The sheriff continued, "The three of them took rooms for Wednesday night in Oreland, then drove back to Elk Hills on Thursday. Nanette left for Indiana on Friday morning. Ms. Hanks said Betty got lucky on the slot machines and won eight hundred dollars."

A call light blinked on his phone. He answered and scribbled a note then hung up. His chair creaked as he leaned back, and his uniform shirt buttons strained across his ample stomach.

He began in a measured voice. "According to Arnold, on the night Betty disappeared, Friday, May twenty-third, she drove from their home on Spruce Street to the Alpine Shopping Center on Third Street at approximately four thirty in the afternoon. Arnold said she'd planned to shop for some new art supplies. Hanson's is the only art store, and the clerk remembered seeing Betty before five o'clock. Her records confirm a sale at that time. They closed at five."

Lynn interrupted. "Did they see anyone suspicious?"

"No, they didn't. As you are aware, her body was discovered in Bright River on Saturday, the morning of the dam break. Her vehicle was not found until early Sunday morning, just after midnight, by my deputy, at an abandoned gas station on Wagoneer Street, across from Bright River. The body was discovered upstream from where the gas station is, so we assume the body was placed in the river at some unknown distance from town. The location where the car was found is about a mile from the shopping area. Mrs. Clay's purse sat on the front passenger seat. A hundred-dollar bill lay on the floor. Her wallet was missing. The deputy checked around the car but found nothing."

Lynn said, "Maggie said she was suffocated."

"That's correct. But she also suffered a head wound."

The sheriff read from a typed report then focused on Lynn. "The coroner indicates it's likely she was unconscious when the plastic bag was placed over her head. It was sealed around her neck, and only a small amount of water had entered when she was discovered. The probable cause of death is suffocation prior to her body being placed in the river."

Lynn's stomach churned. She started to say something, but her voice cracked. She shut her eyes as tears slid down her cheeks.

The sheriff cleared his throat and continued slowly. "The coroner ruled out death from hypothermia. The springtime water temperature dropped close to freezing. It might have been a factor if she'd been put into the river alive." His head lowered as keen eyes peered over reading glasses and rested on Lynn. "However, that doesn't appear to be the case."

"Sheriff, I'm sorry. But to hear about Mom's death in cold facts is almost unbearable."

"It's understandable. Take a minute if you need to."

Lynn started again. "Did they find anything else in the car? A possible weapon?" She heard her own thin voice and tried to overcome the pressure buzzing in her ears.

"Unfortunately, no. We did find that her shoe heels showed signs of being scratched. The rush of water down Bright River obliterated any clues. However, it did dislodge the body. And by washing it downstream into town, we were able to spot it. If it wasn't for the torrent of water, the body might have not been found."

Lynn closed her eyes. "My mother is…was tiny. She weighed around a hundred and fifteen pounds."

"Yes, a strong man might have carried or dragged her."

Lynn blinked and changed the direction of her questions. "What about tire tracks?"

"Footprints, tire tracks pose a problem. We don't know exactly where the body was placed in the river. Easy enough for someone to drive up the river road, dump the victim, then drive back and abandon the vehicle."

Lynn said softly, "So there isn't much evidence."

"Nope, not enough to hang a hat on. Forensics is working on prints and hair found in the vehicle and we followed up on a hunch. Betty had two bank accounts. We reviewed the camera records from the ATMs at both banks and found pictures of her withdrawing money from each of them the night she died."

Lynn leaned forward. "Is it a lead?"

"Definitely. She withdrew the maximum, four hundred dollars, from each ATM. But, dang it, only *her* face showed in the camera recordings."

"You're sure?"

The sheriff rifled through a pile of files on his desk. He opened a large envelope and spread out several pages of pictures.

"These are what we got. You can see the small angle. It's possible someone stood outside of the frame. The attacker may have pointed a gun at her, or a knife, forcing her to withdraw money."

Lynn leaned close to study the images. "Her face is so small in the pictures and her head is down. It's hard to tell if she looks frightened or not."

"True. If the camera had caught a full-face view, we might have a clue to her emotional state. As it is, we're still in the dark."

"When did she withdraw money?"

"At the first bank at 10:59 p.m. and the second at 11:09 p.m. They're a half a block apart."

Lynn said, "The last time she was seen by anyone was at the art store around five p.m. Do you have a theory of where she was between then and 10:59?"

Sheriff Carlson frowned. "Only supposition at this time. We think the attacker held her somewhere in her vehicle until it was dark and the streets deserted. Then forced her to drive to the banks and subsequently murder her. The killer may have placed the body in the river then gone back to the same abandoned gas station and left the vehicle where he'd held her earlier."

Lynn moved the pictures around. "So, your theory is, some unknown mugger approached her at the shopping center parking lot, held her someplace away from view for six hours, then forced her to drive to both banks to withdraw money, and then killed her."

"Yes." Carlson added, "An unfortunate happenstance."

Lynn's agitation forced her out of her seat. She placed white-knuckled hands on the desk. "Mom must have been terrified." She bit her lip then continued, "If she was driving and tried to run the car into a fence, or sound the horn, or even tried to roll out of the car to escape, someone might have seen she was in trouble and helped her. What if she spent those hours trying to talk someone out of killing her? Pleading for her life?"

"Ma'am, there's no way to know what she was thinking or exactly what happened. At least until we find the killer."

"My mother didn't have a strong heart. Being mugged, she easily might have suffered a heart attack, or even a stroke. If the killer knew this about her, he may have been hoping the fear was so great she'd die, right then and there."

The sheriff checked the file. "Considering her age, yes, I agree. Perhaps if the attacker didn't wear a mask, she may have guessed the intent was to kill her."

"Sheriff, what if she knew the person and thought it was possible to talk her way out of it? Maybe she just didn't believe she'd be hurt."

He leaned back in his chair. Metal on metal squeaked in complaint. One beefy hand rubbed his closed eyes. "It's all possible, but there's no way to know, is there?" He examined the camera pictures again. His callused hand moved the pictures around in various sequences for several minutes, then he sighed, and his gaze came to rest on Lynn.

Lynn sat still, listening to the office clock tick off a mechanical minute. *His theory is fuzzy and he has no idea where to find the killer.* She asked, "How far is it from the shopping center to the banks, and then to the place where the car was left?"

The sheriff sifted through the folder and brought out a map of Elk Hills. "The banks are both about one mile to the southwest of the Alpine Shopping Center. She went first to Central Mountain Bank and Trust on Main Street, then to Elk Hills First Bank on Pioneer Street half a block to the west. The gas station is farther to the west and just under a mile from Elk Hills First Bank."

Lynn stood and leaned over the map. "You've circled Arnold and Mom's home on Spruce Street. What's the distance from their home to the shopping area?"

"About a mile."

"What about to the gas station where the car was found?"

"A mile and three quarters."

Lynn's voice quickened. "Arnold said he was alone that evening." Lynn traced the distance with her finger. "It would have been an easy walk for Arnold to intercept Mom at the shopping center then force her to drive to the banks. After she was killed, he'd have an easy walk home from the gas station."

Carlson shook his head. "Lynn, this is a small town. Almost everything is within one or two miles, and an easy walk. We have no reports of anyone seeing Arnold at the shopping center or in the area where the car was left."

"But Arnold has motive. He's the one to inherit—"

The sheriff interrupted, "You can't charge a man with murdering his wife just because he'll inherit her money."

"Arnold has no alibi." Lynn threw up her hand. "You can't think some vagrant mugged my mother. I'm sure Arnold planned the whole thing."

A loud knock on the office door cut the charged air. Lynn dropped into her chair as a deputy handed the sheriff a folder.

He scanned several papers. "Ah, we have the prints from the car. They positively identified Betty and Arnold, but another unknown print came up. We sent the unknown print to Nanette Hanks's hometown. They confirm it's hers." His sharp glance rested on Lynn. "That's logical, since she'd been in the car only a few days before the murder. The plastic bag came up empty. So there's nothing on this unknown mugger. We found one hair that could possibly belong to the killer or to Betty's cousin, or for that matter; to anyone who ever rode in the car. It's a very slim piece of evidence, but we're following up on it. We're running a DNA analysis, and the police in Nanette's hometown will check her results for us. We should have more information soon." Lynn pointed at the sheriff. "I want to know, are you considering Arnold as a suspect?"

The constable drawled, "Yes, among others. We questioned Arnold about any arguments with his wife. He said there'd been none."

Lynn pursed her lips. "Isn't it possible my mom wanted enough money that night, right then, to leave town? She had eight hundred dollars in winnings from gambling, and she still used the ATMs for an additional eight hundred."

"Well, do you know if they were they having problems?"

"Before her murder, I'd have answered no. I thought they were getting along wonderfully, newlyweds enjoying each other. But recently I've changed my mind. After talking to other people, I think big disagreements were going on."

"What kind of disagreements?"

"I was told they centered on money. It's crappy, but I think Arnold married Mom to get her money and property. Her friend Amy told me she thought Arnold was using her."

The sheriff shuffled more papers. "Ah, yes, Amy Nowell. She phoned me."

Lynn said, "After talking with Amy, I think Mom wanted to leave Arnold. I don't believe there was a mugger."

"How do we prove it? Any ideas?"

"Not yet."

The sheriff continued, "Amy thought she was the executor of Betty's will, but she isn't. It was changed recently. Arnold's son, Trent, is now the executor."

Lynn sat up straight. "What? The one thing Mom did discuss with me was no family member should ever act as an executor of a will. She was adamant on that point. And it's not like her to not tell Amy about the change." Her fist came down on her knee. "Why wouldn't she mention it to her best friend?"

"I don't know. Arnold said he called Trent after he found out about Betty's death and Trent showed up by late afternoon. Drove from Denver to reach his father's side."

"He rushed to help his father? It doesn't sound right. Mom told me she was upset when she realized Arnold and Trent weren't even speaking."

"Ma'am, I've examined the will. It was prepared and executed during the first month of Betty and Arnold's marriage by a local attorney in Elk Hills. Arnold is to receive everything: money, homes, property, and savings. You're not mentioned in the new will."

Lynn forced words through tight lips. "Sheriff, my mother and I were on excellent terms. Honestly, I'm shocked to hear this. Amy told me I was in Mom's will. For her to make such radical changes is not like her. And to ignore me…she may have been forced to sign a new will or coerced in some way."

"Are you considering contesting her will?"

Red crept up her neck. "It's possible. Shy of one month, there's a new will, a new executor, and Arnold gets everything, just like he did in his last marriage. Isn't that interesting to you?"

"Interesting, yes. Maggie reported what you mentioned about Arnold's second wife, and Amy went over all the rumors in great detail. I have to repeat, what we have now is not enough to charge anyone with murder."

Lynn stood. "Sheriff, Arnold has motive, easy access to the murder site, and no alibi. What more do you need?"

"We need much more evidence for presentation to a grand jury. Arnold's record as a citizen is spotless. He's been cooperative and forthright during our interviews."

"But, Sheriff..."

Carlson held up his hand. "Along with that, he's an honored, retired policeman, has a clean military record, and calls we made to his previous chief only reinforced his good standing." The constable spread both hands on his desk. "I'm not stopping our investigation. We'll keep going, but we'll check elsewhere, too."

Lynn walked stiffly to the door. "It sounds to me his buddies covered up a suspicious murder years ago and don't want any cause to dig it up again. It's like giving a terrible tenant a good recommendation just to get rid of him. But I hope to God you're not a party to any cover-up in this case."

The lawman squinted as he pointed his finger at Lynn. His voice boomed. "Young lady, that's uncalled for. There never are cover-ups at my station. I can promise that."

He slapped the file on his desk. "We're working to find some physical evidence to lead us to the perpetrator. We have no prints except Betty's, Arnold's, and Nanette's, all easily explained." The big man stood up and tugged on his belt.

Lynn glared at the constable. "So, if the murderer isn't Arnold, then it has to be someone very careful, wearing gloves, cool enough to stay out of the camera frame, and knowledgeable enough to find a secluded place to hold her for six hours, get her to the ATMs for more money, then kill her and dump her body unseen by anyone, with gravel to hide any footprint or tire tracks." She took a breath. "I'd say the killer knew what he was doing."

The constable nodded sharply. "My gut feeling says it wasn't a random crime."

Lynn shook as she lowered her voice. "Do you know how sick this makes me? I'd feel much better to know it was some drifter who killed Mom. Not someone she loved, someone she trusted, who placed a bag over her head. That's so cruel and calculated."

The phone rang. The sheriff listened closely then hung up. "The state police apprehended one of the escaped prisoners from Salida. They hope to find the other one soon. They have his home staked out. It's near Del Norte, way to the south of here."

"You mentioned my mother's wallet was stolen."

"We've notified the card companies, and we'll hear if any purchases are made. Arnold gave us a description of the jewelry she usually wore, and we've got notices out to all nearby pawnshops."

"I hope something works." She opened the door. "Please don't stop searching. Mom just moved here, and no one knew her well. But she was loved, and she deserves justice."

"This office cares about all our residents. This isn't a big, impersonal city." His square chin set hard. "Good-bye, ma'am. Maggie and I will keep you informed. Let us know if you think of anything else we should know."

Lynn sat in her car and banged her head on the steering wheel. *In a pig's eye, it was a random mugging. Arnold, I know you did it, and I'm going to prove it.*

Lynn returned home and started her usual preparation work for the night's dinner crowd, but the phone interrupted her. The instant she said hello, Amy started talking. "I just found out as soon as they release the body to the family, Arnold plans to have Betty's body cremated. And that creep Arnold is not giving us any chance to go to the memorial service for Betty. Can you imagine how insensitive he is?"

"Slow down, Amy. Explain what you mean. I didn't know the plans. I've left several phone messages for Arnold to call me with the information about a service, and he hasn't called me back. I assumed nothing was definite yet."

"He should have called you first. His son called me. Arnold plans to hold a service in Gold Creek. Why Gold Creek? She only knew a couple of people there. All her friends are in Piñon. I told Trent that, but he said Arnold has lots of friends there, and that's where he wants it. Lynn, it's a long way up there. Would you go that far?"

"The distance is of no matter. Of course I want to be at my mother's funeral, but in my gut I'm convinced Arnold killed my mother. I'm afraid I'd spit in his face or punch his big nose. How can I be in the same room with him? His putting on a memorial service is a travesty."

"His son said it was to be very small. Right now I can't leave my sister. She just had knee surgery and has no one but me to help her. It's just another slap. Arnold is terrible. I hate him."

"It tears at my heart to not be at a service for Mom. But, attending a service won't change the fact that she's gone. I'm dealing with my grief every day and it's so hard. You and I have our memories of her, and we still have each other. I won't go to anything he plans, even if he asks, which I'm sure he won't. When Mom's murder is solved, we can do something beautiful and meaningful to remember her."

Amy said, "I agree with you. I called Sheriff Carlson to tell him I was the executor. He said that had been changed. I don't understand. Did he tell you anything?"

"Arnold's son is the executor and Arnold inherits everything. I'm not in Mom's will."

Amy gasped, "No. That's impossible. Your mother would never do that."

"I said as much to the sheriff. He says he is working on the case but he has no real leads.

So many things point to Arnold being involved in some way. It makes me sick. I'll keep you informed as to any news."

"I sure hope they find the killer, and if it's Arnold, so be it."

That night after the restaurant closed, Don asked Lynn about her visit with the sheriff.

"Learn anything new? Didn't Maggie say they were following up on the escaped felons from the correction facility in Salida?"

"That's a dead end. The sheriff said both escapees traveled east, then south, not in the direction of Elk Hills. One was caught in Trinidad, and they figure the one still at large is headed home, down towards Del Norte. He's escaped before and went straight home last time. The sheriff's sure he'll be found soon."

Lynn pushed back her hair. "There's also a new will. Arnold gets everything."

"Whoa. You're not in the will? That must be a mistake. What do you think happened?"

"Amy said Mom was suffering from depression. It was bad enough for her to need medication. I think Arnold took advantage of her condition, coerced her in some way to write him in and me out." She let that sink in. "Mom may have figured she could work around the issue later on, when they were on better terms. But time ran out. I can contest the will, but it would cost money for an attorney and it usually fails. Mainly, if Arnold is guilty, making a big stink over the will could put us in danger. I've thought about this all afternoon. Money's not worth our getting killed. But if I'm careful I can help in the investigation…"

Don gave her a hug. "I think you should try to focus on the summer. You may never find out what happened. Somehow, find some peace over this."

"Sure, I'll just snap my fingers and shut my mind off. Move on, you say." Her temper flared. "My mother was murdered. Hear me? Murdered. It's not whether I'm in the will or not, it's justice. Her time on this planet was unfairly snatched away from her. I'm not letting go until it's solved and the guilty person pays."

CHAPTER 8

Elk Hills struggled through the month of June. Vacationers continued to arrive, and the river water miraculously cleansed itself and looked lovely, even if there were no fish.

Lynn drove to town and pulled into their lumberyard. Last year, Don had convinced her that it would be a wise move to purchase the lumberyard to supplement their income. She'd put up as much resistance as she could, but Don finally had his way.

The previous owner, Toby Yonkers, had wanted to leave town. He was despondent over the death of his sixteen-year-old son who had drowned at the local swimming hole above the Bald Flats Bridge. The twelve-foot falls poured into the river and over time had carved a basin perfect for a swim on a hot day. On the fateful morning, young Mitchell didn't surface after his dive. His friends kept searching for him with no luck then finally called Deputy Maggie Hernandez. As news of the drowning reached The Sport Stop, the owner, Greg remembered that Don had scuba gear and was experienced at underwater diving. Maggie called Don and asked for his help.

When Don finally returned home, he'd told her about the recovery, the details of which made her shiver.

His voice had been somber and full of emotion. "I went under the falls into the water twice and couldn't find the boy's body. The current below the falls pulled me in every direction as though I was in a washing machine. The force tossed me upside down. On my third try, I entered an underwater niche carved by the plunging water and managed to retrieve the boy, who was pinned to the roof of the cave. I hope I never have to do that again. I barely managed to escape being held there myself."

The incident had left a sad memory. Now, each time she looked at the lumberyard, she thought of the heartbroken family. Even the pride she'd felt at her husband's bravery didn't dissolve her fear that he also might have been lost. In addition, she pushed back a tinge of guilt that they'd bought the yard for much less than normal due to the owner's distress. When she'd brought this up to Don, he scoffed. So she'd let it drop.

Their lumberyard took up half a block on C Street on the east side of town. Past the yard, a popular trail leading up to Nugget Top Mountain twisted through forest until it passed the tree line at ten thousand feet, then it struggled along dirt switchbacks to the summit. Today, only one car was parked in front of the office. As Lynn breezed into the office, she was surprised to see Marilyn Lee at the counter talking with Don.

"Hello, Marilyn. Had no idea you were in town."

Marilyn spun around to face Lynn. "It was a quick visit, only here two nights. Scott had to check some things up on Nugget Top Mountain and load up some core drillings." She looked back at Don. "Wish we could stay longer, but Scott's dragging me back to Denver this afternoon. Due to consulting work, he's been away a lot. He needs to catch up on things at home."

Lynn walked around the counter into Don's office area. "That's too bad. Seems like awhile since we got together."

"Much too long." Marilyn opened the door. "Give us a call if you manage to get to Denver any time soon. There are some great new restaurants we can try."

Lynn leaned her elbows on the counter. "I'd prefer to go shopping with you in the city. Frankly, if I get a chance to get away from our restaurant, I'm not eager to spend precious time eating at a competitor's table."

Don tipped his head in Lynn's direction. "Lynn doesn't comprehend the value of research. She'd rather experiment with disaster." He stood as Marilyn left. "Say hello to Scott for me."

When Marilyn was out of earshot, Lynn raised an eyebrow. "What was that about?"

Don shrugged and said nothing.

She dropped the *Elk Hills Daily Journal* on his desk. "I picked this up at The Sport Stop. Quite the headlines. 'All Fish Killed in Bright River.' I know they want news to print, but do they have to pump it up like this? Many out of state summer visitors subscribe to the paper and when they read about this tragedy they might cancel their trip."

Don read the article, then tossed it into the trash. "Don't go nuts over this. Our regular customers will show up. It still gets hot in Texas in the summer, and they're used to coming here for their family vacations, fish or no fish."

Lynn said, "They'd better. It's been one problem after the other. I've about had it with this town."

"You'd quit?"

"Where have you been? My mother was killed in this town. And there's only a slim chance the guilty person will ever be caught by the local-yokel sheriff. After all our work, business is down by half, thanks to a dead river." Lynn's voice quaked. "There comes a time to realize maybe it's been a mistake."

"No one's tying you here."

Lynn blurted, "What do you mean?"

"You're either with the team or you're not." He stood and quickly walked out the back door.

Lynn followed him. She stood mute as he climbed onto his forklift. The rumble of the motor and belch of diesel cut off any response.

That evening when they were alone, Lynn confronted Don. "You were right today when you said I'm not fully committed to this town or our business. I'm sidetracked with anger and suspicion. I don't know when it will let up or if it ever will. If I knew how to fix it, I would."

"I feel for you, and I realize you're working through a big loss. There's a lot on your mind." He faced her and placed both hands on his hips. "But come halfway okay? I'm struggling to keep my nose above water at the lumberyard. It's a big gamble, and I'm as strung out with worry as you are."

They declared a ceasefire. However, between running the lumberyard and the restaurant, they barely spoke.

****

Several weeks later, Maggie stopped by the restaurant to visit. She took a seat near a window, and Lynn rushed to pour coffee.

"I wish I was bringing news on your mother's murder. But I'm sorry to say we have no leads."

"I know you and Sheriff Carlson are working hard. It weighs on me to have no answers, but the real problem is I miss Mom so much."

Maggie said, "I'm as sorry as can be. Just know we're trying our best." She leaned back in her chair and looked out the large window. "I've been curious for some time as to why you built your restaurant on the second floor instead of the first. But, today, I have my answer. The way the sun hits the lake's surface makes the color of the water much deeper and more beautiful from this vantage point."

"It was Don's idea to build it this way, and he was right. Sometimes the water, air, and sunset light generate a magical opalescence that's quite unbelievable. I've been alone, standing on the deck, and I imagine I'm the last person on earth experiencing such a display."

Maggie said, "Sounds poetic, but a bit gloomy."

"I'm too introspective lately."

"I've only come by for dinner three or four times and each time you were too busy to visit with the likes of me. Too often I've had to grab quick food close to the office. With the loss of fishing on Bright River, has your restaurant suffered?"

"Last year when we opened on August first, business was good until the end of September. We don't have a way to compare our receipts. But we've made half of what we'd hoped to see. When we left Denver, we were full of optimism, so much so we overcame huge obstacles without a glance back. But the lack of tourists this summer..."

"How are you and Don doing at the lumberyard?"

"If it weren't for the lumberyard income, I don't know how we'd survive. I was against it, but Don made a good decision buying the business, and he really has improved the place. Sales have increased from what he expected, but competition from the Jeanville Lumber Company is a problem now. They're offering free delivery to Elk Hills, a hundred-and-twenty-mile round trip, just to snag the business. Don's had to stay late, quoting material lists for local contractors that they will accept. His mind is always on the lumberyard."

"Nothing comes easy in the mountains." Maggie checked her watch. "Thanks for the coffee. I've got to go. Everyone is hoping business picks up." She stopped. "I don't want to seem nosy, but are you and Don okay?"

Lynn idly stroked the white linen tablecloth. "We could be better."

"You've mentioned he's made a lot of trips to Denver this month."

"We're both really busy, and there's little time for each other when we're working seven days a week." She avoided Maggie's gaze. "Anyway, lots of times I'm too sensitive."

Maggie studied her friend. "Actually, when at the restaurant, I've been worried when my ears hear Don speak to you like a donkey. Being sensitive has nothing to do with respect."

Lynn's stuttered. "You've noticed? I've brought it up to Don. He says he doesn't know why he talks down to me, and he's promised to work on his attitude and stop picking on me."

"Because I'm your friend, I'm going to ask if you think Don has strayed."

"Strayed? No. Oh, never. I'm sure of that."

"Good." Maggie got up to leave, then added, "My father once told me that even if you are on the right track, you will be run over if you just sit there."

Lynn cocked her head. "Thanks, Maggie, I'll remember that."

Maggie gave a quick wave and left. Lynn continued her chores. *Maggie's words circle around my head, pesky as bees. I better figure out exactly what she meant.*

Early the next morning, Don prepared to leave for work. He carried his thermos and a warm jacket. Lynn stood at the bottom of the stairs, her arms full of clean tablecloths. The mechanical clank of the laundry delivery truck broke the alpine silence as it left the parking lot.

"I'm going to make a quick trip to Denver," Don said. "I'll leave after I close the lumberyard, and I'll spend the night so I can load up early. Jack will open the yard tomorrow morning. I'll be back in town by five at the latest."

"Not another trip to Denver. Why can't they deliver or let Jack make the trip?"

"And pay delivery charges or overtime? Besides, I need to be sure the orders are correct."

Lynn squinted into the morning sun, which formed a halo around his head. "Did you just decide on this trip?"

Don stepped down until they were face-to-face. "No. I considered the timing. The weather's great, and a couple of special orders are ready. Don't worry. I'll be back in time to help in the restaurant."

Lynn's voice was flat. "Have a nice trip."

His truck pulled away, and Lynn leaned against the deck railing. She faced the restaurant and the row of six large picture windows. A brisk breeze blew from the west, and the scene behind her was reflected across the glass panes, a blurred blue sky framed by snowcapped mountains and a lake surface alive with small whitecaps undulating like ruffles on a French can-can dancer's skirt. The intoxicating beauty of the lake and mountains seemed to reach into her every pore.

She rubbed her throbbing temple. *It's hard to argue with his reasons for going to Denver again. But I'm afraid my five-year marriage is slipping over the edge, and I don't know how to stop it.*

CHAPTER 9

Summer was in full swing and the residents of Elk Hills rejoiced. Bright green clumps of aspens stood out against deep-green pines strewn over broad-shouldered hills. Four-wheeled vehicles, SUV's, and family cars with camping gear piled on the car roof, streamed into town. Camper trucks imitating snail shells, propelled by determined round-shouldered retirees gripping wheels with hands gnarled by a lifetime of hard work, hugged hairpin curves and arrived at the campgrounds. The noonday sun warmed the residents, and afternoon thundershowers settled dusty streets. The tourists donned warm jackets as high mountain nights crashed behind the mountain ridges and temperatures slithered downward, leaving a chill in old bones.

Taking advantage of a slow morning at the lumberyard, Don left Jack in charge and arrived home early to do a run to the landfill with their trash. By one thirty, he had finished with his chore and sat in the kitchen of the restaurant, having a late lunch before cleaning up. Lynn joined him. She perched on a stool and waited for him to finish his meal.

"We've been so busy; I haven't had a chance to talk to you. I keep thinking about the murder and what the sheriff said. Everything points to Arnold, not some random mugger. He planned the murder, planned it very carefully."

Don's voice was incredulous. "If he planned it so carefully, why did he leave himself without an alibi?"

"I've thought about that." Lynn leaned against the work counter. "According to the sheriff, without any witnesses or prints on a weapon, they can't directly connect him to the crime. Everything so far is circumstantial, but the sheriff explained that a number of circumstances can create an inference of guilt, such as resistance to arrest, motive, or opportunity to commit the crime, and the suspect's presence at the time and place of the crime. Even denials, evasions, or contradictions on the part of the accused, along with general conduct, can accumulate to sway a jury in a trial."

"Sounds like confusing legal talk to me. What else did he tell you?"

Lynn picked up a pen and drew on a napkin. "I've thought about this a lot. His map showed the art store at the shopping center within walking distance from Mom and Arnold's home. Pictures from two banks show Mom taking out money. Either she was forced to make the withdrawals so it would appear to be a robbery, or she needed more cash for some reason. I think it's too much of a coincidence that a mugger would happen by when she had sixteen hundred dollars in cash with her. And be willing to kill for it."

Don's eyes widened. "Get real. People get killed for a lot less."

He put his arms around his wife. "Honey, I know you're still upset, and I understand why. Please let the sheriff handle this case. He's a professional. You don't know anything about catching a murderer. Stay out of it. Promise me."

Lynn pushed him away. "Come on, Don, that's just it. The professionals only look at the facts. They don't connect the dots. I'm not going off like some superhero crime fighter. I'm just going to keep my eyes open for clues. I may not find anything." She threw a towel down on the counter. "Arnold might have executed a perfect murder. God knows, he's smart enough. It's possible he got away with it once before, and he's conceited enough to try it again."

"There you go, digging up rumor and gossip about Arnold's prior marriage. Put the brakes on. We have two businesses to run and no time to waste on murder mysteries. You sound like a drama queen."

Lynn said, "Don't forget the new will. Arnold got everything. I'm sure he engineered that surprise."

Don's voice had a hard edge. "Is that bothering you? I told you before, we don't need her money. You agreed. Let this stinking mess end. Keep out of it."

Lynn opened her mouth to speak, but the phone interrupted.

Don answered. After his greeting, he stood silent, listening. He answered quickly, "I'll meet you at the yard. We can load up and get to the spot in about fifteen minutes. I'll leave right now."

"What's happened?"

Don called over his shoulder as he reached the front door. "There's a fire up on Divide Mountain Pass. It's not big yet, but we need to get the water-pump truck up there and some volunteers with shovels."

"Please be careful. Don't get hurt." Lynn trailed behind him as he took the stairs two at a time. "Mike will help me. We can handle the restaurant."

Don crossed the landing. "Sure, don't worry."

Standing on the deck, her eyes scanned the green ridgeline, and sure enough, a wisp of black smoke snaked across the blue sky. Don jumped into his pickup. Gravel spewed from the tires as he sped out of the driveway.

At four o'clock, Mike arrived and joined Lynn in the kitchen. As he washed his hands, he asked, "Did you see the smoke? Earlier, I was in town, and black smoke covered the top of the pass. I drove by the lumberyard where five or six trucks were parked. Don was handing out shovels and rakes to take up to the fire."

Lynn asked, "Did you hear how it started?"

"Nope. I'm sure they'll get it out while it's small. It's green up there, but there's thick deadwood around. If it jumps over a couple of canyons, it could reach here." Mike lit the broiler. "Your restaurant sits lower than where the fire is, but the wind could push it this way."

Her eyes grew wide. "Did you see any Forest Service firefighters yet?"

"Heard they called them. I'm sure they're helping by now. I didn't drive up the pass, so I couldn't see them. Our pumper truck's up there. Loaded, it must have crawled up the steep grade. Cross your fingers they'll get the fire out fast."

Lynn peered out the kitchen window. "The lake is our only water source to fight a fire, but we have hoses. We can connect to the water intake if we need to. This spring, we cleared the brush and trees around the building for fifty feet in all directions, and we have the lake on two sides and a road behind us. The road should act like a firebreak."

Mike smiled. "Yeah, and the gravel rock all around wouldn't burn."

Quite a few cars went back and forth on the lake road, but only a couple of travelers stopped to eat. Lynn sent Mike and Wendy home early and shut down the kitchen. The trees across the lake whipped back and forth. The wind had changed direction.

Maggie called at six o'clock. "Lynn, Don's on the line. He can't call you. Probably won't have to, but be prepared to evacuate at any time. They have it almost out, but there are still some spots burning, and the wind is so unpredictable, sparks could jump anywhere."

"Should I go into town or east to Survivor Ranch?"

"Go into town. There's a box canyon to the east. I don't think the fire will reach the lake, but I don't want you trapped. There's a lot of traffic on the road at the bottom of the pass, but you should be able to get through."

"The wind's a vortex here, spinning in a circle."

"If you don't see white smoke soon, head into town. Promise you'll go."

"I will. Don't worry about me. You take care."

Lynn packed a small bag and rummaged through some papers. She tried to figure out what to take. In frustration, she just tucked her and Don's photo album under her arm. She kept going out to the deck. The restaurant sat at the west end of the lake. She checked the northwest, hoping to see white smoke above the pass. The sun had set behind the ridge an hour before, and the sky was now a light marine blue with pinpricks of growing starlight. Again, she heard the drone of an airplane from overhead. Gray smoke blended into the sky. She took a few precious items down to their car. Then, on her second trip, billowing white smoke emerged. She reassured herself, *that's a good sign. The fire is slowing down.*

Lynn paced around their bedroom. Shortly after seven o'clock, she finally heard Don's truck enter the driveway. He opened the door to their bedroom surrounded by the scent of smoke, sweat, and singed hair.

"I'm so glad you're back." Lynn encircled him in a bear hug. "Is the fire out?"

Don grunted. "Yes." He slumped into the couch. "We left some men to watch for any hot spots that could flare up again. All we did since about five o'clock was put out tiny fires. Wind blew hot ash and embers everywhere." He struggled out of his blackened jacket. "I've got to get out of my burned clothes."

"Let me help take off your boots. You smell like a campfire. I'll put your clothes out on the porch tonight and see if I can wash out the smell tomorrow."

"Throw my boots out. I stepped on a couple of embers, and the soles are almost melted through."

"What you need now is a hot shower. Do you want me to get you anything to drink or eat?"

"No food. They brought us some from town. First thing is a shower, then sleep. I'm dog-tired. We worked all over the mountainside. Fortunately, we got the fire out before the wind sank its teeth in and the fire had a chance to take off."

"Do they know how it started?"

"That's the easy part. Our neighbor across the lake started the fire. Pete stood there as we drove up, beating at it with an old blanket. What a dumb shit."

"Pete Langston? Why on earth did he start a fire?"

"He was all doped up. Pot, I'd guess, and drunk on top of it. He said he was going to camp there, but he was cold, so he piled up loose sticks and threw some gasoline on them to get it going. It got going, all right. It flamed up, and sparks flew into the dry brush. Fortunately, a passing car alerted the sheriff's station. Maggie and the volunteer fire department got there as fast as possible."

"How many showed up to help?"

"About fifty." Don continued to undress. "We had to get across the meadow to reach the fire. Only our little Jeep made it. A small stream flows through the meadow there, and the mud went up to the hubcaps. The rest of the trucks got stuck and had to go around. For a while, Jack and I were the only ones shoveling dirt."

"Get into the shower. You can tell me more later."

"The minute I'm clean and my head hits the pillow, I'll be out for the night. One good thing happened today. We all pulled together. For the first time, I became part of the town. Each of us fought to keep our stake in Elk Hills alive."

Don finished his shower and fell into bed. "I hope I smell better."

"You do. Smokey the Bear is gone. I guess Pete's in real trouble."

"Yes, he is. I'm sure we'll hear about it soon enough."

****

When morning came, Don got up later than usual. He joined Lynn in the restaurant kitchen, and she placed a plate of scrambled eggs and bacon in front of him. He ate with gusto.

"You were out for ten hours. I've never seen you sleep that long. How do you feel?"

"Not bad for an old man of thirty-five. There was no way I could keep up with the forestry guys. They were all in their twenties. I figured I was the oldest guy up there. Then I spotted Hal Adams shoveling dirt. He's in his sixties."

Lynn shook her head. "Bless his heart. Do you know if they arrested Pete?"

"Yes. I called the sheriff's office before coming upstairs. Sheriff Carlson took him to jail. Pete's lucky. The fire caused no damage to any homes or structures, and no one was killed. They'll fine him, and I imagine he could go to jail for the damage to the forest land. Fifty acres or more burned."

"I heard Pete planned to fix up his converted school bus to make it more acceptable. Guess he figured he should try to make it fit in. No doubt some people griped about it being an eyesore with the corny smokestack sticking up."

Don shook his head. "A Caterpillar worked over there a few weeks ago, shoving dirt around it to more or less make it blend into the hillside. Joel Conner lets him stay there. Must be okay with Pete living there, so there's nothing anyone can do about it. Don't understand why he was sleeping in the forest and not at his bus."

Don put his plate in the sink. "I doubt Pete pays rent. He hasn't worked since he came back to town, at least, not any honest work. I've got to get into town and open the yard. Expect me by five o'clock. Did you have many customers last night?"

"Only ten dinners. I'm sure it'll pick up soon."

****

Two weeks passed, and one morning Lynn awoke in their small living quarters. She pulled back the curtains, allowing playful sunlight to splash across their bed and couch. The sunrise freed escaping swirls of morning mist playing hide-and-seek among hillside evergreens. Only the bright green tips of new growth stood out above the milky veil.

She entered the kitchen just as Don was preparing to leave. His lips grazed her cheek in a haphazard kiss.

"See you later," he said.

"Okay," Lynn grunted. She glanced at his wide back covered in red-and-black plaid. *We've become strangers. Don works all day at the lumberyard and handles the bar at night. I'm cleaning, receiving deliveries, and serving. We're both either nuts or terrified of failure. One thing's obvious, we're sure not lovers anymore.*

Further introspection ceased as the kitchen phone rang.

Penny Fisher chirped, "Hey, stranger, how are you?"

"Good, just chained to the kitchen like Cinderella. How have you been?"

"I'm frantic. The summer is here and the kids are in my hair already. Don has kept Jack so busy at the lumberyard I've hardly seen him. But, we're thankful for the work. Have you had lots of business at the restaurant?"

Lynn studied the rack of dishes drying on the sink. “Yes and no. It was a pretty good night for the middle of June. We managed two dozen dinners. I hope Texas heats up something ferocious soon so folks will scurry to the mountains for cool days and chilly nights.”

“They will. Your little town will burst at the seams.”

“Don’s in his element, but for me, it’s harder than I imagined, and he’s sick of hearing me gripe. I bit my tongue all winter and dealt with cabin fever. Thank God it’s summer, and there’s plenty of work to keep me busy. Our first full season. It’s make it or die. Maybe my nerves will settle down as we make some money.”

“Just think of what you two have accomplished. I want to come see all the improvements you made in the restaurant during the winter. I’ll call to let you know when the kids and I can make it. I’m anxious for a chance to catch up with all the news.”

“Love to see you. Talk with you later.”

****

By mid-July the high mountain passes were finally cleared of snow, and visitors filled the town. Lynn was preparing vegetables when Don joined her.

“Got to get going.” He loaded his lunch and thermos under his arm. “Don’t forget to listen for fishermen wanting a boat. We need to keep it rented so we can pay for it.”

Lynn gave a perfunctory nod as Don left. She took a sip of her coffee then tossed the rest of the cold brew into the sink. Her thoughts raced. *As usual, he’ll only give me credit for half a brain. No sense arguing. He’ll be at the lumberyard all day, and I’ve got a ton of work to finish on my own. Better snap to it.*

After another bumpy morning with Don, even the glint from snow-filled canyons etched across the Continental Divide ridgeline couldn’t improve Lynn’s mood. She dug into the chores waiting for her and spent several hours checking produce, dairy, and meat supplies. Preparing carrot sticks, she tapped out a thought.

I'm crabby today. Maybe it's because there should be four of us to share the work, but, surprise, once Dad and Mom bailed from the restaurant project last year, it left only Don and me to struggle on our own. It's a miracle we scraped up winter work or we'd have been flat broke. I'm sure Don's anger kept him going. But me? Pure panic and the wish to save my marriage.

Her mind replayed the argument last year that had killed the partnership. She tugged on the vacuum cord as she furiously covered the carpet around forty tables. The machine became a weapon as she avenged the hurt and deceit by banging table and chair legs. *How could my own father have rejected all the work Don and I accomplished last year? All our money was invested in the new restaurant building, and Dad arrived from Denver, looked around, criticized everything, and turned his back on us. Mom said nothing to change his mind.*

She remembered how Dad's face had turned red as he'd looked up at the high ceiling, "The roof's all wrong. The first ten-foot snowfall and it'll cave in. Why didn't you follow the plans I drew?" Even now she cringed recalling how Don tried to explain that the changes he'd made to the building were safe. He'd explained calmly, "We talked to people from here who knew what to expect from the winter." Confused questions still swirled in her mind. *Where'd Dad think we were going to find the money to furnish the place? Why did Mom stand silent?*

Lynn relived the crucial moment. *Mom's face was tight as she held back tears. I'd expected her to say something, make Dad see he was destroying us, but she didn't. That really hurt. Maybe she knew her marriage was failing. And then Dad walked out on her. He managed to dump his entire family so he could chase young women. Last year had been full of disappointment, and now this year has been full of heartbreaking loss.*

A knock on the door interrupted her memories of betrayal.

Before her stood two men loaded down with fishing gear. Each wore a wide grin. Her bad mood evaporated as she took in their smiles.

"Hello, I'll bet you want to rent a fishing boat, right?"

"We sure do. Can't wait to get our lines wet. We pulled in last night. Drove up from Dallas. Aim to catch our limit by noon."

The trio walked down the stairs.

Lynn asked, "Is this your first visit to Mineral Lake?"

The gray-haired man said, "Oh, gosh, no. I've been coming here since I was a kid, sixty years at least. My grandson here, Matt, he's come since he was ten or so. But this is the first time I got a chance to rent a boat on the lake."

"Yeah, our dock's the first one built here." She motioned toward the spillway. "The pullout area across the bridge is too steep to use, and the east end is too shallow and filled in with skunk cabbage and willows."

She wrote down his driver's license number, and they walked down the sturdy dock. "Our shoreline has a gentle drop-off. Out farther, there's a deep channel cut by the current all the way to the spillway. The trout follow the channel."

Standing on the dock with the two men, she stuffed their fifteen dollars into her jacket and carefully stepped down the wooden catwalk to the lower floating dock. She gave the new sixteen-foot fishing boat motor two hard pulls. The engine caught, and she adjusted the idle until the Evinrude purred, ready for action.

Lynn climbed out of the boat and let the motor warm up. "Watch your step getting in and keep the boat away from the river outlet. The current is fast and strong at the spillway. You don't want to go down the river."

The older man settled his bent body into the boat. "What are they biting on?"

"The trout are awake and hungry. Some really big ones may still be up from the bottom, and they hit Super Dupers or Red Devils."

The teenager asked, "What's the chance of landing a really big trout?"

"You might get lucky and hook a twelve-pounder, a mackinaw. Rainbows rarely get that big. I've got worms and fish eggs for sale in case it's not a day for lures."

The old man held up a bright orange jar. "We bought salmon eggs at The Sport Stop."

Lynn waved as they pulled away from the dock. "Good luck. I'll see you back by noon." She smiled inside. *After a year living on the lake, my fishing advice falls short of expert, but at least I sound like a local instead of like a "flatlander" from Denver.*

Blue exhaust plumes left a trail as the fishermen headed east through dissipating mist. At seven in the morning, the calm water mirrored emerald-green pines, a lapis sky, and snowcapped mountains that loomed above the small lake. The outboard motor sliced through the reflection and created curls of liquid satin ending as small waves that slapped the shoreline beneath her. A pair of jays squawked angrily at her for allowing the rude noise to break the alpine silence.

She walked back along the twenty-four-foot wooden dock and reached the foot of the stairs but stopped as a second car drove into the parking area. Suspecting another boat rental request, she waited. Instead, Sandra Steele emerged. Disappointed, Lynn shifted from one leg to the other as the Realtor picked her way across the jagged shale covering the parking area. Her high heels dug into the loose rock and exited with several deep slashes in the leather.

Lynn said, "You're out early today. Sorry about your shoes. It's best to wear boots around here."

Sandra faced Lynn. "Actually, I've come to talk about the rocks." A thin smile jerked her lips then faded.

"Now what makes our driveway of interest to you?" Lynn aped the fake smile.

"Several of us in town are very concerned with the…change…the lack of aesthetic appearance of the shore along your parking area." Sandra waved her arm. "Your property stretches at least a thousand feet from the restaurant to the bridge, and you've destroyed the natural water edge with all this rock."

Lynn folded her arms. "And what's your suggestion? Should we expect our customers to park and walk across yellow gumbo clay, which globs around shoes like cement?"

"We think you should keep the natural shoreline like it was before you built here."

"And who are 'we'?"

"Lots of people in town. They also don't like the dock."

"That does it, Sandra." A flush crept up Lynn's neck. "How can you butt into our business venture here?" Her voice rose. "You're the one who sold us this property. You grabbed the commission check fast enough for the sale, which now includes the water rights we had to secure for ourselves. Your negligence almost made this land worthless." Lynn started up the stairs.

"I'm bringing up our objections at the next county commissioners' meeting." Sandra squinted. "We'll see what they think."

"Go ahead, and we'll sue you for unethical behavior of a real estate agent and have your license yanked. How'd you like that?" She waited for a reply, but heard none.

Sandra strode to her car. Her Range Rover lurched back in reverse then bounced forward. Gray shale tugged at the wheels, and snow tires kicked small shards as she left the property.

Lynn plodded up the wide outside stairs and slammed the restaurant door. She poured a cup of coffee, which sloshed over the rim. Tears came as she held her hand under a stream of cold water. The woman's words reverberated through her. *Sandra, you unethical witch, you'd get a big laugh if you knew we opened last August with only thirteen dollars left to our name.*

Lynn thought back over their ordeal. Buildings don't just appear. We put every board and nail into this place without any help. She examined her rough hand. *And the dock you don't like, we built it in January on the ice as howling wind and frigid sleet stung my face and Don's. We barely avoided frostbite.*

She walked to the large picture window. Her attention was drawn to the nearby lake's edge where a lone uprooted pine was snagged in brush during the spring thaw, its gnarly roots reaching up to the sky and bare branches forming curved ribs across the trunk. Her thoughts churned on a new problem. *We barely had the money to open this spring, and Don keeps sinking more into the lumberyard. Now we're more in debt. It's a crapshoot to make it here. The scenery is fantastic, but we sure can't eat it.*

Close to five, Don joined her in the bar.

Anxiously, Lynn said, "I'm telling you Sandra's out to get us. She'd like nothing better than to see us fail. Sometimes I can't sleep thinking about the balloon payment on the land we have to come up with in five years. What if they shut us down? If she had a chance to list this place again, it would go for a lot more money with our building on it."

"Calm down. No one's shutting us down. But you're probably right. I'm sure the locals bitched about this prime land being sold to newcomers."

"But what if the county cites us?"

"Don't worry. If we get any static from the commissioners, I'll ask Paul to write them a scorching letter. A sharp attorney's letter will shut them up." Don wiped the bar top. "Legally, I'm sure they don't have a case. It's still a free country. " His knife clicked as he sliced lime wedges.

"How can you be so calm about it? I know she badmouths our place to keep customers from coming here. She's so two-faced."

Don leaned his muscular arms on the bar top. "Hey, small towns are like that. Most everyone's living on the edge. They all have to work double time to stay above water, and most aren't afraid to step on the guy on the lower rung."

"I thought we moved here to live among friendly, hardworking people, not phonies."

"People everywhere use one another all the time." He grabbed his cleaning rag and slapped the counter. "I trusted people in the past. I'm not doing that again."

"Here we go again. You mean my father, and you're right. He did a horrible underhanded thing to us. I'm embarrassed whenever I think about it. I guess Sandra's the same kind of person."

Don walked to the steps leading down from the bar into the restaurant. "Anyway, we got this place started against the odds and in spite of...certain people."

Lynn bit her lip in thought. *He'll never forgive Dad or me either. I'm guilty by association.* She followed him into the kitchen. "Don, it's just unnerving when a few men on a county board can sink our plans, and Sandra's husband sits on the board. It makes me scared to be at their mercy."

Don lifted a heavy tray of steaks from the refrigerator and set it on the kitchen counter. He tied on his bartender's apron and glared at Lynn, the muscle in his jaw twitching. "I worked hard to get this place built. I won't walk away a failure. If I have to fight back, I will. Don't worry." As he left the kitchen, he spoke over his shoulder. "Don't go out of your way to pick a fight with Sandra. Most of the town backs her husband on any issue. I've got two businesses to run, and I don't need you flapping your chops and sabotaging me."

Lynn's cheeks burned. "As I recall, *we* built this place. How can you suggest I'd cause trouble? I..."

Before she finished, the front door opened, and their first evening customers entered. Don rushed to seat them and take their drink orders. Lynn walked to the table. Her eyes shot arrows at Don as they passed, but she pulled out her friendly hostess voice as she greeted their guests. The woman and two men beamed with merriment. A twinge of envy passed through Lynn as she heard their cheerful, light banter.

Lynn handed them menus. "Let me guess. You're from Texas."

"Proud to say, yes. I'm Dick, and this is Niki. We're from Austin, and the ugly guy is Steve. He's from Houston."

Lynn shook hands all around. When Steve clasped her hand, a shock ran up her arm. "Static electricity," Lynn offered. "Our thin mountain air is ion-charged."

"That may be, but something else is charged." His smile broadened as he held on.

Recovering, she withdrew her hand. "Did you get in some fly-fishing today?"

Steve answered, "Yes, we made it up to Big Meadow. We caught a couple keepers." He smoothed back a wayward lock from his brow. "We're staying at the Rainbow Cabins." His steady eyes held her gaze, and he changed the subject quickly. "I'm sure I know you. Yes, we both went to high school together in Piñon, Sage High School. I'm Steve Russell. Do you remember me?"

"Oh, yes. Of course. Gosh, it's been over ten years since high school. You're living in Houston now?"

Steve said, "Yes, since law school. When we asked at The Sport Stop for a good place to eat, the clerk mentioned this restaurant. Are you the owner?"

Lynn said, "Yes. My husband, Don, and I built it last spring. We didn't open until the beginning of August last year. Is this your first visit to our area?"

Dick spoke up. "Not quite. Our parents are longtime friends, and our families have met here to camp and fish almost every summer since we were five. But it's Niki's first visit to the high country."

Niki tapped Dick's shoulder. "And I caught more fish than either of you."

"Girls rule." Lynn smiled.

Steve said, "I admire your bravery opening a new business in this small town. I'm sure I'd starve trying to survive here with a law practice."

Dick chuckled. "You'd starve if you tried to live here as a fisherman. I didn't see your creel overflowing today."

Niki giggled. "He could become a trapper."

Dick jested, "Yeah, he almost snagged a beaver when he stepped through the critter's dam up on Big Meadow."

Steve said, "They're right. Not my most graceful move. Caught my line in bushes..."

Dick said, "Bushes. He walked backward right up the side of the lodge, then plop. All we could see was the top half of him sticking out." Belly laughs exploded around the table. Lynn joined in, too.

Lynn said, "Did you notice the beaver lodge off the side of the parking area? She built hers last spring when we built our building."

Dick said, "Whoa, Steve, better stay clear of any more critters. I don't plan to interrupt my dinner to save you."

Lynn said, "Well, I'm happy to have you try our food tonight, and Steve, it's good to see you again. Enjoy your dinner."

She rounded the kitchen door, but the sound of their guests' banter still reached her. She concentrated. *Don't remember him at all. But is he a lady-killer or what?* Still focused on the happy trio, she collided with Wendy, who'd been balancing two plates as she came through the swinging door. One hit the floor, but Lynn rescued the other. The sizzle of steaks on the grill brought Lynn's attention to Mike as he prepared for the first orders.

"Hi, Lynn. Looks like we've got early customers." He adjusted his chef's hat.

"Yeah. Season's in full swing. From now through August, it'll be nonstop. Up at six, fall into bed at midnight, work, work, work."

Mike rubbed his hands together. "Hey, I'm ready. I need the money."

Lynn filled glasses of iced tea. "So do I. It'd be great to go four-wheeling all over the forest, but someone has to do the heavy lifting, right?"

"It's okay." Mike adjusted the charcoal burner. "Our time for fun starts after September."

Don came into the kitchen and frowned as he stepped over Wendy cleaning up the spilled salad. "What's going on? Let's keep the food off the floor, okay?"

"My fault, not Wendy's," Lynn said.

"Well, get your head screwed on tonight, and we might manage to see a profit for a change."

Lynn bumped the kitchen door with her rear as she balanced a tray of glasses. "Just take it out of my paycheck. Oh, I forgot, I don't get one." She heard Don groan as she scurried out in time to seat a group of six. The busy night flew by.

****

Two days later, Lynn worked in the bar cleaning. The meat vendor was due to arrive at any time. Footsteps sounded outside. She caught sight of Steve walking up the stairs. The wind ruffled his sandy hair. Her movements stopped as she waited to hear the restaurant door close.

He breezed in with a big grin and sat down at the bar in front of her.

"Hello. Can the Lady of the Lake find a beer for a tired fisherman?"

Lynn placed a Coors in front of him and admired his cool looks.

A smile spread over his tanned face. "Do you serve lunch?" He unzipped his light jacket, exposing a tanned throat.

"No. Too much to handle by myself. But if you're starving, I can find something for a sandwich."

"I'll just have a beer. I can eat later." He ambled over to the jukebox and pumped in quarters. A country-western song began to play. He enjoyed his Coors, and then his attention zeroed in on her. "I'm curious as to how you chose this place. You don't strike me as a mountain girl." He took a sip. "I mean that in a good way. Your manner is...refined." He pointed at the artwork on the wall. "The other night your waitress mentioned you did all of the beautiful paintings. I'm impressed. She mentioned sometimes you stand outside on the dock in the afternoon painting the lake scene, and then hang the painting in the restaurant. I'll bet people buy them all the time."

"Thanks. The tourists love our scenery. It's extra money, and this beautiful place inspires me."

Steve took his time with his next statement. "You said you remember me, but I doubt it. I sure remember you though. I was a year ahead of you, and you were one of the prettiest girls in the junior class."

Lynn gave an indulgent lift of her shoulder. "Piñon seems a long way from this mountain town. I don't fit here...yet. But I'm working on it. There are trials to pass that aren't apparent until you're called upon to face them. All newcomers have to prove they're strong enough to live here."

"And if they aren't?"

"One way or the other, they get culled. Just like the elk herds, the weak don't last. The locals have paid their dues, and they constantly amaze me. Tourists probably won't hear the stories they have to tell. But after a few drinks in the bar, they open up. I've learned some remarkable things."

"Share some with me."

"Oh, if you get me started, I'll yak your ears off." Lynn dusted a bottle of liquor from the back bar. Then she stopped her cleaning. "It's beautiful out. Let's sit on the deck and enjoy the view, then I can bore you with the life history of the

Mineral Lake Restaurant." She opened a beer for herself, and they went outside to the deck.

Steve said, "Tell me what you've been doing since high school and how you found this mountain berg."

"Well, Don and I met at UC-Boulder. I'd graduated but was taking an art class at night. Don was there for computer classes. After we married, we moved around. Tahoe, Virginia City, Nevada, and then back to Denver before moving here."

Steve said, "I miss the Denver area. Houston is a temporary home. I like skiing and the 'go after it' attitude in Colorado. As I remember, this piece of land your restaurant sits on was a large picnic area. I've come here many times to fish. I was surprised to see a building on it."

"My dad found the town. Don worked with my father learning the construction trade. My parents were supposed to move here as partners in the business. The four of us wanted to live in a small mountain area where there were more opportunities. We fell in love with this parcel of land the minute we stepped on it. It's actually four mining claims, ten acres each. They wrap across the end of the lake in front of the bridge and up the sides."

Steve whistled. "Mining claims?"

"They're nothing to speak of. The forty acres are mostly underwater or under the road going along both sides of the lake. The tax assessor came by when we were building and said, 'You've bought one-third water, one-third pavement, and one-third mud,' but he loved the view like we did. We built the restaurant on this side of the lake because the view is so spectacular from this spot. Also, our property behind us has good views. The soil on this side is clay, worthless for minerals due to a high arsenic content. Water pipes erode fast. We have to pump our water from the lake."

"How do you manage that?"

"Don put on his scuba gear and placed an intake line and pump on the bottom, where the current runs year-round. Even when the lake surface is frozen, water moves under the ice and down the creek. He ran underwater electric cables to operate the pump."

Steve said, "So you didn't buy this land for any mining use."

"Never entered our minds. My mother's land on the other side of the lake from us goes up an acre or so beneath several old mines, which years ago had gold discoveries. And the soil over there is normal and not affected by the high minerals. Anyway, mining's an expensive enterprise with questionable rewards."

"The dinner I had here the other night was great. You must have had some restaurant experience."

"Our only experience was ignorance and nerve. We figured we'd eaten in enough restaurants to know what works and we just dived in. We planned to first build a restaurant then later on cabins along the shoreline and, finally, subdivide the land up the hillside behind the restaurant into home sites, all with lake views. But at the last minute, it all blew up. Then even Mom and Dad's marriage ended."

Steve said, "I sense it's very different living here."

"I think it's because the residents are so invested. Their hearts are on the line along with their money. Also, they pull you into the community by asking each newcomer to join this or that committee. It wasn't like that in the city. No one cared whether you made it or not. If you failed, a 'for rent' sign went up."

Steve asked, "How are new people treated here?"

"They lend you a hand, give you ideas. They want new blood. Some want to keep out anything new, but they're in the minority. Most want to keep the old mining town atmosphere, with buildings sporting fake fronts. They've designated the abandoned mines as historical sites. But the impact of transplants from the city can be seen. We have a new leather store, an ice cream shop, and a T-shirt store."

It was afternoon when Lynn said, "I can't believe we've been talking for two hours." She checked her watch. "My meat vendor is due any minute."

Lynn pointed her finger at Steve. "You clever attorney. I've spilled my story, and you've kept your life in Houston a secret. Give it up."

"My law practice deals with estates and contracts. My brother is a border agent. He's much more interesting." His eyes locked on Lynn. "You're more interesting, too. I've wanted a chance to talk with you since I first recognized you. I'm glad it happened today." His body relaxed as he leaned back. "Your place is beautiful. People in town say you and Don worked together, pouring cement, hammering, even building the first dock."

"Problems grew on top of problems. Some locals took bets we'd never open." A wry smile came and went. "But we showed them. Summer is so short. The window for construction closes fast. We started the building the first of April last year and lived on the property in the half-completed structure. I fished for trout each morning, and we cooked our fish dinner over an open fire each night. After eating fish every night for dinner from April to August, I was sure I'd grown gills." Lynn added, "It was a good thing we planned on a steakhouse without fish on the menu. I compromised with offering Alaskan crab legs. Anyway, most tourists rent cabins with kitchens and cook the fish they've caught."

Steve smiled. "That's what my family always did. When did you finish the building?"

"Everything was done by July Fourth last year. But we were out of money. A lucky meeting with the man who owns Survivor Ranch at the far end of the lake saved our skins. To use the mining vernacular, he 'grubstaked' us so we could open. Once we had the money to purchase furniture, food, and liquor, we were on our way." She gazed across sapphire water, pulling memories from the silent witness to their struggles. "We barely made it. Don and I set a goal and a difficult one. Our backs were to the wall, so failure wasn't an option."

"Sounds pretty stressful."

"Good and bad clashed all last year. We both knew hard work went with the dream we were chasing, but neither of us suspected the toll..." She took a sip of her beer. "The mountains throw challenges at you with no mercy. Enough of that. So far, we're holding our own, and this summer, business should be great."

Steve's eyes scanned the green mountains. "I'd find it hard to stay put and work in the summer with all of this pulling me outdoors."

"It is hard sometimes. And work is seven days a week, all summer long. We enjoy clean air, peace, and tranquility." Lynn perked up. "But by winter, there's time to burn. I've made a very good friend, Maggie Hernandez, our Elk Hills deputy sheriff. Now, she's a real mountain girl, raised here and full of knowledge about the town and mountains all around. She's helped me a lot, even took me target shooting a bunch of times. She convinced me I should know from which end of a gun the bullet comes out—if ever I need to use one."

"Don't tell me you hunt."

"No. I'll never manage to do that, but I've killed dozens of beer cans. We did have a cinnamon bear visit our garbage cans early this spring. I walked around back, and there he was, head in the trash can with his butt sticking out. Believe me; I backed up slow and quiet. Now, Maggie hunts elk by horseback with her husband, Domingo. He's also part Native American and works on the road crew in the spring and summer, clearing the passes at twelve thousand feet. It's dangerous work. Right now, he's up on Cottonwood Pass. Then, in the fall, he guides deer and elk hunters. I'm in awe of both of them."

Steve said, "When we were up at Big Meadow, there was still plenty of snow around. The road was passable, but I could see where the road crew had cleared several slides."

Lynn held out her hand. "Speaking of being up high, did you notice how strong the sun's rays are?"

"I sure did. The altitude got to me, especially while walking upstream. I've never known the lake's elevation."

"It's at exactly ninety-two hundred feet."

He raised his eyebrows. "Exactly?"

Lynn pointed left of the building. "There's a National Geological marker hammered into the ground over there, stamped '9200.' This piece of land was also used as a stage stop. Wagons dropped off supplies for the miners, and they corralled mules here that they used to carry items up to the mines on the mountain across from us. There are fifty-plus mines on that mountain. Sometimes, I hear dynamite going off."

"They're still mining up there?"

"Just small attempts. Nothing large-scale. Guess some claim owners want to try to find a big return on their investment. A hundred years ago, the Golden Cross Mine was the richest in southern Colorado. It had very high-grade ore."

"I've wondered how it came to be called Golden Cross Mountain."

"Driving from Elk Hills north to the lake, as you reach the bridge, there's a cluster of aspen growing close to the highest peak. In the fall, the leaves turn bright gold and form a cross of gold nestled among the green pines. Right beneath the cross is the Golden Cross Mine."

"I've heard some mining history about Elk Hills, but I didn't know about this mountain. And here it is, right in front of me." He focused on Lynn. "You're teaching me new things."

As they enjoyed the quiet view, Lynn reflected on Steve. *I like his charm, but it's a challenge to return his gaze. His eyes are so intense, they seem to enter and find their way right to my thoughts. The years since high school have certainly improved his looks and personality. Whoa, girl, remember you're married now.*

The treetop in front of the deck wobbled as a breeze wove through the branches. A bird passed overhead then dipped and glided above the water. Its white underbelly feathers gleamed against the indigo water. Their shared silence was broken by a rattling truck entering the parking area. The Mountain Meat Company van parked, and the driver jumped out, flinging open the doors with a bang.

Lynn stood. "I need to get the meat delivery. He's always in a big rush. If you're ready for another beer, you can serve yourself."

"No problem."

Lynn made her way down to the parking area and, a few minutes later, followed the burly vendor up the stairs as he carried a large carton filled with New York strip, rib eye steaks, hamburger, and cubed beef for kabobs. They went to the kitchen to unload the meat.

In a few minutes Lynn returned to the bar and opened the register to pay the vendor. "Thanks, Bill. Give me a call if you hear anything."

"I sure will, Mrs. Mason."

Lynn sat down across from Steve.

He peered closely at her. "I can see you're troubled. Can you tell me why?"

"I guess it shows. Bill just dropped a bomb on me. This is our last delivery. There's some kind of meat shortage. He usually comes every week, but what he just delivered is all he has for us."

"They're cutting you off for the entire summer?" His eyes opened wide.

Lynn nodded. "Yes. This was just our two-week order."

"A meat shortage in Colorado with all the cattle around here is bull." Steve added, "Wait, I didn't mean to make a pun. I know this is serious."

"I didn't take it that way." Her voice was low. "It sounds like some kind of joke. But this might close us down. We've been counting on this being a good year for us—to get through the winter. Now, I don't know."

"I'm sorry. Sounds like a bad deal. The fish in Bright River dying must have been a hard blow, too."

"Yes. The entire town lost revenue." Lynn became silent.

Steve said, "I think I need to get going. I wanted to let you know my mom is here in town, and we want to come by for dinner tonight. I'm anxious for her to meet you and see your restaurant. When Dad was alive, they fished here often, way before I was conceived."

Flustered, Lynn nodded. "I'll save a table for you around seven o'clock. Is that okay?"

"Perfect." He stood by the front door. "I sure hope your bad news is some kind of mistake. I'd hate to see a hitch like this hurt you…your season..."

"Thanks. I'm going to call around and see what the other restaurants are doing about this mess. Bill said something about black-market deals." She gave him a weak smile as he left.

Around five o'clock, Don arrived home from the lumberyard. After he showered and cleaned up in their living quarters, he joined Lynn upstairs in the restaurant kitchen. She braced herself. "Bad news. There's some ridiculous meat shortage in Colorado."

"Yeah, Greg mentioned it when I went by The Sport Stop. Jason Steele said this happens every ten years or so. They usually work it out."

Lynn whacked at a head of lettuce. "Quite a novel way to jack up prices, if you ask me."

Don opened the freezer door. "I'll do an inventory to see how long we can last."

"I already did. We have enough steaks to get us through this month."

"You're kidding." Don slammed the freezer door. "Why didn't you order more?"

"I ordered the usual. I never expected a shortage." Flustered, she added, "We can buy black-market meat for August. Bill said—"

"To hell with Bill." Don brushed past her. "I'll drive to Texas for meat before I'll pay ransom."

She knew her voice sounded sardonic as she said, "Well, that's one solution." She ripped the leaves. "Let's hope it doesn't come to that." She spun around and realized she was talking to a swinging door.

Throughout the evening, Don sulked in the bar, and she sent Wendy to pick up drink orders.

Steve's mother joined him for dinner. Lynn reasoned that Steve came by his good looks from his mother, Bea.

Mrs. Russell touched Lynn's arm. "Steve told us about the meat shortage. I certainly hope it ends soon."

Lynn smiled. "Thank you very much." She liked the petite woman.

The dining room was filling, and the bar held a dozen guests waiting to be seated.

Lynn was standing by their table, visiting, when Don stormed over and cut through the conversation. He grabbed her elbow and led her to the kitchen. "Quit gabbing and get the hell back in here. We have orders up. The potatoes aren't even done."

Shocked by Don's rudeness, Lynn's heart dropped to her stomach. Face flushed, she pushed open the swinging door. Don stood behind her as she checked the oven. She slammed the door shut and spun around. She pointed to the back storage room door, propped open for air.

"Pilot blew out. Potatoes aren't quite done. We'll stall for more time to serve the entrées. Tonight, I'll handle the bar. Wendy can use your help serving."

She brushed past Don and walked up to the bar. Acid churned her stomach.

An hour later, Steve stood in front of her, money in his hand. Lynn kept her eyes down. She pulled on her neckline, trying to hide the red she could feel creeping up. As she gave him his change, he pressed a business card into her hand. "Lynn, if you ever need a lawyer, please call me."

She tried to read the card, but her eyes blurred from tears. Her chin tipped up. "Thanks. I'll hang on to this. I don't…know what came over him." A hand wiped her brow, half-hiding her face. "Too much work..." She glanced up quickly. Disbelief crossed his face.

Steve spoke softly. "Not much of an excuse, if there is one."

She concentrated on sloshing a dirty glass back and forth in foamy water. *Steve's probably as embarrassed by the situation as I am.*

He said, "I'm leaving tomorrow."

"Oh. I'm sorry your stay has been so short. There are still some trout waiting to be caught." She swallowed hard after her awkward attempt at levity, but bravely ventured a direct glance into his eyes.

He held her gaze. "I hope I see you next year."

Her cheeks prickled, and she knew her blush was obvious. "So do I."

She caught a last glimpse of him as he went down the stairs. A strange idea surfaced. *I'm watching a man walk away who's exactly what I need.* She moved to the window to keep him in view. Her fingers squeezed both arms as she hugged herself. *My heart is in free fall, and the branch I reached for has snapped.* She retreated to her work with a new question. *What the hell's the matter with Don?*

****

Lynn awoke groggy. Too tired last night to face Don, she'd slept poorly. Wearing her work clothes, she met him in the restaurant kitchen. "Okay, tell me why you went off on me last night. It was totally uncalled for."

"No big deal. There was work to do, and you were standing around yakking."

"You're wrong. Everything was under control. The way you spoke to me was…embarrassing and belittling. Why do you think you can talk to me like I'm a chambermaid? You wouldn't talk like that to an employee."

Don shouldered past her as he responded, "You're overreacting. You make a big deal out of everything. If you don't like working around me, work somewhere else." He slammed the front door.

Lynn charged across the restaurant and down the stairs. Don stood on the dock, unlocking the bait-and-tackle shed. She raced across the parking lot to their truck. Slipping, she fell to one knee. Yellow mud oozed between the shale and clawed at her boots. She gasped to fill her lungs with air as she slid into the seat and cranked the engine. The snow tires groaned and spit rocks, then spun uselessly as they rammed the half-buried fallen tree stretched across the shore edge. Her forward motion halted. She shoved it into reverse as Don dashed in front of the truck, arms outstretched like a bird of prey. Silently, she glared at her husband. *I'd love to put this truck into the water and watch it sink along with my hopes, but I'd never try to run you over. I love you…you…stupid dope.* Her head rested on the steering wheel as she cried.

Don flung open the driver's side door. "Are you trying to wreck our truck? You can't get dumber than this."

"You push me past my breaking point." Her voice was barely audible. "The way you talk to me. Why do you treat me like this? I don't deserve you talking down to me." She wiped away hot tears. "Marriage isn't a game. Do you think I'm some kind of sports award you fought to win then set on the shelf with all of your trophies just to ignore?"

"Please calm down." Don leaned against the van. His head sagged. "I know it's wrong. I just get so uptight; I take it out on you. I know I shouldn't. I'm sorry."

"That's a lousy answer. There's not another woman in this town who's worked as hard as I have—pouring cement, carrying lumber back and forth." She scrutinized Don's face. His head and shoulders were silhouetted by blue water, and her tears blurred his face. "Is it all about money with you? Is success in this town worth ruining our marriage?"

"No, it's not. I'm just slugging it out trying every day to convince the contractors in town to switch from Jeanville and buy at my lumberyard."

"*Our* lumberyard," she hissed.

"You know I meant *our*. Don't be so sensitive. I realize how much you've helped."

She got out of the truck. Don kissed her lightly and held his arm around her as they walked back to the stairs. "Let's forget about this argument. It's just nerves, yours and mine."

He gave her his dimpled Irish smile. "We've got to pull together. This summer will be a real boon to us financially." He squeezed her shoulder. "I'm counting on you. I've got to go now. Are you all right?"

"Yeah. I'm embarrassed. It was foolish to even think of driving into the lake. I'm sorry I blew up."

"Okay. I'll see you tonight."

Lynn leaned against the railing as Don pulled onto the road. Silence enveloped her, and her senses reached out to the body of water before her as small waves lapped against stones mixed with moss randomly woven through driftwood at t he grassy shore. Her anger evaporated, replaced by a deep sadness. *Being married doesn't mean you're not alone.*

CHAPTER 10

During the first week of August, Lynn's friend Penny stopped by to visit. They sat on the outside deck, enjoying the view and sipping iced tea.

Penny smiled. "I finally made it up here to see how you're doing. It's been nonstop this summer with swimming and camping. I heard that the meat shortage ended recently."

Lynn said, "It disappeared into thin air with no apologies from anyone. So much for any concern over small-business owners on the western slope. Our meat vendor told me to get my order in and make it a good one, just in case. Don estimated we lost close to five thousand dollars for each puny month of June and July. But lately our dinner business has been all we can handle, and we're breathing easier."

"Jack told me the lumberyard is doing great, way above Don's expectations. The kids have missed their dad this summer, due to Jack's overtime, but with Don making trips to Denver almost every week, it can't be helped. How are you handling his being gone so many nights?"

Lynn shrugged. "Mike and Wendy help me handle the restaurant. We manage, but I do miss him. Didn't expect him to need to be gone so much." Lynn took a pair of sunglasses from her apron pocket and slid them on, effectively hiding her eyes. "The restaurant business will drop in September. I'd like us to take a week off, but I doubt Don will agree."

Penny raised an eyebrow. "Jack and Don are already talking about hunting season. November will be here fast."

"I thought we moved here to get away from Denver and the constant rush, but running two businesses, there's no chance to breathe. But at least we've made wonderful friends like you and Jack. It was a blessing we left."

"Did something happen there?"

"It was a stupid near miss. Don and I went out one night for dinner at a downtown nightspot. There was a disagreement over a parking space. The jerk pulled out a gun. I thought he was going to shoot Don. He shouted, 'I'll kill you.' The guy's buddy settled him down, and we got the heck out of there fast. We were lucky."

"Wow, I don't blame you for leaving. I've lived in this small town all my life and always thought it safe and kind of dull because nothing ever happens around here. Since the tragic loss of your mother I'm a lot more aware of my surroundings especially at night."

"The drunk in Denver waving a gun at us was a fluke event, but Mom's death was much more sinister. We moved here for the beauty and opportunities. Her death was a rotten blow."

"Please don't give up on this town. It had to have been an outsider. The locals like and respect both you and Don. They can see the result of your hard work." Penny stood. "I've got to get going. The boys have been visiting with my cousin's kids, and I promised them lunch with their dad. I'm bringing hamburgers to the lumberyard. Jack lets them eat sitting on the forklift. A unique type of picnic."

Lynn walked her friend to the door. "Thanks for coming by. It's good to see you."

Penny gave Lynn a hug. "We'll plan some fun girl stuff when our men go hunting. Okay?"

"It's a deal." Lynn waved good-bye then dived into the daily chores. Her mind revolved around an idea. *How nice to have family around to visit. Mom and I hardly got together once she and Arnold met. I should have pinned her down to a lunch or dinner and called her more, just to talk. I thought there'd be lots of time this winter to spend with her. But those chances are gone.*

CHAPTER 11

Soon, the Colorado autumn enticed Elk Hills's residents to stop work and grab their cameras. Excited tourists joined the locals as they crisscrossed the state highways and trails leading to vibrant valleys and sun-tipped peaks. Lynn considered the changes around her. *I wish I could enjoy autumn, but Mom's death has stolen my usual joy over the color-splashed hills.*

It was a crisp September day. Lynn parked at the quaint Gunnison County Elk Hills Justice Center. Eight months earlier, she and Don had subdivided a portion of the land on the hillside behind their restaurant, and their first sale had gone through. She finished filing the papers with the recording clerk and was walking down the hall when Hal Adams, the county assessor, came through the main door and called to her.

He moved in a determined shuffle, and as he reached her, he put his hand on her shoulder. "Lynn, Vicki and I both want to tell you how sorry we were to hear about Betty's death." The big man stood with his sweat-stained hat held over his heart. "We got to know her pretty well last winter. She seemed like a lovely person. We planned to have her and Arnold over to visit but...well; we should have done that sooner. My misses kept telling me how pleased she was Betty was working to open an art gallery in town. She thought it added a touch of culture to Elk Hills. Betty's friendship meant a lot to Vicki. We'll miss her. How are you doing?"

"It was a rough summer. It still doesn't seem real. Thanks for your condolence. I did receive your card. Mom had big plans for her new art gallery, but..."

"Best to keep busy. Time will help, but remember that if we can help in any way, call and let us know."

"Thanks, Hal."

His kind eyes reassured her. "Any word on the investigation?"

"No new leads, but the sheriff's working on it."

"I know he is. He's a good guy. How's Arnold? I haven't seen him since it happened. I got used to him hanging around here."

"Actually, I haven't been able to contact him. It seems he's not communicating with anyone. Hal, do you mean he used to come by the courthouse a lot?"

"Well, at first he almost wore me out with his chattering. I figured he was just another 'ninety-day wonder,' you know, staying in town June, July, and August for the good weather then slipping out when the first snowflake fell."

"What changed?"

"He was more than just curious. He came by every other week or so to file new claims on the property at Mineral Lake. Guess he didn't mention it to many folks, but he purchased a slew of old mining claims near the property Betty owned above the lake. He peppered me with lots of questions. We'd talk for hours. He even went with me to check out property lines on the Golden Cross Basin claim and on some near the Fist-Full-of-Nuggets Mine on Bright River."

"How many claims did he buy?"

Hal touched his patchy beard. "I'm not sure, but the records are public. You can see for yourself if you want."

"I'd like to."

She followed Hal to his office, where he pulled out a book of county maps. As he thumbed through the large book, Lynn looked around his office. Light shone from a window in the high vaulted ceiling and a vortex of dust spiraled through the column. Behind the desk, a bookcase bowed from the weight of heavy books.

As Hal came to the page for Mineral Lake, he slid the book around to Lynn and pointed to the relevant parcels listed by legal descriptions in thin black ink.

She peered at the small print. "Hal, are all of the squares outlined in red new claim filings?"

"Yep."

"I count twenty-five. Did Arnold buy all of these? What did they cost? Are they expensive?"

"Yes, Arnold purchased all of them. They varied in price, but most were around a thousand to two thousand dollars. Course the ones up Bright River are a lot less now. That old mine was played out a long time ago, and since the dam burst, prices have dropped a lot. I guess because of so much damage to the river bank. Still debris to be cleaned up."

"These sales add up to a lot of money."

"Yep." Hal winked. "And Gunnison County is grateful. Our county is dirt poor. We always need income."

"Did he say why he wanted these claims?"

"Arnold talked of finding gold on them."

"He wants to mine?"

"That's what he said."

"Did you tell him they were played out?"

Hal chuckled. "Didn't want to throw cold water on his gold fever. He chose to buy them, and most of the owners were surprised and happy to sell them."

"Do the claims on Golden Cross Mountain change hands often?"

"Nope. Most were filed along with the major shafts on the mountain. When those didn't pan out, they were abandoned. Many he bought are on steep hillsides and rock faces, inaccessible areas for mining, I'd think."

"Would it make sense to spend so much?"

"You may not have heard, but with the rise in gold prices, a mini-gold rush is going on in Colorado and some other places. Experienced hard-rock miners are in high demand, too. Talk is unions are pushing to strike for higher wages in Leadville."

Lynn frowned. "I didn't know. Do we have much mining going on in this area?"

"No. More up in Leadville, Cripple Creek, and points north. I told Arnold about it. He was real interested. He made a trip up to Leadville back in April or May—to see all the old mines and museum there. I told him the same kind of union trouble could come to our area soon. The union isn't strong right now, but if they get some money to back them, we could see trouble. But it's not a big industry around here. In this town it's mostly single guys working pick-and-shovel pockets."

"Thanks for the news, Hal. I guess you never know when it comes to finding treasure."

Hal laughed. "Nope. Say hello to Don for me. He did a great job on the fire. I didn't know he was so strong. He shoveled and cleared brush like Paul Bunyan."

"Don said the same about you. It's good they put it out so fast." Lynn started for the door. "Say hello to Vicki for me, and thanks."

Lynn hurried to the lumberyard. Don was busy pricing stock. "Don, I ran into Hal at the courthouse. He told me Arnold's spent lots of money buying up mining claims on the mountain across from us. I think he has plans to mine for gold there. It could be a possible motive for Betty's murder."

"Damn." Don threw his cap onto the counter. "Lynn, you can't jump to conclusions. Hal's full of hot air and a gossip. I don't want you talking about motives all over town."

"Whoa. I'm not talking all over town. I'm talking to you. I've told you I think Arnold is responsible for Mom's death. I'm sure he wanted her money and property, and he's been adding to her claims. He's up to something. Hal said gold and silver prices are going up fast."

"Anyone can buy those claims. They're worthless. He'll find out he's wasted his money. And, besides, last time I looked, it was a free country. He can buy what he wants. Let it drop. I can't talk anymore. I have a big delivery before I close."

"Big help you are." Spinning around, she stomped out the door.

In a few minutes, Lynn sat across from Maggie and described Arnold's gold-claim purchases. "Please tell Sheriff Carlson about this. Arnold's motive is as plain as can be."

"I'll call him, but don't get too excited. We still don't have any hard evidence to connect Arnold to the murder."

"Again, I hear this, Mr. Innocent, Arnold Clay. It's more than just her money. He has big plans to mine for gold. I'm telling you, he's nuts." Lynn threw up her hands.

"Lynn, it's good information, but believe me, everyone in this town has a secret of some sort. That's how small towns are. I'm just asking you to take it easy. Trust us. We're working on this case." Maggie reached out to put her arm around Lynn, but she sidestepped the gesture and strode to her car.

Before getting into the car, she called back to Maggie. "I thought you were on my side. Let Sheriff Carlson know what I told you. Maybe he'll think it's useful. Then again, maybe he doesn't care, either." Her voice was unusually strident. "I'm not finished with this." Her mouth became a hard line. Lynn slammed the car door and drove off. Her mind was a jumble. *I can work this out; I know it, if only I can avoid the lumps of clay blocking my way.*

****

Lynn needed to get back to Mineral Lake, but she had one more stop before going home. She parked at The Sport Stop and picked up the Thursday edition of the *Elk Hills Daily Journal*. The store carried dry goods as well as sporting goods. She needed a box of toothpicks for the restaurant. She found them on the bottom shelf. She knelt a moment, deciding if she should buy more than one box. In the next aisle, she heard men talking about big times at Stag Horn Ranch.

A tenor voice said, "Yeah, when Pete was around he smoked enough to knock over a horse, or an elk." A slightly lower voice added, "I'd like to know why Joel put up with him for so long. Back in June, when he was still around, all he did was ask everyone for money or food. Now he's in jail. Good thing he's there. Some guys still want to punch his face in."

Their talk stopped. Lynn peeked over the top shelf. Both had ambled to the storage room. She caught only a quick view of two teenagers' backs. Lynn paid for her purchase and hurried home.

That night while closing the restaurant, Lynn told Don what she'd heard in The Sport Stop.

Don grunted as he replaced a keg. "Yeah, rumors are Joel used to supply the area, and since his uncle let him move onto the ranch, he's at it again. But the young people in town who want stuff can find it, either there or somewhere else."

"You're right. Now Pete's in big trouble for arson and will probably go to jail for quite a while. He's not new to jail. Guess he's too stupid to avoid it. Hasn't he had a trial yet?"

"It was postponed. Judge was ill and the public defender was swamped with cases when he returned from his vacation. Should come up soon."

Lynn put the last clean glass on the shelf. "This place is sure a lot different than you and I imagined when we decided to move here."

Don said, "If you mean it's harder to make a living here than I planned on, I'll agree."

"No, we moved here so we could be a part of the community, work to build a better life, and enjoy living close to nature. We wanted out of the big city. I still have nightmares about that guy threatening to shoot you. Anyway, I'm surprised Maggie and Sheriff Carlson haven't arrested Joel if he's the local supplier."

"Who knows? They might be waiting to discover his supplier."

"I'll ask Maggie next time I see her."

"If they're setting a trap, she can't tell you anything. Leave it alone. It's not your business."

Tersely, Lynn said, "I don't get you. First, you don't want to hear anything about Arnold buying up claims because it's just a coincidence. I get that you're tired of hearing about Mom's murder, but then you ignore information about Pete and his friend's drug-peddling. It's not butting in to just ask her."

Don stood. "Do what you want. I've got to get to bed. I need to get up early."

Lynn sat in the darkened bar. She slowly rubbed the back of her neck. *I've got to get through to Don before it's too late. I'm in quicksand. If I can unravel Mom's murder, things will get back to normal. We can be like we were when we first got here, unafraid of the future and in love.* She waited until she was sure Don was asleep before she joined him.

CHAPTER 12

Two days later as Lynn prepared to make a quick trip to town, the phone rang. "Hi, Maggie, you just caught me. How are you?"

"I'm fine. Sheriff Carlson called me this morning about a possible lead in your mom's case. I'm to meet him at the station. Can you join us about noon?"

"Of course. Did he say what he found?"

"No, just something about the murder, but he didn't sound very pleased. I'll see you there."

Lynn finished her errands and went to the sheriff's station. Maggie immediately ushered her into an empty office.

"Lynn, Sheriff Carlson's ready to interrogate Pete Langston again, and I got permission for you to listen with me behind the one-way glass. We'll be able to see and hear everything."

"Pete Langston? What does he have to do with my mother's murder?"

"He's been sitting in jail since his arrest for arson, but he got word to the sheriff he has important information to tell him about something big. The only big thing that's happened around here is your mother's murder. His cellmate also told Sheriff Carlson that Pete mentioned your name and bragged that what he knows will make him a hero. The sheriff wanted you to hear it firsthand."

"I hope it will help."

Maggie led Lynn into the viewing room. On the other side of the mirror, Pete sat alone, eyes downcast, his body bent in a lazy slouch across the metal chair. He cracked his tattooed fingers and then rubbed red knuckles across chin stubble. Now and then he jerked his head to the side as he spit chewed fingernails onto the floor.

Lynn whispered, "I haven't seen Pete in at least three months. Guess it was in May that I bumped into him at The Sport Shop. It was before the fire. He was joking with the help and brushed past me. He said, 'Hi, snooty neighbor.' I hardly recognize him now." Lynn held her breath as she followed Sheriff Larry Carlson's arrival in the interrogation room.

The lawman's wide shoulders and big body filled the room. He dwarfed the young man at the table. Pete pushed himself up straight and folded both hands on the table. The sheriff leveled his gaze at the prisoner. Pete returned the look only a moment then studied his hands. The sheriff pulled up a chair. Deputy Jones entered the room and sat on a chair near the door.

"Now, you say you witnessed something connected to the death of the woman discovered on Memorial Day weekend. I don't have time to waste on liars, drug users, or bums. I don't need to point out it's not your first arrest, and starting the fire is your one-way ticket back to jail."

Pete raised his head. His eyes darted around the room, and he picked at his earlobe, then at his fingernail with shaky fingers.

The sheriff jabbed his finger at Pete. "You can consider time you spent in rehab for drug use a vacation compared to the time you'll do behind bars for arson, and it could be quite a few years."

Pete licked his lips, and his body trembled slightly. He spoke in a low voice. "I do know something."

Tapping the arrest file, Carlson leaned back and studied the young man. Pete dropped his head again and attacked another fingernail.

Carlson cleared his throat. "Well, Pete, are you ready to spend the next fifteen years in prison?"

Pete squeaked, "I can't, Sheriff. You know me. I'd never set a fire on purpose. I was cold and wasted. I tried to put the fire out, but it got out of hand." His voice turned into a thin whine. "I only wanted to get warm. I'm sorry, really sorry."

"You're right, I know you. Just because you grew up in an alcoholic family doesn't excuse your actions. I've seen you and your punk friends slide in and out of trouble since high school. And I'm sure you're sorry. But this is going to be very bad for you. The only reason it's taken so long to get you in front of the judge is the arson report got pushed aside due to the judge being sick."

The sheriff folded his arms across his barrel chest. "The public defender will do his best, but arson's a felony. You'll get jail time. You don't like being in jail, do you, Pete? Well, get used to the idea."

Pete squirmed. The twenty-five-year-old shook nervously and rubbed at red eyes. "I hated it. I almost died in there. I never want to go back." His hands trembled. "I'm just stupid, I guess, too stupid to stay out of trouble. Can't you help me?"

The lawman grunted. He flipped through Pete's arrest file and closed the cover. "My hands are tied. I can't do much. The prosecutor wants to burn you. She'd like nothing better than to remove a druggie, pusher, and fire starter from society. I think she's going to run for judge pretty soon, and winning this case would make her election a sure thing. You can say good-bye to your friends for a long time."

The lawman pushed his chair back and stood up. He leaned over and spread two meaty hands on the table. His broad face was six inches from Pete's. Beads of sweat spread across Pete's face like a bad case of teenage acne.

"Pete, you asked for this meeting, but you haven't given me anything. You said you had something important to tell me." He headed for the door. "Unless it's real good, there's no chance in hell for a plea bargain. Think on it, and if you come up with something, let me know." His hand reached for the doorknob.

Pete leaned forward. "Wait. I can tell you stuff."

The sheriff twisted around. "Well, what is it?"

Pete's lips were pressed tight, and dark sweat marks appeared on his shirt. His eyes became narrowed slits. "I can tell you something big, but you have to give me immunity and get me out of this town, somewhere far away, where I'll be safe."

The constable groaned. "This is bull. Everyone tries to wiggle out of an arrest with made-up stories to waste my time." He shot a bored look at Pete and again touched the doorknob.

"I saw the murder."

A loud scrape made everyone jump. Deputy Jones almost hit the floor as his chair squirted out from under him. The sheriff glared at him. "For Christ's sake, get it under control."

Behind the glass, Maggie touched Lynn's hand. They both strained to hear more.

The sheriff's attention focused on Pete. "Be advised this conversation is being recorded. Do you want your Public Defender here?"

Pete shook his head. "No."

"Okay, then go on."

"I thought it was a murder, but I didn't know for sure. Now I do." He spoke faster. "I know who did it, too. I almost crapped when I bumped into him in town. I got scared. I think he recognized me, so I hid out." He took a big breath.

Carlson raised his hand. "Slow down, what murder did you see?"

"That woman, the one found…her body found in Bright River. I crashed at Stag Horn Ranch for a while. I tried to get out of town, but I didn't have any money. Everyone at the ranch got tired of me hanging around, so they quit bringing me food and stuff."

"How long did you stay there?"

"About ten days. I finally went into town for some beer. I never figured I'd bump into him, but there he was, getting gas at the Chevron station." Pete hissed. "Just my luck."

"So you recognized the man that you think committed the murder?"

"Yeah. I knew it was him."

"What kind of car was he driving?"

"He was in a Jeep. When I went into the convenience store, I kept my head down. I hoped he wouldn't recognize me or my truck."

"Where did you go afterward?"

"I went into the woods where I started the fire. I was going to stay there a couple of days. But I got drunk. I was afraid I'd get shot or something. I didn't want to get my friends in trouble, either. Sometimes they're jerks, but I'm no rat." Pete took a breath. "My friends are all I got. Can you keep them out of this if I tell you what I know?"

"We'll see." He peered over his glasses. "Pete, we don't make deals unless we can verify the information you provide."

Pete sat back in the chair and began to talk. "I was with one of my friends late at night to make a drug buy. We argued. He told me to piss off and left."

The sheriff's finger tapped on the file. "Dates, names, places..."

Pete nodded. "Okay, it was the Friday night of Memorial Day weekend, May twenty-fourth...uh, no, the twenty-third. Jed Noble and I were supposed to make the buy, but I didn't have all the money. We argued. He was mad as hell at me and left. I was about to follow him, but a cop car crossed the street up ahead, a couple blocks away. So I kept my headlights off, and I went in the other direction, north, and pulled in behind an old trailer and stacks of wooden crates. I was in a storage yard next to an abandoned gas station, west side of town by the river."

"What kind of trailer?"

"I don't know, just a wood stake trailer for hauling stuff."

"Okay, go on."

"My truck was still running, but I rolled down the window for some air. I lit a smoke and just waited until no cops were anywhere around. Then a car light went on not very far from where I was parked."

"In the storage yard?"

"No, in the gas station." He used his hands. "Perpendicular to my car. I was looking out my side window and could only see the back of the other car."

Carlson asked, "So what lights came on? Headlights? Taillights?"

"The interior dome light."

Sheriff Carlson leaned forward. "Estimate the distance from the other car to yours."

"Fifty yards…no, less, half that, maybe twenty-five yards."

"How many people did you see?" Carlson squinted. "One, two? Man, woman?"

"I'm sure it was a man in the passenger side. He opened the car door. That's when the dome light came on, and I could see his profile and shiny bald head. He got out and went around to the driver's side and helped someone out of the car."

"A woman or man?"

"It was dark. I couldn't tell. But much smaller than the man. He opened the back door, and the two of them disappeared into the backseat. I figured it was just people parking in a deserted place 'cause they wanted some fun, you know, sex. But then a voice called out, but not real loud, just enough for me to glance again."

"Male or female?"

"I couldn't tell. The dome light was out, and everything was black again. I didn't hear any more noise."

"What did you do then?"

"I finished my cigarette and drove onto the street. Didn't see any cops, so I made a left and drove off. The guy coulda seen me 'cause when I turned, I went under the street light. My truck's unique. Only one in town with an elk head painted on each side door. Painted it myself."

Pete stopped to catch his breath.

The sheriff continued his questions. "What kind of car were the two people in?"

Pete answered, "Don't know the make. It was long. I'm pretty sure it was a new SUV, with roof rails. Not like the Jeeps you see around here. The interior seemed light, gray or white. It was only a silhouette from where I was parked. But it was silver looking."

Sheriff Carlson studied his notes. "Why did you think it was a murder?"

"I didn't until about a couple days later when I read the newspaper with the story about a lady being killed and her car found right where I was that night." Pete raised his chin. "I put two and two together."

The sheriff asked, "What street were you parked on?"

"Don't know."

"Pete, when did you leave the area?"

"After midnight. I'm not sure."

Carlson kept firing questions. "When did you read about the murder?"

"Couple days later, in the Tuesday edition of the *Elk Hills Daily Journal.* The paper was lying around at the ranch."

Sheriff Carlson had listened carefully to Pete's account. When Pete finished, the lawman growled, and his fist hit the table. "Why in hell didn't you come forward sooner? We needed this earlier in the case. That poor woman was killed, and you withheld information."

With each question, Pete slid lower in his chair. "I'm sorry. I was scared. I knew I should tell someone, but I was afraid the guy had seen me, and I didn't know who he was. I figured he was the drifter the newspaper talked about and he'd left town."

The sheriff stood and yanked on his belt. "When did you bump into the man again?"

Pete spoke quickly. "About a week later. No, five days later. He drove up the mountain above Mineral Lake... around May twenty-eighth. That's when I realized he must be a local."

Sheriff Carlson leaned back. "Go on, in detail."

Pete said, "It was before the fire. I left the ranch to meet my cousin." Pete hesitated.

Carlson asked, "Why were you up there?"

Pete slurred over his words. "We had some business to do."

"Go on."

"I heard a vehicle coming up the cutbacks to the old Golden Cross Mine above Mineral Lake. I kept hoping it would veer off, but it kept coming, so I backed my truck into some brush and made sure I was hidden."

The deputy asked, "Then what?"

"I stayed there at least thirty minutes. I was an hour early for our meeting, and I hoped this nosy tourist would wander off, out of my way. The car passed the Golden Cross Mine and moved even closer to my spot. The driver stopped. He was so close I thought he'd seen me. Luckily, he pulled out a big map and opened it. He looked way above my hiding spot and continued to stare up the mountainside."

"Did you see his face?"

"No. But then he took off his hat. I recognized the bald head, and I got a view of his profile. He's a big guy." Pete took a breath. "I realized it was the man in the car. The one I'd seen the night the lady was murdered."

The room grew quiet. The only sound was made by Deputy Jones as he checked the recorder. Pete sat straight, his leg bouncing up and down.

The sheriff picked up the questioning. "What happened next?"

"The man started his vehicle again and moved up the narrow road to the next cutback. Pretty soon he was out of view. I figured he stopped and went into a mine. I didn't hear a motor running. I wanted to get out of there." Pete placed his cuffed hands on the table. "I eased out and took a different route down to the main road."

"What did you do next?"

"I headed straight for Stag Horn Ranch. I stayed there for ten days or so, like I said. I was too scared to come into town."

"This was the same man you ran into at the Chevron station? When?"

"Yeah. The day before the fire. Like I said, I went in to get some beer. He walked right past me. I beat it up the pass and slept there all night. I wanted to get out of town, but the next day I started the fire—accidentally."

"The fire was on June tenth" the deputy reminded them.

Carlson asked, "Do you know who the man is, his name?"

Pete shook his head. "Not his name, but he's the lady's husband. His picture was in the newspaper next to hers." He faced Sheriff Carlson. "I guess her husband killed her, right?"

Deputy Jones and the sheriff remained silent.

Carlson stood up. "Pete, is that everything you can remember?"

Pete nodded. He squinted up at the sheriff. "Will this help me?"

The sheriff stood in the doorway. "If it's all true, and you swear to it in court, then it might help. Jones, have his statement typed and signed then get it to the DA and the public defender. I'll go by there now to give them the heads-up."

The sheriff pointed his finger at Pete. "Keep quiet about this meeting. There's a lot to work on. I'll let you know when we need to speak with you again."

Pete nodded. "You can count on me. I won't say anything. I'm glad to help." The sheriff left the room.

Lynn and Maggie stepped out of the viewing room and went down the hall. Maggie said, "Wait for me outside the sheriff's office. I know where he's gone."

Lynn nodded, but her mind was elsewhere. She sat down and held her head in her hands.

Maggie rounded a corner and came face-to-face with Sheriff Carlson. She was caught off guard by his steely comment.

"If Pete's telling the truth, this case is now smokin' hot. I'm encouraged by this eyewitness placing Arnold Clay at the possible crime scene. The abandoned gas station is close enough for Arnold to walk back to their home. Motive is still weak. We'll have to make the case airtight enough to tie it up with the knot around Arnold Clay's neck."

Maggie trailed behind as the sheriff strode down the hall, his body tilted forward. Maggie said, "I'm angry. Too bad Colorado doesn't still hang killers like they did in the old days." She lengthened her stride to keep pace with him.

Carlson spoke mostly to himself. "A public hanging used to prove the point that crime doesn't pay."

Maggie added, "Now only a few witnesses are left to see the end of a convicted killer's life, followed by a brief notice in the newspaper."

"Yep, many years of appeals have passed before the sentence is carried out. By then, none of the victim's family members are even alive. The swift sword of justice is only a footnote in history now." He entered the DA's office and shut the door.

Maggie returned to the waiting room. "The sheriff will be going over Pete's statement with the DA. We may be able to charge Arnold Clay with Betty's murder."

Lynn hugged Maggie. "Oh, I hope so."

"The sheriff's all fired up. You might as well go on home. I'll call you when I hear what the district attorney says."

"Wait, Maggie. I've been trying to remember the dates Pete mentioned. I'm confused, and I want to be able to tell Don. You took notes. Can you go over them again?"

Maggie pulled out her small notebook. "On the night of May twenty-third, he witnessed two people in a car. On about May twenty-seventh, he thinks he recognized the same man on the mountainside. He stated he read an article in the paper that pictured the husband of the murdered woman sometime after the murder date. He was uncertain about that date, but I'm sure we can substantiate it from newspaper archives. Finally, on June ninth, he ran into the same man, the woman's husband, at the gas station."

Lynn said, "And on June tenth, he started the fire on Divide Mountain Pass."

"At least we finally have something to work on." Maggie walked Lynn to her car.

Lynn said, "I admit, I've been pretty unhappy with Sheriff Carlson. It seemed he was looking everywhere except at Arnold. I thought he was afraid to tackle a former lawman."

Maggie stopped. "Afraid? You're wrong. Once a perp is in his cross hairs, he doesn't waver. I can't say too much, but a long time ago Carlson had a bad experience. He leaned too hard on a suspect, and it ended in tragedy."

"What happened?"

"Rumor has it, when Carlson was a Texas Ranger, a young man was a prime suspect in a case. He became so distraught from the interrogation, he cracked. He jumped off an overpass and died. Awhile later, a witness came forward with evidence that exonerated him. But it was too late."

"That's horrible." Lynn got into her car. "This helps me see why Carlson has been treating Arnold with kid gloves. I thought it was because Arnold's a retired policeman."

"No. He learned a hard lesson. You understand I told you this in confidence."

"Don't worry, I do. Thanks."

****

Two weeks went by as Maggie and Lynn waited to hear from Sheriff Carlson on the district attorney's response to the case against Arnold Clay.

Finally, the call she'd waited for came. "Lynn, this is Sheriff Carlson. I'm sorry to tell you the grand jury denied our request to charge Arnold Clay with the murder of Betty Clay."

Lynn's voice rose, "No...Sheriff, how...can that happen? Pete identified Arnold Clay at the car with Mom. That should be enough."

"Unfortunately, his distance from the parked car and the dark night cast doubt on his ability to identify a specific person. In addition, we have no corroboration for his claims."

"But he's an eyewitness."

"His testimony wouldn't hold up. The DA found a previous conviction for perjury about five years ago. Combined with his drug history and current arson arrest, he's not credible."

"But he knew all about the area where the car was found..."

"Most of what he told us might have come from the newspaper articles. You also have to remember Arnold's unblemished record with his department in Denver.

It goes a long way with a jury. It's a stretch to suggest a man without even a traffic citation would kill his new wife, even if she did have money."

"Sheriff, you can't blame me for being sick about this decision. I think Arnold has slid out of trouble a second time. What can you or I do about his evasion of the law?"

"I'm not convinced of his innocence, but we have to be sure he's our man. I'll continue to follow every lead. Keep your eyes and ears open. We need to locate anything we might have missed. I'll keep you posted on anything I hear. It's not completely over yet."

Lynn hung up the phone and wiped away angry tears. She dialed the lumberyard. "Don, Arnold is walking. Sheriff Carlson just called. The grand jury didn't think Pete's statement was strong enough to go to trial. So Arnold's skipped out of trouble again. I'm so angry."

"I'm sorry. You tried, Lynn. I'll give you credit for that. It's possible something will come up."

CHAPTER 13

A week after the disappointing news from Sheriff Carlson, Lynn received a call.

"Hi, Lynn. This is Amy. I have some news for you about Arnold and his wife."

"You mean Blue Bird?"

"No. His first wife, before he married Blue Bird. I don't know her name, but she died by drowning. How about that?"

"Mom mentioned Arnold's son, Trent, is from a first marriage, but she certainly never mentioned the details of that wife's death. Maybe Arnold never told her."

Amy grunted. "Some omission."

"How did you find out?"

"I can't say exactly, but I was told this came out during the investigation into Blue Bird's death."

Lynn said, "I'm disgusted. I need a scorecard to keep track of this guy."

"I just know he's responsible for all their deaths." Amy's voice rose in anger. "He either killed three women, or he's the most unlucky bastard in the world."

"Amy, I've got to find out more about this."

"The person who told me will only talk to you in person."

"Who is it?"

"He's Bea Russell's son, Steve. He told Bea he knows you. And Bea says she met you. Do you remember her?"

"Steve Russell? He was recently here at our restaurant. We were both at Sage High at the same time, and I met his mother, but I didn't dream she knew Mom."

Amy said, "Betty and Bea were both in Emblem Club when your dad was an Elk. It was awhile back, at least fifteen years. Bea was in the club in Aurora, but the small club in Piñon got together with the Aurora club for lots of events and fundraisers. When Steve introduced you to his mother as Lynn Mason, she didn't make any connection to Betty Thomas."

"But Steve said he lives in Houston. You say he's in Piñon?"

"Oh, his firm's in Texas, but for the last couple of months, he's worked in Denver. Bea's thrilled. He drives up to see her often."

"Steve recognized me, but I didn't remember him at all. He was visiting here on a fly-fishing trip with some of his Texas friends."

"Bea says this information is confidential, so I can't say anything more."

"I'll get back to you tomorrow. I have to convince Don I should go."

That evening, Lynn cornered Don in the kitchen.

"I had a call from Amy today. She said someone has information about Arnold that may make a difference in the investigation. To get this information, I need to talk to the source in person. I need to go to Piñon."

"Really?" Don squinted at her. "What's this about?"

"Business is not that great right now." Lynn spoke firmly. "I could make it there and back in two days. I'd like to go tomorrow."

Don's back went straight, and he loomed over her. "What in the world are you talking about? You're not the police. Keep out of this. I mean it. Talk to Maggie if you feel you must, but stay put at home."

Lynn folded her arms across her chest. "Don, I'm not trying to upset you, but I need to talk to this person. His mother, Bea, was a friend of Mom's in Piñon. Her son has information about Arnold that he'll only tell to me. You should remember him, Steve Russell. He stopped by the restaurant in the spring. I introduced you to him."

Don waved her off. "I don't remember."

"Amy said Bea was very upset over Mom's murder. She kept talking about it to Steve. He's an attorney, working in Denver now. He said he came across information that might shed light on the case, but he'll only talk to me in person, not on the phone."

Lynn took a breath and placed her hand on Don's arm. "If anything can help solve Mom's murder, I owe it to her to at least spend a little time trying to get some answers."

"I give up. Go ahead and go if you feel you must. I'm too busy to argue with you. Are you going to stay with Amy?"

"Yes."

"It might help you to see Amy. Maybe she can talk some sense into you. Promise you'll call me and let me know when you'll be home."

Lynn followed Don out to the deck. "I promise. Could be a dead end, but I have to try. I can't change the fact that Mom is gone, but if I can find justice for her, I'll feel a lot better."

"Don't get your hopes up. There are a lot of unsolved murder cases in this country."

"That's just it. The case is going nowhere. The sheriff's lost interest, and no new leads have come forward. All they found is one unidentified hair. Big deal. If this man can point the investigation in another direction, I need to contact him."

Don said, "You have a point."

"It will be a quick trip."

The next morning, Lynn rushed upstairs to see Don before he left for work. They met at the front door. She grabbed Don's arm. "Good-bye kiss?"

Lynn reached both arms around her husband's bulky jacket.

He gently lifted her chin. "Take care." His grin revealed the crinkle-smile eyes that used to make her knees weak. His mouth brushed quickly over hers.

She wasted no time. She called Amy to let her know she was on her way.

"Lynn, I'm so glad you're coming. I'll call Bea and her son to let them know. I'd like to help more. I'm an old lady, but if I were younger, I'd work with you to find out who did this terrible thing to Betty. I can't tell you how much I love you for trying to help. I'm thankful that Don agreed it was worthwhile that you make the trip."

"Yes. See you soon."

Lynn carried her suitcase to the car. As she slammed the trunk, a crack sounded. She jumped backward, thinking a gun had gone off. Standing only ten feet from the lake, she beheld the beaver she'd named Matilda and realized the sharp report resulted from her tail slapping the water in typical bad humor. Their nearest neighbor had warned Lynn to keep away. The familiar ripple of an aspen branch being pushed by Matilda appeared on the surface. Lynn could see a change in the lodge. The mound, covered with new mud and adorned with branches, now resembled an unfriendly citadel.

Lynn called out, "So you're getting ready for winter. I got your message loud and clear. I'll keep my distance."

Lynn drove through Elk Hills and past quaint churches, Catholic, Presbyterian, and Baptist. She found it curious that the tiny town managed to fill pews of three churches on Sunday with the same two-fisted drinkers who filled the bars on Saturday night. The hamlet was perched on slopes of inhospitable peaks ready to snap off toes from frostbite in winter or pierce hearts in spring with the sight of a baby elk standing on wobbly legs in a meadow of lupine. Perhaps the dichotomy of the place appealed to the people who chose to chisel a comfortable life from the mountain's hard rock.

She spied Sandra Steele talking to a man in front of the Black Bear Café. They stood next to a shiny new Dodge truck. Lynn ducked her head, anxious to avoid eye contact with the troublesome Realtor. She bit her lip. *What a witch. She's probably discussing some new complaint she wants to file against us. She keeps her feud going every chance she gets.*

Lynn began the long drive. After four hours she reached Denver. Once beyond the city, she moved along the highway south on E470 leading to Piñon. Falling darkness crossed the city and the changing sky. Only a short distance away, early stars winked against an ultramarine blanket above a tangerine sunset. Office building lights competed with the stars for attention as their jewel tones sparkled on the horizon.

She continued south on E470, passed under I-70, and drove another ten miles.

City traffic dissolved. The gray ribbon of asphalt stretched ahead, and light traffic moved around her.

She arrived at Amy's to find both Bea and Steve there.

Amy embraced her. "You must be hungry."

"I hadn't thought about it, but now I'm starving."

Steve said, "I'll get your bags, and then I'll take you to dinner." He was already moving out the door. "That will give us a chance to talk."

Lynn looked at Amy, who smiled and shrugged. "Bea and I will get a bite here."

The women barely had time to say hello before Steve returned with her bag. "Ready to go?"

They said their good-byes, and Steve led her to his car.

Soon they arrived at a local resort that advertised a fine dining restaurant. In addition, attractive cabins, nestled among pine trees, graced the river edge. They entered the restaurant and sat at a small table facing the bar. A waitress came over and Steve ordered their drinks.

Steve leaned back.

Lynn broke the silence. "It's been quite a while since we talked."

"Yes. How are you?"

Lynn smiled. "Business is okay. Don's been busy at the lumberyard. Of course, he also helps me in the restaurant each night. We subdivided our land behind the restaurant and just made our first sale." She raised her eyes to meet his. "Are you interested in a building site for a second home?"

Steve answered. "I'd give anything to live on Mineral Lake. But right now it's too far away for me to invest."

"Ah, too far a commute."

"You sidestepped my question, Lynn. I want to know how *you* are. Is there any change?"

"Sorry to say, no change." His direct question startled her. "Don's grumpy, and I put up with it."

Steve's face was earnest. "You know you don't have to put up with anything. A different life is possible."

"That subject's too serious to discuss on an empty stomach. You mentioned food. I sure can use something to eat."

He picked up on the cue. "Right. I thought you might enjoy this place. They serve great Western barbecue ribs. How does that sound?"

"Wonderful. I'm anxious to know how you think you can help in the investigation."

Steve's voice was earnest. "I was very sorry to hear about your mother's death. I know it was hard on you."

"Thanks, it was hard."

He sipped his drink. "Let's unwind, enjoy some good food before we get serious."

"All right, you're in charge."

Their meal was long and enjoyable. Steve entertained her with bright stories of his youth fishing with his dad in the Elk Hills area and good times with Dick Kaplan rock-climbing around the Red Rock area outside of Denver.

Lynn's thoughts stirred. *I'm enjoying this evening more than I ever imagined. I'm feeling feminine all over, right down to my toes. I could pull him into one of those cabins and make mad love all night...*

Over after-dinner coffee, Steve began, "I let my mom know I ran across information about Arnold's first wife and her death in Illinois. I discovered a news article with a police statement that was very clear. No foul play occurred. Arnold wasn't charged."

"Your mother said she drowned."

"She did, but he had a solid alibi, and there was no evidence their marriage was in trouble, so he was eliminated as a possible suspect. The police wrote it off as an unfortunate accident. However, the title for a small farm his wife had inherited from her father a few years before passed to him."

Lynn studied Steve's profile. "It's interesting, but is this what you had to tell me in person?"

"Not exactly. I gave my mother that information to chew on, rather than the real angle I'm chasing. This is all strictly confidential. It means disbarment if it came out I discussed any of this with you."

Lynn answered firmly. "You can trust me."

"My law firm in Houston handles mostly civil suits. Usually, I'm given property disputes, land sales, and estate cases. Since the first of the year, my firm has worked on a murder case. They used a local attorney to represent our client until he took a leave of absence due to illness. They handed me the assignment four months ago."

Lynn said, "Tell me about it."

"It involves the death of our client's father, George Wilson. In January he was murdered by an unknown assailant. George Wilson and Tony Salvatori were partners in the Gold Bar Casino, in Oreland, located a short distance from Denver. My client is convinced Salvatori had a hand in the murder of his father."

"Why do they suspect him?"

"Wilson's son claims his father accused Salvatori of cooking the books. In retaliation, Tony killed Wilson."

Lynn asked, "What do you mean by cooking the books?"

"Wilson figured Tony kept two sets of books and was cheating him out of his fair share of the profits. His son says when his father accused Salvatori, they had a big blowup."

"Didn't the police check on the accounting records for irregularities?"

"They did just that, and there were signs of moving money around, but they didn't find a second set of books. Then there's the practice of skimming."

"Skimming?"

"A lot of cash comes into a casino. It's easy to steal money off the top each day before the amounts are recorded. That way, each day is consistent with every other, and the tax man doesn't notice any variation in receipts."

"Do you think they were skimming?"

"Yes. According to his son, Wilson complained he wasn't getting what he calculated as his share. Salvatori kept all the skim for himself. Seems a good motive to get rid of Wilson. But the case against Salvatori dissolved in March when someone provided an alibi for the night Wilson was killed. So the DA had to let him go. My firm sent me here to tie up loose ends of Wilson's property and close the file."

"It's all very interesting, but how does it connect to Mom's murder? She was killed in Elk Hills."

"Ever since your mother's murder, every phone call I've had with my mother has been filled with sorrow and speculation. When she first gave me the news about Betty, she mentioned Betty'd recently married Arnold Clay. I didn't know Arnold Clay, even though Mom said he lived in Piñon years ago. But while I was processing the documentation for my client's case, I came across papers signed by Trent Clay. He was one of the attorneys working for Salvatori. I did some snooping and discovered Trent had recently closed his Denver office and was working out of a small office in Piñon. When I heard 'Piñon' and 'Clay,' I thought of Betty and her new husband, Arnold Clay. I checked it out. Trent is Arnold's son."

Lynn said, "The sheriff told me Trent's an attorney. He's also the executor of Mom's will. He's been in town helping his father."

"The document I ran across, signed by Trent Clay, is the statement from a Jake Dixon, providing the alibi for Salvatori. The alibi hamstrung the district attorney. The investigation died, then and there."

"Did you find any other connection between Trent and Jake Dixon?"

"Yes. Trent Clay handled his recent assault and battery charge. Jake was in jail for that when he gave his statement for the alibi. The point is Jake Dixon used to work for Salvatori as a bouncer. That's how he was arrested for the A&B charge.

He got a little too rough with a customer. Even though the alibi is suspicious, Jake had no other convictions, so his alibi stuck, and it blew our case to bits."

"Wow, this all sounds so fishy. Did you tell anyone else about it?"

"The previous attorney handled that phase of the case. As long as Jake Dixon is willing to perjure himself, our case is shut down. They're not nice people. They run casinos and may have ties to organized crime."

"Mafia? In Denver?"

"Where there are casinos, it's possible there's Mafia. In the last ten years, Native American casinos have sprung up all over Colorado. I'm sure most are clean, but some may not be pure. Investors and partnerships were formed and think of the number of employees they hired quickly to get open. Some rotten apples can infiltrate at all levels from valet to entertainment, right up to management."

Lynn said, "Even without the Mafia, I can imagine there could be a tough guy involved in the casino mean enough to coerce Jake Dixon and make him lie."

"That's what I'm guessing. I need to find out if Jake was willing to lie about the alibi and I need some time to investigate the relationship between Jake Dixon and Trent Clay."

"You said he worked for Salvatori. Suppose he just wanted to help his old boss."

"It's doubtful. Jake was in jail several months for his assault and battery conviction, and no help came from Salvatori to get him off."

Lynn said, "I can see this web involves Trent Clay, but how does it involve Mom's murder?"

"That's what I need to work on. Trent may have gone over the legal line. I need to dig for motive and opportunity. I've done enough snooping around that I didn't want to phone you about all of this supposition. I wanted to tell it to you in person so you'd understand the danger."

"Danger to me?"

"We can't divulge this information to anyone. Salvatori would stop at nothing to avoid being brought up on murder charges again."

"Salvatori certainly doesn't know me. Trent does but I'm up on Mineral Lake, and you're here. How can I help?"

"You found out Trent Clay is in Elk Hills helping his father. Just keep an eye on him. If he does anything odd or you hear anything, let me know. I'm going to check on cases he recently handled in Denver and what actions he's taken in Piñon since he moved his office there."

"When did he move to Piñon?"

"Around the first of April. I plan to stop in and visit with the local judge and touch base with some old friends. I'm going to feel around for any information that may lead somewhere."

"When Arnold and Mom married, Trent didn't come to their wedding. He was mad. Arnold refused to give him any more money. Mom told me about Trent's gambling problem. I didn't think anything of it at the time, but now I wonder if he owes money to a loan shark or casino."

Steve slapped the table. "That's just the kind of information I've been hoping for. I can check with several sources about who he owes and how far he's in debt. I have a few pipelines I can use."

Lynn said, "We need to get back. I want to spend some time with Amy."

"I'm sorry to say I won't see you again on this trip. After I speak with the judge, I need to drive back to my place. I've got a lot of work to do as well as dig into Betty's murder. But I'll keep in touch. Can you give me your cell number?"

"I have one, but I don't use it at the lake since we don't get a good signal there. It works in town and some other areas, but the canyons and mountains block some calls. The restaurant land line works. That's the best way to reach me." She wrote both numbers on a piece of paper and handed it to Steve. "I'll start carrying my cell phone with me, just in case."

"Just stay in touch and watch what you say. If Trent is guilty, he's going to try to keep his connections secret. Call me at my office or use my cell if there's any emergency." He handed her his card.

Lynn studied it. "I remember the first time you gave me your card. I don't think you had any idea that night how much it meant to me that you cared I was upset."

They parked in front of Amy's house, and he faced her. "Don's verbal abuse went too far. I care about you, and I meant exactly what I said to you. I'm here to help you any time, whenever you need me."

His sincerity was powerful. Lynn took his hand. "Steve, I truly thank you."

He smiled. "Better go in. Amy's on the porch waiting for you."

They climbed the stairs, and her mother's friend's loving arms held Lynn tight.

Amy said, "Bea and I waited to have dessert with the two of you."

"Sorry, I can't stay. Tell her I'll call later." He walked back toward his car. Amy ushered Lynn into the house.

Bea, Amy, and Lynn had so much to catch up on, they didn't stop to take a breath until late. That was fine with Lynn. She didn't want to think about Steve and his affect on her.

The next morning, Lynn stopped, speechless, as she entered Amy's living room. Her father stood at the door. He looked at her, a serious expression on his face. "Lynn, Amy told me you were here. I hope we can talk a bit before you leave."

Amy nudged Lynn forward. "Kurt, I think it's a great idea."

Lynn couldn't think of any excuse, so she agreed to join her dad on the porch. She didn't want to discuss their old issues.

Kurt said, "Amy's call was a surprise. I'm so glad I have this chance to see you. I love you, Lynn. You're my only daughter. Let's just talk about good things today and leave the old stuff behind us. Okay?"

"Sure, Dad. That's fine with me. Tell me what you've been doing."

Kurt rambled on about mundane subjects for about half an hour. Lynn added her own general comments about the heavy winter in Elk Hills, the economy, and the cost of employees.

Kurt finally said, "I want you to know I was saddened to hear about Betty. Her death was untimely and unfair. I wish things hadn't gone the way they did, but I—"

Lynn interrupted, "I know. She was a wonderful woman. She loved you. I'm sorry you were unable to stay together. It's all over now."

They sat in silence.

"I guess I'd better leave. It's a long drive." She embraced her father awkwardly, and he walked down the steps to his car.

"I still love you," Lynn whispered, not sure if he'd heard her.

CHAPTER 14

Fall days were getting shorter. Afternoon sunlight glowed above the ridgeline of Nugget Top Mountain as Lynn drove through Elk Hills. She stopped at The Sport Stop for a newspaper. Her friend Carolyn was handling the register.

"How was your trip to Denver?"

Lynn was surprised Carolyn knew she'd been gone. "It was good. Actually, I was in Piñon, southeast of Denver. The place has changed, and most of my old friends have moved away. Lots of new people in town now."

"Just like here. Strangers come in every day."

Lynn left the store and continued to the lumberyard to see Don. She drove down an alley and passed by Scott Lee's warehouse. The lights were out and the door closed. A black truck parked on the grass drive. *If Scott's in town, maybe Marilyn is here, too.* She drove on.

Don was alone, bent over papers and a calculator as she entered the office.

"Hi, Don, I'm home. What a long drive."

Don leaned back and focused on his wife. "Well, how did it go?"

"Pretty well. Got some news that may lead somewhere. I'll tell you tonight."

Lynn leaned down to plant a quick kiss. "I'm tired, but it was so good to see Amy and Bea. It helped a lot to spend some time with them."

"I'm glad. I thought the trip might do you some good. I've got a late appointment to go over material costs with Tim Watson. It'll take awhile. I'll grab some dinner in town and eat here. Just rest and unwind. Okay?"

"Thanks. Sounds good. What about the restaurant? Are Mike and Wendy still working for us?"

"Nope. Both took off for the ski resorts. Before you know it will be November. They're eager to find jobs and a place to rent. I put a closed sign on the restaurant this morning. We didn't have any customers last night. It's been crazy busy here, and it's too much for you to run it alone. We can talk about opening for hunting season."

"Works for me. Hey, I drove past Scott Lee's warehouse. I wondered if it was Scott's truck parked in the drive."

"Haven't seen him. I doubt he's in town. Told me he would be out of state for a while."

"Hmm. I'll see you at home."

Lynn drove along the river. Evening light began to fade above the dark shoulders of the protective mountains surrounding the lake as twilight stars were caught in a cosmic net. Shards of rock crunched under the tires as she drove into the lot. The sound startled mallards resting on the lake.

Lynn was happy to be home, back under the spell of the primordial lake.

Later that evening, she finished washing up her dinner dishes as Don arrived.

He dropped his keys on the counter. "If we get a good night's rest, how about getting up early and doing some fishing? I'm hoping the trout are still biting. It could be our last chance this fall. Jack mentioned he'd like to get in an hour or so before we open."

"You and Jack go. I need to rest after my trip. I'll fix you both some breakfast when you're done before you leave for the yard. How does that sound?"

"Good. We might even have some fresh fish to fry."

Just after six in the morning, Lynn woke to the hum of an outboard motor. She dressed and walked outside. Jack and Don were a short distance from the dock in front of the spillway, and both were hunched over their lines. Jack's dog, Boomer, was with them. Sunlight caught her brown fur as she stood in the boat, ears perked, watching the action. Lynn smiled to herself. *I'm not surprised she's in the boat with them. Jack takes her everywhere, and after Don heard how she worked the ducks last fall, he wants to find a hunting dog just like her as soon as he can.*

Don had turned on the coffee pot they kept in their living quarters and Lynn carried a cup upstairs to the restaurant. After breakfast, she intended to clean out the refrigerator and thoroughly scrub the kitchen and bar. Sipping her coffee, she stood at the side window and observed the two fishermen. Don sat next to the outboard motor of their aluminum sixteen-foot fishing boat. Last night, Don had mentioned the rental money had paid for the boat, and he wanted to buy two more for next year.

Alarm spread through her as the boat drifted closer to the mouth of the river. Don pulled on the cord to start the motor. She heard it sputter once, then twice, and then no sound reached her. Transfixed, her scalp tingled. Her fear grew as the tiny boat headed for the spillway. *They could be killed going down the river.*

Her coffee cup hit the floor as she bolted down the stairs. She shoved the door open and pulled her car keys off their hook. Running to the truck, she glanced toward the boat and then stopped. Don stood with his arms up, reaching for the bridge spanning the river. He tried to stop the boat by hooking his legs under the boat seat. He quickly disappeared from her view as the boat passed beneath the bridge.

Lynn flung open the driver's door. She twisted her head in time to see Jack jump into the river. *Oh, God, Don, jump. Don't go over the falls. You'll die.*

As she reached the bridge, she spied Jack clinging to a bush. His arm came up, and he waved he was okay.

The boat had disappeared around a bend. Lynn crossed the bridge and sped to the one place she knew the river would be visible, less than a quarter mile from the spillway. Mineral Creek gained speed as it descended from the lake toward the heart of town, where it connected with Bright River. White-water rafting wasn't possible on Mineral Creek due to narrow sides and protruding boulders. Even fishing was impossible due to the steep banks.

She came to the pullout and bumped onto the dirt. Her mind sped over her options. *How can I help Don? I'm not strong enough to handle the current. If only there was a rope in the truck.*

A rocky dirt path led from the parking area down thirty feet to a grassy area used for photo shots and picnics. Grabbing hold of long grass and bushes, Lynn slid and half-fell down the incline to the river's edge. A granite boulder formed an eddy next to the shore. Water circulated in a crescent then rejoined the main stream. The falls were a hundred feet from where she stood. She didn't see anyone, so she called out, "Don, Don."

Abruptly, he appeared thirty feet upriver. He was out of the boat in the water. The current pulled him toward the spillway. Swift water surged past his chest. Holding the tether rope, he slowly pulled the boat behind him. He inched closer to shore on a diagonal.

Lynn's heart thudded in her chest. She called out, "Be careful!" The roar of the falls was deafening. Boomer still sat in the boat. "Let it go."

She shook with fear and prayed. *God help him. Don't let him die.* She watched each agonizing step as Don strained against the force. She chanced a quick glance toward the falls. The current increased as the sheer banks pinched the water until the satin surface disappeared. A terrified thought grew. *Don has to get out here. There's no other place before the falls.*

All at once, she realized Don was no longer headed downstream. He moved sideways toward shore. Hope sprang in her heart. *His feet must have found traction. He's making his way against the pull of the water.* Soon, the water level dropped to his waist. Quickly, his knees appeared.

Don leaned forward, head down, as he dragged the boat to the shallows.

The bank crumbled under Lynn's feet as she reached out as far as possible. Still separated from her husband by a dozen feet, she called, "Let me help you."

Don didn't answer. He grimaced as he fought the soft mud and rocks. His body swayed as his legs propelled him forward. Finally, he reached the embankment and heaved his body onto the ledge, then fell facedown. His fingers still held the rope as the boat bobbed at the river's edge. Kneeling at his side, Lynn pried the rope from his fingers.

Boomer sat at attention and then jumped daintily onto the grass. She bounded off to search the bushes for interesting smells.

Lynn touched Don's shoulder. "Are you okay?" She touched his face. "I was afraid you'd drown, or collapse pulling the boat."

Don gasped for breath. "Almost didn't make it…knew if I didn't get the boat ashore, Boomer would die and the boat would crash over the falls." He coughed and sat up as he took a deep breath. "Jack jumped out. He okay?"

"Yes, he's fine." Lynn wiped away tears. "You almost went over. I was so scared."

Both looked the short distance to the falls. The cascading water roared as it fell ninety feet to be crushed against rock cliffs. Only white mist escaped the deadly drop.

"Yeah. Damn…I don't understand why the motor stalled. It just wouldn't start."

"Let's get you to the car and back home into some dry clothes."

Don rose to his feet. "That dog. She hasn't a clue how close she came to disappearing over the falls. I'll tie the boat to this tree." He securely fastened the rope. "Going to be a job getting it up to the road. I'll ask Greg to help me later."

They reached the truck, and Lynn opened the tailgate for Boomer. Don slid into the seat. His blue lips quivered.

"As soon as we're home, jump into a hot shower and get into bed. That should thaw you out. I'll check on Jack."

As they entered their drive, Jack was getting into his truck. He poked his head out the window. "Hey, I thought we were going fishing, not swimming. Are you okay?"

Don pushed back his damp hair. "Yeah, I'm okay. Glad you made it. Boat's banged up. Prop and a couple of good dents."

Jack hopped out and opened the tailgate to let Boomer out and loaded her into his truck. He came up to Don's window. "I borrowed a jacket I found by the front door. I'm going home to dry out and get some hot coffee in me. I can be at the yard by nine."

"That's fine. Boomer's the only one that didn't get dunked." Don waved him on. "I'll be there soon as I change. Sure glad you're okay."

As Jack drove off, Don said, "Why in the hell did the motor conk? I checked it a few days ago, and it ran great. When I get the boat home, I'm going to find out what went wrong."

After a hot shower and some food, Don made a quick phone call then prepared to leave for work.

"Lynn, Greg is going to help me after I close the yard. I'll use his trailer. We'll take the boat back to the lumberyard. Along with the motor problem, the hull has dents. Jack will take it to Gunnison tomorrow and drop it at Nate's Marine Shop."

"Okay. I'll expect you later than usual."

"I can't understand why the engine fouled. I'm sure Nate will figure it out."

****

A few days later, Don called Lynn at home. "I'll be by after work with the boat and motor."

"Did they find out what was wrong?"

"The mechanic said the fuel line in the engine was plugged with a piece of plastic. The only way possible is if it was put there."

"You're saying someone purposely blocked the fuel line?"

"It had to have been deliberate. I can't think of anyone who'd want to hurt us. No one but us would use the boat this time of year. There was only enough gas in the line for it to start. After that, it would die."

"What should we do?"

"We'll talk when I get home. I have to work at Greg's property on the north side of the lake this afternoon. Delivering cement for his driveway. I'm in the big truck, but I'll have to leave it at the yard for Jack to use in the morning. Expect me home after six. I'll see you then."

"Okay. Take care."

"I will."

CHAPTER 15

Learning the boat had been tampered with disturbed Lynn. *Don doesn't scare easily, and now he suspects something might be amiss.*

A few days after the incident, the phone rang.

"Lynn, this is Scott Lee. I've been out of town for a couple of months. Marilyn told me about the fire up on the pass. Glad you both are okay and your restaurant didn't have any damage."

"Thanks for calling, Scott. The fire was close, but it was uphill from our place, and they got it out quickly. Lots of volunteers jumped in to help. Say, I thought you were in town a couple of days ago. I drove past your warehouse and a truck was parked in the drive. Was someone working there?"

"No. I don't have any employees right now. We've suspended core drilling on the mountain. I'll ask Deputy Maggie to check the warehouse. I left a lot of stuff in there. Thanks for keeping your eye out. Say hello to Don. We hope to get to Elk Hills to see you two before winter."

"Say hello to Marilyn. We miss you both."

Lynn found Steve's card tucked into her address book. She considered calling him. *The boat's plugged gas line may be a sign. Before I call Steve, I need to clear my head so I don't sound hysterical.* She put on her jacket and descended the outside stairs to face the enigmatic lake.

She'd walked for almost an hour on the dirt road that circled the lake when she slowed at the top of a steep hill. It offered a breathtaking vista. Across the lake, dust billowed above the trees, and she pinpointed where Don was hauling building material for Greg's project. Near the construction site, she spotted a speeding truck swerving around the curves on the narrow two-lane road. She frowned. *What an idiot to drive so fast in that area. It's probably a tourist.*

She finished her walk and dialed Steve.

He answered, and as soon as she said hello, his tone softened. "I've been waiting to hear from you. Any news?"

"Not a word from the sheriff. Probably put Mom's case in the deep freezer since they bombed getting Arnold to trial."

"Remember, we want the guilty person to pay. That means there has to be a solid case."

"You're right. Do you have any news?"

"Not yet, but I'm going to Piñon soon to see what I can learn about Trent."

"Can you find out what kind of vehicle he drives? It might be helpful. I drove by Arnold's house several times and the only vehicle parked there was a new Jeep. I think he traded in the SUV he and Mom had before . . ."

"Sure. Call me back tomorrow about this time."

"One more thing, something odd happened to our boat motor while Don was fishing on the lake a few days ago. He went down the river and almost over the falls. I don't know if it's related to Mom's murder, but it really scared me. It appears the fuel line was plugged on purpose."

"What? Lynn, this is dangerous. It may mean someone is after you and Don. They may think you know something that would expose them. Be very careful and keep a low profile. Have you discussed the case with anyone?"

"No."

"I'll find out what Trent drives and let you know soon. Please, be careful."

Lynn ate dinner alone. Evening caressed the lake, and the sunset washed the distant snow-clad peaks in pink. Water rippled in expanding circles as small trout leaped out of the water to catch tiny flying insects as they zigzagged over the liquid mirror. The fish antics made a soft plopping sound, called spooning, as their arched bodies hit the surface. A slice of moon shed a pinch of light, but soon night clouds covered its face, and darkness surrounded her.

CHAPTER 16

Steve woke to a crisp October morning. A blanket of gray clouds, plump with moisture, hovered above Piñon. He ambled into the kitchen and encircled his mother's ample figure in a bear hug.

"Mom, I think you've lost weight. You're almost a twin to Linda Evans."

Bea swatted the air with her kitchen towel. "Like your Irish father you are." She patted her hair in place. "I'm so glad you're able to visit again this weekend. Do you want sausage and eggs for breakfast?"

"Thanks, but I'm going to breakfast in town this morning, though I'm sure your food's much better."

He entered the town's popular meeting spot, the Gray Squirrel Café. The smell of pancakes and sausage met him at the door.

As he ate, he overheard a couple of locals discussing fishing.

One man said, "I was at Aurora Reservoir yesterday, and they were really biting. The judge is down at the first cove right now."

His breakfast companion said, "Situation normal. He's there every chance he gets."

Steve finished his omelet and the last bite of a warm biscuit. Back at his mom's, he rummaged in the garage until he located his favorite fly rod and fishing jacket. He went over his plan. *If I can locate the judge today, I won't have to wait until Monday.*

Driving along the reservoir, he spotted a parked car near the first cove. The parking area hugged a wide bend in the lake protected by large granite boulders and trees. He parked near the other car. Quickly, he pulled on waders and boots and entered the shallow edge of the lake a polite distance from the lone fisherman.

Slate-blue water swirled over submerged rocks and around secret pools as the feeder creek entered the lake. White ripples fluttered down the current fifteen feet into the water. Both men stood knee-deep in cold water. Their practiced movements mirrored one another as each man whipped his line back and forth.

Steve's cast attracted a brilliant rainbow. As it flashed by, it took the fly. Arching like a bow, the pole tip touched the water. Time seemed to stop as water, fish, and man formed a unit. The big fish flailed heroically in an attempt to free itself. Steve skillfully brought the large trout to his net. He removed the barbed hook and fought the urge to release him. *You're a tough soldier. I'd let you stay, but Mom is hoping for fresh fish today.* As he headed back to shore the fisherman upriver gave a congratulatory salute.

Steve picked his way across the rocky bottom and bank. Soon, he stood next to his car.

The other fisherman also left the water. He called, "Nice catch. How big is it?"

"About fourteen inches, maybe two pounds."

As both discarded their fishing gear, Steve called, "Get your limit?"

"Yes, the trout were a little sleepy this morning. I was able to sneak up on them."

Steve walked closer and extended his hand. "Judge, we haven't met before, but I recognized you. I'm Steve Russell, Bea Russell's son. I overheard at the Gray Squirrel you like to fish here. I realize it's the weekend, but I was hoping to speak with you."

Judge Miller's face showed surprise, but he took Steve's hand and pumped it firmly. His face was lined, and a day's beard showed patches of white, but his eyes were sharp as he surveyed the young man who stood before him. "So you're Bea's son. She's one of my favorite people in town." He cocked his head. "As I recall, you're an attorney."

Steve said, "Yes, sir, in Denver."

"This must be urgent or you wouldn't bother with a wet line and cold fingers to meet me."

Steve said, "I apologize, sir. I'm hoping you can tell me about Trent Clay. He's an attorney. We've crossed swords in a case, and I hear he has an office now in Piñon."

"That's right. I haven't had any contact with him yet. He hasn't been very active. As a matter of fact, he let his secretary, Cindy Becker, go shortly after he moved his office here from Denver. She's trying to find work now. Very smart girl who happens to be my niece." The judge pulled a large kerchief from his pocket and cleaned his glasses. "Know of any openings in Denver?"

Steve flashed a smile. "Good timing. I need an assistant for a new project. I'm here for the weekend. Maybe I can meet her."

"Are you staying with your mother? I can tell Cindy to give you a call."

Steve handed his business card to the judge. "Ask her to call my cell number. I'll be there all day. Thank you so much for your help."

"My pleasure, young man." The judge slammed the car trunk. "From the color of those clouds, you and I enjoyed the best part of the day."

Steve drove back to his mother's house, cleaned his fish, and set the fillets in the refrigerator. When Bea came in a few minutes later, he showed her his catch.

She smiled. "We'll have them for dinner. You're a good fisherman."

"Not as good as Dad, though."

"He was wonderful." A tiny spark of sadness crossed her face. "But I know they'll be delicious."

Steve gave his mother a hug. "You and Dad had something special."

"That we did. Too bad Lynn's taken. She's quite a girl. You best get busy and find yourself someone like her soon, before you become an old bachelor."

"You're right on all counts, Mom. Trouble is there aren't many around like her." He ambled upstairs. *I missed out for sure. Now she's married and unhappy. I may be able to help her find closure over her mother's death. At least I can try, but her husband…I sure don't understand him.*

Steve showered and dressed and sat in the living room. Bea shouted down the hall, "You have a call."

Cindy Becker had wasted no time making contact. She agreed to meet Steve at one o'clock the next day at the Thunderbird Restaurant.

****

Midday arrived crisp and cool. Steve and Cindy sat at a window table facing the town square. They were alone in the large dining room.

After they ordered their meals, Cindy handed him a well-prepared résumé. He reviewed it. "You worked for Trent Clay for two years. Why did you leave?"

Cindy replied, "He had a tragedy. His new stepmother died, and he went to help his father."

"Hadn't he just opened up his office in Piñon? I'd think he'd need you to keep it running while he was away."

Cindy hesitated. "There wasn't much business, just phone calls now and then. Actually, Trent and I were somewhat involved for a short time. He not only terminated my employment, he also ended our relationship."

"Oh, I'm sorry."

"I'm okay with it. I knew his marriage was in trouble. It was wrong I got involved with him. What really upset me was I did all the work to set up the office here, and then I got the boot and no check."

"Does he still owe you salary?"

"No. I got a final check this week, so we're square. I worked extra hard to get all of his papers and records sorted out and stored here. He asked me to hold on to the office key just in case he needed something, but he hasn't called even once."

Steve said, "I actually need someone to assist me with a new project from my office in Denver. I should disclose I represented George Wilson in the case against Tony Salvatori. Trent Clay was Mr. Salvatori's attorney of record. Do you know that case?"

Cindy perked up. "Oh, yes. I did some filings and typed plenty of letters regarding the case for him."

"I'm also interested in Jake Dixon. Did Trent's office handle anything for him?"

"Yes, an assault and battery case back in February. I believe he was in jail until sometime in May."

"Did you answer any calls from Jake Dixon?"

"No, not from Jake, but in March we got several calls asking about him. All of them came from a woman named Rosalie Loomis. I remember her name because she called at least six times. She was very insistent that Trent was to help her and another woman, a Maria something—oh, yeah, Garcia."

"Was Trent representing either Rosalie or Maria?"

"No. I gave all her messages to Trent, but each time he denied knowing either woman. He said she was mistaken and to tell her not to bother him again. When I told her, she kept saying Trent had agreed to help Jake and Maria and their child. She became more upset each time she called."

"Did she leave a phone number? I'd like to contact her." Steve added, "Since Trent never did any work for her, there's no ethical reason for you to withhold her number."

Cindy answered thoughtfully, "I know that. Trent avoided contact with her and denied he'd agreed to represent her or Maria. I packed all the old phone message pads and I know I emailed Trent about her calls. I'm sure I can find her number. Her first calls were from a Colorado number, but in her last call she said she was moving to Shiprock in New Mexico."

"My new project may involve Trent Clay. Do you have any reservations about working for me?"

She was pensive, and then answered, "Our relationship never really went anywhere. He had too much baggage, and I didn't quite trust him. I signed a confidentiality agreement, so I won't be able to talk about any of his cases. Is that okay with you?"

"Yes. Here's my cell number. Your experience is acceptable. I'll prepare my offer and email it to you for your signature. Can you start in two weeks, in Denver?"

"Yes. Thanks."

They shook hands, and she left.

He got into his car and picked up his cell phone, then stopped. *No. It's too soon to call Lynn. Better wait until I fill in more gaps.* He slid the phone back into his briefcase.

****

Cindy Becker called before dinner with a phone number for Rosalie Loomis.

"Thanks for being so prompt. I'm glad you'll be working for me soon. Did you get the offer?"

"Yes, thanks. I'll put the original in the mail today. I'm happy to help and anxious to get started."

****

On Monday, Steve paid a visit to the Downtown Denver Detention Center. He went straight to booking. At the back of the office, an officer was busy making copies. The officer was as wide as he was tall. He glanced up to face Steve at the counter.

"So they let you in here, did they?"

"I slid past security."

Officer Gomez stuck out his square hand, and Steve smiled until the vise-like grip made him wince.

"Hey, easy, Eddy. I don't work out anymore like you, gorilla man."

"I miss you at the gym. There aren't any skinny, bird-legged guys to pick on since you got so busy with lawyer stuff."

"How's your kid brother? Is he behaving?"

Eddy looked serious. "He is, thank God. Ricardo's working, and I keep a close eye on him. He's on the right road now, thanks to you. Like I said, I owe you one."

"I was glad to help. He deserved another chance. To change the subject, I need a favor."

"Anything within the law, amigo."

"Two things, I need a license number, make, and model for a vehicle owned by Trent Clay. My other favor is also legal and ethical. I need to locate Ms. Rosalie Loomis. She has some kind of tie to Jake Dixon who's been a guest in your jail. I have a phone number for her, but I would prefer to visit her in person. Can you help me out?" He handed Gomez a piece of paper with the phone number.

"Can do. Give me a minute."

Gomez sat down at his computer and read aloud. "Jake Dixon. Let's see. When he was arrested in late February for his A&B, he listed an address for next of kin in Black Bear, near Oreland, Colorado. He said he wasn't married but his girlfriend lived with a friend in Black Bear. His sentence was shortened, and he was released May twenty-third, got picked up in Shiprock, New Mexico, for drunk in public on May twenty-sixth. New Mexico constables found he was on parole and restricted to Pueblo County so they delivered him to Cortez, Co. where his vehicle was impounded and stored. From Cortez, the Montezuma County Sheriff's Deputy escorted him back to Pueblo, where he was put back in jail for violating parole. Not too smart, I'd say. Here's the address he listed for his next of kin, in Shiprock. This may be where the lady in question lives. He spent from May twenty-seventh until October twenty-seventh in jail. Didn't behave well this time and didn't pay the impound fee to get his vehicle back. He's out and about since then."

Gomez punched some more keys, and the printer spit out a sheet. He handed it to Steve. "Here's the info on vehicles owned by Trent Clay. Will this help?"

"Possibly. Thanks, Eddy. I hope the lady is still around. We're even."

"No, we're not. You saved my brother's life. Anytime you need anything I can help with, call. Got it?"

They shook hands. "I'll keep it in mind. Take it easy. See you around."

Gomez made barbell-lifting motions and called out as Steve walked to the door. "Don't avoid the gym. Those toothpick legs need help."

****

Steve wasted no time. He stopped by his condo, packed a bag and drove out Interstate 70 to Denver International Airport. He had an hour wait for his flight. He dialed the number for Rosalie Loomis. It was busy. He tried it again before he had to board. Busy again. He got on his flight to Cortez, Colorado. Within an hour, he had landed and stood at the rental car counter.

He drove south from Cortez on Highway 160/491. To the east was Mesa Verde National Park. Billboards blinked past depicting ancient Anasazi cliff dwellings nestled in pimiento-colored caves. He drove along the flat monotonous road for eleven miles until he came to Towaoc. A glaring-white stucco building with bright red and yellow geometric designs sprang up from the sand. The Flaming Arrow Casino's sign shrieked in neon against a cloudless blue sky. He continued on past distant stair-step mesas as sand snaked across the highway pursued by a constant warm wind.

After a forty-five-minute drive, he could see the large volcanic plume, serene on the desert as a clipper ship at sea. As he approached Shiprock, Highway 64 angled east, and he followed it for one mile then made a left at the first light by the Ayani Nez Shopping Center. The paved road surrendered to dirt as houses became smaller and landscaping blossomed into junk cars and small mounds of used tires. Slowing at each road crossing, he examined street names. After the sixth one, he found Navajo Lane. Light was fading as he made a right. Every three or four hundred yards, he passed a mailbox, each mutilated in some manner. Faint light shone from windows as he passed squat adobe homes set back from the road, where barking dogs in fenced yards performed sentry duty. He stopped at a tilted mailbox. The black lettering said: Loomis. Steve pulled out his cell phone and again dialed the number Cindy had provided.

A woman answered. "*Hola*."

"Hello, do you speak English?"

"*Si*. But not so good."

"I'm an attorney from Denver and need to speak with you about Jake Dixon. I got your number from Cindy Becker. She spoke to you several times when you called Trent Clay's office."

"Yes. Trent Clay."

"I'm on the road outside your gate. May I visit with you?"

The woman hesitated then said, "*Si*. Gate not locked. Come in. My dog, he no bother you. It okay."

The woman opened the door and held her dog's collar as Steve entered the unpainted cinder block house. He ducked his head as he moved into the low room.

She motioned for him to sit at a small table. He waited as she filled a glass of water and placed it in front of him. A small child clung to the flowered tablecloth. Two dark eyes peered at him. Steve smiled at her. *Do toddlers ever blink*?

The woman sat down. "You talk to Jake?"

"No. That's why I'm here. I need your help to find him."

Lines furrowed her brow. "Do you work with Mr. Trent Clay?"

"No. I'm working on a case that may involve Trent Clay."

Her eyes opened wide, and she took a quick breath.

Steve spoke to reassure her. "Please, something went wrong. I'm sure you went to Trent for help..."

"*Si*, yes, he was to find Maria Garcia, my friend. She disappear long time ago."

"Rosalie, please trust me. Was Maria here illegally?"

"*Si*...I no can go to the sheriff to find her." She tapped her chest lightly. "I, no papers."

"Did Maria work in Oreland?"

"*Si*, at Gold Bar, but she no come home since March. I call, and they say she go to Towaoc casino to work. She a dancer. Sometime she gone for one, two days, but always she come home. My cousin bring me to Shiprock so I can be close to Towaoc casino."

Steve considered this news. *Trent Clay was connected to Gold Bar Casino.*

"Rosalie, did you go to Towaoc casino to find Maria?"

"I no can go there. I no have car. I call there, but they not know anything about Maria. They say she never come there." Rosalie's voice rose. "She never call me." The little girl snuggled close, and Rosalie stroked her silky hair. "Before, she always call. I not know what to do."

Steve spoke slowly and gently. "Why did you contact Trent Clay for help?"

"Jake call me in February. He tell me he in jail and for me to tell Maria. He give me Señor Clay's number for Maria."

"Did Trent help you in any way?"

"No. I call many times. I give lady my number. She say he call me, but he no call."

"Rosalie, I'll try to help you."

Rosalie smiled. "I can trust you?"

Steve nodded. "Yes, you can."

She put the small girl on her lap. "This is Maria's baby—and Jake's baby. I take care Juanita for Maria. Then she no come home. I know Jake in jail, but I no can go to the jail."

"I understand. Rosalie, did you ever call the jail to talk with Jake?"

Rosalie leaned forward. "*Si*. I call the jail in Denver. They tell me he no there anymore. He in Pueblo jail now. I call there. He say to me he know Maria taken to Mexico by border men. He tell me Maria's father very bad man. He mean man, do bad things."

Steve interrupted, "Did you know about her father?"

"*Si,* Maria tell me her father want her to stay in Mexico and not live in America. Jake say Señor Trent Clay promised he bring Maria home to me and Juanita. He ask me if Maria call me. I say no. I tell him I not see her for many months."

"Did you talk to or see Jake again?"

"Jake call me when he out of jail in May and come here to see baby. He spend two night here and use my phone to call Mr. Trent. His voice very loud, and he... he say he take care of him. He drink much. Then he tell me keep Juanita until he come to get her. He say he call me soon. He leave and I no hear from him for long time."

"He called you again?"

"*Si.*" Her hands trembled. "He say he in jail again. I not know why. He say when he get out he come get Juanita. He tell me November he will come."

Steve nodded. "I understand."

Rosalie patted the small child. "I have Juanita. She not mine. Police think I take baby. If they take me away...where Juanita go?" The woman wiped tears away with the back of her hand. "No Maria, no Jake."

Steve's voice was soothing. "You did the right thing. But Maria hasn't come back. I'll try to find out why."

Rosalie placed her hand on his. "I have no money. My cousin give me some food and say I can stay. Shiprock close to Towaoc. I think maybe Maria come back there soon. Please help me."

"Rosalie, the case I'm working on involves Trent Clay. We both need to find out about Maria and Jake." Steve opened his wallet and placed a hundred-dollar bill on the table. "This is for you and the baby. Here's my card. Call me if you need anything. Here's my cell phone number. Don't hesitate to contact me anytime."

He stood up, and Rosalie walked with him to the door. They shook hands.

"Gracias, Señor Russell." She crossed herself. "I pray many time someone come to help."

Steve smiled at the small child. She held tight to the woman's worn jeans. Her smile was pure as sunshine.

Steve drove back to Cortez and spent the night in a motel. He read and reread his notes. He paced his room as he pondered what to do about Rosalie and the little girl. Legally, they could yank his license to practice law if he failed to report the illegal woman and abandoned child.

He was up before dawn. He dropped off his rental car and booked a flight for Denver. He landed at nine o'clock and made his way to short-term parking and picked up his car. By ten, he was in his office. As soon as he arrived, he called the local Immigration Customs Enforcement office.

"I need your help to determine whether a client of mine was picked up some time in the spring. She's an illegal, Maria Garcia. She worked as a dancer first in Oreland then was to work at the Flaming Arrow casino south of Cortez."

After five minutes, he had his answer. Maria Garcia was picked up before she reached the Towaoc casino and was sent back to Mexico first week in March. He jotted down what he could deduce from his investigation so far. Jake expected Trent to find Maria and bring her back. Not an easy feat, time-consuming and costly to arrange. From what Rosalie said, she, Maria, and the little girl had been living on Maria's meager wages. Once Jake landed in jail, any help from him stopped.

Steve's mind raced. *The alibi for Salvatori was provided in March by Jake. What did Trent need that Jake could provide? Trent's profile doesn't appear to include kindness. Offering to help must mean he needed something more than the alibi Jake already provided. And I'll bet it was big.*

CHAPTER 17

Steve called Lynn at home. As he talked, he undid the top button on his shirt and yanked his tie loose. "Lynn, I found out Trent worked some kind of deal with Jake Dixon. Trent promised to get Jake's girlfriend back into the US. She was deported to Mexico."

"You sound excited."

"I am. It directly ties Trent to Jake."

"Jake's alibi seemed fishy to me, but I'm not an attorney."

"The whole thing's complicated and not nearly complete, but I know I can pull it together. You asked about Trent's vehicle. It's a black 2013 Dodge Ram truck." He read off the license number. "A friend in the police department got it for me."

"My God. It was a black Dodge truck at my friend's warehouse. I'll bet it was Trent. He's up to something here in Elk Hills. I promise I'll keep everything secret."

****

The next day, Lynn went to see Sheriff Carlson. She sat waiting outside his office for ten minutes. Through the glass window, she noted the visitor ahead of her stand and exit the office as the sheriff picked up his phone.

The secretary called, "Lynn Mason's here to see you."

Lynn stood and went through the office door. The man leaving glanced quickly at her as they passed. The sheriff motioned her to sit.

"Lynn, there are no new leads. Even the hair found in the car is useless unless we can compare it to a suspect's sample."

Lynn said, "What we need now is something solid. Right?"

"That's our aim."

"Honestly, I can't get my mind around the thought it was a random mugging. Arnold has motive, yet no evidence points to him. And he doesn't have an alibi."

The constable squinted at Lynn. "He's still our prime suspect."

"He hasn't been charged. What about his son, Trent?"

"We drew a bead on him right away. He has a solid alibi. Was in court in Oreland until five that day, spent a couple of hours at the courthouse, then had a late dinner with his client until ten o'clock. Impossible to have gotten from there to Elk Hills by midnight or one."

"Please keep trying." Lynn stood. "I'll be going. I can see you're very busy." She stepped to the doorway.

"Mrs. Mason, speaking of Trent Clay, he left as you came in."

Lynn turned quickly. "What? I've never met him. Only spoken to him by phone. Your secretary called out my name while I waited to see you. He didn't even stop to introduce himself."

The sheriff said, "I take it he's not the friendly type."

Lynn sputtered, "Guess not."

She left, hoping to catch sight of Trent as she walked to her car, but the parking lot was empty.

She spent several more hours in Elk Hills grocery shopping and completing errands. With her chores done, she drove back to Mineral Lake. Her mind sifted through the evidence. Nothing fit together.

As she approached the bridge at Mineral Lake, Don's delivery truck appeared less than a quarter mile ahead on the lake road. It rested tilted on its side in a ditch at the entrance to Greg's lot. She quickly drove to the site and stopped in a narrow pullout. Don squatted near the rear tire.

Lynn walked quickly over to him. "What in the world happened?"

"Just awhile ago, some idiot drove around the curve as I was backing down the dirt road. To miss being hit, I had to shift into forward and, bam, I slipped into the ditch." He touched a small wound on his forehead.

Lynn pulled a tissue from her purse and handed it to him. "How bad is that cut? Maybe you need stitches. Are you hurt anywhere else?"

"I'm okay. It's nothing." He dabbed once at the small cut.

"What kind of truck was it?"

"New model, black. I didn't see the driver. He went by fast. I'd like to get my hands on him."

"Don, a couple of days ago a black truck was speeding right here. What if it was Trent's truck? He might have tried to kill you."

Don screwed up his face. "What are you talking about? Are you nuts?"

"I can't tell you everything, but I know we're in danger. Remember the boat? If he fiddled with the engine..."

Don stomped around to the other side of the big truck, climbed into the cab and grabbed his cell phone. Lynn picked her way over a deep rut until she was near the cab where Don sat. After a short conversation he climbed down and leaned against the stake bed. "Jack is getting a big-tow truck out here. Please do me a favor. Go home and shut up about the murder nonsense and Trent Clay before I really lose it."

"Okay, okay. I'll go home. Don't listen to me then. We'll see what happens. I'm warning you. I feel it. Trent is evil."

Don walked off. "Yeah, yeah."

Lynn drove home. She dialed Steve's cell number.

"Hi Steve. We have trouble here. Someone tried to run Don off the road. He's lucky he avoided serious injury. It was a black truck, maybe Trent's. I'm afraid someone's after us. The boat motor was fouled on purpose, and now this..."

"Lynn, lie low. Don't do any snooping around. I'm worried. Trent may have acted alone or with someone else to kill Betty. One or both might still be in Elk Hills. There's no knowing what they will do to avoid detection."

"I wish you were here. Don won't listen to me. I've tried to tell him, but he thinks I'm being paranoid or crazy."

"Lynn, I'm going to drive up there soon. I need to follow up on a few more things here before I leave. I think it's time you talk with Maggie. Will you do that?"

"Yes. I'll see her as soon as I can. Please keep in touch."

"I will, and be careful. I mean it."

Their call ended but a thought grew. *Steve is working hard to help me and he's coming here.*

After a moment Lynn called Maggie. They arranged to meet in town. Lynn picked up a couple of sandwiches and followed her friend's car to a deserted area. The road moved in and out of shadows from cottonwoods and pines as they followed C Street along its sinuous curves parallel to the river. The sharp fall air made it too chilly to lunch outside, so they sat in Maggie's vehicle.

The deputy listened closely as Lynn recounted the boat incident with the fouled gasoline line and the wild driver on the road, which resulted in Don ending up in the ditch.

"Maggie, my nerves are jangled. Trent Clay and possibly another person may be behind the incidents."

"What does Don say?"

"He was really concerned about the fuel line. Couldn't figure how that happened and he said the reckless driver forced him into the ditch. But he thinks I'm nuts. He's angry about my bringing up Mom's murder all the time. I can't even mention it without starting a big argument."

Maggie's voice was level. "Don's a hands-on person. If he sees a problem, he fixes it. But he can't fix Betty's murder. I think his emotions fight like a tarantula and a scorpion over your persistent digging."

"Honestly, I don't think he cares about finding out who killed Mom, and he shrugs off everything I say. I'm sure I irritate him, and he insinuates I'm ridiculous to try to find a lead. He's made it plain he thinks I'm a big nuisance."

Maggie closed her eyes for a moment then looked straight at her friend. "I see a wagon being pulled by two mules going in opposite directions, and I sense you feel torn between wanting to make Don happy and getting closure on Betty's death."

Lynn gave Maggie a playful elbow jab. "Thanks for the character analysis. I get it." She stuffed her lunch remains into the bag. "You may be right, but there's more to it. I've got a friend who's helping me with some leads. I'll be honest with you. He's more than a friend. I feel a lot for him."

Maggie's face was stern. "Are you sure you want to tell me about this?"

"You're my closest friend, and I need to talk to someone."

"Does Don know about him?"

"He knows he offered to help. That's why I went to Denver a couple of weeks ago. My friend discovered things about Trent Clay. His name is Steve Russell and he's coming here soon."

Maggie measured her words. "If what you've told me is true, you and Don are in danger. And now you've added another man into the mix. Why place hot coals in your path? Are you sure you want to heap more trouble on yourself and Don?"

Lynn considered for a moment. "I can see my emotions are strong, and my mind is trailing behind." She hesitated. "I've tried, but Don ignores me. He goes through the motions, but I don't think he cares about me anymore." She closed her eyes. "It's agonizing to feel like an unnecessary part of his life, not significant. It might be the end."

"Well, it wouldn't be the first time something like this happened." Maggie squinted into the distance at the mountains. "Men and women can't always make it, but to me, you and Don appear to be a good match in many ways."

"We were...but now there's a big disconnect." Lynn twisted a lock of hair. "I don't know who he is anymore. He talks down to me every chance he can and embarrasses me. I'm sick of it."

Silence built between them. Finally, Maggie said, "Do you think the murder caused this rift between you?"

"We were already having problems before the murder, and running two businesses kept us apart. Don's focused on making money. Everything else is secondary."

Maggie frowned. "That's pretty cold. I've seen Don do a lot for other people. I was there last summer when he dived into the swimming hole under the falls over and over, searching for the body of that young boy who drowned. He almost died himself bringing the body up. And this spring, he beat down flames like two men, with fire around his feet. I'd say he's a good man."

"I'm not saying Don isn't a good man. At times he's heroic, but around me, he's...preoccupied. We're more like coworkers than lovers. Honestly, I don't think he needs me to complete his life." She leaned back on the headrest. "Steve believes in what I'm trying to do. He's helping me find justice. He's a good man, too, and he's happy when he's with me, not grumpy all the time." She closed her eyes. "I feel happy around Steve."

"I think you'd better decide what you're going to do before he shows up here. Questions will be asked."

"You're right. I know."

"If this man has any useful information regarding Betty's death, he needs to talk to me or Sheriff Carlson immediately. Promise?"

"We'll see you as soon as he arrives and share with you everything he knows. But I'm worried."

"Someone has said worry sucks away your strength. Push aside worry and become alert. You have a lot to think about." Maggie reached over to hug Lynn. "Remember, I'm your friend. If I can help, call."

Chapter 18

After lunch with Maggie, Lynn went by the post office. She sat in her car sorting her mail. Backing up to leave, she spotted Arnold Clay driving past. Deciding to follow him, she hung back far enough to blend into traffic. *Just as I thought, he's driving straight to Mineral Lake. Maybe up to his claims.*

Lynn observed him as he took the road leading to the mines. She decided to call Maggie.

"Hi, it's me. I'm at the lake. I followed Arnold. He's driving up the mining road across from my restaurant. I'd like to see if he's meeting someone."

"Wait for me. I mean it."

"Okay, I will."

Lynn began to dial Don and then stopped. *There's no cause for alarm. All we'll do is tail Arnold to see what he's up to. Besides, Don will tell me to not get involved.*

Within fifteen minutes, Maggie arrived, and Lynn got into her vehicle.

Maggie said, "We're only observing Arnold. Understand? Ordinarily, I wouldn't bother with following a guy like Arnold, but my instinct is piqued from recent events." They started up the first switchback then hooked into another smaller road. The mountain was so steep each switchback was longer than the one before. The mining road abruptly narrowed, and large boulders pinched the road on both sides. Maggie's Jeep scraped by one, receiving a long scratch.

Maggie peered ahead. "I hope this road widens around this next curve or I'll have to back up."

Lynn said, "We came up this road almost as far awhile ago for target practice, but went to the left. Hey, there's another trail to the right. Let's try it."

"Okay, here goes."

"The mine opening ahead is much wider." Lynn pointed to the left.

"Well, there's no sign of a vehicle, and from all the brush around the opening, it appears no one's been here in a long time. I'll back around, and we can try higher up."

"Maggie, I've never been up the mountain. I've lived in its shadow since we moved here, but haven't had time to explore."

"I was only here once, years ago. Just poking around, but it's more overgrown than I remember. The trails twist back and forth, and with so many trees and underbrush, we may not be able to see Arnold. There are a dozen roads going every which way."

"Let's keep going. There's a fork ahead. Which should we take?"

Maggie downshifted. "I'll go to the left this time."

"Ouch. That hole almost swallowed the car."

Lynn leaned away from the window as thick brush scraped past. She checked her watch.

"We've been going up for twenty minutes. How long do you think it will take to get to the top mines?"

"Four-wheel drive is slow going. You know, they used mules to haul ore down this mountain when the mines were in full swing."

"Hal Adams explained to me part of our property on the lake was used as a stage stop and a corral for the mule teams. When our restaurant was under construction, I found one small mule shoe in the dirt."

"There's another mine up ahead. The area around it is really narrow, and there's no room for me to back around. I better not pull in there. Do you want to keep going?"

Lynn said, "Sure, I do. He can't be very far..."

They heard a loud explosion. Maggie braked, and they listened to the rumble. The vehicle jiggled.

Maggie said, "What was that?"

She got out and turned in a circle, studying the area. She pointed to the right. "Over there. Dust above the trees."

Lynn got out and stood next to Maggie. "Was someone blasting in a mine?"

"Might have been dynamite, but it could be a cave-in."

Maggie reached into the car, grabbed her cell phone. "Violet, this is Maggie. I'm on the mountain at Mineral Lake near the Golden Cross Mine with Lynn Mason. We heard an explosion. Some demolition may be going on. Contact Burton Cook and ask him to call me. He should know if anyone is mining up here. His number's on the computer."

Violet's voice crackled back, "I'll call him right away."

"Hard to hear you. Reception is bad on this side of the mountain. Lynn and I'll try to find out where the noise came from. If it's a cave-in, we might need a rescue crew."

Maggie and Lynn got back into the patrol vehicle and followed the switchbacks leading to the right. Fine dust still hung in the air as they located a Jeep parked near a mine entrance. Maggie opened the door to check the registration. It belonged to Arnold Clay.

Maggie called Violet back. "There's been a cave-in. I think the front of the mine has collapsed. Arnold Clay might be inside. Call the rescue team and let the volunteer fire department know. The site is close to the peak on the right side. Hurry. Wait, call Hal Adams. Ask him to get a map of Arnold's mines. If we can tell which one this is, we can locate any other mines running alongside or above. The rescue crew may need to punch through from an adjacent shaft to reach Arnold."

Lynn and Maggie walked to the entrance. Large beams and boulders filled the opening, and fine dust still floated in the air. They both yelled into the mine.

They heard the clang of metal on metal. Lynn said, "That must be Arnold. He's alive."

"For now, anyway. There's no way to know what condition he's in or if he has enough air. Let's try to move some of the wood and small stones."

Both of them pushed rocks to the side and tugged on broken wood. Most of the debris was wedged tight.

Lynn said, "It's pretty pointless for us to try to move this stuff by hand. Only a backhoe can dislodge the boulders."

Maggie went to her vehicle and rummaged in the back. She brought out a tire iron. She banged on a rusted piece of machinery near the mine opening: *bang bang bang* then *bang bang bang* again.

She called to Lynn. "Listen near the opening and let me know if you hear any response. I want him to know someone's out here."

Lynn listened and waved to Maggie. "Yes, I hear noise."

Soon, a siren sounded in the distance. The whine became louder. Maggie called out, "That's the rescue truck. I hope they get here quickly."

Maggie phoned Dave Roach at nearby Lakeside Resort. "It's Maggie. I'm up on Golden Cross Mountain at a cave-in. Can you get some men and equipment up here to move the rocks and beams? Someone's trapped inside the mine. It may be Arnold Clay."

"I heard an explosion. Sounded like dynamite. I'll call everyone I can reach. The roads are too narrow for a full-size backhoe, but maybe a small skip loader can maneuver the switchbacks. I'll ask Garret Hicks to get his up there. I'll call back as fast as I can."

Maggie's phone rang. It was Burton Cook. "Maggie, we're on our way up the mountain now. Violet says you think Arnold Clay's in the mine."

"His car is outside, and he banged to signal he's alive. If you get air to him, he should have a chance. Dave Roach is rounding up more men, and a small skip loader is on the way to move the rock."

"How much room is there around the mine entrance?"

"Not much. It's a small area, maybe fifty by one hundred feet. I'll move my unit up the road away from the area and off the road so you have more room, then I'll do the same with Arnold's Jeep. I'll expect you soon."

Maggie found the keys in the ignition and moved Arnold's Jeep up the road away from the mine entrance while Lynn moved Maggie's vehicle and parked it next to Arnold's. They walked back to the mine entrance. Maggie moved back and forth, checking around the entrance.

Lynn asked, "What are you doing?"

"The dynamite may have gone off by accident, but I'm checking to see if there's anything unusual around here, before everything gets trampled by the rescue workers. It might not have been an accident."

"Oh, God. Do you think someone else caused the cave-in?"

"After what you've discovered, anything's possible."

****

Spectators from Elk Hills parked at the lake and followed the progress of the rescue team as it snaked up the mountain. So many came, they started parking on Don and Lynn's property. The heavily treed mountain hid any sign of the cave-in, but curious onlookers pointed and stared at the green growth just the same.

Dave Roach stood on a large log near the bank. He put his hands in the air. "Let's have some quiet, please." The talking stopped. "The vehicle at the mine site belongs to Arnold Clay. Hal Adams is pretty sure the cave-in site is in an old mine recently purchased by Arnold. We don't know how extensive it is, but we have to clear it out fast to get to Arnold. The condition of the surrounding rock face is shaky. The lives of the rescue team are at stake as well as Arnold's."

Someone called out, "Did they hear anything from inside the mine?"

"Yes, someone banged on metal. We think he's alive. It's possible he may be injured."

Another man called out, "Has the rescue team reached the mine yet?"

"Yes, our local team is there. They're working now to insert an air hose." He scanned the crowd. "Some of you have worked at hard-rock mining and may have assisted in rescues. We'd like you to help. The deputy needs to know if anyone else is in the mine. We need to let Maggie know immediately if anyone's missing."

Dave held up a clipboard. "Sign this list if you're able to help clear rock and debris from the entrance, then get your equipment and come back here. Our team will do as much as they can, but it'll take forty-five minutes at best for the Gunnison rescue team to get here. Hal has a few maps of the mountainside with details of other mines and shafts that may offer a way to send down a listening device if needed."

Men and women formed a line to sign the volunteer list. Don elbowed to the front.

He reached Dave's side. "Someone said Lynn was up there with Maggie. Did anyone say why she's there?"

"Yes, she's there. Violet mentioned it, but I don't know why."

Dave raised his hands and addressed the crowd. "When Burton Cook calls me to send help, I'll call out the first five names. One four-wheel vehicle at a time will go up, and then come back down for more volunteers."

****

Within half an hour, Don was at the mine. He stood among several men. Lynn ran over to him, and then shrank from his stormy face.

Don demanded, "Why are you here?"

"We were following Arnold to see if he was meeting someone. We didn't know where he was going. The explosion sent dust above the trees, and we followed it here."

"It was reckless to come up here. You had no idea what you might face. You don't belong here. Go down the mountain the first chance you can and stay at home. Promise you'll do as I ask."

"Maggie already told me to go. There's a lot of confusion around here. I'm in the way. Don, be careful." She grabbed his arm in a haphazard hug. Don brushed past her and strode over to a clump of men receiving instructions from the rescue captain. His broad back dwarfed the other volunteers.

Lynn got into the empty vehicle. She held the grab bar tight as it bumped down the trail. After a few sharp curves, the noise diminished. *Arnold's in a terrible situation. I'm not happy thinking he may die, but maybe he deserves it. Anyway, it's out of my hands.*

Her Suburban was where she'd left it earlier at the bottom of the mountain. She drove over the bridge and straight to the restaurant. She started a pot of coffee. In a short while, she handed out coffee and sandwiches to the volunteers milling around the bridge.

Light faded as the rescue work went on. From the upstairs window, Lynn tracked winking headlights as they moved between the trees.

Don entered their bedroom late that night. He shed dirty clothes and kicked off muddy boots. Then he started the shower. "Well, a rescue isn't certain. There's a lot of rock to get through. We moved boulders the size of VW Bugs just to get twenty-five feet inside."

Lynn paced past the window. Don finished his shower and climbed into bed.

She asked, "Do they have enough equipment?"

"They have what they need. They got an air hose in, and if he can reach it, he has a chance. The rescue crew is still working on that hope. They have trained mine rescue workers there now, and equipment is moving the rock. It's a small area with very little room, so they sent the rest of us home."

Lynn said, "I'm afraid to ask, but do you think they'll get him out in time?"

"Everyone's working hard. He may make it if he's lucky and close enough to the entrance. It could go either way."

"It makes my skin crawl to think of him dying in there. The dust was so thick. How can he breathe? If he dies, they still have to get his body out, don't they?"

"I guess so. I'm glad it's not my problem." He added softly, "Don't worry. It's not your concern. How would you feel about Arnold dying right across the lake from us?"

"It seems strange. If they can't save him, then I guess he got what he wanted. He's surrounded by the gold he's been chasing. I know I'll picture him dying in there, breathing in the dust and dirt." She turned off the light and snuggled under the covers. "If I knew for certain, without any doubt, he killed Mom, then his death wouldn't bother me. As it is, it gives me shivers. Some kind of fate took hold of the mountain today. Arnold may be done for."

****

Don had predicted doom the night before, but by breakfast, good news arrived. Their neighbor, Dave, called to say Arnold was safe.

Don hung up. "He's at the hospital. He's banged up some, but he'll recover."

Lynn set a plate of eggs and bacon on the table. "I'm relieved. I didn't like the thought of Arnold dying in the mine. I'm glad his ghost won't lurk around our lake."

"I'm sure Arnold would agree with you. I'd like to know how he survived the cave-in."

Late in the day, Maggie called Lynn. "Sheriff Carlson called awhile ago. Arnold will be okay. He has some cuts, bruises, and his back is tweaked, but he should recover in a day or two."

Lynn said, "Quite a close call. He's lucky."

"He told the sheriff he was saved because a shadow crossed the mine entrance. He knew the old mine was pretty unsafe, and he didn't want anyone coming in, so he went back towards the entrance. Then the explosion happened."

Lynn interrupted, "He was near the entrance?"

"Yes. Close enough for the air hose to reach him. The crew dug him out so fast. He said when the dynamite went off, he was standing right by an ore cart and he dived into it. A big beam shattered above and fell, sending the ore cart onto its side, which protected him even further from rocks falling from above."

Lynn asked, "Did he have any idea who might have been at the mine entrance?"

"I'm pretty sure he didn't, but I'll get more information from Sheriff Carlson. I'll let you know what I learn."

"Sounds strange. Call me as soon as you can."

CHAPTER 19

Ragged brown grass stretched across the lawn in front of the Elk Hills Sheriff's Office. The fall wind blew from the north, and next to imperial green pines, stood brave leafless cottonwoods, ready to withstand another winter. Each gust of wind issued a screeching rasp, as desolate branches raked across the window glass and semi-transparent, hummus-colored leaves gathered in corners.

The receptionist ushered Sandra Steele into Sheriff Carlson's office. He motioned for her to sit down. Deputy Maggie Hernandez placed a recorder on the desk and positioned herself to the side. She held a notepad in her lap. The sheriff opened his mouth to speak then stopped. His secretary opened the door, clutching some papers.

"Sheriff, pardon my interruption, but it's most important that the papers I discussed with you earlier get signed before the courier leaves for Denver."

"Humph, it will only take a minute..." The sheriff put on his reading glasses and flipped through the stack.

The middle-age Realtor cast the sheriff an irritated smirk, then pulled out a small mirror and lipstick. She finished her lip touch-up and closed the mirror case.

The constable handed off the signed documents and signaled to close his door.

"Sandra, you need to explain your relationship with Arnold Clay."

Sandra dropped the shiny lipstick case into her handbag and snapped, "I have no relationship with Arnold Clay."

"Let me put it this way, Arnold and I had a long visit yesterday, and according to him, you and he have been very close ever since he came to Elk Hills. That's over a year ago."

"Arnold would never say something like that." She concentrated on smoothing her skirt. "Besides, I'm a married woman. You know that."

"Yes, I do. Arnold was also married for a short time. It seems that since his near-death experience, he's feeling religious. He was eager to unload all the details of your relationship, which went on while he was wooing Betty and continued even after he married her."

"Well, Arnold can say what he wants. I would never do that to Jason." Sandra stood up.

The sheriff said, "Sandra, sit. You handled the sale of mining claims to Arnold, right?"

She perched on the chair, as if ready for flight. "Sure, I did. I sell property to many people. That doesn't mean I have affairs with them as part of the deal." She nudged her chin in Maggie's direction. "I've worked hard for ten years to build my reputation as the best real estate agent in this town."

"Hold on, Sandra. Don't waste my time. We've got more to cover today. Arnold wasn't lying about this. Remember, he just escaped death in a mine cave-in, which may not have been an accident. I've got his written statement about your involvement. But, if you prefer, I can call Jason in, and we can go over some dates and where you were. I may need to see if Jason has proof of where he was on the day of the cave-in."

The sheriff reached for the phone on his desk and glared at Sandra. "Arnold came by to visit with me about once a week. He'd spend ten or fifteen minutes shooting the breeze, then say he was going to his property. Maybe he went by Hunter's Bar to visit with Jason. I'll give Jason a call to see if he remembers all those visits."

"No, Larry, please don't do that. Jason will kill me if he even suspects I was seeing someone. He's insanely jealous. You know how rough he can get if he's angry." Her eyes widened. "He might make me quit my job if he thinks I flirt with my customers."

The sheriff leaned back and was quiet. Sandra twisted her wedding ring. Her air of confidence faded, and she seemed older than her forty-five years.

The sheriff said, "Tell me about Arnold's son, Trent, and don't skip details. You were seen by a witness talking with him in town a few weeks ago."

Sandra impatiently brushed at her blond bangs. "He called and said he had important information for me from Arnold. I met him at the Black Bear Café. He ordered coffee and kept me there for at least a half hour talking about the mining claims his father had recently purchased."

"What else did you talk about?"

"Nothing important. He finally said Arnold wanted to clear out some debris from one of his old mines, and he wanted to know where to get some dynamite for the job."

"Did you tell him about the restrictions on explosives?"

"Of course. I explained only a certified miner, like Scott Lee or his employee William Short, can buy dynamite or store it."

"What did he say?"

"He said, 'Oh, well, Dad will need to work that out for himself.'" She choked out, "Oh, Larry, you don't think he got hold of some dynamite and caused the cave-in? His father might have been killed. I didn't mean to say anything to hurt Arnold." Her head pivoted to Maggie then back to the sheriff. "I just relayed common knowledge. Everyone in town knows who has dynamite."

"I know, Sandra. Settle down. We're checking all angles. I know Jason was at the bar working the day of the cave-in." The sheriff stood. "Thanks for your help. If I need anything more, I'll give you a call." He added, "It's best you keep all of this to yourself."

Sandra nodded curtly as she left his office.

"Maggie, give the recording to my secretary so she can type it up."

"Sheriff, we took some tire-track impressions at the cave-in site before the rescue vehicles arrived. There were loose rocks and debris, so the only area where we found decent partial prints was back in the trees. They're probably from Arnold's vehicle, but if we can compare them to Trent's truck, they might tell us something."

Carlson tapped his pencil. "The imprints will have to be examined in Denver. Arnold said Trent owns a black Dodge truck. But even if they belong to Trent's vehicle, it's possible he drove his truck up to the mine site before the cave-in to check out some of the old mines his father bought."

"Yes, it's possible. But the road's gnarly. Most tourists wouldn't go up that high to just snoop around."

Carlson added, "Did Lynn mention to you there was in unfamiliar truck parked next to Scott Lee's warehouse? Scott called me about it. Deputy Jones checked it out. He didn't see any sign of a break-in, but he may have missed something."

Maggie scooped up her notebook. "I'll go by, but it's been several weeks, and we've had a couple days of rain. I doubt any tire tracks would still be there."

"Let me know what you find. Also, have William Short open the warehouse and look inside. Check for prints near where the explosives are kept. We'd need proof to tie Trent to this event."

CHAPTER 20

October had brought no progress in her mother's murder. Lynn sat at a table in the restaurant and sorted through the day's mail. She opened an envelope from the Elk Hills Chamber of Commerce. The orange flyer announced, "Don't Forget the Hunters Ball Saturday, November Eighth at the Armory." Her fingers drummed on the table. *That's tomorrow. Now what in the world is the Hunter's Ball? I'll have to ask Carolyn about this.*

The phone rang. She recognized the voice. "Steve, where are you?"

"I'm just leaving Cortez, Colorado. I'll fly into Elk Hills, rent a car and check in at the Rainbow Cabins. Should be there by eight or nine."

"That's good. Give me a call in the morning."

"I will. I'm at a truck stop, and it's really noisy here. I'll see you before long."

"See you soon." She closed her eyes and pictured Steve's face.

She decided to go to The Sport Stop. Carolyn stood at the counter.

"I'm glad I caught you. I got a notice about a Hunter's Ball. Do you know anything about it?"

"They went out to everyone. Weren't you here last November?"

"No. Remember, last year Don and I went to Denver to purchase material for your remodel. I didn't bring any clothes for a ball when we moved here. I wondered what I should wear and if it's a dance with a band."

Carolyn choked back a laugh. "That's not what this ball is like. Last year, Greg roared when I fussed about what I should wear. The Armory fills up with close to five hundred hunters, all wearing Day-Glo orange hunting jackets and camouflage. Everyone in town contributes food, and the hunters each pay ten dollars for the dinner. They play poker and chuck-a-luck. There's a big raffle and someone wins a new rifle."

Lynn laughed. "I'm glad you told me. I'd be a jackass showing up in a fancy dress. Does the town make a lot of money with the raffle?"

"Last year they made almost eight thousand. They used it to by a new water pump for the fire truck. The mountains around here will be crawling with hunters over the next couple of week. The season starts Monday."

Lynn said, "Can I help with food for the ball?"

"Give Vicki Adams a call. She'll tell you what to bring. I'm taking a turkey, and I'm going to help serve. They usually have four or five turkeys, four big pots of chili, rolls, vegetable dishes, and lots of mashed potatoes and gravy."

"I could make some chili or what about desserts?"

Carolyn said, "They raffle off the desserts and cakes to the hunters. You should see them bid. Sometimes they go for twenty-five dollars or more. It's wild."

"Sounds like fun. I'll let Vicki know I'll help. Guess I can wear jeans."

"Absolutely."

Lynn called Vicki and signed up to serve and bring food. Then she drove to the sheriff's office to see Maggie.

The deputy sat with her head down, reading. A pile of papers filled her in-box.

"Hi. Can you spare a few minutes?" She motioned to the stack as she sat down.

"Of course." Maggie got up and poured Lynn a cup of coffee. As she handed Lynn the mug, she automatically tugged on her uniform cuff.

Lynn made sure her eyes avoided Maggie's wrist. She'd asked her about the deep scar once and vowed to not go there again. Maggie had explained curtly how life on the reservation involved fighting off things other than just poverty.

"I came by to tell you Steve should arrive tonight."

"Yikes. That's fast. What are you going to do?"

"About Steve? I don't know. Actually, he needs to talk to you. He has some information you need to know about Mom's murder. Can we meet with you tomorrow morning after breakfast?"

"Come at nine. I'm anxious to hear what he's found. You look tired. Not getting enough sleep?"

"Not much. I'm not used to such indecision."

"Dig deep. Listen to your heart. I know you can do it."

"I'll try."

****

At eight the next morning Lynn received Steve's call.

Lynn said, "Before we see Maggie, I want Don to hear what you've found out. Is that alright?"

Steve said, "Sure. I'll meet you at the lumberyard in thirty minutes."

Soon Lynn parked next to Steve's rental Jeep. As they walked in, Don's head came up from his desk. His jaw clenched when he spotted Steve.

"Don, this is Steve Russell. He's been helping me. He found some important information about Trent Clay. It may help to find out who killed Mom. Do you have time to talk with him?"

Don gave no greeting and stayed seated. A crimson flush crept up this neck. "No, I don't have time to visit, but Steve, why are you so interested in Betty's murder?"

"My mother, Bea, was a good friend of Betty's for fifty years. It was a terrible shock to her. She asked me to do whatever I could to find the person responsible. Lynn deserves to find out what happened, too."

Lynn said, "Maggie's expecting us. Do you want to come along to hear what Steve's found?"

Don glared at her. "Like I said, I don't have time."

"Okay, then, we'll be leaving." Lynn and Steve walked toward their cars. Lynn said, "Steve, wait a minute." She went back and opened the door again. "Thanks, Don, for your help." She slammed the front door hard enough to rattle the glass.

Soon Lynn and Steve entered the sheriff's office. Once introductions were over Maggie offered them both coffee. "Made it myself, campfire style. It'll grow hair on a scalped polecat."

Steve smiled. "Better let me have a cup."

Lynn said, "I'm fine. I've had my week's quota of your coffee." She sat down in a chair near the small potbelly stove.

Maggie placed her recorder on the desk. "Tell me what you know, for the record. Start where you think best. I want to hear all of it."

Steve began with his case for the Wilson family against Tony Salvatori and the questionable alibi provided by Jake Dixon. He relayed his conversation with Rosalie Loomis about Maria Garcia, and Jake's little girl, Juanita.

Steve leaned forward. "Trent's the connection between Jake and Salvatori. It appears Trent benefited somehow when Salvatori was freed. With Betty out of the way, Trent may have expected to wheedle more money from his father. Lynn told me about the possible attempt on Arnold's life at the mine. My guess is Trent orchestrated the cave-in when his father refused to share Betty's estate with him."

Maggie's face remained impassive.

Steve grew more intense. "This spring, while Jake was in jail, his girlfriend was deported to Mexico. In exchange for Jake providing the alibi, Trent agreed to get her back into the US. Either Trent didn't succeed or he didn't bother to follow through."

Maggie said, "So you think Jake's alibi for Tony Salvatori was part of a deal."

"Think about it. The plan was a win-win for Trent. The alibi was way too convenient. It freed Salvatori and made him happy. He might have paid Trent, but more likely he wiped out his gambling debts. All Trent needed to do was get Maria Garcia back across the border to make Jake happy."

Maggie tapped her pencil on the desk. "Well...how does this deal between Jake and Trent tie into Betty's death?"

Steve stood up and paced around the small office. "Trent got greedy. He controlled Jake. Rosalie told me how desperate Jake was. He'd do anything to get Maria back and reunited with their baby. I think Trent convinced Jake to murder Betty as a part of the deal."

Lynn said, "You think he's that evil?"

Steve placed his hand on Lynn's shoulder. "Trent lost his home. His wife left him and took away his only child. His law practice was in shambles, and he was flat broke. He was just as desperate as Jake to get his life together. My sources said Trent racked up close to a hundred thousand in gambling debts at the Gold Bar Casino in Oreland. Even his life may have been in danger. And then, after the alibi came forward, his debt seems to have disappeared."

Maggie studied Steve. "Have you found anything that points to Jake killing Betty rather than Trent or Arnold?"

"I've got only one clue. Jake was picked up in New Mexico near the Colorado border on May twenty-sixth."

Lynn's eyes widened. "That's three days after Mom's body was discovered."

"Right. He broke his probation by leaving Colorado. He must have had a pretty big reason to risk losing his probation. They nailed him with a drunk in public and sent him back to jail for five months. I checked. He never had any visits from Trent."

Lynn said, "Trent seems totally selfish. His father was grieving, and he asked him for more money."

Steve said, "If Arnold said no, I have a feeling Trent may have tried to get rid of him."

Maggie said, "When Betty was murdered, we found no solid evidence. The river carried off any clues as to where she was placed in the water. The vehicle came up clean, no unidentified fingerprints or murder weapon."

Lynn interrupted. "Except for Arnold's prints. Do you have the newspaper account of the murder? I'd like Steve to see it. It has a picture of Arnold."

"Sure." Maggie went to her file cabinet, pulled out a folder, and removed clippings showing pictures of Betty and Arnold. Steve studied the pictures and read the account.

Lynn said, "I was devastated when they didn't charge Arnold. I was sure he had killed Mom. But when Steve told me about Trent and Jake, another possibility opened up."

"Hold on, Lynn." Maggie raised her hand. "Let me finish. If Jake killed Betty, and we can examine his car and find some evidence, we might solve her murder. Of course, we'd still need to prove Trent put him up to it."

Steve pinched the bridge of his nose. "It would be tough. Jake was originally arrested in Oreland and placed in jail in Denver. He was moved to Pueblo then released. He may have used a rental car, which I doubt, or more likely he made it back to Oreland somehow to get his own car and drive to Elk Hills where he then killed Betty. Elk Hills is located just about midway between Pueblo and Shiprock. It was a few days after the murder when he was picked up in Shiprock, and returned to jail in Pueblo. My Denver source said Jake's car was impounded in Cortez, and as of a few days ago, the fee had not been paid. If it was examined it might tell us something."

Lynn asked, "What about the one hair they found in Mom and Arnold's car? They never identified it, and Sheriff Carlson said if they found a suspect, they'd compare it for a match. Maybe they could find a hair in Jake's car."

Maggie said, "We'd need hard evidence to link Jake to the crime scene."

Steve sipped his coffee. "Well, we need to locate Jake and check out his car. He's probably out of jail by now."

Maggie reached for her phone. "I'll get the information on your theory to Sheriff Carlson. We'll need his help."

Lynn said, "You think this is just a theory?"

"For now, yes." Maggie straightened her shoulders. "We have a lot to verify, but we have something to investigate. Steve, where are you staying?"

"I'm at the Rainbow Cabins, number five. Here's my card with my cell phone number."

Maggie placed the card on her desk. "Sheriff Carlson or I might have questions, so stay handy. Also, we have a busy weekend coming up. The Hunter's Ball is tonight. Hunters will be crawling all over town. Monday is opening day of the season, and I'll be busy locking up drunks and checking hunting tags."

Lynn said, "I'll be at the Hunters Ball. I volunteered to serve food. Steve, you should come. It starts at six o'clock."

Steve said, "Thank you, Lynn. I'd love to go."

Lynn blushed and walked to the door. "We need to let you get back to work. Bye, Maggie."

As they left the building, Lynn said, "I have to get home. I also volunteered to do some cooking for the ball tonight."

"I'll be there for sure. Where's it held?"

"At the Armory. It's the big red building at the north end of town on Quartz Street. You can't miss it."

"Fine. I'm going to drive around town for a bit."

"Be careful. Call on the sheriff if you sense any danger."

"I will. Don't worry." Steve waved as Lynn drove off.

She took her time to drive the four miles from Elk Hills to Mineral Lake. Camouflage-painted Jeeps passed by her, all filled with hunters, most with rifles displayed on racks behind the drivers and passengers. The busy morning filled her thoughts. *Steve's information made an impression on Maggie, but it's hard to know how Sheriff Carlson will view it. It's a relief to have someone actually trying to solve Mom's murder. Don sure acted like a jerk this morning. He made no attempt to hide his dislike of Steve. Good. I've shown my cards, now it's up to him to do something about it.*

CHAPTER 21

After they left, Maggie called Sheriff Carlson. She went over the information Steve provided. He wasted no time asking Arnold to come to the station.

Within an hour, Arnold hobbled into the office.

"Reckon you're on the mend." He motioned to a chair.

"I am, thanks to Maggie, Lynn, and all the volunteers. I owe them huge thanks."

"We take care of our own."

"I did a lot of thinking in the hospital. I need to set things right with Lynn. I avoided calling her after Betty's death." Arnold folded and unfolded his hands. "I'm embarrassed about how I betrayed Betty. I lied to a wonderful woman." His mouth curved down. "Now she's gone."

Awkward silence hovered between them. Finally, Carlson said, "Well, I can't tell you what to do. But you're lucky to have the chance now to make amends."

Arnold's sat up straight. "Yes. I am."

"Before Betty was murdered, did Trent ask you for money?"

"Sure. He's asked me for money several times in the past nine months. I know he's got a lot of debt, but I wasn't going to bail him out this time." Arnold's eye twitched. "It's not the first time he's been in over his head."

"Your inheritance from Betty was substantial."

Arnold's face went florid. "I didn't kill Betty for her money. Your office came up empty. That's why you never charged me." Arnold started to get up from his chair.

"Hold on. I didn't accuse you. My question was, did Trent have a motive to get his hands on her money? We have new information that may point to Trent's involvement."

Arnold stood up and pointed his finger at the sheriff. "If you're going to accuse my son of killing Betty, you better spit out facts, now. Trent's a gambler, may even use drugs. He's sick. But murder...?"

"Please sit down and hear me out."

Arnold used the chair arm to steady himself as he sat again. A frown creased his brow.

Carlson tapped a file. "This time Trent could be in deep trouble. We have a witness who says Trent made a deal with a man desperate for help with a family matter. We think he may have convinced this man to come to Elk Hills and kill Betty."

"What man? Do you have proof? I can't believe this."

"I can't reveal his name. We believe he was in this area at the time of Betty's death. He may be here now. My men are searching for him and for Trent. Trouble is, it's the start of hunting season with hundreds of strangers in town, and they all have rifles."

Arnold's eyebrows went up. "Do you think this man may be after Trent or me?"

"It appears Trent may not have fulfilled his agreement with the guy. I'd guess he might be looking for your son and anxious to settle a score. But if you're in the way, or if he has revenge in mind, you also could be in danger. We put your home under surveillance this morning. It stands to reason that if he killed Betty, he knows where you live. He might have followed Betty from home the night he killed her."

Arnold sat quietly. He studied his hands. Finally, he said, "Trent or this other man won't come around my home if police are in the area. What you need is bait."

Carlson's eyebrows went up. "Are you volunteering to act as bait?"

"Yes. I can go up to my mine and see if anyone shows up. It'd be easy enough for someone to ask around to find out where it is. Talk must still be going on about the cave-in. Today's paper still has it on the front page, along with mine-safety interviews."

"One of my men could follow you. But before you agree to do any of this, consider it carefully. It's dangerous. Do you still want to act as decoy?"

Arnold stood. "Yes. I'd like to clear my name and Trent's at the same time. And if Betty's killer is caught, she can rest in peace."

The sheriff held out a booking photo of Jake. Arnold studied it.

Carlson said, "We got this by email this morning. He might be the man in question." The sheriff jotted his phone number on his card. "Check in every hour. We don't need a hero. Let us do the heavy lifting. Understand?"

Arnold nodded. "Yes. Here's my cell number if you need to contact me. I… also want to call Lynn. Do you have her number handy?"

"Yes, I do." The men shook hands. Neither smiled.

****

Arnold left the sheriff's office. He sat in his car and dialed Lynn. "Hello, this is Arnold. I want…need to thank you for your help at the cave-in."

She stammered. "Sure. Well…it was mostly Maggie. She knew what to do. I'm glad it…you were safe."

Words tumbled from Arnold. "I just left Sheriff Carlson, and realize I should tell you…Sandra Steele and I had a thing going on which should have stopped when Betty and I got married. I'm sorry it didn't." He cleared his throat. "I can't apologize to her, so I thought..."

Lynn gulped. "I…don't know what to say."

"You don't have to say anything. I avoided you after Betty's death. That was wrong. I was rotten to her and figured you'd see it in my face. In the cave-in, I thought about lots of things. I did want to take care of Betty. We had plans to travel, but money was so short..." His voice quaked. "I've been alone, too. My son and I, we never got along. My fault again. I've screwed up."

Lynn said, "Thank you. This helps with some of the feelings I've had over... my loss. Why did you have Mom's memorial in Gold Creek?"

"Another mistake. No one knew Betty in Gold Creek—just me. I was selfish. I just needed to be around my old friends. Again, I'm sorry."

"Well, nothing can change the way things were handled. Anyway, thanks for your call, Arnold."

Before leaving Elk Hills, he stopped at the post office to pick up his mail and then parked in front of the old courthouse. He strode down the familiar hallway until he came to the tax assessor's office. Hal Adams sat at his desk with a large map spread out. The faint odor of old books lingered in the air. Binders and maps were stacked on shelves behind the elderly man.

Hal raised his head. "Arnold, by gosh." He reached out his hand. "Here, let me put this old map away, and I'll get you a cup of coffee."

Arnold raised his hand in protest. "No time today. Just stopped in to say hello. I'm heading up to check my claims and see how it is at the cave-in."

"Sure glad you recovered. Those old mines are dangerous with a capital D."

"You're right. Learned my lesson. I won't be going inside any more rickety mines for a long while."

Hal stroked his beard. "I suppose you know it wasn't a natural cave-in. I've heard it had some help."

Arnold's lips formed a wry smile. "A lot of help, I'd say. Like dynamite."

"Yes. Very odd indeed..."

Arnold tilted his head. "The sheriff's working on it. He may come up with something." He shoved his hands into his jacket pockets. "Anyway, today, after I visit the cave-in, I'm going around the back side of Golden Cross Peak to the two small claims above the creek. You know the ones I mean?"

"Sure. I helped you find the property stakes after you bought them. Enjoy the day, and watch where you explore."

Halfway out the door, Arnold called, "I will. Need to check things out while I still can. Snow will be falling soon."

Hal said, "Don't forget the Hunter's Ball tonight. By Monday, you best stay out of the woods. Don't want to get shot by some trigger-happy Texan."

Arnold pulled out onto Main Street. Vehicles filled with hunters passed him. The Hunter's Ball kept most visitors in town Saturday night, but by Sunday evening, it would be deserted. He used the rearview mirror. Any vehicle could contain a deputy assigned to follow him. He drove to the Hunter's Bar. It was filled with strangers and laughter filled the bar as hunters met old friends and talked of camp sites. Arnold drank a beer and talked to the bartender over the din. He mentioned his plan to check out his mine on Golden Cross Mountain.

Next, he planned to visit The Sport Stop, the busiest place in town. He threaded his way through the full parking lot and past a dirt bike parked in front. Inside, the store was packed with burly men buying buck scent, ammo, sticks of Slim Jim, and beer. Arnold pulled a bag of chips off of the rack and a six-pack of beer. *I'm doing what I normally do when I spend the day up at my claims. Hope someone's watching.* He took out his cell phone, dialed, and then slid his cell phone into his back pocket.

Phil, the store manager, stood at the cash register. "Hi, Mr. Clay, going up to your claims?"

"Yes, want to check out the cave-in. You're sure busy here today."

"Loads of business the past few days. Hunters are coming in by the score. We're hoping for a good season." He extended his hand to Arnold. "Glad you're okay, Arnold."

"Thanks. Say, have you seen a new Dodge Ram truck pull in here today? My son, Trent, may be in town. Like to see him. Can't seem to get a call through to his cell."

"No, sir, I haven't, but it's been crazy here today."

"I can see that. The Hunter's Ball will be packed. See you around."

****

After Steve and Lynn's Saturday morning meeting with Maggie, Lynn returned home while Steve left to cruise through the bustling small town. After a couple of hours, he ended up at The Sport Stop. He weaved through the packed store and made his way to the back by the beverage cooler and selected two cans of beer. Hunters, holding everything from liquor to long underwear, surged around the register. Cars outside pulled in and out. As he stood in line, his attention fixed on the conversation between the store clerk and a customer. The store clerk called the man Arnold. Steve paid for beer and slipped out of the store at a discreet distance from the man and kept his head down as he got into his own car.

Steve dialed Lynn. "I'm at The Sport Stop and from the picture Maggie showed me, I'm sure I just found Arnold Clay. The store clerk called him Arnold and asked if he was all healed up since the cave-in. He said he was going up to his claim today."

"Steve, do you know if Maggie talked to Sheriff Carlson?"

"Yes. She called me. Got hold of him after you left. He already spoke to Arnold and said Arnold offered to act as bait to try to lure Jake out of hiding."

"That means he thinks the information you gave him is important."

"I'm sure of it. In spite of all this pre-hunting season activity, he assigned a man to tail Arnold."

"What are you going to do?"

"I'm going to follow him. I'll keep in touch."

"Wait, Steve, following him might be dangerous. Call Maggie."

"Don't worry. I'll be okay."

"I'm worried. Promise to be careful."

"I will. He said he's making a quick visit to the cave-in site. The Hunter's Ball is tonight, and I'm sure Arnold doesn't want to miss the biggest night in Elk Hills."

Steve backed up and waited for traffic to clear so he could follow Arnold's vehicle at a prudent distance. A dirt bike pulled alongside and merged into traffic ahead of him.

Steve let several vehicles pass then positioned his vehicle behind Arnold's Jeep to blend in with the heavier-than-normal traffic on the lake road. Arnold reached the lake, and then went up a mining road. Steve drove past the trail Arnold took, went a half mile farther, made a U-turn and returned to the trail. He waited ten minutes to give Arnold time to maneuver several switchbacks. Then he followed the billowing dust trail. After a few direction changes, Steve stopped. His vision was blocked by tall trees. *Damn it. I missed the trail he took.*

Steve phoned Maggie. "It's Steve. I'm up on Golden Cross Mountain. I've been following Arnold. I overheard him say he was going up to the cave-in. I followed him for two switchbacks, but somehow I lost him. I'm on the left side of the mountain. Can you tell me which direction I should go to reach the cave-in site?"

"I'll do better than that. I'm just below you at Lynn's restaurant. I'll drive up there. I have an idea where you are. Did you see any other vehicle following Arnold up the trail?"

"No. Traffic was jammed-up in town; the deputy could have lost Arnold."

"Well, stay put until I get there."

****

Maggie explained to Lynn where Steve was and gathered her coat. She quickly opened the restaurant door.

Lynn was right behind her. "Maggie, I'm going with you." She pulled her jacket off the wall hook and bent to find her boots on the floor. Her mind raced. *I'm not being left behind, no way.*

Maggie said firmly, "No, you're not."

"Steve's up there because of me. I need to follow this through."

"I don't have time to argue. We need to get up there fast. Promise you'll do what I tell you. Agreed?"

"Yes, I promise."

They started up the mountain in Maggie's vehicle. After four switchbacks, they still hadn't spied Steve's rental vehicle. Maggie drove farther and swung around the next curve.

"He should be right here. I asked him to wait for me."

"I see a vehicle." Lynn pointed. "There, to the right, past the big boulder. Maybe it's Steve's."

Maggie stopped in the middle of the narrow mining road and stepped out.

"Stay in the car, Lynn. I'm not sure who it is." She walked a few steps down the side of the road and then motioned for Lynn to join her.

Steve had his shoulder against his Jeep, trying to dislodge it from the mud.

"Maggie, good to see you. Lynn, what are you doing here?"

"I'm here to help."

Maggie asked, "How did you end up in the ditch?"

"I was waiting for you when another vehicle started up the road. A black truck. I figured it might be Trent." Steve caught his breath. "I didn't want to be seen, so I backed into the trees here, but I went too far and slid into the mud."

Maggie said, "Did he see you?"

"No. He went far to the right. Maybe it's a hunter."

Maggie bent down next to the stuck wheel. "There's no game in this area of the mountain. It's too close to the lake road." She pointed. "If you keep to the right, you end up at the explosion site, Arnold's old mine. What bothers me is if you keep going, you cross a saddle that leads up to Schofield Pass. Someone could leave town unseen over that pass."

"And the next stop is Aspen." Lynn frowned. "My bet is Trent's going to meet Arnold."

Steve kicked the front tire. "This has had it. It's not going anywhere soon. I'll call the rental agency later."

"Don't worry about it now. Let's find our way up to the old mine. Arnold's in danger. I feel it." Maggie walked to her unit. "I've got to let Sheriff Carlson know what's going on, and I need to find my map of this mountain. It's in the back somewhere. We may need it."

Lynn moved to the backseat and produced the map as Steve got in front.

"I don't want to lose him. He may go to another claim before the cave-in site." Maggie motioned. "See that next fork? I hope that's the right trail. The rescue vehicles damaged this road so badly I don't recognize any of it. All I remember is we kept going to the right at each fork until the last one, when we made a left."

Lynn said, "It gets really steep as we reach the top of the mountain where the cave-in happened." The engine growled in low gear. "Wait, did you hear that noise? It sounded like a giant bumblebee."

Maggie stopped the vehicle and listened. "I heard something. Maybe it was a dirt bike on the lake road." She started up again.

After the second switchback, she had to back up several times to navigate the trail. The mining road was rugged, very narrow with brush and broken-off trees branches that scraped the side doors. New ruts gouged from the rescue-vehicle traffic impeded their progress.

She brought the vehicle to a stop. "This is taking longer than I thought. I've got to stop for a minute and call the station." She dialed the Elk Hills Sheriff's Office.

Maggie turned to her companions. "You may have gathered Deputy Jones, Sheriff Carlson, and Deputy Hayes aren't reachable now. They're at an accident scene near St. Elmo. Couple of hunters went over the side in a very inaccessible area. I told Violet we might need backup and asked to have the first available deputy or the sheriff get back to me as soon as possible. I don't know who was assigned to follow Arnold. He must have gotten sidetracked. If I don't hear back soon, I'll try the Gunnison station. It's a distance from us, but..."

A loud bang went off.

Steve said, "That sounded like a gunshot."

Lynn pointed to the left. "I think it came from over there."

"It was close, but I think it came from the right, past that next fork." Steve asked, "How long before we reach the cave-in site?"

Maggie said, "We're not far, but that shot could be from miles away, bouncing across canyons."

Steve said, "Arnold may be in trouble."

"I'm afraid he is, and we need to get to him." Maggie started the engine.

CHAPTER 22

Maggie kept her eyes on the narrow track. She drove a short distance over the rutted road then cut the engine. "I hear voices. It sounds like an argument. There are two forks ahead. I think the voices came from the left one."

Steve said, "I heard voices, too, but I think they came from the right. What should we do?"

Maggie spoke in a low tone. "The cave-in site should be around the curve. I'm going to walk ahead to the left—"

Steve interrupted, "I can take the right, check it out, and meet you back here in five minutes."

Maggie nodded. "Just listen. Don't do anything. You know how to shoot?"

"Sure do. Been hunting my whole life."

"Okay. Take my rifle, just in case, but listen. Don't confront anyone and come back here and report. Lynn, stay in the car and here's my phone. If you don't see me in five minutes, back up fast and head down the mountain. Try the sheriff's office in Elk Hills again for backup. Do you understand what I'm saying?"

Both Steve and Lynn answered yes. Lynn whispered, "Please be careful, both of you."

Steve gave her a small wave as he disappeared around the bend. She sat in the vehicle listening to the silence. Time was measured by a bird call and the soft rustle of parched fall leaves. She strained to listen. *Calm down, you know how noises echo off the mountain around this lake. Maggie should appear any second. It's getting late. Where's Steve? I should go find them, but which one?*

Lynn went the direction Maggie had taken. The trail was eroded and littered with tree stumps and fallen limbs strewn from side to side. She picked her way around the first bend then suddenly halted. Maggie lay facedown in a deep rut. Lynn knelt and gently turned Maggie's face to the side. As she did so, a moan came from her friend.

Lynn spoke softly, "Can you hear me?" She wiped away leaves stuck to Maggie's forehead and found a bump. She started to roll her on to her side when Maggie groaned louder. Then Lynn discovered Maggie's ankle twisted beneath a root. She gently pried at the trapped foot, but a sharp whimper made her stop. *God, you're really hurt. What should I do? Your ankle may be broken. Where's Steve? He should be back and looking for us.* Then she spied Maggie's handgun. She touched it and drew back as if it was a hot coal.

"Maggie, please wake up." She gently moved her friend's shoulder. Maggie's head turned toward her and her eyes opened, then closed again as her back curved forward and her knee bent in an effort for her hand to reach her ankle. Lynn carefully extricated Maggie's foot from the tangle. A whimper escaped from Maggie as her face screwed up, and she collapsed back on the ground. Lynn held Maggie's arm as the injured deputy tried again to raise herself onto her elbow. Maggie's head hung forward as she mumbled, "My foot."

Lynn put her arm around her friend and whispered close in her ear, "God, Maggie, I need to get help right now, for you and…maybe Steve." She looked into the trees and spoke under her breath. "Where's Steve? What the hell should I do?"

She removed Maggie's weapon from the side holster. The gun was heavy in her hand, much heavier than when she'd used it on targets with Maggie.

She whispered, "You're hurt. You have to stay still. The wound on your head has you all foggy. I'll be back. You're my friend, but it's my mother who was killed. I've got to go."

Maggie looked at her. She whispered, "Careful. Keep hidden."

She walked into the trees. Maintaining cover, Lynn moved from pine tree to boulder as she edged closer to the mine entrance. A voice yelled. *God, was that Steve?* She couldn't make out what was said or whether the voice was male or female.

Moving fast, she stepped over broken branches and pulled back the limb of a large fir. She gasped. Steve stood with his hands in the air. Twenty-five feet away, a big, bald man pointed a rifle at him. It looked like Arnold. Another man lay on the ground. A dirt bike rested on its side next to the fallen man. *Oh my God. What should I do?*

Behind her, Lynn heard Maggie call out. *How could she be here?* Just then the stranger pointed his gun in Maggie's direction. Lynn ducked behind a boulder as one shot rang out. Chips of rock hit her arm and neck. She dived forward and rolled onto her belly into the clearing.

Lynn aimed Maggie's nine millimeter at the man and pulled the trigger. He took a step back and then fell to his knees. He crumpled to the ground.

Maggie shouted, "Steve pick up his rifle. Hold it on him. If he moves, shoot."

Lynn got to her knees and tried to stand, but her legs were too weak. Maggie hobbled toward her and asked, "Are you okay? Good thing his aim was off."

"I'm okay. But your ankle...how did you get here?"

Maggie pointed at a forked stick under her arm. "Once I got my senses back, I used this as a crutch. I'd fallen on top of it."

Lynn rubbed both her eyes. "I shot a man. Was it Arnold?"

Maggie said, "Catch your breath. You did a good job. Whoever he is, he's not going anywhere. He's shot in the chest. Not sure how badly he's wounded."

Lynn asked, "Why'd you call out?"

"The man had the drop on Steve, and I wanted you to take the shot. I knew you wouldn't shoot first, so I drew his fire in my direction. You did what I thought you would. You shot to protect me. I'm glad he wasn't as good a shot as you are."

Lynn managed a weak smile for Maggie. "Guess the target practice you gave me paid off." The two women stood. Maggie leaned on Lynn and used the makeshift crutch to limp into the clearing.

Steve put an arm around Lynn's shoulders. "Little gal, your bravery paid off."

Maggie hugged her friend and whispered, "Yes, Lady Bear, you saved us all."

Steve held the wounded stranger's rifle. "He's not going anywhere." Next, he knelt beside the body of the younger man and felt for a pulse. He shook his head, "This guy's dead. The first shot we heard must have been when the big man shot the other one."

They all froze when a man's voice called out. Steve moved to the edge of the ravine and called back to Maggie. "Hey, another man is down here. He's on a small rock ledge. Whoa, it looks like Arnold. We need to get a rope to pull him up."

Steve yelled into the ravine. "Arnold, hold on. We'll help you. Are you hurt?"

Arnold shouted, "My elbow is bad, but mostly I'm just stuck here. Do you have a rope?"

"We'll get one from the car. Hang on."

Maggie rolled the dead man onto his back. "This is Trent Clay. Sheriff Carlson emailed me a picture of him this morning."

Lynn said, "You're right."

Maggie knelt by the wounded man near the dirt bike. "Lynn, bring back the first aid kit and the rope in my car. There might be something we can do for him."

In a moment, Lynn handed the rope to Steve. Then she also knelt by the wounded stranger. "I thought I'd shot Arnold. From a distance they look alike."

Steve moved to the edge of the ravine and tossed the rope over the side. It dangled twenty feet above the stranded man.

"Arnold, it's too short. We'll call for help. It won't be long."

Lynn opened the stranger's jacket. A red circle stained his shirt. She pressed a bandage over the wound and heard staggered gasps escaping from the man along with a gurgling wheeze.

Lynn said, "He may be Jake Dixon."

"I think you're right. He looks like the man in the picture Sheriff Carlson showed me. He may have followed either Trent or Arnold up here. My guess is he shot Trent."

Lynn checked his pockets for identification but found none.

Maggie glanced at Lynn. "Are you all right?"

"I'm okay, just shaken up."

Maggie stood and dialed her phone. "I'm calling the Elk Hills station."

Maggie's voice was crisp. "Maggie here. Got an emergency. We're up on Golden Cross Mountain at the cave-in site. Send help. Arnold Clay fell into the ravine, and his son, Trent Clay, is dead. It appears he was shot by a stranger who might be Jake Dixon. The stranger is also wounded."

She listened and then said to Lynn, "They're at your restaurant. They should get here in twenty minutes. Don's asking about you."

Maggie spoke on her phone. "Tell Don she's with me."

Steve knelt next to Lynn and put his arm around her.

Lynn said, "How Maggie dragged herself out of the ditch she'd fallen into is beyond me. She'd hit her head, too, and was barely conscious."

Steve stroked her cheek. "And you were to stay in the car."

"I had to find you. Maggie couldn't, so..."

"It's a good thing you did. He was ready to shoot me, and you nailed him just in time. His shot was awfully close to you." Steve gave Lynn a gentle squeeze. "I thought you'd been hit. I don't ever want to feel that way again. Let me see your neck."

Lynn tilted her head. Steve said, "Yep, you need some first aid, too." She leaned against Steve's shoulder.

Maggie said, "Deputy Jones and Don will get here as fast as they can. I hope this guy will last that long."

Lynn said, "There's not much I can do. I'm holding pressure on the wound. He looks so much like Arnold."

"He and Arnold are the same size and both are bald." Maggie knelt by the stranger and gently shook his shoulder. "Mr. Dixon? Jake Dixon?"

The man moaned, "Yeah."

Maggie spoke into his ear. "I'm Deputy Sheriff Hernandez. You're seriously hurt. Tell me, did you kill Betty Clay?"

"Hurt bad." The man coughed, and a thin line of blood slid from his mouth. "Got Trent…shot the rat."

Maggie spoke louder. "Did you kill the woman in Elk Hills in May?"

His eyes opened. "Yeah." He tried to raise his head.

Steve leaned close to the man. "Did you lie about the alibi for Tony Salvatori?"

The man squinted. He raised a trembling hand. "Yeah…Trent…promised. Can't breathe." He coughed and wheezed. "Had a deal. Maria, help…my angel." His head rolled to the side, eyes open, fixed on blank space.

Steve touched the dying man's neck, checking for a pulse, and shook his head.

Lynn whispered, "He confessed. Did you hear him? He said yes. He admitted he killed my mother." Lynn stood up and backed away.

Maggie went to Lynn and put an arm around her. The two women held each other. Lynn's shoulders trembled, and tears ran down her cheeks.

Maggie cooed, "It's over now. It's over."

Steve stood. "Lynn, you need to get into the Jeep and lie down. Maggie, I'll see what's in the first aid kit for your ankle and the goose egg on your forehead."

Lynn pointed toward the ravine. "What about Arnold?"

"The rescue team will be here soon." Steve went to the edge of the ravine. "Arnold, help is on the way. We'll get you up here soon."

Arnold replied, "Thanks."

Steve helped both women into the backseat. He wrapped Maggie's ankle and dabbed antiseptic on her forehead. Next, he cleaned Lynn's cuts on her arm and neck from the splintered rock.

Soon, the sound of motors vibrated up the mining road. Deputy Jones parked his vehicle behind Maggie's Jeep, and Don jumped out. A second vehicle held their neighbor, Dave Roach. All the men ran up to Maggie's vehicle.

Don opened the door and leaned in. His eyes bulged at the sight of white bandages on Lynn. "What reckless stunt—"

Deputy Jones interrupted, "Both of you need to get to a doctor."

"First, someone needs to help get Arnold out of the ravine." Maggie pointed to Steve. "This is Steve Russell. He helped us find Trent and the other dead man over there. We think he's Jake Dixon."

Jones said, "Was he shot?"

Maggie said, "Yes."

Don gingerly touched Lynn's cheek. Scarlet moved up his neck. "Are you okay?"

"Yes, only some cuts."

"Thank God."

Deputy Jones said, "I've got a long rope. Dave, why don't you take Maggie and Lynn to the doctor? Don, Steve, and I can get Arnold up from the ravine. Sheriff Carlson will be here soon."

Maggie tilted her head in the direction of the dead bald man with the chest wound. "He said he was Jake Dixon and confessed to killing Betty before he died."

"You shoot him?"

"No, Lynn did, in self-defense. She saved Steve's life and mine."

Jones asked, "Who's the other guy?"

Maggie answered, "He's Arnold Clay's son, Trent. Jake also confessed he shot Trent. You'll have to talk to Arnold to find out how he ended up over the cliff."

Jones looked at Lynn. "Well, well. You both need to get down the mountain and to the doctor."

Maggie didn't move. "I want to see Arnold safely back up here. Then we'll leave."

Lynn held Maggie's arm. "I agree."

"Okay, it shouldn't take long. Sheriff's driving down from St. Elmo along with Hayes." He looked at Maggie. "You get my meaning?"

Maggie said, "I do. Poor Hayes. After riding with the sheriff, he'll be pale and white-knuckled when he gets here."

Lynn asked, "What do you mean?"

"Sheriff Carlson only uses two wheels per side coming down a mountain road. Riding with him is an extreme ride at Six Flags. We think he learned to drive in West Texas doing gully-hopping."

Jones went to his vehicle and pulled out a long rope. He motioned to the men. "Secure the rope to that tree. Then toss the rope to Arnold. All four of us should be able to pull him up."

They stood on the rim of the cliff. High pines blocked the weak evening light. Near the edge, Jones propped a bright flashlight against a rock and angled it on Arnold.

"I'm tossing the rope down now. Tie it around your waist. Do you see any footholds?"

Arnold answered, "Yes. Here at the ledge I can go up a bit, but then it's only sheer rock."

Don said, "I can climb down using the shorter rope. You, Steve, and Dave can pull Arnold up to where I am. I can help him up the rest of the way. What do you think?"

"Sounds good. Here we go." Jones tossed the rope over the side. "Got it?"

"Yes. I'm ready."

Lynn watched as Don tied the second rope to the pine and climbed down. Steve and Jones strained to pull Arnold up. Soon, Don disappeared from sight, and she heard the sound of small rocks cascading down the rock face.

Don called out, "I'm alongside Arnold. Dave, start pulling us up."

Soon, both men were making progress up the cliff. Don steadied Arnold and guided him. Steve and Jones pulled on Arnold's rope as Dave pulled on Don's.

The pine tree bent from the weight of two men. Seconds ticked by, punctuated by heavy breathing. Finally, Don and Arnold rolled onto the edge.

"We made it." Don wiped his brow, leaving streaks of blood from his torn hands. He sought Lynn and found her standing near the Jeep with Maggie. He gave her a small smile. She waved back.

Arnold cradled his elbow. His voice was barely audible. "Thank you." He walked to where Trent lay on the ground. He bent to his knees and touched his son's arm. He covered his eyes and bowed his head. His shoulders trembled. After a moment, he stood up and wiped his eyes.

He reached out to shake Deputy Jones's hand. "Thanks for saving my life. I'd been here for about five minutes when my son walked into the clearing. He must have parked his truck farther up the road. We were by the cliff edge when the arguing started. He was very angry and not in his right mind. I don't think he's been sane for quite a while."

"I'm sorry for your loss. Seems you've had more than your share of tragedy." He pulled out a bandanna and wiped his brow. "What did you argue about?"

"Money. He knew I'd inherited Betty's estate and he wanted some of it. I refused. He'd just gamble it away, and I told him so. I refused to keep feeding his sickness." Arnold pointed to Jake. "We heard a motorbike. That man drove his dirt bike into the clearing and fishtailed right at our feet. Dirt flew everywhere, and Trent jumped back, knocking into me. I slipped backward over the edge. I tried to slow my fall by grabbing tree roots. For a minute, I dangled close to the rim, and I heard them shouting, then a gunshot went off. The root I grabbed pulled out, and I slid farther down the ravine to the lower ledge."

Jones asked, "What did you hear?"

"They cussed back and forth. Then the stranger said, 'I took care of the woman like you wanted, and I told you I'd kill you if you didn't bring Maria back.' I realized then it had to be Betty they were talking about. Trent used this man to kill my Betty."

Arnold slumped to the ground. "I suspect Trent also tried to kill me in the cave-in. He failed, so he followed me up here to try again." Arnold looked up at Lynn. "I'll never be able to change what happened. Betty is dead because of my son." He rubbed at his eye. "I didn't realize how troubled…sick he was. I never realized my poor parenting affected him so badly. There's no way for me to undo any of it. I'm sorry."

The deputy said, "Why don't you rest in your car? We need to wait for the sheriff. You'll need to give him all of the details when he arrives." He pointed. "How bad is your arm?"

"Banged my elbow on a rock. Just bruised."

Maggie said, "Deputy, before it gets dark we should get some photos."

"Yes. I'll get my camera. I've got some blankets to cover the men."

Lynn and Maggie got into Dave's vehicle. He backed it up several times to reverse direction in the narrow road. Light was fading as they rode down the mountain.

****

A short while later, Sheriff Carlson's patrol unit cast headlight beams on green needles and black bark as he pulled into the clearing at the mine. He walked over to Steve and Don and shook their hands.

"Thanks for your help." He gave Steve a stern look. "I stopped Maggie on her way down the mountain. She told me what happened." He pointed to the large, bald man. "She said this man is Jake Dixon, and he confessed to killing Betty Clay. Is that correct?"

Steve replied, "Yes, sir, it is."

The sheriff then knelt by Trent. "He was already dead when you arrived?"

"Yes, he was."

The sheriff made a note. "Well, we'll need to verify the bullet in Trent's body came from Jake's rifle. It may belong to him, but we also have a hunter report his rifle was stolen from his truck last night in Elk Hills." The sheriff stood. "Maggie said the dying man said he killed Betty. Did he mention her name?"

Steve answered, "No. But when Maggie asked him if he killed Betty Clay, he said yes."

The sheriff nodded. "Good enough to close the case." He pointed at the two bodies. "Coroner is on his way up here. Jones, you took pictures?"

Jones answered, "Yes."

"Good. Stay here and help the coroner and his assistant. I'd like everyone off this damned mountain before it's any darker."

Deputy Jones asked, "Do we leave Trent's truck here along with the dirt bike?"

"Yes, for now." The sheriff slapped mud from his pants. "I'll send someone up tomorrow to put them in the storage yard." He motioned at the official vehicles. "Steve, ride with me. I'll drop you off where you're staying. I'll take Arnold into town. I'll need to get his statement at the station. Tomorrow is Sunday. Let's meet at my office Monday at one o'clock to complete the rest."

****

The two injured women sat in the back seat. Don sat up-front with Dave. As the vehicle swayed across ruts, Lynn blinked as jagged pieces of sky skipped past. Night sped to pull a dark blanket over the mountain. Shy stars balanced in their mysterious dance across the black night between fan-shaped tree arms moving in time to the night breeze. Descending headlights bounced back like sonar bleeps across the dirt trail.

Lynn sniffed. "Do you notice the air? It smells strange."

With her eyes closed, Maggie replied, "Yes. The air is filled with the stench of evil souls released. I feel they are being swept from the exhausted mines populated by secrets of murder and deceit from years before."

Lynn said, "Then let's get off this mountain as fast as we can."

Don spoke up. "We'll be at the hospital in no time. Lean back and relax. Everything's going to be fine."

Forty-five minutes later, Dave pulled up in front of the Elk Hills Hospital. He helped Maggie out and led both women to the emergency room. The ER doctor examined Maggie first. "We'll get an X-ray to be sure your ankle isn't broken and check out that nasty bump on your head. Best to have you spend the night so we can monitor any sign of concussion. Lynn, we can clean those cuts and send you home."

Maggie said, "Wait. I need to say something to my friend." She took Lynn's hand. "You must consider things wisely tonight."

Lynn gave her friend a thumbs-up. *She's giving me wisdom from her grandmother again. I think she feels a clash coming between Don and me.*

CHAPTER 23

The sound of mallards calling to one another awakened her. Sitting up, she had a narrow view of the lake. A half-dozen ducks skimmed across the water as four or five migrants bobbed on the remaining open water, which diminished more each day. Thin ice covered the lake, etched in a tapestry of lines. Clear, lacy fingers filled every small inlet, leaving only gray-blue circles as clues to the location of the up-welling warm springs.

Lynn threw her legs over the side of the bed and wiggled her toes in the soft pile of the area rug. She rose and immediately sat back down. A marching band high-stepped through her head. Only her need to wet her parched throat propelled her into the bathroom.

She did a double-take. *Bad idea to look in the mirror. First priority, a hot shower, then coffee, and some major work on my face and nails.*

Wrapped in her robe, Lynn held the hair dryer and let it warm her sore neck as she circulated hot air through her clean hair. Don appeared at the door with a mug of steaming coffee.

"So you're awake. Good. How do you feel?"

"I'm fine. The cuts are minor, and the shower helped."

Don came up behind her and reached both arms around her and nuzzled her neck. "You worried me. Will you promise to leave police work to the experts?"

Lynn clicked off the dryer and set it on the counter. She faced Don. "God forbid. I hope I never again have to shoot a man and experience such fear for my friends as I did yesterday."

"That's what I mean. Now it's all over. Nothing will bog us down, and we can get back to our lives as they're supposed to be."

She pressed her temples. "My head is pounding. I think I need to take it slow this morning."

"Sure, anything you want. How about breakfast? I can whip up some eggs."

"Sounds good. I'll come upstairs in a few minutes. Just need to put some clothes on."

"Okay. I'll get breakfast started."

Lynn walked to the bed and fell facedown. She placed her pillow over her head.

It took several minutes to gather her strength to dress. She entered the restaurant as the phone rang. Don picked up the call.

"Lynn, it's for you. It's Penny."

Lynn sat on a stool at the breakfast bar. "Penny, how are you?"

"I'm fine. What I want to know is, how are you? Everyone in town is talking about what happened yesterday on Golden Cross Mountain. Jack related the most unbelievable news. Tell me everything."

"I will Penny, but not right now. I just got up, and I'm still in shock. I'm taking it easy today. Monday I have to go into Elk Hills to see the sheriff. I'll try to stop and see you while I'm in town."

"Perfect. See you then."

Don placed a plate of scrambled eggs and toast in front of Lynn. "Sheriff called, wants to see you at one o'clock."

Lynn nodded. For the next ten minutes, she ate in silence.

"Thanks for breakfast. I feel better."

"You need to stay home today. I have to go to Denver for a pickup. I'll spend the night and drive home on Monday. Will you be okay?"

"Sure. Today I want to check on Maggie, then come home and rest. I think it will take most of Monday to finish my report for the sheriff. What time will you be home?"

"I've got to go to three different yards to pick up appliances and lumber. Should be home by eight o'clock at the latest. I'll leave the truck loaded at the yard and drive home in my pickup."

Don gave Lynn a long kiss and went out the door.

Lynn walked outside to the deck. All was quiet. She listened for the lake's heartbeat. *Sometimes I can touch the isolation. It surrounds me in a lover's embrace.*

She walked inside, picked up the phone, and dialed Steve's cell number. He answered, and Lynn held her hand over her heart. "Steve, I hope this isn't too early to call."

"No, I'm glad you called. I've been up for hours. Maybe it's the mountain air. Have you had breakfast? I'll buy you some in town."

"Thanks, but I just finished eating. The sheriff left word for me and Maggie to meet with him Monday around one o'clock. Did he mention anything to you?"

"Yes. Said he needs to formalize all our statements. Can you meet me in town before we see the sheriff?"

"Noon would be best. I'll meet you at the Elk Hills Café. Today, I need to rest."

"I'll see you."

Lynn checked her watch then located Amy's phone number and dialed. Hearing Amy chirp hello made her smile. "Amy, this is Lynn, and there's so much to tell, you better sit down with a cup of coffee. Yesterday was unbelievable."

Amy squealed. "Lynn, my wonderful Lynn. Bea called last night. Steve phoned her to share the news. It was all so dangerous. Thank God, you and Steve are both okay. That bastard Trent plotted to have Betty killed for money. Such a miserable man. Forgive me, but I'm glad he's dead. I really am."

"Steve figured it out."

"Yes, and Arnold is innocent. I thought he was involved, but I can admit I was wrong."

"So can I. He's innocent of the murder, but he wasn't honest with Mom."

Amy's voice was soft. "Poor Betty. She thought he loved her. I'm glad she never knew about the other lady in town. At least when it all came out, Arnold was willing to do something to find the killer."

"There are still a couple of loose ends to be tied up. I have to meet with the sheriff on Monday. I'll be in touch. Love you."

Amy said, "I'll keep praying that all of this is over soon and you can feel real peace. I love you. Thanks for calling."

Later, Lynn went to see Maggie in the hospital.

Maggie greeted Lynn with the brightest smile in Elk Hills. "Good to see you."

The two friends hugged.

"You just missed Domingo. He came home last night, but he had to get back to his hunting clients. The season starts tomorrow."

"Last night I was worried about you. You looked pale."

"That's a good one, a white woman calling a Native American pale." Both of them chuckled. "How are the cuts on your arm and neck?"

"They're nothing, just nicks. Are you doing what the doctor says?"

"Oh, sure. I expect they'll let me out of here this afternoon. Need to stay off my foot for a while, and the headache should fade. But no walking over rocks for a while. Guess I won't be going hunting this year."

"Lord, no. The elk can breathe easy this year."

"Speaking of walking gently, what did Don say about Steve?"

Lynn fidgeted and glanced away from Maggie's strong gaze. "He didn't say anything."

"Then he sidestepped the whole issue?"

Lynn locked her hands around her knee. "I don't think he sees an issue."

Maggie huffed. "What kind of husband is Don? He must be blind. If he can't see what's going on in his own home, then he needs glasses."

"I didn't bring anything up. Not yet. I'm working out what I should say and when."

"What about Steve?"

"We're supposed to meet with the sheriff Monday afternoon. Afterward, we'll have a chance to talk. I need to know how he feels." She twisted her jacket belt. "Don's on his way to Denver today. He won't be home until later, so I can spend some time with Steve." She peered at Maggie's face. "It's all so confusing."

Lynn stood and picked up her coat. "I've got to go now. I promised Penny I'd stop by for a few minutes. I'm so glad you're going to be okay."

Maggie frowned, "Girlfriend, sit down. Please."

Lynn complied.

"I don't mean to hurt you, but I've seen how Don acts around you. The tone he uses with you makes me sense he doesn't respect you. Tell me, why did you marry him?"

Lynn stroked the rough corduroy of her pants. "It's hard to sum up in a few words. When we met, I'd just landed my first job out of college. Things started to work out for me. But the years leading up to then were a struggle. I never mentioned it..."

"Your parents, family?"

Lynn took a breath. "I was married to someone else before Don. We met in college. He was a senior. We planned to live together, work, and finish college. We got married."

"How long did it last?"

"Four years. No children. I went to college full time. He worked part time and finished his master's degree. Once he had a full-time teaching job, we drifted apart. I realized we'd propped each other up so we could finish school. Once I graduated we ended our marriage."

"Eighteen is young to marry. What were you looking for?"

"I'm not sure. No one got hurt, but it was a mistake."

"How long did you know Don before you married him?"

Lynn flushed. "The truth is, Don proposed one week after we met. I knew I should take more time, especially having goofed once before, but I wasn't going to let him get away. My dream man was right in front of me, and it was me he wanted. I said yes. The next weekend, we eloped to Las Vegas. Maybe I wanted to be envied. I married the handsomest man I'd ever met and a jock on top of it. Don was first string at Boulder. I'd watched him play, but was never in the clique who dated the football players."

Maggie said softly, "Two weeks."

"I'm embarrassed to admit, I really didn't know Don—and he didn't know me. But our hormones marched us to the altar. It's been good up until the last six months or so..."

Maggie closed her eyes. She rocked back and forth and hummed. "Two days." Her black eyes flew open. "I was a tree top; he lightning." She pointed her finger up. "The bolt ran from me up to the sky or from him down to me. Neither of us ever knew which."

Lynn stared. "You married Domingo after only two days?"

"Yes. I've been proud my love for Domingo started as fireworks from a tree hit by lightning."

Lynn shook her head. "You never mentioned this to me."

Both women laughed until Maggie held up her hand. "Please, stop. My side hurts."

Lynn became sober. "I should have confided in you sooner. I've been hurting since we moved here and trying to hide it. This past year, I began to sense Don believes he made a mistake marrying me. I've hung in because I didn't want another failure. It's hard to face, but..." Lynn wiped away a tear. "I've tried to talk to him, but he shuts me out."

"And Steve? Where does he fit in?"

She twisted her wedding ring. "Steve acknowledges me...he listens to what I say. I know he's smart, but he makes it seem like my opinion matters. Maybe it's my weakness, being considered a person with a brain, but I've missed it with Don. You've seen how Don ignores my opinions." She stood and gathered her things. "In truth, I'm torn. I want to do the best thing for me, Steve, and Don. But, right now, I'm lost, and I'm afraid my need for recognition is driving the bus, not my head."

Maggie stood and placed both hands on Lynn's shoulders. "Lady Bear, I know you will do the right thing. Life is a flowing stream. Blurred reflections are a part of it."

Lynn said, "When you get released can I drive you home?"

"Not needed. Domingo insisted that he take me home. I'll let him fuss over me for one day." She snapped her fingers. "Then it will be back to normal."

"Then I'll go. Thanks for caring…helping. I'll see you soon." Lynn walked a few steps then looked back and gave a small wave. Maggie waved back, but her smile had vanished.

****

On Monday morning, Lynn drove along the river to Elk Hills. Low clouds filled the sky and a threat of snow pressed down. Intent hunters traveled the road. One vehicle passed her with an early kill strapped to the roof. The formerly regal elk appeared pitiful as brown fur blew in the wind and horns dangled across the windshield. Its destination was either the butcher shop in Elk Hills or the taxidermist thirty miles away to the west in Jeanville. Either way, its existence was over.

The spectacle of the dead animal's flopping neck caused Lynn to shiver. Instead of enjoying the Hunter's Ball, she'd spent Saturday evening on the mountain, involved in the deaths of two men responsible for her mother's murder. Instinctively, she clutched the wheel. *There'll be another Hunter's Ball next year.*

As Lynn drove, Maggie's words crept into her thoughts. *Somehow I need to find clarity in my life.* She yanked her attention back to the moment as Penny and Jack's log cabin came into view. Penny waited on the porch as Lynn parked. She greeted her friend with a hug. Seated at their kitchen table, Lynn leaned down to smell a plate of warm, chocolate-chip cookies.

"Don't tell me. Your famous Chuck Wagon cookies?"

"Yes, and I baked them for you. Dig in." She poured tea as her friend savored the treat. "It's been too long since we had time together."

"I agree." Lynn drank her tea and finished off a cookie.

"You and Don are always working, and so are Jack and I. It takes a lot to keep the bills paid. At least our two men will have some time to hunt together by the week's end."

"Yes. They need to get out in the wilds. I hope they get lucky."

"I'm counting on it. Have another cookie. You're thinner than the last time you stopped by."

"I have a huge story to tell you, but I have to meet the sheriff, so I can't stay long."

Lynn recounted the events at the mine site. "It took Steve, Dave, and the deputy to pull Arnold up from the ravine to safety. He got some bruises and cuts, but he's okay."

Penny said, "So Jake murdered Betty, and he followed Trent to the mine and shot him before you got there?"

"Yes. Arnold said Trent accidentally bumped him off the cliff, and then Jake killed Trent. It was pitiful to see Arnold kneeling by his son. He seemed horrified. I don't think he imagined Trent capable of what he'd done. I give Arnold credit. He'd volunteered to act as bait to help the sheriff. The sheriff thought Jake might make his way to Elk Hills to find Trent. He was right. Jake got even with Trent forever."

Penny shook her head. "You read about shootouts. It's always someone else. But it happened right here and involved my friends."

"Trent attempted to kill his own father and orchestrated Mom's murder." Lynn propped her elbow on the table and rested her chin in her hand. "I'm sure he was insane. I say good riddance."

Penny said, "I hope you feel some closure now."

"Some. Nothing will bring Mom back, but it's the best I can expect." She blinked back tears as she pulled out her keys. "I've got to get going. I'll get in touch once things settle down."

Penny touched Lynn's arm. "Are you sure you're okay? You seem distracted."

"I'm fine, just tired. Saturday was physically exhausting and very emotional." Lynn smiled. "But things are going to change. Wait and see." She'd omitted the information about her shooting Jake. And she didn't explain who Steve was and how he had become involved in the capture. Those details would have to wait.

CHAPTER 24

Monday arrived and as Lynn crossed the street, she caught sight of Steve in the restaurant window. He was watching her. She lowered her head as the wind whirled specks of corn snow. Her long stride brought her through the door of the café.

Lynn grinned at him. "Okay, what are you smiling about?"

"Your cheeks are pink, and you look beautiful."

Lynn sat down, reached across the table, and tentatively touched Steve's hand. "Thanks for the compliment. And thank you for everything you did to solve Mom's murder. If you hadn't made such an effort, nothing would have worked out like it did."

"You sparked the investigation. I'm proud of you."

The waitress waited for their order. Lynn glanced at the menu then looked up. "I feel like a big hamburger with everything on it and I'd like a cup of coffee."

"Sounds good to me. Make that two, and please bring me a coffee also."

Lynn slipped out of her jacket. "I stopped to see Maggie. As you thought, her ankle was just sprained. She'll get to go home this afternoon. The sheriff was to drop by and have her sign her statement."

Their coffee arrived, and Lynn stirred plenty of sugar and cream into her mug. Steve sipped his black brew as his eyes followed each movement she made. "I called my firm and told them about Jake's false alibi. They're filing a second charge with the Denver DA as we speak."

"That's great. His fake alibi must put Mr. Salvatori in a worse situation."

"Yeah. Our client wants us to reopen the case immediately. Our position is much stronger since there's no alibi. However, we're still dealing with circumstantial evidence."

Lynn cocked her head. "That wasn't enough in Mom's murder."

"That's not necessarily always the case." He stroked his chin. "Circumstantial evidence is most often employed in criminal trials."

"I don't understand. They let Arnold go because they didn't have enough to make the charges stick."

"A popular misconception is that circumstantial evidence is less valid or less important than direct evidence. In practice circumstantial evidence can have an advantage over direct evidence in that it can come from multiple sources that check and reinforce each other. I'm sure there's direct proof out there somewhere. I intend to find it. And the more evidence of either type I can find will help us. I've got a lot of work to do."

Lynn's smile faded. "Then you have to go back to Denver right away."

"Yes. And there's another thing I need to clear up. Rosalie Loomis."

"Oh, gosh, of course. Without her, we'd never have been able to discover the link between Trent and Jake. How can we help her?"

"Right now, I don't know. I need to let her know that Jake is dead and figure out a course of action."

Lynn said, "Rosalie is still caring for his little girl?"

Steve nervously tapped his spoon. "Hopefully, they haven't been picked up as illegals. I've been thinking about the whole deal Trent made with Jake. Jake must have given Trent information so he could find Maria and bring her back."

Lynn's enthusiasm shone. "Maybe he had a map or notes on friends or family. Can we check his office?"

"After he closed his Denver office, he opened a small place in Piñon. He hired a young woman to help him, but he let her go after a couple of months. She's the person that gave me the lead on finding Rosalie. Trent's papers are still stored there. I hired her to help me in my Denver office. I'll see what she can find."

Lynn said, "I'm happy that Mom's killer is dead, but it doesn't seem right that his little girl and Rosalie should suffer."

Steve nodded. "I agree. I want to find out more about Maria Garcia."

Their meals arrived, and both ate ravenously. Their small talk continued as they finished their lunch.

Steve spoke first. "I should leave today." His gaze locked on Lynn. "I'd feel a whole lot better if I knew where I stood with you before I leave."

"I know." Lynn's gaze was intense. "I plan to speak with Don tonight. I want to clear the air. He needs to know how I feel about a lot of things. I was too exhausted to say anything Saturday night and he was gone Sunday."

Steve leaned back. "I think he knows I feel more than friendship for you."

"I'm sure he does, but he seems to be ignoring it—and me."

Steve held Lynn's hand. "I'll be there with you, if you want."

"Not a good idea."

"You're sure you'll be okay?"

"Yes. Don would never get physical—ever. No matter what."

"Will you call me in the morning?"

"Yes." Lynn sat still. "I'm going to tell him I'm leaving him."

Her hand trembled slightly as she took a last sip of coffee.

"What you just said makes me happy, and I'm glad you're being honest with Don so we can start with a clean slate." Steve stood. "Let me walk you to your car. We need to get going."

When they reached the sheriff's office, they parked next to one another. Steve put his arm around Lynn as they walked inside the building.

Sheriff Carlson's secretary showed the couple into his office.

The big man stood and shook Steve's hand, then Lynn's.

"Please, sit. Thanks for coming by. We've got a lot to cover." He leaned forward to gather papers from the corner of his desk. His ancient wooden seat squealed as he settled back. "Maggie gave me a detailed report. Each of you needs to provide a statement as to yesterday's events. We'll record each of your accounts. It won't take very long. When you're through, you'll come back here."

They were escorted to separate rooms and questioned. After she finished, Lynn entered the office where Steve was already seated across from the sheriff.

Carlson said, "I think we're through. Thanks."

Steve stood up. The sheriff's piercing eyes peered from under his bushy eyebrows. "One more thing. In the future, let my office chase the bad guys." He scowled at both of them. "You were both mighty lucky you weren't injured. Neither of you has good sense." Then he smiled. "Lynn, I am glad to see Betty's murder solved."

Lynn held back tears. "I'll never get over losing my mother, but seeing Jake and Trent pay for...what they did helps a little. Thank you for all your help."

Steve and Lynn left the office and headed quickly for their vehicles.

Lynn giggled. "Wow. I was reduced to a fifth-grader being scolded by the principal."

"I checked on him. He comes off like a hick, but he served as a Texas Ranger for ten years before he moved to Elk Hills. Been wounded and received medals several times."

"I'm glad he's on our side."

Lynn unlocked her car. She leaned against the door as Steve reached his arms around her and pressed his body against hers. His breath against her throat singed her skin. He kissed her with purpose. A switch inside flipped, and her body responded.

He whispered, "I've wanted to do that for a very long time."

Linking her hands around Steve's neck, she kissed him back as her heart skipped to match the pounding in his chest.

Her eyes still closed, she said, "My knees are jelly. I can't breathe."

Steve's finger traced the curve of her cheek down to her chin. "I love you. Let me make you happy." He kissed the tip of her nose.

Lynn snuggled deeper into his embrace as a car pulled into the lot a few spaces away. Steve murmured, "Let's go somewhere we can be alone. I want to make love to you. There must be a hundred motel rooms in Elk Hills. We only need one."

"We can't. Everyone knows…sees everything." The desire to be with Steve teetered opposite logic. *Damn it, I've kept a rein on my emotions long enough. I need to feel alive and wanted.* Lynn's body relaxed. "But I know a quiet place north of town, outside of the Divide Mountain Ski area. It's only a ten-minute drive."

****

Their time alone together flew by. As evening fell, Steve got into his car. His eyes followed Lynn's vehicle as she left for Mineral Lake. His watch indicated three hours since they'd left the parking lot, but the earth must have rotated twice since then. Pulling himself back to reality, he wiped his hand across his chin. The fragrance of gardenias wrapped around him, the scent of the woman he loved.

He dialed Rosalie Loomis. "Rosalie, Steve Russell here. I have bad news. I'm sorry to have to inform you, but Jake Dixon is dead. He was killed in Colorado."

Rosalie's voice trembled. "Oh, Santa Maria, Mother of God. Did…did he do something bad?"

"Yes. He killed Trent Clay. He was angry when Trent didn't bring Maria back from Mexico."

"God forgive him. I afraid. He be so angry sometimes. He love Maria very much, but to kill is wrong. Señor Russell, I must care for Juanita. What can I do."

"I'm returning to Denver today. I can get down to Shiprock to see you in a day or two. I'll try to find a way to help you and Juanita."

"Señor Russell, you are good man. Gracias."

Steve hung up. He put a notation in his Smartphone: Help Rosalie somehow.

****

After her brief rendezvous with Steve, Lynn drove home. She surveyed the sky, crisscrossed with jet contrails. *Steve's on his way by now. He'll be immersed in work getting the George Wilson murder case rolling again.* Contrary thoughts flooded her mind. *Goody-Two-Shoes just committed adultery. How am I supposed to feel? Guilty, happy? I don't know how I feel, unless you count satisfied.*

Arriving home, she parked in the empty drive. Wearily, she ascended the stairs and flipped on the dining room lights. She walked through the restaurant. Closed for the season, it was strangely quiet. Without the hum of customers and the smell of food, the room's aura seemed cold and uninviting. Lynn dialed Maggie's number. The line was busy. *Darn, I want to tell her I came to a decision to leave Don. Don't want to just leave a message. I'll try again soon.*

She poured a glass of wine and fixed a plate of cheese and crackers. She sat at a small table in the nook off the kitchen that she used to do paperwork. Head bent, she focused on what to write. *First, a list of what I need to do before I leave—money, prescriptions.* She took another sheet of paper and wrote down a few lines she might say to Don, wadded them up, and tossed them into the wastebasket.

Her concentration was so deep it was past seven o'clock before she stopped writing. *Don will be home soon. I've got to face my failed marriage now. Steve's passion rocked me...I've been a rusty bicycle leaning against the garage wall, unused and unnoticed.*

Heavy footsteps sounded on the outside stairs. Her back was to the door. Expecting Don, she hadn't locked it. As it opened, she pivoted in her chair. A menacing stranger moved toward her. "Who are you? What do you—?" She stood quickly and backed into the kitchen.

Taking long strides, the big man crossed the dining room and loomed over her. He'd covered his face with a bandanna and wore a hat. His arm came up and then down. The blow to her head sent blinding light behind her eyes, and she fell to the floor.

CHAPTER 25

Steve leaned back in his seat. He let his mind drift to Lynn. *It's going to be painful for her. She took marriage to Don seriously, and the failure will hurt. I hadn't dared to dream we'd be together. Certainly didn't see us solving a murder together. Now she's faced the rift in her marriage and unhealthy relationship with Don. Tomorrow, when she calls, I'll know for sure she'll be with me soon and in my arms.*

He made it home and fell into bed and a deep sleep. The phone jarred him awake at six. Before he could utter a word, an angry voice bellowed, "You asshole! Why didn't you face me like a man? You took off with my wife like a coward. I want to talk to Lynn. Put her on."

"Don? Lynn's not here. She's at home."

"No, she isn't. I called Maggie and Penny. She's not with either of them. I know you wanted her. I got your number from Maggie. Now where is she?"

"Don, calm down. I have no idea. She left the sheriff's office when I did, around four o'clock yesterday. She was headed home. Did she leave a note?"

"Don't you think I thought of that? There's no note." Don's voice rose. "I know you two are up to something. So come clean."

Steve gathered his thoughts, and then decided it was the time to let Don know where he stood. "Look, Don, Lynn said she intended to tell you when you came home last night how she and I feel about each other. She wants a separation, a divorce."

There was a long silence, finally Don spoke. "I figured as much. We can sort it out later. Right now I'm worried about Lynn. If she's not with you, then where is she? I'm calling Sheriff Carlson. I've got to find her. Something's very wrong. If you care about her at all, tell me where she is."

"I swear I don't know. I'll call you if I hear from her. I'm as worried as you are. I'll check with Mom and also Lynn's friend Amy."

"Good enough." He hung up.

Steve took a quick shower and dressed. All the while, his mind considered possible reasons for Lynn to leave home without a word to Don. *She was steady and seemed confident she could face Don about the divorce. Why would she leave mysteriously? My God, it better not be foul play. Who would want to hurt Lynn?*

After he dressed, he called Maggie. He'd barely said hello when she lit into him. "Steve, is Lynn with you?"

"No, Maggie, she isn't. Don called me earlier this morning. I don't know where she is. I'm really worried."

"We're all worried. We found her purse missing, but her clothes are still here. She'd started a letter to Don and a list of things to do. We're mystified as to why she'd disappear. Please help."

"Maggie, I love Lynn. She planned to tell Don last night she was leaving him. She said she'd come here to Denver to be with me."

Maggie said, "I'm aware of her feelings for you. But we're close. She'd have called me before she left. Lynn wouldn't just disappear and hurt Don without explanation. Something bad happened to her. I can feel it. We have to act fast. Think hard. What reason would anyone have to take Lynn?"

Steve's voice rose. "You think someone kidnapped her?"

"Yes, I do. Maybe to hurt her for some reason, or to hurt Don…or you?"

"I'm racking my brain. No one I know would want to hurt Lynn, or Don. Did you talk with Penny? They're pretty close."

"Yes. She's very worried. She suspects Don may be involved with another woman."

Steve said, "Don—an affair? Someone local?"

"Not local. A friend from Denver, Marilyn Lee. But Penny's speculating."

Steve spoke deliberately. "I'm not surprised. The way he treated Lynn—"

Maggie interrupted, "What about you? Is there anyone who'd want to hurt you?"

"Certainly no angry woman or husband, except maybe Don. I've been so immersed in my work I haven't had a life. No dates or..."

"Wasn't there a woman and child involved with Jake Dixon, the mother deported back to Mexico?"

"Yes, Maria Garcia. I don't know much about her. I'll keep thinking and let you know if I come up with anything. Promise to keep me informed?"

"Yes, I will."

Steve hung up. Next, he dialed his new assistant, hoping she was still in Piñon. "Cindy, Steve Russell here."

"Oh, hello, Mr. Russell."

"I need your help again. Can you search through Trent's stored files for any information about Maria Garcia? She's somewhere in Mexico."

"Sure. I'll call you with anything I find."

"Thanks, Cindy, and I'm sorry to give you bad news over the phone. Trent was shot yesterday in Elk Hills by Jake Dixon. It's pretty clear they had a deal that went sour. Trent's dead."

He heard a gasp.

"Are you okay, Cindy?"

"Yes."

"There's more to tell you, but I want to do that in person. How soon can you come to Denver?"

Cindy hesitated. "I was packing my things. I can stay with a friend. I could probably be there by tomorrow. But first I'll review Trent's notes for you."

"Good. Please call me when you arrive. I'm sorry about the bad news."

"I'm okay. Trent and I were through awhile ago. It's just a shock."

Steve left his office and went to the Denver Downtown Detention Center. He needed to talk to Eddy. He arrived just before noon.

Eddy recognized him and motioned him in. "Come on, let's get some food. I want to hear everything about the shootout at Golden Cross Mountain."

Steve gave Eddy a shocked look. "How'd you know about that?"

"Sheriff Carlson called us right away. When he did a fingerprint check on Jake, he found he'd recently been released from our jail. The sheriff had questions about Jake's car and other stuff. He said Jake killed Trent Clay. Course, we all know Trent. He was here on and off, and then he defended Tony Salvatori. I want to hear all the juicy stuff."

They walked toward the cafeteria. Then Steve stopped and said, "Look, I'm seriously worried about Lynn Mason. She's missing. Maybe kidnapped. I'm at my wits' end trying to figure why someone would take her."

Eddy's manner changed. "I'm sorry, Steve. Let's sit down and you can tell me everything you know."

Steve nodded. "I'm really worried."

The two men went through the cafeteria line and found a quiet corner. Steve had no appetite, but drank coffee while Eddy ate.

He finished a bite. "Tell me what you know from start to finish. Don't leave anything out."

Steve summarized the deal between Trent and Jake.

"So Jake confessed he killed Betty Clay."

"Yes, he did. His last words were, 'Help Maria.'"

Eddy's eyebrow went up. "His girlfriend and the mother of his child?"

"Yes, Maria Garcia. She's somewhere in Mexico. I think her father may be heavily involved with drugs if what she told Rosalie is true. Trent failed to get her back across the border, so Jake killed him. After Jake killed Trent, he was shot and died at the scene."

"So where does your case against Tony Salvatori go now?"

Steve leaned forward. "Well, it's obvious Jake's alibi was a lie. My firm intends to again file charges against Tony for George Wilson's murder. We had a strong case before the alibi caused it to be thrown out."

"I see." Eddy drummed fingers on the tabletop. "So now Salvatori is worried."

"You've got it. Go on."

Eddy raised his hands in mock surrender. "News of Trent's and Jake's deaths spread fast. Your firm is reopening the case. Salvatori will be arrested shortly, and the woman who helped you goes missing. Buddy, I think they'll put the squeeze on you soon, very soon."

Steve rose. "I need to talk to the district attorney right away."

Eddy put his hand on Steve's arm. "Hang on. Let's think some more about this."

"Eddy, Lynn's in big trouble. If your guess is right, they might call me with a deal for her release."

"Hopefully, they'll call. What kind of deal will they want? What can you deliver?"

Steve slumped. "I don't know. I'm out of my depth here." He rubbed his temple.

Chapter 26

Dry cold marked the mile-high city's winter. At five o'clock, the sun crouched behind the mountains, and the night wind stung. Steve's headlights cut across the road. He pulled up to his garage and hit the opener. The door creaked open. A metal clank caused him to pivot. He spotted a dark green garbage truck rounding the corner.

Quiet surrounded his vehicle as the door thumped close. He squeezed past his own trash cans. Gone for a week, he realized he hadn't put his out. *It's pretty late for a pickup. They usually finish in this neighborhood before noon.*

He flipped on the kitchen light, unloaded his briefcase on the counter, and went straight for the scotch in the end cabinet. A faint reflection in the dining room mirror caught his eye. He squinted and quietly rocked back on his heels to avoid being seen. Silently, he stepped backward through the kitchen and put his hand on the knife block. He began to slide a knife out, but changed his mind. Silently, he slid open the drawer under the small kitchen desk nook and located the key to his gun case, located just off the kitchen. His hand moved past his rifle and silently removed a small-caliber pistol. He took a deep breath as he considered his options. A plan formed, and he moved slowly around the corner where he had a clear view of the intruder. Startled, he recognized the figure on his sofa. This changed everything. Afraid someone may still be in his house, he crept down the hall and checked each room. Broken glass in the half bath off the spare bedroom indicated the entry point through a window there. He quickly returned to the living room.

He spoke softly as he touched her arm. "Lynn, my God…what in the world?"

Jerked as if prodded by electricity, only a mumbled cry escaped her covered face. "Mmelp…mmelp."

"It's me, Steve. Honey, are you okay? Tell me you're okay."

She nodded as he knelt and lifted the hood from her head. Red-rimmed eyes peered back at him. He gently pulled the tape from her mouth. A small piece of skin came off, leaving a tiny droplet of blood on her lip. He pulled her close and cooed reassuring words into her ear as her shoulders quaked. He gently patted and stroked her in an attempt to calm her.

Her scratchy voice demanded. "Steve, oh, God, I thought they would kill me. Where am I? They took me..."

"Honey, let me untie your hands. You're safe now."

The moment he freed her wrists, she flung her arms around his neck, sobbing and gasping, all the while trying to talk. Her dry, splintery voice asked, "Where am I?"

Steve cradled her in his arms. "You're at my house in Denver. I'm here. Thank God, you're not hurt."

"Your house? Why here? I was at home. A man came into the restaurant. He hit me on the head. I don't know why."

"Show me where he hit you."

Lynn bent her head and pointed to the left side of her head.

Gingerly, Steve checked the spot. "Got a goose egg but no blood. Does it hurt? We should call a doctor."

"No, not necessary. It doesn't hurt, and I don't have a headache." She cleared her throat. "The restaurant is closed for the season. I thought Don was home from work, but it wasn't him. The man wore a ski mask. When I came to, my eyes were covered and a hood covered my head. Can I have some water?"

Steve quickly poured a glass and brought it back to her. "How long have you been here?"

"Not sure...several hours... maybe longer. What day is it?"

"Monday, about five in the evening. I'm so glad you're safe." Steve held her tight. "Got to call the police right away."

"I was scared to death. Why did they bring me here?" She took a big breath. "Why Denver?"

Steve started to answer, "I don't know..."

Lynn rushed to speak. "No one talked. I didn't know where they were taking me. I was in a car, then in a plane, and then a truck of some kind. Then they led me in here. I was afraid they'd kill me." She wiped away tears, and her arms tightened around his neck again.

"They put something in my pocket before they left." She handed Steve a folded piece of paper.

Steve read the note out loud. "We can reach anyone, anywhere. Drop the case. Next time she'll disappear forever."

"My God, they said that?" Her hand went to her throat.

"It's a warning for me..." Steve kissed her tenderly. "You're okay now. I'll keep you safe. Don't worry."

Steve pulled out his cell phone. "We must call Don and Maggie right now. They're both worried about you—and the police."

"Yes, oh, yes."

"Let them know you were kidnapped. Don needs to be warned, too. I'll call the Denver police as soon as you finish. I wish I had a landline." He handed her his phone.

She continued to rub her wrists. "They're going to ask a lot of questions I don't know how to answer..."

"Do the best you can. Maggie will let Sheriff Carlson know."

Lynn called Don first. She tearfully assured him she was all right and explained where she was. She assured him they'd call the Denver police as soon as she hung up. Next, she explained things to Maggie.

She hung up and wiped away fresh tears. Steve put his arms around her. "Please, don't be afraid. It's over now. The police will find who did this."

"They both said they were relieved to know what happened and that I'm all right." Lynn stopped. "I ache all over. I need to freshen up." Head bent, she massaged her neck.

"You'll find the bathroom down the hall on the left."

Steve phoned Eddy. "You won't believe who I found in my living room. Lynn Mason. Thank God, she wasn't harmed. I discovered her on my couch, hood over her head, hands tied, with a note in her pocket." Steve went over Lynn's story and then read the note to Eddy.

"Damn it. That points to a leak here at the station. Someone got wind of the call from Elk Hills. Sheriff Carlson asked us to send someone to Cortez to search Jake's impounded vehicle. And rumor had it Salvatori was in hot water again."

"Of course. And I called the DA to let him know about Jake's phony alibi so he could reinstate the charges against Salvatori. You may have more than one mole."

"Tony had nothing to lose, so he put scare tactics in play immediately." Eddy added, "Try not to touch anything until we dust for prints. It's doubtful we'll find any. These guys would know enough to wear gloves. Don't talk about what happened inside the house. It may be bugged."

Steve said, "I understand."

"I'll go to my boss and call you back real soon. I'm so glad your friend is okay."

"She's very frightened, and I am, too."

Lynn came into the living room. "I feel pretty ragged."

"You look wonderful to me. The police will be here soon."

"Who sent the note and what do they want you—"

Interrupting her, Steve held his finger to his lips. He pulled a tablet from his briefcase and wrote, "They may have put a bug in here, so we need to talk outside."

Lynn said, "Can I have a drink?"

"How about a glass of wine?"

"Great."

A secluded lanai formed the center of the house. Lynn leaned back on a lounge chair. She sipped her wine and took pleasure watching Steve as he lit the outdoor heater.

Steve asked, "Feel better?"

"Much."

Steve poured himself a scotch. "The heater will warm it up quickly." He sat next to her and kissed her cheek. "You're wearing a Mona Lisa smile. What are you thinking?"

Lynn sat up. "Oh, gosh. You made me remember something I heard."

"What is it?"

"Someone said 'Mona' when the plane stopped."

"Be sure to mention that to the police. Could be a lead."

Lynn laid her head on his chest. "I feel safe with your arms around me."

"Good. Try to calm down and let yourself breathe. It's been a terrible ordeal for you." They held each other for several minutes. Steve sought her lips and kissed her over and over. He pulled back as a loud knock sounded.

He reached the front door and greeted Eddy and two officers, both carrying satchels.

Steve came back to Lynn. "They're going to examine everything and search for bugs. They'll want to talk with you as soon as they're done. For now, stay here and rest."

Steve returned as Eddy surveyed the living room. He pointed to the light over the dining table and to the corner lamps and cocked his head. "Steve, let me see the note."

After reading it, he placed it in a plastic bag. "We'd like to speak with Mrs. Mason now."

Steve took Lynn into the kitchen, and Eddy quickly shook her hand. "I'm Officer Eduardo Gomez with the Denver police. Steve and I go back a long way. I'm glad you're okay."

"Thank you."

Just then, an officer stuck his head in the door. "It's all clean in here now." He held out his hand with a small listening device disassembled in his palm. "Found it in the sound system."

Eddy nodded. "Good, now we can talk. Please sit down at the dining table, and we'll go over a few things. Tomorrow you'll need to come into the office to sign the report. You, too, Steve, since the note was addressed to you."

He set his recorder on the table. "Start at the beginning, and tell me what happened."

Lynn glanced at Steve then began, "I was at home in the restaurant. About seven o'clock, a man walked in and hit me on the head. I was knocked out, and when I woke up, I wasn't sure where I was. My eyes were covered. Tape covered my mouth, and my hands were tied in back. Soon, I realized I was on a plane. I could hear the engine and sensed a swaying motion. I was afraid they were going to kill me…"

"What kind of plane? Could you tell?"

"I'm not sure, maybe a small single-engine. The seats weren't very large, and we sat close to each other. I've ridden in a Cessna a couple of times. It was similar to that. I think there were two men, but they said very little."

"Did anyone use a name in your presence?"

"No. Someone asked the time and mentioned food. But we landed after maybe an hour, and someone opened up the plane's door. I heard, 'Good old Mona,' and then they slammed the door real quick. We sat there a long time."

"How long?"

"At least an hour or two. Then they took me to a building nearby to use the bathroom. They untied my hands and gave me a sandwich to eat, then tied my hands again. They put the tape back on my mouth. I was so frightened I didn't sleep. I listened to small talk but didn't hear anything like names or places. This morning, they let me use the bathroom again."

Eddy stopped writing. "How did you know it was morning?"

"It was cold, and birds were singing. Next, they put me in what I think was a van. They slid a side door closed and then drove a short distance. Plane engines whined. I think we were still at the airport."

Officer Gomez said, "How long were you in the van?"

"From morning to late afternoon. I kept trying to think of a way to escape, but I couldn't think of anything. I was praying most of the time. They gave me a little water and half a sandwich to eat. It was cold. Finally, they helped me into a big truck. It was loud and bumpy. They pushed me down in a backseat and drove for a while."

"How long do you think you were in the truck?"

Lynn closed her eyes. "Not long, maybe half an hour. Then they brought me in here. I was so scared. I thought they were going to kill me. It seemed like I sat here for several hours. I was afraid to move."

"You said they put the note in your pocket as they left."

"Yes. They put something in my pocket. Then I heard the door close. I had no idea where I was until Steve found me."

Gomez stood up. "Anything else?"

"Not that I can think of now. Why would they do this?"

"I can't answer that yet. But calm down. We'll find them. We'll work on what you gave us. When you come by the station, we'll go over everything again. I'll have a car stationed out front all night. Try to get some rest."

The officers left.

Steve said, "It's in their hands now. Let's get some sleep. You must be tired."

"Dead on my feet. How about you?"

Steve embraced Lynn. "I'm rejuvenated. Being close to you makes me crazy. But it's been an exhausting ordeal for you, and you need rest. I'm going to tuck you into bed."

****

In the morning, Lynn smelled coffee before Steve placed it on the nightstand. She spoke softly as he opened the drapes. “Coffee. Please just pour it into my vein.”

“Nope, you have to sit up and greet the day.”

Steve kissed her gently then placed a pillow behind her. “You have some calls to make. Then it’s off to the sheriff’s station.”

“Did you call Don?”

“Yes, and Maggie, too. I updated them on the police visit and let them know you’re fine. Don expects to hear from you this morning. Are you ready for that?”

She frowned as her eyes met Steve’s. “I’m not conflicted anymore. I’m clear about where I want to go. Don may not be ready, but he’s going to have to handle it. The night I was taken, I was struggling with how to tell Don I was leaving him.” She sipped her coffee and then touched Steve’s hand. “It took something remarkable to shatter my inertia, and in a way, I’m glad it happened.”

Steve exhaled in relief. “I’d hoped you’d say that.”

Lynn stroked his face. “Being so scared made me think. I don’t want to waste one more day without real love in my life.”

Steve kissed her neck. “We don’t have to be at the station right away. I intend to make time for you from now on, if it’s okay with you.”

Lynn back-stretched like a cat. “Oh, yes, I have plenty of time for you. Can’t you tell?”

Chapter 27

After formalizing the statements from Steve and Lynn, Detective Zucker sat with Officer Gomez in his office at the Denver Downtown Detention Center. He motioned for Officer Sparks to join them.

"Lynn's kidnapping is complex." He scrawled on a white board. "Steve Russell was working on a case involving Tony Salvatori when the connection between Trent Clay, Tony, and Jake Dixon became clear. He discovered Rosalie Loomis had tried to reach Trent numerous times asking for help. Steve visited her. She explained she was caring for the child of Maria Garcia and Jake Dixon."

The detective's eyes went from man to man. "It's probable Trent used Jake's desire to get Maria back to the US to coerce him into providing Tony's alibi and commit murder..."

He held up a paper. "Gomez, we have a list of all employees of the Gold Bar Casino. I want you to review the list and see if any name appears even vaguely familiar."

Before beginning to read, Gomez said, "Maria worked as a dancer at the Gold Bar Casino. As Jake's girlfriend, she might have spoken to Rosalie about other people there."

Zucker made notes. "We need to talk to her. Steve's been to her house?"

"Yes. But she's very fearful. Steve gained her trust. If Steve comes along she might cooperate. Several months ago, she moved to Shiprock, New Mexico, when she learned that Maria was to start work near there at the Towaoc casino. Some relatives helped her with a place to stay. Maria never showed up there, but Rosalie held on to the idea Maria might return there."

Zucker motioned to Detective Sparks. "Ask Steve to go with you. I want her brought here for questioning. We'll meet again when you get back."

Gomez read the final page of the list. "I see a name I know, Paco Lopez. He was in jail a couple of years ago. When we booked him, he strutted around and made a big stink about how important he was to Salvatori. Course, we never heard from Salvatori and, as far as I know, he served his time. He was picked up for drunk and disorderly. We can check his record and see what happened to him."

"Good, Gomez."

Gomez barked into the intercom. "Pull up Paco Lopez and print off his entire file and bring it to me ASAP."

A clerk arrived within a few minutes.

Zucker quickly scanned the pages. "Paco listed Salvatori as his employer. No job description. Jake was sent to jail for beating up Paco. In jail, Jake was worked over by four of Paco's family members. He almost died. It will take most of the day to reach Rosalie and bring her back here." He checked his watch. "Gomez, you speak Spanish?"

"Yes, sir."

"Good, stick around. We may need you to translate for her. In the meantime, please take Lynn to the cafeteria for lunch. Let her know we intend to protect her while she's here."

Gomez said, "I'll do that, sir."

"And keep me posted on finding the mole in this station."

Gomez nodded. "Will do, sir."

Zucker slipped the file on Paco Lopez under his arm and went down the hall.

****

That evening, Rosalie sat across a table from Detective Zucker in the interrogation room.

He clicked on a recorder. "We will record our conversation. We appreciate your cooperation. Juanita is in the visitors' reception area with a dish of ice cream."

Rosalie was silent as she perched on the edge of the metal chair.

Zucker read his notes. "Detective Gomez is here to translate anything you may not understand. Detective Sparks told you we want to ask you about your friend, Maria Garcia, and Jake Dixon and Juanita."

Rosalie nodded, her brown eyes riveted on Zucker's face.

"We understand your worry and appreciate how you've cared for Juanita under difficult circumstances. Do you understand me?"

Rosalie nodded. "*Si,* yes." She tore at a tissue in her hand.

He continued, "Detective Sparks told you about Jake Dixon's death and his confessions to killing Betty Clay and providing a false alibi for Tony Salvatori. He also killed Trent Clay."

Rosalie bowed her head and crossed herself. She faced the agent. "I pray for his soul."

"We all do." Zucker cleared his throat. "Please tell us everything Jake said to you. Start when Jake was released from jail May 23rd."

Rosalie replied in a small voice, "He find me in Shiprock. He come to see his baby. He very angry Maria not back here. He said he going to find Mr. Trent Clay and fix him good." She wrung her hands, and then placed one to her heart. "I no think he mean to kill him. Maybe beat him. He very angry and drink much tequila. Is drunk maybe. Then he leave my house."

Zucker nodded. "I see. Did he ask you anything else?"

"Oh, *si*. He ask me to keep Juanita a little longer. He said he mail money to me. Week later I get call that they take him from Shiprock and put him in jail again. He say he be out early November and come to get Juanita. He give me number to call if Maria come here. But, she no come."

"How long have you cared for Juanita?"

"I come here two year ago. Maria and me go to school together in Mexico. Maria help me, and I help with baby."

"How old is Juanita?"

"She two."

Zucker nodded, then rose and paced slowly around the room. "Do you know a man by the name of Paco Lopez?"

"Si, he is cousin to Maria Garcia."

Zucker's head jerked sharply. "Cousin?"

"*Si, señor.*"

Zucker said, "We know Paco worked for the Gold Bar Casino. Did Maria tell you what Paco did there?"

Rosalie answered slowly, "She say he make lots of trips to Juarez for the owner."

"Did Maria tell you the name of the owner?"

"*Si,* same man Jake work for, *Señor* Salvatori."

"Did Maria ever talk about Salvatori to you?"

Rosalie looked away from Detective Zucker. "I no remember."

Zucker's eyebrows went up. "You don't remember? That seems strange. You and Maria lived together. You've been caring for her baby for almost two years. You knew Jake. You're worried about Maria...come now, try to remember."

"Maria tell me he do much business with her father." Rosalie's voice grew quiet. "Maria's father, he own many business in Juarez. I afraid to talk about him."

"You can tell me. What kind of businesses does Maria's father own?"

"Some good, some bad business."

"Drugs?"

"I not sure." She lowered her eyes.

The investigator leaned back in his chair. He studied Rosalie. Then he said, "You are here illegally. You tell me that Juanita's mother has disappeared for several months with no word. How do I know that you didn't just kidnap Juanita? Maybe you loved this child so much you wanted to keep her for yourself. People will go to jail a long time for taking a baby from her mother."

"No, *señor*, no. I never take Juanita." Rosalie trembled. "They leave her and not come back. Jake go to jail, and Maria not come home from work. I care for Juanita." Tears welled up in her dark eyes.

"Rosalie, if you withhold information from us, we can't be sure if you are telling us the truth about Juanita. We need to know everything. How else can we help Maria and Juanita?" Zucker said, "Gomez, translate that so there's no misunderstanding."

Gomez spoke to Rosalic in Spanish.

Rosalie squirmed. "Maria's father dangerous man. Many people in Juarez do this business. But Maria no like business and want to live here, away from father, with her baby and Jake." She wiped at perspiration on her brow. "Maria's father no good. Very bad man."

Detective Zucker extended his hand to Rosalie. "Thank you for your help." Rosalie's small hand disappeared in his. "Detective Sparks will arrange for you to speak to someone regarding assistance."

"*Señor*, I afraid to go home. People maybe see men take me away today. They talk. Maybe someone tell Maria's father I come here."

"All right. We'll find a safe place for you and Juanita until this is all sorted out. Don't be afraid."

Rosalie stood. "You help Maria come home?" Emotion caught in her voice. "She love her baby."

"We're looking into it now."

Rosalie left with Detective Sparks. Zucker gave the recorder to his clerk. He excused Officer Gomez and walked into the waiting room, where he found Steve and Lynn.

"Maria Garcia is the key to nailing Salvatori for drug trafficking. Paco Lopez is Maria's cousin, and I intend to squeeze Paco to get her back here so she can testify against Salvatori."

Steve said, "There's a chance Maria may be able to help in the George Wilson murder." Through the frosted glass, he followed Rosalie's exit. Then he faced Zucker again. "Wilson may have threatened to turn Salvatori in for drug trafficking and was killed for it."

"Quite possibly." Zucker added, "But you may have to settle for less than a murder conviction. It all depends on what Maria knows. I think Salvatori had her sent back to Mexico so her father would keep her quiet. Salvatori's too smart to just have her killed. His relationship with her father is important. Let's see what we get out of Paco."

Zucker said, "Lynn, we haven't forgotten about your abduction. This afternoon, we followed up on the name Mona. Had an idea it may be the name of the plane you were on. Found out Salvatori's private plane is the Mona Loa. The details you gave us regarding the time you spent on the plane helped us narrow our investigation. We got a lead on an employee at a nearby private landing field who has a serious drug problem. We're going to pull him in and see if he witnessed your transfer from the plane."

Lynn said, "I'll be relieved when the kidnappers are arrested." She reached out to hold Steve's hand. "Do I stay here or go home to Mineral Lake?"

"I'd appreciate it if you stayed a little longer. I think you're safer under Steve's care." Detective Zucker motioned to an officer. "Keep someone at Steve's around the clock."

Steve and Lynn stood. Zucker shook hands with each of them. "Steve, your lead to Rosalie Loomis was critical. Now we'll bring Paco in and grill him."

"Good. Let me know what you find out. I'm going to take Lynn to a doctor to check the bump on her head. I'll work from home for a few days. I won't let Lynn out of my sight."

Zucker opened a file. "Good."

Steve ushered Lynn through the door.

CHAPTER 28

That afternoon Detective Sparks drove as Zucker ate his sandwich and read through the file on Paco Lopez. Their black SUV sped west on Interstate 70 and then went north at exit 244. They were now on reservation land. He finished his half of the foot-long Subway sandwich and washed the last bite down with black coffee.

Zucker said, "It shouldn't be hard to locate Paco. The report says he hangs around the Gold Bar Casino poker room. If he's not there, he's at one of the small gambling spots outside of town listed in his file. Seems he has a strong affection for poker but is not very lucky. Been in arguments at several poker clubs and received warnings but no recent arrest."

Sparks pulled into the nearly deserted Gold Bar lot and found an empty space. Sparks took a long drink of bottled water.

Zucker asked, "Do you want to finish eating first before we go in?"

"Yeah." Sparks carried a big appetite along with his wide shoulders. He inhaled the food.

Zucker said, "I think they used Lynn to slow Steve's investigation. Salvatori must be getting worried. A year ago, Paco was picked up in Denver for selling drugs, but the arresting officer changed his report before Paco could be charged. I want to know what Paco does for Salvatori."

Sparks mumbled through a full mouth, "That's odd. No officer I know ever changed a report. What made him change his?"

"Says he realized he was too far away to confirm the suspect actually made the trade-off to the buyer. He never caught the buyer." Zucker whistled low. "Hold on. Officer Arnold Clay made the arrest. Steve said Trent Clay was gunned down by Jake Dixon in the shootout he briefed us about. Arnold Clay was Trent's father."

Detective Sparks wiped his mouth, balled up the napkin, and tossed it into the backseat. He took a long drink of tepid water and yanked on the door latch. Then he stopped. "What an unlikely coincidence. Trent Clay was defending Salvatori, and his father changed his arrest report regarding Salvatori's employee, Paco Lopez."

Zucker mopped sweat from his forehead. "Coincidences make me nervous. We best throw out the names, just to see if anything sticks. Right now, I want to know if Paco can tell us anything about Maria Garcia and her father."

"Yeah, or why he makes so many trips to Mexico. Such a busy guy."

They failed to find Paco at the first two gaming clubs. At the third, Sparks stepped out of the car. "Paco's harder to find than a virgin showgirl."

Blue nicotine air hit them as they circled around the grimy casino. They scanned the table games and identified Paco from his booking photo as he hunched over a blackjack table. At two o'clock in the afternoon, Paco sat bleary-eyed as the dealer scooped away his money.

Sparks handed Paco his card. "The George Wilson murder case is reopened. You've been questioned before. We'd like you to come with us. We need a few details regarding the Gold Bar Casino partners at the time of Mr. Wilson's death."

Paco swayed on the stool. "I'm pretty busy right now. Maybe later." He barked at the dealer, "Deal."

Zucker signaled the dealer. "Hold up. He needs to spend a little time with us." He gave Paco a peek at the warrant. Paco swayed on the stool. "I don't know nothing, and I don't want no trouble. I'll go, but I gotta finish my drink."

"We'll get you black coffee." Sparks spoke to a waitress, and she handed him a cup from her tray. "Now we can go. It should only take a little while. Glad you're so cooperative."

"Yeah, yeah. I'm very co-oper-ative." Paco got off the stool and straightened his pants. He scratched at the stubble on his cheek. "I better clean up before we go."

"Not needed. We only have a couple of questions." Zucker nodded to Sparks. "Our car is right outside."

Paco rattled off more questions in the car. "Why you need me? I don't know anything."

The detectives took turns humoring him. Soon, Paco was boasting about his many friends in the police force in Oreland and other towns nearby.

Agent Sparks said, "Know anyone in Denver?"

"Yeah, lots." Paco pressed his hands to his temples. "Gives me a headache to remember one of them." He held up two fingers twisted together. "Good friend of mine. Close acquaintance. I was going to get to go to the western slope, up in the Gunnison National Forest. Never been there. Wanted to see those cool mountains. Maybe fish..." Paco waved his hand and coffee sloshed onto the seat. "Too damn crowded here. Smoggy, too. Where'd the smog come from? Huh? Tell me. Then, poof. No job. Over and done with, he tells me."

Zucker asked, "What kind of job?"

Paco smirked. "The best kind. Good pay for a few hours of work."

Sparks said, "Paco, your record says you got picked up in Denver."

"Yeah, but he let me go. First time a cop go easy on me. He wanted help with something, so he let me go, just like a bird." He flapped his hands in mock flight.

"You're talking out of your ass. Why would a cop ask you to do something?" Detective Sparks winked at Zucker.

Paco belched. "Because...he knew I work for Salvatori. Clay used to work for Mr. Big, too. Seen him at the Gold Bar lots of times."

Sparks cranked the engine over. He said, "You talking about Trent Clay, Salvatori's attorney?"

"No, Officer Clay." Paco wagged his hands, "Pig in blue...oink, oink." Paco croaked, "Hey, where we goin'?"

"To the station," Zucker said. "Got to sober you up so you can make a statement. You've got information we need."

Paco belched again. "I do? Okay, we go." He fell back on the seat and closed his eyes. Before they reached the station, his snoring drowned out the radio chatter.

Chapter 29

Maria grimaced. Her feet burned as she staggered across the searing-hot sand. *I can't waste water on my pain. Elena will be back before long, and once she sees I'm missing, they'll start searching. Please, Eric, be at the café like you promised.* Her face angled to the sun, Maria stopped and drained the small canteen. Gingerly, she touched her burned cheeks as she peered into waves of heat. Dizzy thoughts formed words that slid over her split lips. *I see you, Juanita. Soon, I will hold you, my sweet baby.*

She stopped often to pull thorns from her feet. Her mind retraced the quick plan. The fifteen miles from Elena's home to the border crossing seemed easy when the American planned it. She shook her head in disgust. *I never guessed ugly Elena would take my shoes to keep me from escaping across the cactus and rock-strewn Mexican desert. My hope of freedom had worn thin as the months of captivity weakened my chance of reunion with my baby and Jake. But hope sprang when Border Agent Knox touched my arm in the marketplace and passed me a note. I had to stifle my joy. Someone wanted to help me. Now, my part is to reach the café. I must make my body fight, and soon I will rock Juanita and kiss away her tears.*

She gazed down at the earth. Her shadow formed a circle around her feet. The noon sun pounded on her head. Bleeding feet covered by torn strips of her dress kept moving forward. Ahead, a black crow was sitting on the sand. Heat waves rose with the bird's wings—going up and down—waving at her. The bird had long legs.

She thought she recognized the face of Agent Eric Knox as she fainted.

****

Four hours later, Maria stood before the sink in the women's restroom at the El Paso airport. It swirled with pink water as Maria placed first one foot and then the other into the bowl. Her flexible dancer's body allowed the contortion necessary to extract more of the stinging cactus nettles from her feet. Next, Maria sloshed cool water on her face and yanked off the auburn wig.

She closed her eyes and thought of Juanita. *My baby won't mind her mother's blistered cheeks or nose. My arms will pull her close, and I will tell her I will never leave her again.* Maria's eyes flew open, and she slid her hand down the mirror, leaving a streak of blood. Her chin came up in defiance as she pulled her shoulders straight. Her mind conjured up the cause of all her pain. Her father's face appeared in the mirror. She spit at the mirage. *You, my father, will pay for your cruelty.*

CHAPTER 30

Detective Sparks deposited Paco Lopez in the interrogation room, placed a large cup of black coffee in his hands, and then went to Zucker's office.

He found Zucker rifling through the messages littering his desk. His lined face crinkled in a smile. "Good news. Our contact in Juarez found Maria. They'll be on a flight out of El Paso in an hour."

Sparks gave a thumbs-up. "Where'd he find her?"

"He spied her at the marketplace and slipped her a note. She'd been kept nearby. The next day, she snuck out while her cousin was gone. She hadn't even seen her father. The agent put a wig on her and flashed his badge." He waved the air. "Sailed right through. The best news, she's anxious to testify against her father. Seems there's plenty of bad blood between those two."

Sparks said, "Hope she realizes it means the witness protection program for her and the little girl."

"No doubt she'll welcome a new start safe from her father's reach. Paco's small potatoes, but Rosalie said he made trips for Salvatori. We'll get the information out of him, and we hope what he gives us will back up Maria's testimony of Salvatori's connection to the cartel. And, I just know Paco's gonna throw shit on Arnold Clay."

Sparks tossed a quarter. It spun in the air. "Tails, good cop; heads, bad cop." Sparks joked. "Get ready for my Oscar-worthy performance."

The two detectives sat across from Paco. Being in the hot seat, he sobered quickly. His head twisted from one to the other as questions flew. Soon, he provided dates and places he'd traveled to, but he held back details on amounts of cocaine and marijuana and who received them.

Zucker unloaded. "How many deliveries to Arnold Clay?"

"Can't talk about my work." His small eyes became slits. "Don't want no trouble. I need immunity, or I'm not saying nothing more. Nada." He folded his arms across his chest and burped.

Sparks stood. His tall frame cast a shadow over Paco. He spoke softly to Zucker but loud enough for Paco to hear. "Listen, Paco is important. If what he tells us is usable, he's not going to be bending over in jail. Work with me here."

Zucker raised both hands. "Okay. He's got immunity, but only if what he coughs up is good." He tilted his head at Paco and gave him a weak smile. "Now, tell us about your contact with Arnold Clay. Did he receive drugs from Salvatori?"

Paco's eyes darted between Zucker and Sparks. "We were talking about Arnold Clay. I never said nothing about Salvatori." He shook his head. "Count me out."

Sparks spoke in a conspiratorial manner. "Paco, we're working with you here. Understand, we're giving you the heads-up. Salvatori's going down. We got a mountain of testimony from folks that really have it in for Mr. Big, and it'll be hard time for sure. Make no mistake, he'll give up everyone as fast as he can to save his own skin. What does he owe you? I'll tell you. Nothing. He doesn't give a crap about you. We're giving you a chance to save yourself. Talk now, or go to jail later. You pick."

Paco fingered a gold nugget dangling from a chain around his neck. His upper lip sprouted sweat, and he wiped it away with the back of his hand.

"Remember, I got immunity." He wiggled in his chair and then closed his eyes. "I made trips to Mexico with gold and back across the border with drugs."

"Gold?" Zucker gave Paco a hard stare. "Where does gold come in?"

Paco did a little bounce in his chair. "Cool, right? I picked up the gold from Arnold, took it to Juarez, then on my way back, I made a small drop of drugs at Clay's place in Denver before I slid into Oreland and delivered the rest to Salvatori."

Zucker leaned forward. "Gold from Arnold Clay. How long did this go on?"

"About two years been delivering drugs, but maybe for six months I been picking up gold. He wasn't a cop anymore. While he was on the force, Arnold had a sweet deal going with some bimbos and pimps. He always said the dope was for his snitches. But he's a liar. Haven't seen him for a while and don't want to. He wanted a job done over on the western slope, and he cut me off." Paco snapped his fingers. "Left me hurting."

"What kind of job?" Zucker leveled his gaze at Paco.

"I don't know if I should say. Could be I'd get in trouble."

Zucker raised both hands. "Whoa. If you didn't do any job, then how could you be in trouble?"

Paco's leg bounced up and down as he deliberated. Finally, he caved. "He wanted me to off some bitch in Elk Hills. Never gave a name, and for sure, the bastard never gave me any money."

"That's helpful. When were you supposed to do the job?"

"May. But, like I said, he never called back." Paco's eyes glared. "Asshole knew I was tapped out, real bad. The two thousand woulda made a difference, and he shut me down."

Zucker spoke softly. "You never heard from him after the business offer?"

"Nah. Disappeared into thin air."

Zucker stood. "Paco, go with Detective Sparks. He'll take down your full statement. You'll need to stay with us for a while so we can protect you. Keep cooperating, and you'll make it through this mess in one piece."

****

Later, Zucker phoned Steve Russell. "Wanted to let you know I'm sending over papers to the district attorney as we speak. Salvatori will be picked up by the end of the day. Paco folded like a tent to save himself, and Maria Garcia is on her way here to give information on her father's connection to Salvatori."

"That's great. I'm eager to tell Lynn." Steve said, "How about the kidnapping charge?"

"The attendant at the private airport is here now. He'll be easy to crack, considering he's still on probation. His statement will tie the plane to Salvatori and implicate him in the kidnapping. We can build the case that he used Lynn to threaten you to back off on your murder case."

"So we have kidnapping, drug trafficking, and perjury plus a false alibi to arrest him on. Even without proving the Wilson murder charge, he can expect life in prison. I'm buying you a bottle. Name your label."

Zucker said, "Thanks, but let's wait for the bang of the gavel. He's a slippery guy, and we're still a long way from seeing him in numbered coveralls. Keep this quiet. We got some interesting details about Salvatori laundering gold in Mexico in return for drugs."

"Gold?"

"He had help from Arnold Clay."

"You mean Trent Clay."

"No. You heard me right. Somehow, Arnold funneled gold from Colorado to Mexico in return for drugs that ended up with Salvatori. On one occasion, Paco met Arnold along with two miners from up in Leadville. There's been a lot of trouble with unions in Leadville. We think since the rise of gold prices, they wanted money to fund their union so they could strike for higher wages and secure cushy union positions for themselves. We have Paco going through pictures of union strong arms to see if he can identify them. Sparks and I are digging deep. We won't quit until we have the goods on these guys. We still need more evidence to prove the connections, but we have a good lead."

Steve let out a soft whistle. "Arnold had a bad case of gold fever, and he was dangerous to boot."

"You're right about that."

"I'm worried. As you poke around more, Maria and Rosalie may be in danger. I'm guessing Maria's father is involved with Salvatori."

Zucker replied, "You're right. We have to place them in a safe house until the trial and then eventually relocate them. Paco gave us useful information as well, bless his alcoholic liver. By the way, he brought up another interesting angle on Arnold Clay."

"You can't shock me more than you just did, but spill it."

"Lynn will be interested to learn that Paco was approached by Arnold Clay to do a job for him in Elk Hills."

"To do what?"

"Kill a woman."

"That's where Betty was murdered. You don't mean he hired Paco to kill Betty?"

"Almost. Seems Paco was ready to do it, but she was killed before he got the final order."

Heavy silence hung between them. Steve repeated. "Trent had Betty killed before Arnold's contract was put in motion. Arnold had all of us fooled, except Lynn."

"Don't get too excited about nailing Arnold on that point. Paco's not really credible, and his story is weak. Says he never got paid and didn't know the name. He only knew she was in Elk Hills."

Steve said, "But he gave up information with no knowledge of any connection between Arnold Clay and Betty. Hope they can charge Arnold. He wiggled out before."

Zucker said, "After our trial, there may be no need to file charges on the Wilson murder. Let's wait and see."

"Yes." Steve added, "I'll explain to Lynn. Do you think Arnold's a flight risk?"

"Yes, if he gets wind of Salvatori's arrest. Your friend Eddy has a good idea who the leak is in his department. Mick Riley has a history of getting in over his head gambling and makes frequent trips to the Gold Bar. We've got eyes on him. Until we nab him, we're keeping this investigation as quiet as we can. We need to locate Arnold, so Lynn is safe." Zucker asked, "Who handled the Betty Clay case?"

"Sheriff Larry Carlson in Elk Hills. Arnold's still living there, or at least he was." Steve added, "I think Lynn should stay here in Denver with me until Arnold is locked up. He's dangerous."

"Agreed. I'll keep in touch."

Steve took a moment to gather his thoughts and then asked Lynn to sit with him at the kitchen table. Lynn leaned forward as Steve related his conversation with Agent Zucker. As he described the connection between Paco and Arnold Clay, she became agitated. She stood, then sat down, and stood again. "No. No. Monster..."

Steve reached for her, gently holding her tight.

Lynn screeched, "That man admitted Arnold asked him to kill my mother?" Her face flushed. "I thought it was over. Jake killed Mom. He's dead."

Steve said, "Lynn, please calm down."

Lynn rocked back and forth. No tears. "He planned to kill Mom. His son beat him to it. What vile monsters they are...were. I hate them both."

"So do I." Steve moved close. "Sheriff Carlson will find Arnold. He's dangerous and unstable." He encircled her in strong arms.

CHAPTER 31

Lynn's hand clenched the phone receiver tighter as she listened to Don. Her back curved as she slumped on the kitchen stool.

"I've bungled things. I realize that now," he stammered. "It hasn't been perfect, but can we try? We've been through a lot."

Lynn answered, "I'm sure about this."

"Give me a chance. Don't decide this over the phone. Come back so we can talk, for Christ's sake. I'm your husband. Don't I deserve at least..."

Lynn said, "It's clear we're done. They want me to stay here awhile longer, but I'll get home when I can to tie things up."

Don tried again. "I haven't told you everything. Come home. We can talk."

She listened to Don's choked good-bye.

****

The painful conversation buzzed in Lynn's head. She joined Steve on the lanai, where dappled sunshine crossed strewn newspapers. She moved stiffly to the chaise lounge.

"He's very upset—angry and hurt. He wants me to come home to talk. I told him I had to stay here a few days due to the investigation and with Arnold on the loose. There was a loud crash. I think he kicked over a stool."

"Let me get you some coffee." He quickly brought a mug and placed it in her hands. He waited quietly for her to speak.

She tucked her hair behind her ear and sipped her coffee. She picked up the front page then let it fall. "I told Don I'm leaving him. He said he knew why it wasn't working anymore." Lynn hid her eyes. "I didn't think he'd care if I left." She clenched both hands. "So typical. He growled like a dog over a bone he doesn't want but won't let any other dog have. Oh, I didn't mean…"

Steve laughed. "I'm going to let that comparison slip by without comment. Don't worry. I know what you meant to say." He reached for her hand, and their eyes met. "Take it easy. You don't have to talk about it. You're off balance right now. After a bit, everything will clear up. You know I love you with all my heart."

Overwhelmed by his words, she curled up next to him and reveled in his warmth. Closing her eyes, her thoughts scattered. *I'm in a strange place. I no longer feel forced to strain against an obstinate, immovable object.*

She opened her eyes and kissed Steve with emotion so full, they both cried.

****

The news Detective Zucker shared crackled across the lines from Denver to Elk Hills. Sheriff Carlson clutched the receiver as he listened intently to the detective. He scratched his chin.

"Yep. Arnold was around after the shootout, but I haven't seen him since. I'll let you know as soon as he's in custody." He held the phone pinched between chin and left shoulder. His chair squealed in protest as he swung around to face the credenza against the wall. Papers dropped to the floor as he rifled through files. Holding the Betty Clay murder file, he heaved himself up. His wide shoulders hunched as he thrust his head forward. "Don't worry. I'll find him. We'll figure out the jurisdiction later."

The sheriff bellowed, "Hayes, Jones, get in here pronto." The two deputies rushed into his office. "We're picking up Arnold Clay." He stretched his six-foot-four frame up and yanked on his belt. "Suspicion of attempted murder of his wife, Betty Clay." He handed the file to a shocked Deputy Hayes. "Get over to the DA and have the forms back here in thirty minutes. Get the warrant to search his home signed by Judge Nickel. I'll call him with the details. They found a mole at the Denver station who's been feeding info to Salvatori and Arnold, so it's likely Arnold knows we're looking for him. I'm thinkin' this scalawag might be armed and dangerous, so put your vests on." Both deputies filed out of the office. He yelled, "I mean it. Vests on. We're bringin' in the bastard."

CHAPTER 32

A few days later, Steve and Lynn left the Denver courthouse. As they crossed the parking lot, Steve said, "The preliminary case brought by the district attorney against Tony Salvatori seems solid. Testimony from Rosalie Loomis implicated Paco Lopez in drug running for Salvatori. Paco's testimony against Salvatori backed her accusations. Maria Garcia is a key witness regarding the drug trafficking between her father and Salvatori. He won't wiggle out of that charge. Your testimony about your kidnapping is strong, but you can't actually say he was involved. You only heard the name of his plane."

Lynn frowned. "What about the false alibi Jake provided?"

"Jake admitted to killing Betty Clay. Trent used Jake to kill for him. We have Jake's admission that he lied about his alibi. We can use all of our statements to reopen the case. Pinning a murder charge on Salvatori based on a dying man's statement should hold up, but cases have been known to flop in front of a jury."

They got into Steve's car. "If we can connect him to your kidnapping, Salvatori will land in jail. The false alibi and our wish to push for a murder charge in the Wilson killing could be trumped by the stronger evidence and better chance of putting him away. I'm just not sure which crime will take precedence."

Lynn reached for Steve's hand. "If that happens, you could be staying in Denver for quite a while."

"I won't be the one handling the case since I'm a witness to a lot of what happened. But my firm can keep me in Denver longer. I still have a lot to clear up for the Wilson family." Steve faced Lynn. He held her shoulders gently. "I have a lead on a place to rent on Blue Spruce Lake. It's close to Denver but far enough for peace and quiet. How does that sound?"

Lynn kissed him. "It sounds beautiful and thoughtful."

"I want a smooth transition for our new life together." He took a big breath. "They haven't located Arnold yet. Detective Zucker said they've combed the area, but there's no sign of him." Steve eyed Lynn. "How does that make you feel?"

"Worried, I guess. But we've got to live. We can't hang in limbo, waiting for him to be found."

Steve started the car. "Paco will testify against Arnold, not you. Unless he wanted revenge, I don't see him bothering you."

"I agree. He's protecting his own scalp. That should keep him busy."

Shortly, they reached Steve's house. He closed and locked the door. "Zucker said you can return home if you wish. And I think you should. Let me explain. I'm more concerned for your safety here in Denver now that Salvatori is scheduled for trial. Your testimony puts you in his sights. He has friends."

Lynn sat down on the couch. "I agree, and I need to clear things with Don. Right now, I need to lie down." She stretched out on the couch and closed her eyes.

Steve offered, "Do you want anything to eat?"

"No. I'm tired. I guess everything has finally caught up."

"Take a nap. I'll be in my office. I'll wake you before dinner."

Lynn stayed in bed and passed on food. Steve reserved a flight for her to leave early in the morning.

The next day, Lynn called the lumberyard and left word for Don to pick her up in Elk Hills.

She and Steve were both quiet as they drove to the airport. They held each other in a long embrace. Lynn whispered, "I don't want to say good-bye." They kissed again. Lynn touched his cheek.

"I'm planning on you returning to me soon—very soon." He kissed her one last time. "Okay?"

Lynn squeezed his hand. "Soon." As she entered the security area, she looked back searching for Steve in the crowd behind her. Finding him she touched fingers to her lips in an air kiss. He waved and smiled.

****

Returning was a shock. In the time she'd been gone, winter managed to unload both barrels of ice and cold. Puffy white snow swooped down the valley and mountain canyons. Ice covered the shallow end of Big Mesa Reservoir. Silence accompanied her ride home with Don. She made no effort at small talk, and her eyes never left the road ahead. As they arrived, reality hit.

Lynn opened the car door. "I know there's a lot to talk about. But can it wait for tomorrow? I'm awfully tired."

"Sure. I have some things to clear up at the yard. You'll find food in the refrigerator. If you feel like going to bed early..." He glanced sideways at his wife. "I'll sleep on the couch."

"Thanks." She bent her head and massaged the back of her neck. *Yes, fire and ice. Body heat and icicle toes. How different Steve is from Don. Around one of them, my senses race, and the other, I'm a dry twig ready to snap. Such an easy choice.* As she lay down on her bed, her eyes closed with that final thought.

She awoke in the morning to a quiet room. After she dressed, she found the coffee made. The hot brew warmed her instantly. Don had taped a note on the door. She pulled it off and read. *Gone to the yard. See you later. Love, D.* She crumpled it and dropped it into the wastebasket.

She went upstairs, opened the refrigerator, and pulled out eggs and bread for toast. Waiting for her breakfast to cook, she sipped her coffee and glanced around the restaurant. A shudder went down her spine. *I'm disappearing from this picture. So much I worked for is gone.* She carried her food to the counter and ate slowly. A big sip of orange juice sent her flying to the bathroom. She heaved until nothing remained. She hung on to the basin and splashed cold water over her face. Her reflection in the mirror told her nothing. No reason for the violent reaction.

Still queasy, she sat at the nook she used as a desk. *Should have known I wouldn't get through this ordeal without any emotional punishment.* She picked up recent mail and sorted through a stack of bills. *Better let my nervous stomach quiet down.* After several hours, she started across the restaurant when the phone rang. She smiled at the sound of Maggie's voice. "I'm so glad it's you."

Maggie said, "I'm close. Can I stop by?"

"Of course. See you soon."

The two friends sat at a window table, and Lynn brought Maggie up-to-date on all the events since she was kidnapped.

Maggie sat back in her chair. "Sheriff Carlson put the word out to all the surrounding towns to be on the alert for Arnold, but he's nowhere to be found. We've checked under every rock and pulled up every stump. I figure Arnold hightailed it out of town and he's far away by now."

Lynn nodded. "Steve thinks Arnold found out Paco was picked up. He may have called someone at the casino, or there's a leak at the police station. Arnold knows Paco will protect his own skin and talk his head off. He probably heard about charges against Salvatori being resurrected now that Jake's alibi is null and void. Arnold's smart enough to know he may be netted along with Salvatori and Paco. The Denver detective working this case told Steve there's an indication that Arnold used miners in Leadville to funnel gold to him, which he gave to a man in exchange for drugs. The man worked for Salvatori."

"We've had some miners with ties to Leadville float through town now and then looking for work. I'll talk to Sheriff Carlson about it. I can check with Burton Cook to see if he has any names. He's the contact for mining jobs in town."

Lynn said, "Arnold wove very convoluted plans. Father and son were both involved with a drug kingpin, and both plotted to kill the same woman."

"I suspect they did it independently from each other."

"I do, too." Lynn's eyebrows went up. "They traveled down parallel tracks. Same basic goals. Imagine what damage they might have done if they'd worked together."

"The number of bodies is proof enough of the evil they shared." Maggie studied her friend. "You're flushed. Do you feel all right?"

Lynn wiped her brow. "No, I don't. Probably just nerves. If I don't feel better by tomorrow, I'll get in to the doctor and see if I have the flu or something."

Maggie rose. "I need to go. Try to get some rest. Don't neglect yourself. Speaking of neglect, any backlash from Don on your friend Steve?"

"Actually, Don and I have barely talked. He refused to accept the news I was leaving him. Probably figures our problems will fade away."

"Is your mind made up?"

"Yes, but Don and I have difficult details to work out." Lynn reached out to Maggie. "I'll hate not being near you." They hugged. "I'm trying to face another failure. I prayed my marriage to Don would last forever. But now, looking at the end, all I feel is a kind of relief. I was the only one trying to keep our love alive. Don should have cared, and he didn't. But, even recognizing the truth, I'm filled with guilt. I keep asking if there was something I did or missed doing which pulled us apart. And I'm wrestling with leaving my home, everything we built here, and my friends. I don't want to go, yet I must. I feel a part of the mountain. It's funny how I've adapted to the lake's rhythms."

Maggie hugged her. "Living here is not like the city. Here, you have to become regulated to nature's tempo. You've evolved since I first met you." She opened the door. "But you're not gone yet." She smiled and left.

After Maggie's departure, Lynn made an attempt to finish her paperwork but gave up. Her mind spun. She walked slowly out onto the dock. Beneath her, the lake's surface was frozen hard, but down deep, a determined current steadily moved toward the spillway. Her mind merged with the water, and she pictured being under the ice. *I hear cracking noises around me. I'm being dragged by the current, moving with the water, searching for a way up from the cold.* She slowly walked upstairs. *The lake makes no judgment. Nor does it forgive.*

Fatigue settled into her bones. She left a note for Don that she needed to go to bed early.

****

It was after nine when she awoke the next morning. A rumpled blanket spilled off the couch. Don had left for the yard. As soon as she was dressed, she called Maggie.

"Wanted to let you know, I don't have the flu." She hesitated. "But I do have a condition. It's called uncertainty." She sobbed softly.

"Last time we spoke, you were sure of what you wanted. Or I should say, who you wanted."

"I was, but being here and thinking of leaving—starting over. Maybe I'm just chicken."

Maggie said, "Not on your life. Cautious, yes. And that's okay. But be honest with Don."

"I can't tell Don I slept with Steve. He'll hate me. I've ruined everything..."

"Well..." Maggie hesitated. "Listen, I've got to tell you something. I wasn't going to bring it up unless…well, never, I suppose, except if I had to."

"What are you talking about?" Lynn reached for a tissue and blew her nose. "Tell me..."

"All right, here it is. When you were missing, I talked with Penny. She brought up something she and Jack suspected."

"Maggie, what are you saying?"

"Jack said he thought Don's trips to Denver were to see a woman, Marilyn Lee. He said most of the trips were unnecessary, and Marilyn called Don often for no real reason." Maggie waited for a response. "You know her, don't you?"

"Yes." Lynn's voice was a whisper. "Don mentioned she and Scott have been having problems."

"Lynn, Penny said it's been going on for at least six months."

Lynn's voice grew stronger. "Damn it. She's my friend...well, was. No wonder Don was so anxious to go to Denver." Lynn blew her nose again. "I never thought she'd do something so rotten to me, or that Don would sneak around. I knew we were in trouble. Maybe I drove him away. We hardly made love anymore. Oh, I've been such a fool."

"Lynn, don't beat yourself up, okay? You're not the first woman to go through something like this."

"So Don cheated on me. Well, I was so needy, I jumped into bed with the first man who paid attention to me. Maybe I'm just setting myself up for a fall again." Her voice cracked.

"You're focusing on what the situation isn't instead of what it is. Maybe your life with Don is over, but by some lucky twist of fate, Steve truly loves you."

Lynn's sniffling stopped. "Yes. But I hurt. I'm embarrassed and angry all at once."

Maggie growled, "If you don't concentrate on the positive, I'll drive up there and shake you until you do." Her voice became soft. "It's time for you to confront Don. Tell him you know everything. What's that saying about people in glass houses?"

"They shouldn't throw stones." Lynn chuckled through her tears. "We're talking about stones the size of cars. I hope you're right."

"If you need me, call. I'll be there. Be strong, Lady Bear. I know you can do it."

"I'll talk to Don tonight. I'll call you tomorrow. Thanks, Maggie."

Lynn's mind spun. She continued to sit at the kitchen counter, her head cradled on her arms. Her thoughts raced. *I must act, but how can I confront Don?* Finally, she recalled something her mother used to say, something she had learned as an Indiana farm girl. *You can't plough a field by merely turning it over in your mind.*

Chapter 33

That evening, Lynn paced the restaurant, anticipating Don's arrival. Winter light fled behind the mountains to the west, and evening stars appeared above peaks penetrating the darkening sky. A half moon crept high, and shadow fingers crossed the frozen lake. Lynn added extra logs to the fireplace. Warmth radiated into the dining room as she prepared chicken breast and a tossed salad for dinner. She ripped the lettuce roughly. *I doubt either of us will eat this damn salad tonight.*

Soon, Don entered the restaurant. He called out, "Hello," and went up the short stairs into the bar. Lynn joined him at one of the small tables.

"Can I fix you a drink?" Don asked. "Hope you're feeling better."

"Yes, I am. A glass of wine would be good." She followed Don's motions as he moved back and forth behind the bar. He took a sip of his drink.

"Do you want me to light the potbelly stove? We can eat dinner up here in the bar or sit closer to the fireplace in the dining room."

"By the potbelly stove."

"You look better. The extra rest must have helped." Don placed her glass in front of her and sat down. He took a sip of his drink and leaned back, rubbing his eyes. "This week's been a heavy one. Been quoting jobs and making deliveries nonstop."

The spinning in her head hindered her speech. "Yes, you've been doing double-duty, that's for sure." She spread her hands on the tabletop and avoided his eyes.

"Actually, I took time today to examine our relationship." Her fingers tightened around the slender stem of her wine glass. "Our marriage is over."

Don choked on his drink, and his eyes flew open. "That's some statement." He stuttered, "We…we…I know it's been chilly around here, but…"

"I'd call it downright frigid." Lynn pressed her lips tight.

"I know. We should have talked..."

"I've tried talking." Lynn's attention became fixed on a section of stained barn wood above Don's head. "You haven't listened."

"What does this mean?" Red crept up Don's neck.

"I'm leaving."

His brow bunched in a frown, and he kept blinking. "I know. You said that earlier, but I figured it was just because you were upset, or frightened after being kidnapped. I told you it was not what I want."

Lynn studied her clasped hands. In a controlled voice, she said, "I'm in love with Steve." Pressure pushed blood to her brain. *There, I said it. It's out. Now he'll know. God, what'll he say?*

A flush reached Don's face, and his eyes widened. His finger jabbed at her. "Are you telling me you had sex with Steve…you...?" He pushed back abruptly and jumped up. The captain's chair crashed to the floor. His arms rose as if to ward off more discussion. He loomed over her and then spun around. In two strides, he reached the bar.

Lynn shuddered as Don's fist banged the solid-pine counter top. Glassware rattled. With shoulders hunched, he propped his long arms on the bar and swung his head back and forth between muscled shoulders.

Lynn stood, still holding her glass. "Don..."

He faced her. "You're my wife, and that's it." He set his jaw and pointed at her. "That's all there is to it. Don't try to change things..."

Her knees trembled. "Steve loves me, and it's obvious you don't."

"Don't bring other people into this. It's between you and me, not..."

"You're wrong. Steve's involved whether you like it or not." She walked to the stairs then stopped. She held the handrail to steady herself. "Don't act like I'm the bad person in all of this. I know about you and Marilyn. I thought our marriage meant something to you."

Color faded from Don's face. His mouth opened.

She hissed, "Did you think I'd just sit here for the past six months while you trotted back and forth to Denver imitating a bull elk in rut?" She threw her glass at the potbelly, hitting the isinglass door. Broken shards splattered everywhere.

She turned dry eyes to him. "You can clean it up when I'm gone. Or not… I don't care."

She strode into the kitchen. Tears of loss, anger, and mourning blurred her vision.

Don appeared in the doorway. Keeping his distance, he leaned his shoulder against the frame. Lynn remained before the kitchen sink. Neither spoke. The wall clock ticked off a paralyzed minute.

Don said, "Tomorrow, in the morning, when we've both cooled down, we'll talk. I'll sleep on the couch again." He started to leave, and then stopped. "For what it's worth, I'm sorry." He went downstairs.

"I am, too. I really am." Her words were too soft for him to have heard.

She sat on a stool at the kitchen work counter and cradled her head on crossed arms. All energy seemed to drain out of her. She picked up her phone.

Maggie answered.

"I told him. I told him everything."

"Are you okay?"

"He's really mad, but everything's calm. Maybe I'm in the eye of a hurricane. I can't be sure. He wants to talk again tomorrow."

"That's your decision. Did you mention Marilyn?"

"Yes. That's when he calmed down. He started getting holier-than-thou, but after I brought up his…affair, he pulled his horns in." She took a deep breath.

"What's a vow nowadays anyway? He was so earnest when he said he'd love me forever."

Maggie said, "The willow tree, graceful and thin, vows to stand in spite of wind. Yet, a strong enough force can litter the ground with branches no matter its pledge."

Edgy anger seeped into Lynn's voice. "I invested myself in our marriage, and he returned only meaningless words of love. I don't get you. You sound like you're excusing him."

"Consider that he gave you what he had, probably all he had. It clearly wasn't enough. The decision about your future lies with you."

Lynn took another breath. "He said he was sorry. I am, too. I have to live with what I've done."

Maggie said, "Have you talked with Steve yet?"

"No. I'll call him tomorrow. Today, Don was all I could handle. I'm going to get some sleep. I just wanted to let you know the house didn't blow up when I told him."

Maggie said, "People can handle surprises. You did the right thing confronting Don with truth."

"Thanks, Maggie. I don't know what I'd do without you. I'll call you tomorrow."

In the morning, Lynn met Don in the restaurant kitchen. He quickly poured her a cup of coffee and motioned toward the counter. They both sat. Lynn studied the swirled cream as if it were a Rembrandt painting.

Don spoke first. "We can start over, Lynn. Marilyn and I spent time together—my trips to Denver. It was wrong." Don reached for her hand.

Lynn pulled hers away.

Don said, "Please look at me."

Lynn faced him. "Why?"

"I was stupid...comparing you to her and trying to convince myself she was the one I wanted, not you." The corners of his mouth pulled down. "I'm sorry. I screwed up."

Lynn studied eyes that used to confound her when she tried to determine their color. Today, they were like gray smoke from an open fire. The hands that reached for hers were rough and showed how hard he worked. She studied him as he held his coffee mug. *Hands that used to mean protection now have become large paws pulling at me.*

Lynn stood. "Only one thing's for sure. I'm leaving."

She went to their bedroom and started the shower. Once the mirror fogged over and she was unable to see herself, she entered the spray. The showerhead pulsed water over her head, shoulders, and back. Both her arms pushed against the shower wall as she supported herself. The stream poured over her head as hot tears mingled with the flow. She couldn't tell if she was crying or not. Jarring thoughts raced through her head. Her finger traced droplets as they zigzagged down the tile. Finally, she shut the water off and wrapped her hair in a towel. She cleared a circle on the mirror. *Every girl feels better with clean hair.*

Later, as she dried off, she pulled back the bedroom curtains and noted Don's truck was gone. She tugged on her jacket and walked outside. A clump of snow fell from a bough in a nearby pine. Even at zero degrees, the air was dry and the sky blue. Sunlight ricocheted off windswept ice, still deepening in late December, and diamond dust was visible above patches of sunshine. Alpine atmosphere waited, it would stay suspended until the April thaw, to once again merge with the fluid entity of an awakened lake.

She deeply inhaled the mountain air then went inside and sat at the kitchen counter. She dialed Steve. The ring buzzed in her head. His cheerful hello and concern caressed her in a soothing balm.

"Yes, I'm feeling much better. Steve, I wish I could tell you this in person, but…I told Don about us, and I'm leaving." Hand over her heart, she pushed to keep its pounding inside. Each beat raced from her toes to her head.

"How'd he take it? I'm sorry, I shouldn't ask that."

"He didn't want me to leave, but I have to."

She squeezed her eyes tight, held her breath, and awaited his reaction. *I told him everything. Steve's smart. He'll get the picture.*

"Of course."

"He understands." She gulped air. "I'm sorry. I should have made a clean break of it before we were together."

"No apologies, Lynn. Remember, I was there, too. And I'm not sorry. I'm coming to be with you. I'll get a flight right away. I can be in Elk Hills tomorrow by noon. Can we meet? Just tell me where and when."

"I have quite a lot to do. Can you come here to Mineral Lake around two o'clock?"

"I can make that easily."

Lynn took a breath. "Steve, Don may be here. He wants me to stay. You may not want to confront him."

"Would you feel better if Maggie was with you?"

"I know she has rounds to do, but I'll ask if she can stop by."

"Lynn, I'll be there tomorrow. I love you. Remember that."

"I'll see you tomorrow. I love you, too."

Lynn tried to organize her things, but gave up by noon. She called Maggie.

"I've been trying to sort things out, but I'm too keyed up. Steve is flying in tomorrow and should be here by early afternoon. Don may be here, too. He doesn't want me to leave."

Maggie said, "I'll come by. Don will listen to me if he gets out of line."

As Lynn hung up, Don came in the door. He strode into the kitchen and placed both hands on her shoulders.

"How about if you put on a coat and we take a short walk?"

"All right." She slid into her jacket and followed him down the stairs. They walked along the lakeshore to the bridge. As they stood by the railing, he reached for her hand.

"Remember when we first came to this spot?" Don leaned back against the railing and swept his arm in an arch. "We both pictured a beautiful resort built on this property."

"I remember." She studied his face.

"A lot of what we envisioned has come about. Some is still to come." He pointed down at the spillway. "Look down."

Lynn followed his gaze to water flowing under the ice cover beneath the bridge and exiting as a river on the other side. The unusual natural spillway, created by a massive earth slide hundreds of years ago, had always intrigued her. The displaced material blocked the river, and in time, snowmelt backed up to form the four-mile-long lake. From here on, large boulders and rocks of all sizes filled the creek between Mineral Lake and Elk Hills. Their bulk formed a maze, which slowed the speed of accelerating water as the flow descended a thousand feet in elevation. The river merged in town with Bright River, then again at Big Mesa Reservoir. Finally, it collided with the Green River. Her mind tripped along the rivulets' small beginning, which eventually disappeared into the deep-red Colorado River. In front of her, the truth was so evident: without the tiny feeder streams, no massive river would exist.

Don walked to the other side of the bridge. "This site is like us, you and me." He put his arms around her. "Things…backed up, then released. All water under the bridge…all to be forgotten as it speeds down the river to a new phase. We can do the same thing. Put the past behind us, start again, fresh, together." His gloved hand touched her chin as he brought her face close and kissed her. His lips were warm and searching.

His eyes were intense. "I chose you to spend my life with, and I love you. What do you say?"

"You've confused me. What you just said is the first expression of how you feel about us you've ever mentioned since we met."

Don said, "I don't talk about how I feel." His eyes held her gaze. "But I do feel things. I've been too busy working all the time to let you know. I realize that now." He tilted his face to the winter sun, seemingly to soak up its pulsing energy, and then looked back at Lynn. "I don't want us to lose everything we both worked so hard to build. Do you?"

"I don't like the idea of losing everything we've accomplished. But I can't just look away from the problems between us." Lynn stomped her feet on the hundred-year-old planks covering the bridge. "I'm getting cold. We'd better get back."

Walking back to the restaurant, Lynn contemplated their building. Thoughts of their struggle surged through her as low clouds, forming wisps of cotton, bunched together across the winter sky.

After lunch, Don went back to the lumberyard. Lynn sat at the table, her mind replaying his words. *His speech certainly fell short of any declaration of undying love. But he did try. It moved me in a way. But is it enough to base the rest of my life on? Shit, I didn't want to end up in a divorce again, and here I am facing it. Can I continue to live with Don and exist on watered-down passion and the hope our marriage improves?*

Chapter 34

The following day, Steve caught a late afternoon flight. Bored with the foggy view from the window, he flipped through a magazine he found tucked in the seat pouch in front of him. After reading about how to win poker tournaments, he closed the magazine and leaned his head back. He analyzed his footing with Lynn. *Don is pushing to keep Lynn. Well, so am I. His stack of chips is bigger than mine. A five-year marriage beats my new relationship with her. But I'm holding aces down. I'm the one who supported Lynn in her quest to find justice for Betty. Lynn's got to read his "tell." He lied to her and cheated on her for six months. She's got to see he's bluffing now, promising her it will never happen again.*

The jet parked on the snowy runway. Steve deplaned, and as he weaved through the narrow concourse and past a tight line of passengers waiting to board, he checked his watch.

"Excuse me." Steve bumped the shoulder of a man in line dressed in a puffy jacket that reeked of campfire smoke. The man glared at him then abruptly moved away. Intent on reaching Mineral Lake as soon as possible, Steve made a beeline for the car rental desk.

In a few minutes, he was cranking the engine of an old Toyota 4Runner. The town streets had been plowed, and he drove down Main Street next to a six-foot wall of snow covering the center line. He came to the one stoplight at the intersection of Highway 50 and Main. A city truck and skip loader crossed in the opposite direction and began working to remove the dingy snow before the next storm. He shook his head. *It's a different city than the summer paradise of green meadows and fly-fishing streams I'm used to.*

Elk Hills was quiet. The Sport Stop had only one vehicle parked in front. It reminded Steve of the last outpost before entering no-man's-land ahead. At the bridge across Bright River and the Mineral Creek juncture, the sparkling water flowed past quickly, dotted by boulders topped with white pillows of snow. The road ahead was snow covered with ruts made by vehicles and snowmobiles and his eyes scanned the sloping hills for elk. He passed two ranches nestled in cushions of snow. All appeared deserted except one that offered up smoke from a rock chimney to an opaque sky. He breathed the thin air as he passed eight thousand feet and climbed steadily for the next fifteen minutes to Mineral Lake, higher and even more isolated. Soon, he reached the parking lot at the Mineral Lake Restaurant. A tall pine near the building cast a blue shadow across the wide outside stairs leading up to the restaurant.

****

Steve rapped on the door.

Lynn answered, "Come on in." She gave him a gentle hug. "Have a seat by the fireplace, and I'll get you a cup of coffee."

"Thanks. Is Don here?"

"Yes. He's up in the bar right now. I've been packing. I'll take most of it to Penny's."

They sat near the fireplace.

Shortly, Maggie peered into the restaurant window and gave a wave. Lynn met her at the door.

Maggie's sharp eyes circled the room. "Don here?"

Lynn pointed to the bar. Maggie nodded to Steve then went up the short stairs and sat next to Don.

Lynn sat close to Steve and reached for his hand.

"I can tell you're stressed." He touched her hair. "I'm glad Maggie's here. She's a good friend."

"Yes. To both of us. She'll say something to help Don through this. He's not accepting my decision, at least not yet. But he has to." Lynn stood. "If you're warmed up enough, let's go down to the dock. We can talk there."

Holding hands, they walked to the end of the pier. The December sun had slipped behind the mountain ridge and a twilight evening surrounded them. The frozen lake level was ten feet below the dock, and as the ice had hardened, winter winds left misshapen chunks along the shoreline. Winter ice controlled three feet of the surface, but below, silent water waited patiently for the spring thaw.

Steve leaned against a post and drew Lynn close. They kissed and embraced.

A loud male voice jolted the silence. They turned to see a see a man bundled in a parka stumble onto the pier. The yard light backlit his silhouette. His shoes were covered with snow, and a fur hat with earflaps hid most of his bearded face. Neither of them had caught what he'd said.

Lynn called out, "The restaurant's closed. What do you want?"

He took several steps forward. His feet shuffled as he reeled from side to side. "You son of a bitch," he shouted. "I found you."

He lurched forward. "Ruin my life, will you? I'll kill you first." The man's arm raised a pistol waist-high at Steve. "You and that bitch screwed up everything."

Lynn stifled a scream as Steve quickly pulled her behind him to shield her.

The man continued toward them. His walk was unsteady, and the pistol wavered.

Steve said, "Steady, buddy, let's talk. Put the gun down."

The man ignored Steve and continued forward. With no room left to back up, Steve whispered to Lynn, "Get off the dock."

Lynn didn't move and clung to Steve's jacket. She peered around him. Behind the man, Don descend the front stairs, two steps at a time. He was five feet from the dock. The stranger rubbed his eyes. He seemed disoriented as he moved closer to them.

Quickly, Don was right behind him, and he hurled his two-hundred-pound frame in a right-shoulder tackle. His arms went around the man's waist. The two crumpled forward then rolled and twisted half off the dock. Don held on to the attacker's hand that grasped the gun. A flash and loud report echoed as the gun fired harmlessly into the air. Arms locked, both combatants fell from the dock and landed in a tangle on the ice. An audible crack echoed.

Maggie had followed Don's rush down the stairs and now half-slid down the embankment with her own gun drawn and aimed at the stranger. She called out, "Don, back away from him."

Don had landed on top. He got to his knees then stood, holding his arm. The stranger lay still, facedown.

"Anyone hurt?" Maggie called out.

Don said, "I'm okay. My elbow's banged up. But he's out cold. Got the air knocked out."

Maggie called to Steve, "Do you see his gun on the dock?"

Steve answered, "No, he must still have it."

Maggie walked carefully around the man. She located the gun a few feet away from the inert man and tucked it into her parka. She yanked at the man's arms as she snapped on handcuffs, holstered her pistol, and then rolled him over.

Blood from his nose smeared his face.

Maggie said, "He landed pretty hard. Looks to me he was taken out by an ex-jock."

Don nodded. "Did my best."

Steve and Lynn made their way down the embankment onto the ice and slowly moved close to Maggie.

Lynn faced Don. "How'd you get down here so fast?"

Don shoved his bare hands into his pants pockets as he explained. "I noticed a car parked near the entrance to the parking lot through the side window in the bar. Thought maybe someone had trouble. When I came out the front door, this guy was staggering towards the dock. He seemed to be up to no good. By the time I was halfway down the stairs, I heard him swearing at Steve."

Lynn studied the man. "Who is he?"

Steve leaned close. "Don't know...wait. Could it be Arnold Clay? His face is mostly hidden by the full beard and fur hat, hard to recognize him. Hey, this morning when I got off my plane, I think I bumped into this guy. Didn't take any notice, never dreamed..."

Maggie said, "Arnold must have recognized Steve from the shooting at the mine site." She added, "Luckily, Don saved both of you from being shot."

Lynn edged close to Steve. "He must be crazy. He'd have killed us both."

Steve placed his arm around Lynn. "I'll bet he heard the authorities found out about his drug dealing and connection to Salvatori. That's why he's been hiding out."

Maggie spoke on her phone.

Lynn moved a little closer to Arnold and peered into his face. "He looks awful. Smells like a skunk." She shrank away. "I'll bet he tried to stay the winter in an old cabin somewhere near here."

Maggie clicked her phone closed. "Sheriff Carlson will be here in under an hour. They'll take care of him. We should get him off the ice."

Don said, "Doesn't look serious, but he hit the ice hard."

Arnold twitched and groaned. His arm thrashed out, and he reached for Lynn's coat. Both women moved out of his reach.

"You don't deserve the gold. It's mine." His words spit from clenched teeth. "Stupid Betty didn't know what she had. It was me. I knew it was waiting for me. Your big nose got in the way. Why didn't you give up?"

Maggie stepped in front of Lynn. "Calm down. You're under arrest. Do you understand me?"

Arnold mumbled as his head rocked from side to side.

"Don, Steve, help me get him up." The two men and Maggie managed to help Arnold to his feet and maneuver him up the stairs. Once in the restaurant, Maggie read him his Miranda rights. Crumpled in a chair, he sat as if in a stupor.

Don added wood to the fireplace for warmth. Lynn dropped into a chair near the front door.

Steve sat next to her. He took her hand. "You're trembling. You've had a lot of trouble from that man. You can relax now. He'll be taken care of for good. Are you okay?" He studied her.

Lynn answered, "Yes. It's so odd. Mom's misplaced trust in Arnold caused three people to die. It's so sad. All she wanted was to be loved."

Don left the fireplace and headed to the kitchen. He walked past Steve and Lynn.

Steve looked Don in the eye. "Thanks for taking him out. He was bent on shooting me and possibly Lynn, too."

"Anytime." His lips formed a wry smirk.

Lynn asked, "Is your arm okay?"

"It's nothing. I'll be fine."

As they waited for Sheriff Carlson, Maggie made notes.

Arnold mumbled to himself as he sat handcuffed by the fireplace. Before long, the sheriff and two deputies entered the restaurant. Maggie and the sheriff talked for a while, and then Arnold was led downstairs by the deputies. Lynn stood at the front window and watched as her stepfather was placed into the sheriff's SUV.

Before he left, Sheriff Carlson spoke to Lynn, Steve, and Don. "Maggie's told me what happened. You all know the drill, so come by my office and we'll record your statements."

The sheriff faced Lynn. "The Clay family has been one damned bunch." He scratched his chin. "Any more members you know of?"

"No. I think this is the end of them."

"I hope so." The burly sheriff strode out of the restaurant and took charge of his prisoner.

Steve stood. "I'll head to Elk Hills myself and find a room for the night."

Lynn went out onto the deck with him, and they said good-bye. She stayed on the deck awhile, pulling strength from the stars.

****

The next day, Don and Lynn drove to Elk Hills together. Conversation was strained. They reached the sheriff's office and, with Steve, provided their statements. The sheriff excused them, and they walked outside into an overcast afternoon. Don sent Lynn a crooked smile, dipped his head, and walked to his truck. Steve and Lynn lingered behind, then hand-in-hand, reached Steve's rental car.

Steve said, "Let's go someplace quiet where we can get a drink."

He opened the door for her and kissed her as she got in.

The Wishing Well Café was almost empty. Both were quiet as they finished a light meal.

Lynn said, "I was so thankful that you were there yesterday. I didn't know how you might feel about seeing Don." She folded the napkin smaller and smaller. "I was so anxious to see you, but never in a million years did I expect to see Arnold there, intent on killing you…us." Lips quivering, she tried to hold back tears.

"I'm with you, Lynn, one hundred percent." He reached across the small table and held her hands. "Go ahead. Let it out. There was way too much tension yesterday."

"I hope to God the killing is over." She wiped away tears. "If you'd been hurt..." She quieted down. "The Clay family's been the source of so much grief for everyone I love. I hope Arnold is put away forever."

"This morning I called the Denver DA. He's reviewing information from another one of Salvatori's men. This guy has confirmed Salvatori used two men from Leadville to kidnap you. They're up there now to arrest them. He said since Betty was murdered by Jake before Arnold's agreement with Paco was fulfilled, they'll have to amend the charge to conspiring to commit murder. However, Arnold sealed his fate when he tried to kill me and you."

"Do you think they'll try him in Denver or in Elk Hills?"

"The sheriff's a tough buzzard. I think he'll push for jurisdiction, but he may get pushed aside for a bigger venue."

Steve leveled his eyes on Lynn. "As a material witness, I'll have to be here for the trial. Will that be okay with you?"

"Of course." Lynn fiddled with her water glass. "I've decided to stay with Penny for a little while. I can't...don't want to be at home with Don any longer."

"Lynn, I'm not going to pressure you." He reached across the table to hold both her hands.

"Thanks."

Steve's eyes blazed. "I'm not backing off, either. I want us to be together, however difficult it is to work things out with Don. I'm fully committed to you. I love you." Steve stood. "Let's get out of here so I can hold you in my arms."

****

Later that evening, Steve dropped Lynn at Penny and Jack's home. She took her small bag into the guest room. As she sat on the patchwork quilt, light flickered from the antique glass lamp next to the bed. It cast a rosy glow on the log wall and illuminated a hand-hooked rug.

Penny entered with her arms full. "I have towels for your bathroom and water for your nightstand. I hope the room is warm enough for you. If not, I can push the heat higher."

"It's perfect. I can't thank you enough for putting me up. It will only be until after Don and I meet with our attorney. I hope I can handle what needs to be done, chopping up my marriage, home, and business." Her shoulders sagged.

Penny sat next to Lynn on the bed and put her arm around her. "Don't worry. You can stay here as long as you want. The worst is over." She stood. "Take your time. Too much has happened all at once. Let everything calm down. Then you can make right decisions." Penny walked to the door. "I'm glad I got to meet Steve. I can tell he's a really nice guy. Get some rest."

Lynn slipped under the covers. She closed her eyes. Small noises scratched at her senses. *I'm going to pretend I'm in my own bed, listening to wind moving the pine outside the window and hearing sharp booms as ice shifts on the lake.*

Soon, she was asleep.

The next day, Steve called. "I know you need some time alone, but I can't wait to see you. How about dinner?"

"Of course. I know a nice place in town."

The evening was filled with happy plans.

Don called the next morning. "Before we meet at the lawyer's on Friday, let me take you to our favorite place. I promise to behave."

Lynn agreed. That evening, they arrived at The Ranch and ordered their meals. They'd been seated at a table near the stone fireplace.

Lynn studied Don. "How's it going at the lumberyard?"

"Fine. Busy for December, but I think I can close over Christmas, and no one will mind."

"Close down over Christmas? I'm surprised." Lynn eyed his fresh haircut and new shirt.

"You'd be surprised at several changes I've made."

She leaned back slightly. "Really? Tell me."

"First off, Jack will make all the pickups in Denver." He cleared his throat. "He's a better driver than I am and can use the extra pay." He managed a half smile. "Also, from now on, I'm closing the lumberyard on Sunday."

Lynn said, "Those are good changes."

"I want us back together, and I intend to make a home for us."

"That's quite a promise."

"I mean it. I'm hoping you'll give me another chance."

Firelight flickered across his eyes as Lynn once again strained to identify their color. She glanced away. *I would settle for seeing honesty in his eyes.*

"Penny's been a real friend letting me stay with them." She halted. "It's been difficult..."

Words tumbled from Don. "I'm not pushing you. Honest. Just want you to know I've changed. I plan on putting our marriage first...before business." He squared his shoulders and offered her his most engaging smile.

"I'm glad to hear it. Considering our marriage has already crashed on the rocks." Lynn pushed harder. "Why did you abandon me?"

Red crept up Don's neck. "I...hard to explain...Lynn. I got itchy, I guess."

"Really?" She digested his words. Lynn raised her chin. "And what's to say you won't get itchy again? Am I to worry forever if I please you? Do I look good enough? Am I fascinating and sexy enough?"

"Come on, Lynn." Don signaled for a second drink. He tapped the tabletop, making his point. "I already told you. I was stupid. I risked losing you, our home, our business—everything we'd built—on a whim." He rubbed his hand through his hair as he examined his wife's face. "I'm being honest. I got the hots for Marilyn. She gave me the come-on and, like an idiot, I went for it."

"Will you miss her?"

"No. Not at all. We didn't really have anything except...you know." He concentrated on his drink.

Lynn sat still. His statement hung in the air between them. She traced the design on the drink napkin. "Then Marilyn is okay with you two breaking up?"

"Yes. She and Scott are considering moving to Texas. They're trying to stay together." His voice dropped but was emphatic. "Like I want us to."

Lynn said, "I'm full of remorse, too. We both made a mess of things. Learning about you and Marilyn hurt, but your inattention and neglect for months before pushed me to stray, and I slept with Steve. I broke my marriage vows as well."

"That's what I mean. We know what we did wrong, and we can come back. We owe it to ourselves to make the effort, like we did building our place against the odds."

Lynn studied Don's eyes. She didn't respond.

Don's voice sounded earnest. "I know we can pull together to make everything work as it should."

"You make a good case. But there's something I've figured out. I realize that in the beginning I used you for security, acceptance, even prestige. I gave you my love…at least I thought I did. Now that I'm truly in love with Steve, I can tell the difference."

Don stood stiffly, and together, they drove back to Penny's home in silence.

CHAPTER 35

Steve showered and shaved. Not being used to the cold climate, he put on layers—T-shirt, wool shirt, and vest—then pushed the wall heater higher. He peered out the frosty window as he dialed Detective Zucker for an update.

"Good to hear from you, Steve. The DA filled me in on your brush with Arnold Clay. Glad you weren't hurt."

"Thanks. What's the status on Maria Garcia and Rosalie Loomis?"

"Maria's in a safe house. Got excellent info on her father's operation. She gave up names of mules as well as bankers. Sure took a beating getting away, but she's recovered."

"Has she seen her daughter?"

"Yep. Made sure of that. Lots of tears. Had me and Sparks choked up as well. Rosalie and Juanita are also in a safe house. Her statement will support the case. Due to the dangers, we're pushing this case to the front of the line. Six months to get to court. You'll have to be here as well as Lynn."

"I'll be back soon. Have things to tie up here."

"Your friend, Officer Eddy Gomez, is working with us to plug the leak at the office. We're tracing back as best we can to find out how Arnold learned of our moves to implicate him."

"He went nuts. Are you going to have him stand trial in Denver?"

"Yes. He's tied to Salvatori and the drug business. I'll contact Carlson soon. That's about it for now. I'll get back to you soon. This case sure made some twists along the way."

"You don't know how true that is. Talk with you later."

CHAPTER 36

As Lynn stretched in Penny's guest bed, the smell of morning coffee reached her. *God, everything comes to a head today. It could get ugly with the lawyer.*

She rolled over and checked the clock, then propped her pillows and pulled both knees up. *Don wants to try to breathe life back into our corpse of a marriage. Staying with him would be foolish. Steve wants to start a new life with me. It'd be a different life, new place, a new love to experience.*

Her feet hit the icy floor, and reality crawled up her legs. She donned a warm sweater and jeans. Bending to tie her boots, she yanked so hard she broke the lace and fell backward on the bed. Her eyes traced the nicks and cuts along the beams of the ceiling above. Rugged hand-hewed logs, put in place by some unknown pioneer a hundred years ago, held the weight of heavy snow and had provided a safe home for generations. *Damn. Am I making the right decision? Maybe I should take more time, be sure.* She twisted the broken lace around her finger.

She finished dressing and put on her makeup.

The phone rang, and Penny called to her. "It's for you Lynn. It's Maggie."

Lynn stood by the wall phone. "Thanks for the ride offer. I should be there by twelve. See you soon."

Penny motioned for Lynn to sit at the kitchen table and placed eggs and bacon in front of her. "Dig in. You'll need your strength." She glanced at Lynn. "You look better today. So much stress is not good for anyone." She sat across from her friend and sipped her coffee. "I was going to offer you a ride to your attorney's office, but Maggie beat me to it."

"You've helped so much already. I didn't want you to miss work because of me. Maggie has to be at the courthouse anyway." She pointed at the empty plate. "Breakfast was delicious. Thanks."

"A good appetite's a good sign. So much has happened lately I don't know how you've managed to handle it all."

Lynn shook her head. "Not very well." Downcast eyes focused on her empty plate.

"Don't say that. Think of everything you've been through. Your mom's murder, a shootout, a kidnapping, and a murder attempt." Penny pointed at Lynn. "You're the only person I've ever known who's been kidnapped."

"I'm the only person I know who's been kidnapped." Lynn laughed.

Penny jumped up and rummaged in a kitchen drawer. "Wait, I want your autograph. I need some paper and a pen." Laughing, she placed a half-finished crayon drawing next to Lynn. "Here, write it on Carrie's picture. It's the only paper I can find."

"Leave it to you to see the funny side of all this."

"I've been waiting to see you smile." Penny cleared away the dishes. "Have you made any decision yet about...I shouldn't ask. I'm sorry."

"It's okay. The only thing I know for sure is maybe, with some practice, I can be a good wife. I don't want to fail again." She leaned next to the sink. "Don says he'll change."

Penny said, "That's a big promise."

"Steve is wonderful to me. I think we're a good match—spiritually and physically. He's easy to talk to and be around. We enjoy every minute together." She folded and unfolded her napkin, lost in thought.

"I'm happy to hear that. What's he like?"

Lynn's eyes sparkled. "He's thoughtful and caring, in spite of all the danger and difficulties I've involved him in. He's positive and puts me first."

Penny asked, "Do you think he'll continue to be that way?"

"I hope so. He's stood by me through everything. It's all been life-changing. Some men run for cover. They don't want any baggage. But he didn't blink."

Penny nodded. "He sounds committed to you."

"It's hard because Don said the same thing."

"Speaking of honesty, can you trust Don now?"

"He's worried about losing so much. I know it's bothering him. I can't be sure if his roving is over. I don't want us to stay together just because it's the best financial decision. I'd feel used. You know Don. What do you think?"

Penny slapped the counter with the dishtowel. "Don's had his chance."

Lynn barely caught her words as she dashed for the bathroom.

Penny called, "Are you okay?"

In a few minutes, Lynn came out, holding a cold rag to her forehead.

"Oh, boy. Nerves have gotten to you." Penny took down a package of Alka-Seltzer. "Want a couple of these?"

"Yes." She drank the fizzy mix. "I'll be all right. Just my nervous stomach." She sat at the table again.

"You look a little green, but it'll pass." Penny placed her lunch in a bag. "If you're sure you'll be okay, I need to leave for work in a couple of minutes. Make yourself comfortable, and I'll see you tonight if you decide to stay. You know you're welcome for as long as you want."

Lynn gave Penny a squeeze. "I'm fine. Don't worry. I'll give you a call later, after I finish at the attorney's office."

Maggie and Lynn drove the short distance to attorney Paul Stirling's office. The December day was overcast. Christmas decorations graced the city light poles and storefronts. Parked outside the office, Lynn sat in the car. Her hand rested on the door handle.

Maggie waited for her to speak. Finally, she said, "My grandmother used to say, 'Don't waste your breath chasing a butterfly. He is much too fast. Be still and let the butterfly come to you, as it surely will. Then act with no hesitation, and you will have the butterfly in your hand.'"

"Thanks. I wish I had met your grandmother. She was so wise."

Maggie smiled. "Just family stuff."

"I'm finally beginning to comprehend a little of your Native American wisdom." She opened the car door.

"It's about time." Maggie's grin brought out the sun.

Soon, Don and Lynn sat across from their attorney. Don placed a paper on the desk that outlined the split of assets, money in the bank, and jointly owned real estate.

Paul said, "This appears to be an equal split."

Lynn reviewed the list. "Don, I want you to keep the lumberyard as your own. You're the one who has worked to develop it."

Don said, "Are you sure?"

Lynn nodded. "Then we're done here?"

Paul answered, "I'll send you duplicate copies to sign before the end of the week." As he shook each of their hands, he added, "I'm sorry it worked out this way."

Don replied, "We both are."

After the meeting, the two women picked up Lynn's things from Penny's house and drove back to Mineral Lake. Conversation was at a minimum.

At about three o'clock, they reached the restaurant. Lynn waved good-bye and opened the door to their downstairs living quarters and dropped her bag in the room. She closed the door and pulled her parka hood tight around her face and walked out onto the dock. Sifted powder snow covered the wooden pier. Shivering, she raised her face to the sky and soaked up feeble winter sun. Cold air stung her lungs as she breathed in the sharp air. Silence draped across the lake, dressed in ice, as sunbeams shot through the fine mist swirling over the surface. A rhythm beat in her heart. Lynn repeated the words Maggie had said as she'd left, "God gave us each a path." *I want to follow mine.*

Lynn walked up the stairs. Inside the restaurant, her breath made white puffs. She increased the heat and built a fire. She moved around the kitchen, still in her parka, and started homemade soup for dinner. She found ham and country bread in the refrigerator. Soon, the kitchen warmed, and she shed her parka. She rummaged in her purse for her phone. She pushed the speed dial, and her heart skipped when he answered.

"Steve, Maggie brought me home after the attorney visit. I wanted to talk to you in person but thought I'd better get home. So, here I am again, discussing huge issues with you by phone. Sorry."

"That's okay, baby. Just give me good news."

"With all my heart, I want to be with you, if you don't mind the baggage I'm towing." Tears spilled down her cheeks.

"That's great news. I don't know what to say. When can I see you?"

"How about tomorrow? I want to discuss some final issues with Don tonight and pack so we can be together."

"Just tell me what time."

"How about two o'clock?"

"Perfect. Will you be all right staying there tonight with Don?"

"Yes. He'll be fine. He was very calm today." Her voice became smooth. "I just knew everything would work out."

"Honey, we're going to have a wonderful life. It's hard, but I can wait one more night. I'll be lying awake thinking of all the things I want to do to make a home with you."

"It'll happen soon."

"Not soon enough."

Lynn said, "I'll call you early tomorrow."

"Good. I love you."

She paced as she kept one eye on the soup pot and the other on the clock. After discussing the property split, Don had left in his own vehicle to spend some time at the lumberyard.

Lynn called Maggie. "Hi, do you have a minute? I'm having a meltdown."

"Is Don at home with you?"

"No. He's not home yet. But I just called Steve."

"Bet he's happy."

"Yes, he is. But I'm being hit with waves of guilt. I feel like a failure. I've had to face the fact that Don's not the only one to blame for the failure of our marriage. I let Steve woo me and fell into his arms. Maybe too fast."

"Do you still feel that way?" Maggie spoke slowly. "Lady Bear, you're wavering. I see holes in your canoe that could sink you before you put a foot on the shore."

"Well, I'm the one holding the ax." Lynn wiped at tears. "I've done a lot of thinking and realize that somehow I failed Don, too, or he wouldn't have jumped into Marilyn's bed when she crooked her finger. I'm afraid I just can't hold a man."

"Lynn, you have a true heart. You know when something is good or bad. Not every person is like that."

"But I've made a mess of things. Steve came to me right when I needed someone. It feels like true love, but how can I be sure? Maybe it's gratitude for helping to find justice for Mom. I fell for his attention. Honestly, Maggie, I've never been so confused."

"Why do you think Don wants you to stay?"

"Well, now he says he loves me."

"Let me ask you this: for the past five years, has he shown you that he loves you?"

"I have to say no, but he has worked hard to provide us with a home and security."

"So, can you see his priority? And what's the reason you hesitate to leave? Steve has demonstrated his love. Don has not."

"Oh, dear. I've loved Don in blind stupidity. Maggie, I've been just like him. I haven't wanted to lose what we worked so hard for, and starting over has scared me."

Both women were silent.

"The answer is with me, isn't it? Maggie, you've helped me so much. I'm going to miss you and your wisdom."

"It's good you look inside. Through all your trouble, you have gained wisdom. And I remain your friend."

"I know what I need to do."

The phone barely had hit the cradle when Don opened the door. He called out, "Hello," then shed his jacket and gloves. He ambled to the fireplace and stood with his hands out to the heat then sat on the hearth as he unlaced his boots.

Lynn approached.

Don raised his face. "I know you have things to say. Sit by me, okay?"

Lynn sat. "I can get you a drink if you want one."

"No. I'm fine. Just anxious to talk with you." Small beads of sweat appeared on his upper lip.

Lynn swallowed. "Well, now that you and I have agreed on the property settlement, I'll file for divorce."

As he spoke, his shoulders sagged. "Did you tell Steve?"

"Yes I did."

Don rubbed at a twitch in his eyelid. "Is there any way I can talk you out of this? I want you to stay with me." He tapped his chest. "In here, you're my wife." Nervously, he rubbed both hands on his thighs. "I love you, baby. What happened with Steve doesn't matter. We can keep our home and someday have a family, when the time is right."

His words mesmerized her. Firelight shone in his eyes. "What you just said are wonderful words, but not enough for a second try. It's too late. I love Steve."

Don raised his hand and touched her cheek. "Then I've lost you, and it's my fault."

Lynn said, "You're a man of few words. But they're good words when you say them. We're both responsible."

"The last few months have been something else."

"Maggie would say we must use this experience to grow."

"Maggie's the genuine article. I'm glad she's your friend."

Lynn turned toward the kitchen. "I fixed some soup. It's ready, if you want some."

"No. Too miserable to eat."

"I understand." Lynn put away the food and went downstairs to bed alone.

****

Morning provided one of those rare sights that only occur in the high mountains. The sun painted the snow pink as it climbed the sky.

Lynn started to pack. Don wasn't home. She presumed he was at the lumberyard. She phoned Steve.

As soon as he answered, words rushed out about moving arrangements.

Lynn interrupted, "Don just came in. I'll see you early this afternoon. I need to hang up."

Don walked into the kitchen. "Jack's handling the yard. I wanted to come home. Lots of things around here need fixing."

"I've got plenty of mending to do myself."

Lynn had piled her clothes and personal items by the downstairs door. She and Steve each planned to drive a vehicle to Denver, and she eyed the items, wondering if she was taking too little or too much. She put on her jacket and walked out to the end of the dock. She reached both arms out to embrace the lake and mountains one last time. On the side of their building, Don stacked firewood. Neither heard the car until it parked next to Don's truck. Lynn turned to see Steve standing at the bottom of the stairs.

Steve smiled. "Are you ready?"

Lynn rushed to Steve, and they kissed. "Yes." This time, she knew she meant it.

Don appeared from the side yard. He started toward them. His voice rose. "Steve, why don't you get in your car and leave us alone?"

Steve ignored him. "Lynn, I'll start loading."

"I realize you're in love with my wife, you devious bastard. But I'm not rolling over and letting you take her from me."

Steve faced him. "I don't want trouble, but I'm not backing down."

Don placed his hand on Steve's shoulder and shoved. "I told you to leave."

Fists clenched, Steve's anger landed on Don's jaw. Don's head snapped back as he plowed his right fist into Steve's stomach. Steve bent over but brought his clenched hand up under Don's chin. Don staggered back and tripped backward over the end of a log protruding from under the deck. He sprawled on the snow in a heap. The fight ended before it started.

Lynn grabbed Steve's arm. "Are you okay?"

Don scowled. "You disappoint me, Lynn. I thought you were the one. I've been carrying you all the while, and this is my thanks. I'll sign all papers needed to cut everything in half for good." He spat his words. "Any questions? Have your new lawyer send me a letter." He brushed past Steve as he stomped upstairs and slammed the restaurant door.

Lynn let out her breath. She used her sleeve to dab at the blood on Steve's lip.

Steve gently rubbed his chin. "Don't mind taking a hit for my woman any day." He flashed Lynn a smile. "Let's get your things loaded and get out of here."

"Come on." Lynn took his arm as she opened the downstairs door.

Steve stopped before entering the living quarters. He cast a look over his shoulder, taking in the silent scene of dark pines and snow-covered peaks. "You know, this is going to be the best Christmas ever."

Light danced across the frozen surface like tiny newborn stars. Lynn's mind raced in thought. "Whether or not I deserve it, I've got another chance and I'm taking it with humility."

She winked at her lake. "Yes, it is."

About the Author

Raised in Southern California and educated at the University of California, San Bernardino, Sharon Langdale lived an adventure building a restaurant on a lake in the Colorado mountains. Her commitment to Colorado runs deep. This experience was the basis of her first novel, *Vein of Justice.*

A full-time writer since 2010, she also finds time to travel and enjoy other interests, such as rock-specimen collecting, landscape painting, and photography. Her paintings have received positive adjudication in contests and shows, and she has belonged to several art associations.

She and her husband now live in northern Arizona and enjoy wilderness hiking and Jeep rides on the slopes of the Mogollon Rim.

She is working on her next mystery novel, *Maggie of Ute Tribe*, which is about Native American reservation life and the struggle of a young woman to attain her dream of being a deputy sheriff in Colorado.

Learn more about Sharon on her website, http://www.sharonlangdale.com, and visit her on Facebook.

Made in the USA
San Bernardino, CA
13 July 2015